WHITE FLAG

AMERICA'S FIRST 9/11

Carolyn —
I hope you enjoy the book!
Wayne A. Capurro
12/21/17

BY

WAYNE ATILIO CAPURRO

Bloomington, IN   authorHOUSE™   Milton Keynes, UK

AuthorHouse™
1663 Liberty Drive, Suite 200
Bloomington, IN 47403
www.authorhouse.com
Phone: 1-800-839-8640

First published by AuthorHouse 6/4/2007

ISBN: 978-1-4259-9564-5 (sc)
ISBN: 978-1-4259-9565-2 (hc)

Library of Congress Control Number: 2007902154

Printed in the United States of America
Bloomington, Indiana

This book is printed on acid-free paper.

DEDICATION

To the victims, the survivors, and their descendants, with my sincere and heartfelt apology for the murder my great-great-grandfather committed and for the murders he failed to prevent.

ACKNOWLEDGEMENTS

I want to thank my brother Dale, my mother Mariellen, and my wife Shelly, for their encouragement and support and for their help in editing this book. Also my children—Jeff, Logan, Kaylie, and Kierra—for their patience and sacrifice during the process, and my father, Atilio for teaching me the value of hard work and decency.

Special thanks to Scott Stewart of Street Corner Press for his help as writing coach in the early chapters. Your assistance helped set the tone I wanted to carry throughout this book. Also my friend Ernie Pike, of Pike Line Design and Photography, for the work he did on the cover. Your willingness to brave long walks and cold weather and to scale barriers to make shots was beyond my expectations. Also my friend Chuck Buckingham for allowing me to divert our summer excursions to sites related to this research effort. It really did help me conceptualize this work.

To all my friends and relatives who encouraged me to write this book, your encouragement was necessary and much appreciated.

I owe everything to those authors before me who worked so hard to discover the truth about Mountain Meadows; its planning, execution, and attempts to suppress it. Most notably they are: William Bishop, John D. Lee, and Judge John Cradlebaugh for *Mormonism Unveiled;* John H. Beadle and William Hickman for *Confessions of Wild Bill Hickman;* Harold Schindler for *Orrin Porter Rockwell;* William Wise for *Massacre at Mountain Meadows;* Juanita Leavitt Brooks for *The Mountain Meadows Massacre,* for *John Doyle Lee* and for *Emma Lee*; Anna Jean Backus for *Mountain Meadows Witness;* Charles Kelly for *Caleb Greenwood;* William A. Linn for *The Story of the Mormons*; Sally Denton for *American Massacre;* Jon Krakauer for *Under the Banner of Heaven*; Hart Wixom for *Hamblin;* Gene Sessions and Donald Moorman for *Camp Floyd and the Mormons;* Hope A. Hilton for *Wild Bill Hickman and the Mormon Frontier;* and last, but certainly not least, Will Bagley for *Blood of the Prophets.*

Other influences relative to this work are too numerous to remember, but here is a feeble attempt: Abraham Lincoln; Samuel Clemens (Mark Twain); Horace Greeley; Josiah Gibbs; John C. Freemont; Captain John Gunnison; John Wesley Powell; Judge William W. Drummond; Judge Jacob Boreman; General Albert Sidney Johnston; Colonel James H. Carleton; Captain James Lynch; Dr. Jacob Forney; Superintendent Garland Hurt; John I. Ginn; Joseph Smith Jr.; Hosea Stout; William Law; Thomas Marsh; William Leaney; Governor Michael Leavitt; Secretary Stewart Lee Udall; Lucretia Stout; Hubert Howe Bancroft; David L. Bigler; Jim Bridger; Jedidiah Grant; George Albert Smith; Joseph Morris; Heber C. Kimball; William Kimball; Nephi Johnson; Laban Morrill; William Godbe; Daniel Hamner Wells; Heber J. Grant; George Grant; Thomas L. Kane; Governor Alfred Cumming; Congressman Luke P. Poland; Brigham Young; Dimick B. Huntington; Gordon B. Hinckley; Ann Eliza Webb Young; Emmeline Free Young; Parley Parker Pratt; Thales Haskell; Ammon Tenney; James Holt Haslam; "Pony Bob" Haslam; William "Buffalo Bill" Cody; Susan Staker; Scott G. Kenney; Cynthia B. Alldredge; Ernest Tietjen; Leonard J. Arrington; Jennifer Dobner; John L. Smith; Bryan Haynes; Warren Steed Jeffs; Robert D. Crockett; Glen Johnson; Marjorie Sill; Guy Foote; Douglas O. Linder; Nellie M. Gubler; Samuel Knight; Samuel McMurdy; Ira Hatch; Orson Hyde; John Taylor; Marinda Johnson Hyde; Gerald and Sandra Tanner; Charles Penrose; Sidney Rigdon; Josiah Rogerson; Fawn Brodie; John M. Higbee; Wilford Woodruff; Joseph F. Smith; Erastus Snow; Judge Charles "Argus" Wandell; Wallace Stegner; T.B.H. and Fanny Stenhouse; Frank J. Cannon; George L. Knapp; David A. White; Malinda Cameron Scott Thurston; John Steele; Robert N. Baskin Esq.; Ellen Adelia Klingensmith; Philip Klingensmith; Patrick Fitzgerald; Hannah Creamer Klingensmith; Dave Palmer, Patrick Capurro; Philip Capurro; Steve Djukanovich; Dave Enzler; Debbie Armand; Rick Sorenson; Kevin W. Reid; Keith Lee Jr.; Richard Joiner; John DeSoto; Dennis Wilson; Don Brown; Phil Klink; Angela Frazzitta; Albert M. Souza; Elwood Koenig; Cherie Humphreys; Kathryn Landreth; Kathleen Moore; Carl Kelly; Harry M. Callahan; Google; Yahoo; LDS genealogical web sites; the Book of Mormon; Doctrines and Covenants; and the Holy Bible.

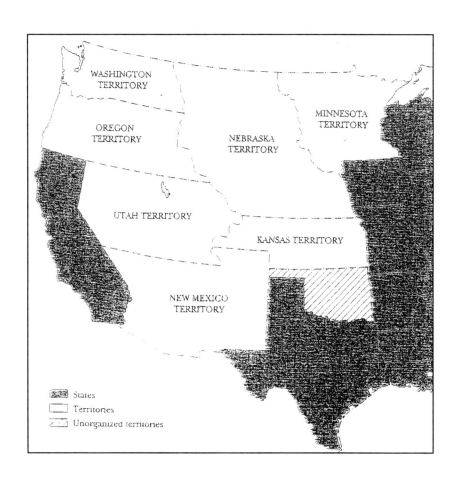

U.S. TERRITORIES 1857

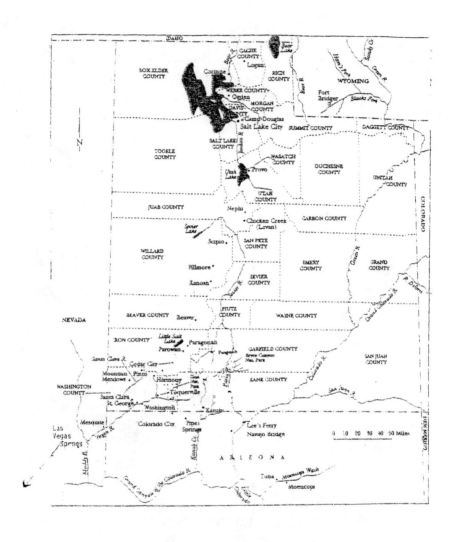

CENTRAL UTAH TERRITORY 1857

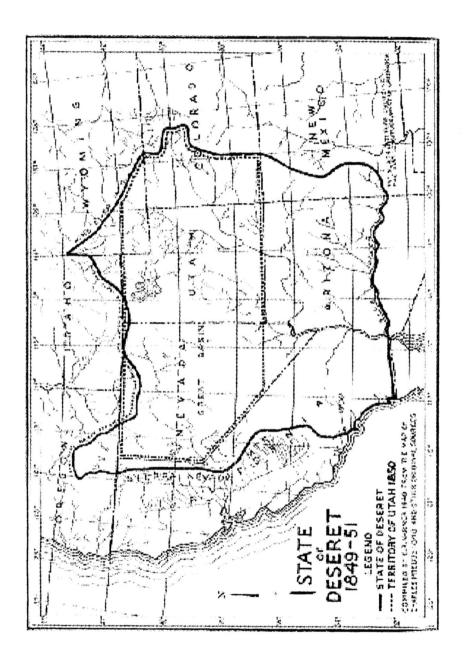

PROLOGUE

Most Americans believe that the "War on Terror" began September 11, 2001, when religious zealots took the lives of over three thousand innocent civilians by piloting commercial airliners into the World Trade Centers and the Pentagon and, when Americans began to fight back, on United Flight 93 in Pennsylvania.

Some would say the first act of terrorism occurred earlier with the truck bombing at the Murrah Federal Building April 19, 1995, in Oklahoma City. They would correctly overlook the October 12, 2000, attack on the USS Cole; the August 7, 1998, attacks on U.S. embassies in Kenya and Tanzania; the June 25, 1996, bombing of the Khobar Towers in Saudi Arabia; and the November 13, 1995, bombing of the U.S. military headquarters in Riyadh.

More would say it began with the first attack on the World Trade Centers February 26, 1993. But this would ignore the December 21,1988, Pan Am explosion over Lockerbie, Scotland; the September 5, 1986, hijacking of a Pan Am jumbo jet in Karachi, Pakistan; the October 8, 1985, seizure of the Italian cruise liner Achille Lauro; the June 14, 1985, hijacking of a TWA Boeing 727 to Beirut; the September 20, 1984, car bombing at the U.S Embassy annex in Beirut; the December 12, 1983, car bombing of the U.S. embassy in Kuwait City; or the October 23, 1983, suicide bombing of the U.S. Marine barracks in Beirut, Lebanon.

An astute scholar of American foreign policy might point, with some credibility, to the 444-day hostage taking of 52 U.S. diplomats in Tehran, Iran, beginning November 4, 1979, as the starting point of the modern day "War on Terror."

With the exception of Oklahoma City, motivation for all of these attacks was directly linked to Islamic fanaticism. These attacks coupled with the wars in Afghanistan and Iraq have, at this writing, taken the lives of more than six thousand Americans and wounded nearly thirty thousand. These numbers pale in comparison to the hundreds of thousands from other countries killed, most of whom themselves were members of the Islamic faith, otherwise known as Muslims.

But few Americans are aware that the very first act of such inspired murder on American soil, and the first American resistance to it, did in fact occur on the morning of September 11, . . . 1857.

The attack occurred on a remote mountain meadow in the Southern Utah Territory. It was planned and executed, not by dark-skinned Middle Eastern-ers, but by light-skinned European Americans, mostly of English, Danish, and German decent. Though their religious beliefs contained significant cor-relations with the followers of Mohammed, they called themselves Christians. They appealed to the poorest in society. They followed the teachings of a Prophet, the book he wrote and the revelations he published. They were told they were the chosen people destined to inherit the earth. On the judgment day, they were to be rewarded with all the riches of the earth's bounty, with kingdoms in the celestial world, and with the brutal destruction of their en-emies—the Gentiles.

These people embraced the doctrines of consecration; of blood atonement; of communalism; and of millennialism; of white supremacy; the principle of polygamy; and governance by theocratic rule. They believed they were being relentlessly persecuted. They failed to anticipate how others would react to their aberrant, antisocial doctrines and practices. The resultant clash led to one of the least reconciled tragedies in United States history. Members, and many of the original founders, of the Church of Jesus Christ of Latter-day Saints, otherwise known as Mormons, perpetrated a monumental transgression in what is now the state of Utah.

While there were other incidents of fanaticism involving America's early history, this is the story of America's first grim encounter with religious obedi-ence mutating into the totalitarian rule of a people. These same people, and their successors, successfully suppressed the story and the lessons that could have been learned. The facts were nearly lost in the firestorm of the Civil War, which closely followed this horrific and largely unrelated event. Fortunately, a number of dedicated historians have painstakingly documented this piece of American history that is not, but should be, common knowledge.

Against the defining prelude to our modern day "War on Terror," what happened in the Southern Utah Territory at Mountain Meadows in the early fall of 1857 can be considered, without hyperbole, America's first 9/11.

PART ONE

CHAPTER 1

LAS VEGAS SPRINGS NORTHWEST NEW MEXICO TERRITORY

SEPTEMBER 15, 1857
6:15 AM

He slung the last of his coffee tin onto the campfire and half-heartedly cursed the sun as its first rays broke over the eastern range. It had been unexpectedly warm since Henry Young had left San Bernardino with his brother Cao. Henry had argued and succeeded, he thought, in convincing his brother to delay their journey until later in the season. The desert weather would be cooler and the sun more a friend than an enemy. His little brother, however, was in the throes of young love, and the virtue of patience was lost on the young buck.

Henry filled a coffee tin for Cao, setting it close and upwind.

"Wake up," Henry said. "We've chores to do before the sun gets much higher."

Cao grunted and rolled over.

Henry knew that the next couple of hours would be the best part of the day. Day of rest or not, stock still needed tending. This practicality didn't persuade Cao. Even in his hurry, Cao had lobbied hard for a day of rest. After six straight days out of San Bernardino, it seemed smart to take a day at the "Springs." They'd made good time, and it would be good for the stock too.

Even in September, the trek from San Bernardino to the Utah Territory was subject to a hot and unrelenting sun. The Young brothers were well prepared. They had crossed through here before. But the horses and pack mules had noticeably lost weight. They all needed to replenish their reserves before pushing on. There would be some water between here and Cedar City, but the first fifty miles would be very dry, and the heat would make it seem even drier. Some day, this landscape would be prominent with monolithic sets of high-rise mega-resorts called Las Vegas. For now, looking outward in all directions produced only visions of a vast nothingness. Yes, after six straight days traveling from San Bernardino, it did seem smart to take a day at the "Springs."

A dry cough from Cao broke Henry's thoughts. Cao still lay in his bedroll, but a hand had snuck out and was reaching for his coffee tin. It had taken less than a minute after the first whiff met his nostrils. Henry knew the power of his brother's cravings and how to use them against him and his lazy tendencies. Henry proceeded to unpack some tools. Each of the pack mules had lost a shoe, and their horse's hooves needed tending to as well.

Henry scanned the horizon of their vacant desert surroundings, rubbed his eyes, and then looked again with his right hand raised to shield the sun.

"We got company, Cao. Get up."

Cao took another sip of his coffee and began to stretch.

"Looks to be about a mile out. I'm sure he's packin' a carbine."

Cao swallowed hard and bolted for his pants.

Henry recognized the dull glint of light flashing off the blued steel. Practically every man carried armaments in these parts. This was to be expected.

"He's comin' out of the northeast . . . . He's afoot."

Cao had his boots on in seconds, and both men inventoried their own firearms. There was reason for concern now. If their visitor had come out of the south or east, he could have been a night traveler from the Colorado River. A considerable distance, but survivable. The trail northeast was dry hard traveling. It was where Henry and Cao were heading. And a man coming out of there . . . without a mount? The brothers sensed trouble.

The figure headed straight for them. There really was no alternative. They were camped at the only water within fifty miles. Henry stoked the campfire. Cao walked over to the horses and steadied them with his hand. "Whoa!" Doc's eyes were wide with excitement. Casey's ears strained toward the walking man.

"What do you make of it?" Cao asked.

"He looks worn out . . . draggin' his feet some."

"How long you 'spect he's been afoot? Injun?"

"No," Henry concluded but not knowing why.

The man was still too far off for them to speculate with any degree of accuracy. A long minute or so passed. Just as well. The brothers welcomed time to gain an edge against any surprises.

"Ain't dressed like no Injun. He's packing a side arm too."

Henry emptied and rinsed the coffee pot and refilled it with spring water and grounds. "It don't appear he's tryin' ta get the jump on us. We best be ready to be hospitable."

The stranger's strides were growing shorter and his tack was slightly side-to-side. But he was steadily closing on their position and slowly coming into view.

"Is that blood on him?" Cao asked.

Henry strained his eyes to see. Then he looked in all directions as if more stumbling wounded gunmen might be descending upon them. Seeing none, he turned his gaze back to the stranger.

"It does look like he's wounded pretty good. His right sleeve is blood-soaked sure enough."

"Arrow or gunshot?" Cao asked.

"Maybe knife," Henry speculated. "I expect he'll tell us."

They watched silently as the man grew near. Cao steadied the horses as he peered out from behind them. Henry hunkered down tending the campfire and starting the coffee for a boil.

The closer he got, the clearer it became. This man was exhausted and worn beyond good reason. His wounds, while not fresh, were far from healing. His clothes were torn rags, and what remained of his boots was nearly worthless. His exposed flesh showed festering cuts and scratches. His right arm was clearly wounded . . . probably gunshot . . . his sleeve blood-soaked. His eyes flickered between the weight of extreme fatigue and the sharpness of incessant pain.

The stranger shuffled into camp holding his rifle with both hands, but making no threatening moves. He stood like a specter silenced before returning to its grave. The brothers measured his approach and responded with their own stillness.

"You boys Mormons?" The stranger spoke first.

The question stumped the brothers. Neither quite knew how to respond. If the stranger had asked for water, for help, for their names, but . . . Finally, after an awkward moment, Henry started.

"I'm Henry Young . . . and this is my brother Cao. We're both Catholic, I expect."

Cao's first thought was to qualify his brother's statement. After all, he would be a Mormon soon, being baptized in the faith so he could marry the girl he loved. Cao was generally comfortable letting his thoughts immediately pop out of his mouth. But there was something in the stranger's register. The way he had asked the question. Maybe it was just the unusual nature of the question itself.

"What's your name . . . and what difference does it make if we're Mormons or not?"

The stranger started wavering.

"You're not . . . you're not Mormons?"

The butt of his rifle hit the ground. The stranger's torn hands slid up the barrel as he grasped it for support. His body buckled and swung down as he tried to hold himself, even as his grip slipped off the upright barrel. Just before he lay sprawled and still in the dust, the brothers heard him gasp . . . followed by the choking escape of two words, "Thank God."

CHAPTER 2

MOUNTAIN MEADOWS
COMMAND POST
UTAH TERRITORY

SEPTEMBER 11, 1857
12:05 AM

The night air carried an early fall chill in this midnight hour. Low cloud cover kept the frost at bay, but also hampered the nighttime visibility as it obscured the moon and starlight. A campfire kept the immediate area well lit. But beyond its reach, a cloak of blackness rose so thickly that when Ira Hatch strode into camp, he materialized as if he'd stepped through a wall of smoke.

The three men already sitting around the campfire, however, were not startled. The late hour would usually call for the men to be asleep in their bedrolls. But these men had been waiting and were in a state of full readiness. They had been waiting for Ira Hatch. They had been waiting for his report. A report they knew was likely to spell trouble.

The tall guide and Indian agent stooped before the fire and rubbed his hands above it as if washing them in the warmth. Across from him sat John D. Lee with a determined look. Major John Higbee and Bishop Philip Klingensmith flanked Lee. Though anxious to hear what Hatch had to say, both Higbee and P.K. (as he was known) remained quiet in deference to Lee. It was his place to speak first.

"Well, let's have it."

"Three made an attempt . . . one was killed . . . two got through our south perimeter. Two Ute sentries killed, two wounded. All from Tutsegabit's camp." Hatch was not known for wasting words.

"Two got through? Are the Utes pursuing them?" Lee's exasperation at this turn of events was apparent.

"They say it's too dark . . . Be too easy getting shot like their brothers. The Utes won't pursue them until sunrise." The picture Hatch was painting frustrated Lee all the more.

"The escapees were well armed. Looks like they used the creek as cover. They were most ways past our perimeter by the time they were detected." He poked the fire with a stick as he let the news sink in further.

The corners of Lee's mouth cringed with disgust. His face turned to Higbee, then P.K., and back again to Hatch. "I don't need to tell you Ira, what will happen if those two men are able to deliver the word of what's been going on here these past four days." Lee was fuming. "Can't these worthless Lamanite savages carry out the simplest of tasks? More'n three hundred of 'em! And every time I get their chiefs to agree on a plan, they botch it. Battle Axe of the Lord, my ass!"

The Mormons had long considered the Indians throughout the territory a great potential resource. The Book of Mormon had portended their eventual conversion in great numbers, and at over three hundred thousand strong, the Mormon militia leaders were counting on them. They were counting on the day they would rise up in a military alliance with their Zion against the Gentiles.

Hatch sensed that it was time to be proactive. "Give me two of our best men and let me pick a dozen warriors. I'll head after them at the first sign of daybreak."

"Don't be waitin' for mornin' light, Ira. Those boys aren't going to stop and wait for you to catch up to 'em. The sooner you get started, the sooner you'll be able to put a stop to this. See that all of your company has good mounts and rifles." It wasn't a suggestion from Lee to Hatch. It was an order.

"What if I can't get any of the Utes to leave before sunup?" Ira didn't much care for the prospect himself.

"Promise each man an extra cow to go. Promise five additional for whoever takes out the quarry." Lee was determined. "We got ourselves into a real shit hole here! The longer it takes to climb out of it, the worse we're all going to stink."

CHAPTER 3

LAS VEGAS SPRINGS NORTHWEST NEW MEXICO TERRITORY

SEPTEMBER 15, 1857
7:20 AM

Milum was not dead, but apparently close to it, and tending to his wounds took a toll beyond the injuries he'd already received. All of them had been incurred over the past few days, and most exhibited some degree of infection. It was easiest to treat him when he wasn't conscious. Each time Henry would administer the liniment, it would burn through the wounds like a white-hot iron. If he were awake, he would soon pass into a faint or become lost in his delirium and then pass out. Although this enabled Henry to more easily complete the dressing of wounds, both he and Cao were exasperated at the time it would take before their visitor could explain his circumstance and how he had sustained himself through the desert crossing. They were also worried. Worried as to what this may pertain to the stranger, to the crossing, and to themselves.

The "Springs," or as titled on some maps, Las Vegas Springs, was located in the vast New Mexico Territory, comprised of present-day Arizona, New Mexico, and the southern tip of Nevada. It was known to travelers as one of the most dependable watering holes along the "Old Spanish Trail" named for the Dominguez-Escalante expedition of 1776. There was no settlement, though a Mormon fort had been built there—a one hundred fifty foot square compound that stood next to the creek flowing out of the springs. It had been built only two years before and within its fourteen-foot-high adobe walls, several buildings had been constructed, including a post office.

But the fort had been abandoned for reasons unbeknownst to Henry and Cao. It had served as an outpost for Deseret, a land comprised of all of the Utah and portions of the New Mexico territories. Mormons and Native Americans populated the Utah Territory, it being the vast highlands to the northeast, comprised of present-day Utah, Wyoming, Colorado, Idaho, and the northern bulk of Nevada. The Mormons believed it to be the "Promised Land" and were carving a nation from it of their own. But it appeared that even with the promise of good water, this empty land and desert sun had proven a harsh mistress. Or perhaps there was some other reason such a well-constructed compound had been abandoned.

Cao was first to conjecture about their patient. "You think this character might be running from the law? Ain't no kinda man gonna be comin' through the trail like he did if he didn't do somethin'. Bank robbing? Maybe he's runnin' from a killin'. Hell, Henry, we maybe got us some reward money comin'." That pushed Cao's adrenaline a bit. "And what's that business about what kind' a churchin' we do? Them's some mighty queer ramblins."

"Well, look at him. More'n half dead. I've no cause to think anything I might say'd make any more sense in the same condition." Henry was less prone to follow his brother's logic and more conservative in his estimate. "The closest bank I know of is more'n three hundred miles north. The closest law's at least half that far. That's a long run, an' he don't appear to have any sacks full a money. He's got his guns, some ammo, an' what's left of his clothes. If he was part of a killin', it looks like he came pretty close to gettin' kilt hisself."

For a moment the brothers were silently bothered. It was clear that the man lying before them had found trouble. Either someone had shot him or he had shot himself, though the latter didn't appear likely. And where was his mount? Someone had tried to cut him down. But who? If there was another shooter, where was he now? Or worse, where were they now and were they still looking for him? They'd have to wait until the stranger told them. But would he be telling the truth? None of the possibilities sat well with either of them. Their discussion shifted to anticipating their options.

"So what are we going to do with this guy?" Cao asked. He didn't care for the burden this man posed. "I don't want any of the trouble he's carryin'. And I sure don't want any posse thinkin' we're takin' up with him."

Henry countered. "Well, if the law shows up, I don't think we've got much to be worried about at this point. It's the other side of the fence I'm worried 'bout. If someone wants him this badly and they're not the law, they might not want us in the picture either."

That troubled Cao even more. "How 'bout we start on our way now?"

"A little late for that."

"Suppose we leave in the early morning but leave him a little food with some bandages and liniment."

"And maybe when he comes to, he'll want to keep headin' south." Henry attempt at facetiousness was lost on Cao.

"Course in his condition, and on foot, he probly wouldn't make it from here to the river." Cao almost wished he hadn't spoken that last thought.

"We weren't planning to do any ridin' today anyhow." Though Henry wasn't one to assume responsibility just because it was thrown his way, he wouldn't assume the judgment of leaving another to die when he didn't know their story. "Either we stay here with him until he's well enough to head out on his own, or we're gonna have to take him with us."

Neither option appealed to Cao. A delay in getting back to Cedar City was hardly acceptable to him. "How long do you think it'll take to get him ready to ride?"

"When he comes around, we'll be havin' that discussion. He might have some helpful cautions about the road ahead." Henry started to reason with optimism. "Most of his wounds don't run too deep. Even the gunshot turned out to be clean. At least as clean as a bullet may get. He's still gonna move with a lot of pain but I think he'll make it. Some more rest and some food and water might see him up in a day or two."

"I guess we stick to our plans for now . . . get rested up and see how he does." Cao knew a choice had been made.

CHAPTER 4

MOUNTAIN MEADOWS
COMMAND POST
UTAH TERRITORY

SEPTEMBER 11, 1857
12:20 AM

"I want Mathews and Haskell. I'll ask for two of the best shots from each tribe. We should be able to track 'em pretty easy. I doubt they'll leave the creek much if any. It's the only dependable water for forty miles this time of year. We should catch 'em before sunset tomorrow." Hatch was confident.

Ira Hatch was an expert tracker and could speak every Ute dialect within the Deseret Territory. Only Jacob Hamblin and Dimick Huntington were more respected in these skills. But Ira was the better soldier. He was an avid game hunter, but this would not be his first manhunt. Though he preferred the kind of prey that didn't shoot back, few doubted he would catch them. The question that lingered in the minds of those present was what would happen when he did.

"What makes you so sure?" P.K. cut in. P.K. was one of the few men around with enough moxie to challenge a man like Ira Hatch.

Hatch ignored the question long enough for John Higbee to intercept. "We all know you got a gift, Ira. It jus' seems more important than ever, that you prove right."

"I'll find 'em, you don' have ta worry bout that." Ira's eyes caught and held P.K.'s.

It was Lee's turn to speak, and the answer to the question must be unequivocal. He straightened himself and looked to Ira and then to Higbee and P.K. Though his tone was grave and his tenor markedly lower, his voice was clear. "By sunset tomorrow this whole business is going to be over. The commanders' orders are clear. It's going to be over here at the Meadows . . . and it's going to be over for those two that got through our lines." He looked back to Ira. "Don't bother bringin' prisoners back, Ira. Just see that they get buried where you find 'em. I expect we'll be doing a whole lot more burying than you . . . so when you're finished, get back here and give us a hand."

Lee's affect was one of commanding inevitability betrayed by disgust and self-loathing. The gravity of their situation had become increasingly evident. Actions had been taken on decisions made by a small group of men. Decisions had been made based on haughty judgments, with reasoning mixed and clouded. As their willing tools, he and the others had set in motion a series of events that were moving out of their grasp and would, from now on, govern their actions. Here at Mountain Meadows, things had gone quite poorly, gone off course, and gone too far. There was no erasing the actions taken, no pulling back from what they must now do, but perhaps their deeds could be hidden.

For Lee it was clear what was now warranted, and there could be no more mistakes. Time had become their enemy. His men had to be told in no uncertain terms—no matter how repulsive—what must now occur.

"Ira, I want you to take Rosmus Anderson with you. Have him carry the surplus and ride behind the troops." Lee's voice bared the quality of a man caring for his brother, but his eyes darkened under the consequences to be visited. "I don't think he has the stomach for what we have to do here."

Ira leaned forward toward Lee. "What makes you think he'll stomach what I'm going to be doing?" Hatch thought it was a fair question.

"He's got a wife and five young girls at home." Lee retorted. "I expect the two you'll be after are grown men."

All four men at this meeting lowered their gaze. Lee's point was well made. As loathsome a mission as Hatch was being sent on, its undertaking paled in comparison to the work that would take place tomorrow across the cresting valley of the Meadows.

Hatch stood up from his place near the campfire, nodded, and left camp without another word. Lee turned his attention to P.K. and Higbee. "Boys, we've got work to do. Hard work. We've been tested by fire before and it's only made us stronger. I know you have the strength and presence to carry it through. Here's how it lays before us." And with that Lee proceeded to advance the plans with his lieutenants.

For the past four days he'd known what would happen tomorrow. Each day his vision increased in clarity. He'd kept the word closely guarded. He had only shared it with a few others, and then, only shared what was needed to prepare, until it was time, and now it was time, for the others to know. Time to defend their nation. Time to submit to Zion's rule. Time to enact God's will.

CHAPTER 5

LAS VEGAS SPRINGS NORTHWEST NEW MEXICO TERRITORY

SEPTEMBER 16, 1857
12:05 AM

The stranger had remained unconscious throughout the day. There were intermittent episodes of delirium where the man would shout out in obvious distress and fear. Nothing he said, however, seemed to make any sense to the two brothers. Henry tended to the man's wounds as best he could by applying poultices. This was Henry's first time playing nursemaid. He had seen women perform these services in the past, and so he was just doing his best to recall how it was done. He was successful in getting the stranger to drink a significant amount of broth. At times, his patient would perspire freely and then shake almost convulsively . . . but mostly the man slept. The level of his exhaustion became evident as the day passed and the night followed.

Henry had considered bringing the wounded man into the confines of the fort, but decided to keep him close to the fire. The brothers had purposely remained outside the compound. They did not want to be mistaken for brazen interlopers if, by some remote chance, a Mormon militia returned. Besides, after sleeping outdoors most nights over the past several years, they were more acclimated to the open sky than the confines of walls and roofs.

It was midnight as Henry Young rose to stoke the fire near the man he had been tending to for the past eighteen hours. As the new flames burst forth illuminating the immediate area, Henry stopped as if a rattler had suddenly coiled before him. Instead, he saw the fire's flickering light reflecting in the icy gaze of the stranger's eyes. The stranger was dead. A deep chill shook his bones as eyes stared at him from a face void of all expression. They stared in a silence that seemed to quiet the sharp crackle of the fire. The unfolding revelation wrapped itself around Henry as if to squeeze all the air out of his lungs. His only breath came as a single slow inhale.

Then Henry nearly threw himself across the fire as the eyes flashed and blinked. It was not death staring at him after all.

The stranger stretched his neck and winced at the pain. He closed his eyes and spoke. "How long have I been out?"

"All day. Half the night gone by too."

In a voice rough but clear, the man searched. "You told me your name was . . . was . . . "

"Young, Henry Young." He was regaining his regular breath, but his pulse was still pounding in his ears.

"You have a brother with you . . . if I'm rememberin' right."

"Yeah. Cao." Henry was taken aback by the lucidity of the man's speech as well as his recollection from the previous morning.

"And you're not kin to the mighty Brigham Young?" The man's suspicious nature was beginning to show again.

There it was again, the odd question. "I told you me and my brother was Catholic. Still don't know why that matters a lick or why I should even be bothered to tell you." Henry never liked being put on the defensive, and it was time to start pursuing the answers to some of his own questions.

A few moments passed in silence. It became apparent that Henry was not comfortable with the one-sidedness of their conversation.

The stranger coughed and produced a string of phlegm that hooked on his lower lip and stopped at his chin. He wiped at it with a torn sleeve. "Sure could use a drink."

Henry grabbed a flask, poured the water into a tin, and handed it over as the man tried to sit up in some measure of comfort and to face Henry as they talked. The stranger held the tin to his lips so that the water soaked into the dryness and then let it cool the stinging of the cracks crisscrossing his lips. He held the cup away from his mouth and slightly waved it in Henry's direction.

"Thank you for this." He took a small swallow. "And it wouldn't be right to not tell you I appreciate your help. I reckon I'd be lying in the sand for the buzzards by now if you hadn't been here. Maybe worse." He dipped two fingers into the water and then wiped them across an eye, then did the same for the other. "My name is John Milum Jones. Lots of folks call me John. Most friends call me Milum. I reckon you've earned the right to call me by either one." He brought one knee up, then the other, so that he was more in a crouch than a sit. "Excuse me while I take a piss." The man rose slowly, carefully stepped out and away from the edge of the firelight, and then began to relieve himself. While he stood in the shadows with his back to Henry, Milum said, "I reckon you've got a few other questions for me besides just my name."

Henry had a flood of questions. What happened? Where? Who did this to you? Why? Were there others, or were you alone? But what he said was, "As many questions as you'll answer."

Milum took a seat back on the bedroll he'd been lying on for the last day and a half. "It's a long story and I want to tell it to you. But it ain't a pretty one and I'd just as soon not have to tell it twice." With that, Milum cocked his head and glanced in the direction of Henry's snoring brother.

"Cao!" Henry shouted as he threw a branch from the woodpile at his brother. "Wake up!"

CHAPTER 6

MOUNTAIN MEADOWS
MOGATSU CREEK HEADWATERS
UTAH TERRITORY

SEPTEMBER 11, 1857
12:35 AM

Ira Hatch approached the sentry position and walked directly up to Thales Haskell, who was standing guard. They were near the meadow's Mogatsu Creek's outlet. Hatch had stationed him there a little more than thirty minutes prior. Haskell glanced at Ira's approach and then turned his attention back in the direction of the recent skirmish between the guards and the three members of the wagon train. The Gentile's company remained positioned some two hundred yards north of this position. The meandering creek, which ran past their encampment, passed south not twenty-five feet from where he now stood.

It had only been an hour since three men had died here. One from the escape party, two from their rank. The Indian guards posted at this spot had not paid close enough attention. Haskell would not make that mistake.

Hatch joined Haskell and silently looked into the darkness that covered the scene of the recent deaths. The quiet following the shootout increased the intensity of each sound that now dared to break the night's chill.

The tribe had moved all three bodies away. By now they were preparing their braves for burial and probably stripping the fallen Gentile and desecrating his body.

"Nothing lately," whispered Haskell, anticipating his superior's question.

In one hour I'll be sending a replacement to your position. . . . You, I, and Mathews will be leading a party to find the two that got through." He waited for Haskell to nod, then proceeded to the creek.

He carefully made his way to the bank. His thoughts focused on the three Gentiles who had immersed themselves in the creek. Dipping his hand in well past his wrist, the water's icy coldness was shocking. The Gentiles would have been floating in near freezing temperatures for over two hundred yards. The distance could be walked in a casual few minutes. Floating down it with a slow imperceptible movement would take much longer. It must have seemed an eternity. The escape was a daring move by desperate men. Desperate but calculated. They had to have guessed that the creek's outlet would be heavily guarded. Yet it was the only escape route with any cover leading from the Meadows.

Hatch's arm began to ache, but instead of withdrawing from the water, he reached deeper to test its depth. His shoulder was nearly submerged before his hand struck the mossy bottom. Deep enough for a man to drift with the current, yet shallow enough to keep his head, and his rifle, above the surface. The force of the water's flow would assist in their forward progress.

How vulnerable they would be if detected. The ache in his arm intensified, but still he did not withdraw. The one Gentile they stopped was heavily armed. He carried a Winchester repeater rifle and two handguns fully loaded. In addition, he carried thirty rifle and thirty pistol rounds. He'd only gotten off one rifle shot . . . probably a reflex after being hit in the chest by the Hawken ball that killed him. One of Tutsegabit's braves had been lucky with that shot.

The other two Gentiles must have been equally armed as they both got off several rounds from their rifles and pistols. They had made those shots count, seeing as two of the Indians were now dead. Another two were wounded. One of them would not live to see the sunrise.

Finally the numbness set in. It was the final answer he had sought. Their plan had worked. Not as well as they'd hoped, but it had worked. The cold water was agonizing at first, but after a minute or so it was bearable. They would hope to drift by their guards undetected, but were prepared to fight their way through. As it was, they made it past the first two sentries unnoticed. The brave who actually sounded the alarm wasn't even assigned a sentry post. He was simply taking a creek-side stroll mistakenly thinking he was safely behind his tribe's perimeter line. That mistake cost him his life.

The heavy cover of willow and alder along the creek only contributed to darker shades of blackness. Had they not been discovered, the original three would have made a clean escape. The breech wouldn't have been discovered until the next day, and probably not at all.

Being found out, and with the chaos of guns blazing in the darkness, the two survivors had only to keep to their plan and head quickly downhill. Confusion would hamstring their enemies. But now they'd be on foot, dripping wet. Cold but generating their own warmth . . . getting lighter as they ran . . . further from the Meadows and the gunfight. With two, one could look to the dangers ahead, and one to the dangers behind. Lee was right about one thing. They wouldn't wait for the danger behind to catch them. Their plan would be to charge ahead, get away, and get help, whatever it took.

It made sense. It made more than sense. It was a run for survival. Hatch would have done the same thing had he been in their shoes. A call to action was always his preference to idleness in the face of danger. An escape attempt like this one was one of the few options this adversary had available. Unfortunately, it was a move no one in his company had anticipated. Ira Hatch viewed their determination, the sheer boldness of their effort, with reluctant admiration. He had to give them their due. Though born from desperation, it took real strength and courage to carry out such a plan.

Ira withdrew his arm and flexed his hands. It would have been difficult to fire a weapon, he thought. But of course they must have kept their hands out, holding their weapons and ammo above the water. He deftly leapt the stream, an easy four-foot-wide hop to the opposite grassy bank. "They had a good plan," he thought. "Lucky for us they didn't pull it off undetected. Challenging enough situation as it is." The odds were still very much against the Gentiles. The success of the escape would only be temporary. Ultimately they would fail. It was his job to see to it . . . and Ira Hatch was very good at his job.

CHAPTER 7

LAS VEGAS SPRINGS
NORTHWEST NEW
MEXICO TERRITORY

SEPTEMBER 16, 1857
12:20 AM

Cao instantly spun to his hands and knees. He knew immediately that his brother had thrown the branch. Henry often kicked or hit Cao when he wanted him to wake up. It was one of the many little things about Henry he grudgingly had to endure. The slight was quickly forgotten when he realized that the stranger was awake. With the stranger in their camp and unanswered questions swirling in Cao's mind, a deep sleep had not been forthcoming. Now, maybe, they would learn the stranger's story.

Cao had only to slip on his boots to become fully dressed. He walked over to the campfire and poured himself a cup of coffee. The flavor had been burnt away, replaced with a scalding bitterness. Cao actually preferred his coffee this way at night. It felt like a weapon. A hard-boiled coffee seemed to sharpen his senses in the darkness. Less than a minute after being rudely awakened, Cao set himself next to his brother and looked across the fire at the stranger. He wasted no time revealing his thought and agenda. "Well, what d'ya know? Maybe we'll be able to ride out of here tomorrow like we planned."

Henry was in no mood to let Cao initiate a debate over trip itineraries. "Mr. John Milum Jones here was about to fill us in on what may lie ahead." Henry had already waited too long to hear the wounded man's story. Recognizing this and edged with his own curiosity, Cao allowed the derailing. The brothers turned from each other and looked at their guest.

With a nod to the northeast, Milum spoke. "I started out part of a wagon train headin' to California. Moved out of Carrol County, Arkansas, near Crooked Creek just over four months ago–May 1 or 2 once't we got to rollin'. Cap'n Alexander Fancher headed us up. He said there was eighty-nine in our train the first night we made camp and we were drivin' four hundred head a cows. Most all of 'em were Texas longhorns, and I reckon they were the first such long-horned cattle ever brought out to this country the way all the folks west of Council Bluffs reacted to the sight of em."

Milum picked up a stick and drew a trail line in the dirt as he continued describing their route. "After we crossed the Big Muddy we commenced to makin' pretty good time and did real well 'til the Rockies rose up, then the going got pretty slow. It took a lot to git over and around the mountains in Colorado. By the time we got to Jasper, we'd picked up another fifty odd travelers, mostly friends and family. When we got out close to Green River, a big Dutchman joined up with us. He called himself the 'Missouri Wildcat.' He was a loud one, always crackin' jokes."

"Ain't nothing wild comes outta Missouri 'cept a jackass," said Cao. A whistling snort gave evidence of the pleasure he took at his own wit. Henry just lifted an eyebrow towards his brother.

"Well that's how he touted himself, 'Missouri Wildcat.' He was a handful, but he didn't mean no harm. Anyways, by now we was pushin' over a thousand head. We had some rough young drovers helpin' out. We had another boss named Cap'n Jack Baker. He and Cap'n Fancher divided up responsibility for the command a the outfit.

"We pulled into Salt Lake City in late July, and Cap'n Fancher went talkin' to the locals. It's pretty much all Mormons there. The cap'n came back and reported their leader had asked us to keep to ourselves and not to do any trading with the settlers along the way. The cap'n was also told we should be takin' the southern route to San Bernardino. They were pretty insistent about avoidin' the Donner route; said it was too late in the year for such a long train to beat the snow. That set off quite a debate among our group. Both Fancher and Baker had intended on the Donner."

Henry added, "All depends on what route you're takin' and the reason you're gonna come to California. Chasing the gold, you stay north. Ranching? Might want to come south." With that thought out, Henry let Milum continue.

Milum knew the purpose of his party included neither. The entrepreneurs intended to set up businesses in supply of the mining boom. The cattle would sell well and provide capital. He decided to let it pass and continue with the telling of his tale.

"Old Brigham Young offered to let us camp and graze our herds at a valley called Mountain Meadows. That's at least a hundred miles northeast a' here. He said the property belonged to the church and we could get the animals ready to cross the desert along the 'Old Spanish Trail.' Everyone seemed to feel it was a generous offer in light of the restrictions being imposed. We were even offered a guide to lead us to the Meadows.

"The guide was supposed to be a fellow named Hamblin. We met up with him at Corn Creek and he also claimed he owned the ranch at the Meadows we were headed for. He was ridin' with about a dozen Indian chiefs headed north. Hamblin claimed to have business he had to get back to in Salt Lake City. That's when he turned us over to a man named Hatch."

Henry and Cao looked at one another. Hamblin they had not met, but his reputation was known beyond the lands he frequented—towering mountains, forbidding salt flats, and a maze of canyon walls. They had met Ira Hatch. They had met him on their first pass through Deseret. He was a man of business, no-nonsense. He performed with an aloofness and stoicism that some found admirable and others found chilling.

"We stayed clear of the settlers in the towns we passed through like we was told. The few people we saw were a scornful lot. I was just as happy to pass them by. Hatch was a good guide, but not very friendly. His eyes looked right through you."

The description matched their memory of the Mormon tracker.

"He's known to be a hard man," Henry added.

Cao agreed. "Seemed like a real taskmaster. He's got a look that rides hard on you."

"No law 'gainst bein' unfriendly." Henry stated. "Or havin' a cold stare."

Milum Jones rubbed his shoulder and looked out past the brothers. His eyes squinted as though looking past the darkness. Then, blinking at the fire as if to clean them, he raised his eyes with a new sharpness. "Cold as he looks when you first see him, he looks even colder when the son-of-a-bitch is staring at you over the sights of his rifle."

CHAPTER 8

MOUNTAIN MEADOWS
COMMAND POST
UTAH TERRITORY

SEPTEMBER 11, 1857
12:30 AM

John D. Lee turned to P.K. and John Higbee, aware that their full attention was riveted upon him. It was time to lay out the full course of plans; what was expected of them; what was expected of others. He knew they would find it ugly, and he expected resistance from his old friend P.K. Keeping this in mind, Lee opted for a soft approach. A touch of diplomacy could only help when broaching delicate subjects or redefining boundaries.

"Thank you for getting here, P.K. I know you had reservations about all these doings. I do believe we'd be in better circumstances if we'd all listened to you at the council last Sabbath. But in fact . . . "

P.K. interrupted Lee. "You're still planning on killing all the Gentiles, aren't you?" Anger ruled over any sadness or misgivings. "And now you want me to help you do it . . . Is that about right, John?"

It was a hard truth, Lee admitted to himself, but he would not mince words with the respected Mormon bishop. "Hear me out, P.K. Once you've got the whole picture, if you can come up with a better solution, I'm all ears."

"Let's have it," Higbee interjected, trying to stop an argument before Lee could present his proposal.

"As I'm sure you've surmised by now, the initial plan to overwhelm the Gentiles failed. Chief Jackson, in his Lamanite wisdom, ordered his braves to attack ahead of my command."

"Chief Jackson says a chief waits for the command of no other. So he and his braves attack the train. Fifty of 'em against a well-armed wagon party of over one hundred. Arrogant savage! All they accomplished was putting the train on defense and giving them a chance to dig in. Now were stuck with a siege that's going on four days. We're finding out these Gentiles are not only well armed but are also good marksmen. The upper hand we've held is slipping away with each mistake and each day."

P.K. had heard enough. Somewhere devils were pointing fingers and laughing at this travesty. "Haven't these folks been punished enough? We have their cattle and other stock. So far it's only the Indians who have blood on their hands. We should not be pulling any triggers."

"That won't be the case once Ira stops the two that breached our lines." Lee's voice lowered.

"He hasn't left yet. Call off the order." P.K. knew there was no turning back, but this was his way of letting Lee and Higbee know he wasn't ready to join them.

Higbee was determined to help Lee with this one. "I beg ta differ. Bill Stewart shot one of 'em that tried to escape to the north a couple of nights ago. So blood is on our hands and they know it. There was two of 'em to start out and the one that got away turned round an' rode right back into the Gentile camp. Our reports have it that there's $100,000 in gold on that train, P.K., not to mention that one of those Missouri boys is said to have been the very one who murdered the Prophet."

P.K. ignored Higbee's revelation of spilt blood and bristled at his other comments. "That's such a heap, Johnny. Most o' those boys was still nursin' their mammas when the Prophet was killed. And if this is about gold, you can count me out."

Higbee was at least fifteen years younger than the older men. In fact P.K. had been his bishop for years. Though P.K. held no rank in the militia, he would not be intimidated by the ambitious young Higbee's rank of major.

"It's not about gold, P.K." Lee could sense P.K. setting his heels. "Haslam rode in a half hour after you arrived with the militia. We've got to end it after the sun rises tomorrow. Besides, the Lamanites are threatening to kill the Gentiles and us if we don't help them finish the job. We asked them to start it and now we have to finish it. We've worked too hard to rope these savages in to allow it to all unravel now."

"Are the orders written?" P.K. was ashen. "Were written orders made and delivered?" He was beginning to realize that the situation was more hopeless than he'd feared.

Lee reached into his shirt pocket. He pulled out a square of parchment and handed it to his old friend.

P.K. looked at the folded parchment. He rubbed his thumb over the broken seal as if to repair the break, then slid his thumb under the edge to lift the message open. He anticipated what the message contained. Still, he was shocked by what he read.

> Captain John M. Higbee,
>
> Regarding the standoff between the emigrant train and our southern Lamanite allies, you are to take no action that would antagonize the Lamanites present nor which would otherwise turn them against the Saints. If possible, proceed as planned with the Indians completing the mission so that the Saints can maintain the appearance of neutrality. If possible, innocent blood should be spared. This provision refers to young children only. If necessary, you are to employ whatever means as may be required to assist the Lamanites in completing the task. This may include decoying the settlers out of their encampment so that the Lamanites can more easily get at them. Let there be no misunderstanding, 'You are to use up everyone old enough to talk.'
>
> Your brethren in the Eternal Gospel of Jesus Christ
> Isaac C. Haight, Commander Iron Military District

CHAPTER 9

MOUNTAIN MEADOWS
MOGATSU CREEK HEADWATERS
UTAH TERRITORY

SEPTEMBER 11, 1857
12:45 AM

Ira climbed the opposite bank to where Thales Haskell was posted. He spoke quietly. "Start visiting the chiefs of the seven tribes and tell them we need the two best shots from each one. Tell them we are giving big prizes. Each brave will get a mount, a long rifle, and a handgun." Ira held up his right-hand index finger. "We leave in one hour."

Haskell had expected something along these lines and he knew he'd be involved. But he did not like having to be Ira's messenger under these circumstances. "Some of the chiefs are raising hell. They're blaming us that four more of their people were shot. Sayin' we should have finished things days ago."

Hatch listened unwaveringly. "Everything that's gone wrong so far has been their doing. I'm beginning to think these vagrants couldn't get a possum out of a sapling if you gave 'em a hatchet. I'm not too worried with what they're sayin'."

Haskell continued, "I wish I had your confidence Ira, but they've got us outnumbered here three hundred to fifteen. I don't like the odds."

"The Cedar militia arrived about an hour ago. They're camped beyond the hill there 'bout a quarter mile. I figure we can handle whatever needs handlin'. You tell the chiefs that I'm going to kill the men who shot their brothers and I only want shooters brave enough to help me kill them." Ira stood his ground while Haskell headed to the east side of the tribe encampments. Ira then climbed the rest of the way up the stream bank to where his horse was tied, mounted up, and headed west.

Haskell didn't know it, but Ira would also be visiting the chiefs encamped around the meadows. He would secure his gear and watch Haskell proceed with his order. Whatever direction Haskell took, he would proceed in the opposite direction. By the time Haskell had completed relaying his orders to the second camp, Ira would have gained compliance from the other five. For Hatch, proving his superiority over the other men was a common occurrence. Haskell would be embarrassed but not surprised.

Tutsegabit would be the first chief Ira visited. This was good. Tutsegabit's was the strongest of the seven tribes present and commanded the most braves. His influence would hold sway over chiefs from at least three of the other tribes. After tonight's skirmish, his group and Chief Jackson's had clearly taken the heaviest casualties. Ira had done business with the old chief many times before. This part of his plan was going to work. It was just a matter of implementing it.

Within five minutes he was riding into the Ute camp. One of the braves on watch immediately dispatched a messenger toward their chief's tent. By the time Ira was dismounting, Tutsegabit was standing between two of his armed braves betraying no sign of having been asleep. He waited motionless for Ira to initiate the discussion.

CHAPTER 10

LAS VEGAS SPRINGS
NORTHWEST NEW
MEXICO TERRITORY

SEPTEMBER 16, 1857
12:40 AM

Henry and Cao had been expecting a story concerning any number of scenarios. Being hunted by one of the militia leaders of the Mormon community was not one of them.

Milum paused, measuring the acknowledgement of the brothers. He was about to further indict Hatch and Hamblin. How would the brothers accept that action? Would they accept the facts? Would they turn against him? Well, there was no backtracking now. Milum was committed to telling his story. These boys had saved his life. He was going to tell what those white devils had done. He was telling the truth. He'd come by it in a hard way. The brothers would either take it or dismiss it, but they were going to hear it.

Milum lifted his eyes straight to the brothers. Neither his look nor his voice wavered. "We arrived at the Meadows on the sixth. We'd been pushin' hard from Salt Lake Valley. There was plenty of feed along the way. That is until we reached Cedar. But most of that was settled property, and we had all we could do to keep our cows out of their fields. After Cedar the feed stayed scarce until we got to Mountain Meadows.

"They was everything we'd been told they would be. High altitude with plenty of grass and water. Hamblin had a nice little herd, and it got mixed up with ours as soon as we arrived. Hatch didn't seem concerned about that. We figured they knew their animals and would separate them back out by the time we left.

"We made camp where Hatch recommended. It was a perfect spot . . . flat . . . creek nearby . . . plenty of room for the wagons to spread out and give the families a little privacy. It was a perfect spot for an ambush too. Surrounded by rocky ridges and outcroppings. But the Mormons assured us we was safe and that the Indians in this region was their friends.

"Before sunrise next morning we woke to whoopin' and gunshots. I've never seen nor heard the like of it before. By the time I got to my feet and my rifle cocked, there must have been fifty braves in camp. They all had rifles and side arms and plenty of ammo the way they was a firing. Me and the other folks in the company commenced to firing back at 'em, and for a few minutes there was so much lead flying around the camp it's a wonder anyone lived. We had twenty-five casualties in that attack. Eight were killed outright and seven more died over the next four days. There's still a couple just a hangin' on when I left about four days ago."

Milum's narrative had just crossed over from being the characteristic frontier account of the American westward movement to the rare and nightmarish report all such travelers feared. Henry and Cao sat spellbound by the gravity of it. The brothers had ridden up on a number of tense situations over the past several years. Guns had been pulled on them a couple of times. It usually turned out to be a misunderstanding easily negotiated. They had often felt the need to be ready to fight. In three years time, that necessity had never materialized.

The three men sat quietly taking in the cool dark of wilderness of territorial New Mexico. The brothers were struggling to fathom the story they'd just heard. For the moment, the story of the Indian attack had eclipsed the mention of Ira Hatch's part in Milum's telling.

Milum was swept with memories of those he'd left behind and the dreadful plight he'd left them in. His own survival the last few days had forced the train's predicament to drift from his concerns. Now his memories returned to their ordeal. He thought of his beautiful young niece Matilda Tackitt, of how smitten by her beauty his friend Able Baker had been. He worried for all their safety, but mostly he worried for his wife, Eloah Angeline, and their baby daughter Zabrina.

Even if he'd known more, and were his powers of imagination greater, his thoughts would fail to meet the full measure of the horrors he had escaped, and that they had not.

CHAPTER 11

MOUNTAIN MEADOWS
COMMAND POST
UTAH TERRITORY

SEPTEMBER 11, 1857
12:40 AM

P.K. allowed the parchment to drop to the ground. Holding it was like holding a summons from hell. "Isaac could not author such a command."

"It's in his hand but not his order, P.K." Lee let the line stretch.

"Colonel Dame?" P.K., sensing he was about to step into a snare, needed to know the identity of its author.

"He's part of the chain.'" Lee's eyes riveted P.K. in place. "Haslam's order was relayed through Colonel Dame to President Haight."

"Haslam would not dare to exert such authority." P.K. was grasping at straws.

Lee shook his head. "Haslam stopped in Parawan just long enough to get Haight's signature as commander of the Iron militia. The order was drafted in Salt Lake City pursuant to a war council of General Wells, Jake Hamblin, George Smith, Charles Rich, and President Young."

"Brigham Young would not issue such an order." The Mormon bishop was speaking almost in a whisper now. Those listening could sense that his stance had been defeated.

The unfolding scenario and its nightmarish stranglehold silenced P.K. He had entered the Meadows under orders from his military superiors, orders that said men were to bring shovels and armaments. A loathsome vision harangued his mind under the thoughts of burying the numbered he'd seen passing through Cedar City less than ten days ago. He had rehearsed the daunting task in his mind over and over as he followed the trail to the Meadows, trying to balance his contempt for the action against his responsibility to his church and community. The only solace he found was that it was not he who had approved the attack necessitating this task.

Lee closed in. "Prophet Young is a leader. He's a man of strength and great vision. We are at war with the Gentiles, or will soon be. Our Zion hangs in the balance. Should we allow our enemies to invade Deseret without putting up a fight? The Gentiles must learn that Deseret belongs to the Saints and that they must submit to whatever toll we proscribe. Entry and safe passage will be subject to our will . . . not theirs." Lee was gaining ground.

"Is our will God's will?" P.K. parried his friend, but he was not the more devout of the two and they both knew it.

John Doyle Lee had become, by LDS proclamation, the adopted son of the Prophet Brigham Young. He was also a Mormon bishop, of New Harmony, and the longtime friend of the man he now quarreled with. Lee was a major in the Iron Militia. Along with Higbee, he held highest rank over seventy plus Mormons presently stationed at Mountain Meadows. Deep loyalty to the Prophet compelled Lee to persuade his friend to engage in actions he himself would normally find repugnant. Lee had spent the past four days agonizing over his options. Under the weight of Haslam's express message, all options narrowed to what now must take place.

Lee needed P.K., as bishop from Cedar City, to make it take place. The nature of the action now contemplated could be more than the men from the Cedar City militia would be willing to partake. But presented a direct order from their major, with sanction of their bishop, Lee was convinced that the brethren would respond to his side. Friendship aside, John D. Lee needed P.K. as an ally tomorrow. Lee needed to move his plan forward. His response could leave no room for further debate.

CHAPTER 12

MOUNTAIN MEADOWS
TUTSEGABIT'S CAMP
UTAH TERRITORY

SEPTEMBER 11, 1857
1:00 AM

Ira greeted the chief in their customary manner but did not waste time on extra formalities, partly because he knew Tutsegabit did not care. Taking his hat off, Ira told the chief that two of his braves were needed to help track down the two men that had escaped.

Tutsegabit responded, "We have lost two braves, and two others are preparing their spirit's journey because of their wounds. How many of your white brothers have been killed or wounded over the past days here at Mogatsu Creek?"

Ira regarded the chief's question as the shakedown it was. He responded in kind. "No white brothers were killed and none have been wounded. You will do well to remember, we were not the ones to charge ahead before the command was given, which is why casualties were sustained four days ago. It is my men who stand guard at the creek's outlet now. Those that escaped and killed your two braves tonight must be caught and killed. I am to lead a party of the best hunters from each of the tribes to catch them and we must not wait to pursue them any longer."

"My braves do not care for this darkness. It is too easy to catch a bullet from the shadows. None of my braves will go with you until the sun lights our way."

"My chief will provide a horse and a long rifle for your two best shooters and five cows to any braves that shoots either one of the men we chase." Hatch expected negotiation. Now he hoped Tutsegabit would settle.

"We now have many cows and most of my braves have long rifles already. They will not go." The old chief wanted more.

The chief stood his ground, but that he did not turn and leave told Ira the negotiation was still on. Unfortunately, Ira had nothing left to offer. "If it's a hard winter, five cows would be a welcomed gift. I have seen the condition of your weapons. Many may not be worth carrying a year from now. If you are not worried about the season coming upon us, so be it. I will not force stock upon you as tribute. The Cedar militia has arrived and tomorrow they will divide the cows not spoken for among those present."

Tutsegabit bristled at the veiled threat that the militia, and not he, would decide how the cattle would be divided. "We are strong enough to kill all the Mericats and all the Mormons as well. Your chief is weak. He cries at his own chief's orders to kill the Mericats. My people are calling him 'No Guts.' Why should my people fear any white man?"

Ira did not care for the debate nor the reference about Lee's lack of bravery. He decided to make one last attempt to elicit the chief's help. "The reason we came here five days ago is the reason we are here still. All the Mericats here at the Meadows will die. The two that got through your guard tonight must die as well. I am going after them. Give me your two best braves and we can finish this part of the task. Or . . . keep your braves and more will be awarded to others."

A few moments of silence ensued. The final worth between the two men was being waged in the complete stillness of this late night hour, on the high desert some thirty miles from Ira's small settlement at Fort Clara. The chief looked piercingly at the white lieutenant. Hatch met his look with his own unwavering stare. All comfort zone advantages belonged to the Indian chief. However, it was Tutsegabit who acquiesced. "We do by our choice, not another's command. For the words shared with the white chief in Salt Lake City we will help." With that Tutsegabit ordered the braves on each side of him to go with Ira. "This night is done." The Indian chief turned and walked back into his teepee.

CHAPTER 13

LAS VEGAS SPRINGS
NORTHWEST NEW
MEXICO TERRITORY

SEPTEMBER 16,1857
12:50 AM

The two brothers were riveted by what they were hearing, and Cao couldn't handle the suspense of not knowing. "What happened with the warriors that attacked your group?"

Henry nodded in association with his brother. Milum's experience was a fear that hung in the back of most men's minds while trekking across this new, open country.

Milum answered. "We kilt two of 'em once't we commenced a return fire. Several others were hit and scrambled off, wounded. I reckon all the lead flying around, and seein' some of their own go down, was enough to put a scare into 'em. Once't a few started a runnin' they all took off. Some of our boys began a chase, but retreated when they saw a band that appeared to be in the hunderds. Cap'ns Fancher and Baker did a good job organizin' a barricade by getting the wagons circled and tipped over. Then they got the folks to diggin' trenches. Unfortunately, both cap'ns were badly wounded by the time it settled down.

"It became pretty clear that we was surrounded. Anybody so much as waved a hat, a rifle balls was like to hit it. We put a half dozen of our best marksmen behind good barricades, and they got off some good rounds. We got the red devils to pull back some. No doubt 'bout our boy's shootin' skills. After a while, they was so far out of range the shooting stopped from both sides.

"Cap'n Fancher's cousin Matthew took over the leadership position. Four days we was pinned down. The only time you felt anyways safe to be movin' round was after dark. We was close enough to the creek so's at night we could sneak down for water. But we's in a fix with the wounded and the dying."

The chill of the night air mixed with the chill of the storied account. Henry reached down for several branches and dropped them onto the campfire. Cao duplicated his brother's actions and said they might as well keep the fire going to last the story. Milum started again.

"On the fourth night, Matt Fancher asked me and two others to make a run for it an' look for help. He took me into the middle of the camp and we hunkered down with him, the two cap'ns, and the two others. One was Baker's son Able. The other was a fellow by the name of Tillman Cameron. Cap'n Baker was wounded pretty bad. Gut shot. Cap'n Fancher had taken a round in the neck and could barely talk. None of the three of us thought either of the cap'ns was goin' to make it very much longer, and aside from both bein' in a great deal of pain, they still had their wits about 'em.

"Able tried to talk his pa into letting him stay, but he wouldn't hear of it. He said the group needed men to get out for who had the best chance of makin' it. Matt Fancher came up with the plan that the three of us would be armed and provisioned with enough to get us to California. The moon would be down 'til a couple of hours past midnight. Using the low cloud cover, we might be able to float down the creek past their lines. We might have 'til sunup to get a good lead. If we had to, we'd blast our way out and try'n outrun them if they chased us. Maybe they wouldn't even chase us. Matt Fancher made it clear that if the company had any chance, it was for us to bring back help."

As Milum recalled these moments, the clouds slowly drifted from the sky, revealing new stars. A weight was lifting from him, and speaking these words seemed to clear his thoughts. For the first time in several days, it felt like Matt Fancher's plan was working.

"We made our way into the creek. God in heaven! Didn't know how cold that water'd be. But once we got in, we started driftin' with the current. Quiet as fish. We was in the water a long time. Course the cold made a minute seem like an hour. We was almost through when Able drifted closer to the bank. Able was our lead man. Wouldn't you know there's a redskin fillin' a water bag right there along the creek. The Injun jumped back tryin' to shout, but it seemed to get caught in his throat. Able put a .45 slug in him to keep him quiet, but the shot attracted more attention than the Injun. In a second we went from floatin' in the stream to runnin' down the side of it. And then the bullets commenced to whistlin' all round us. Tillman must'a took one in the back. I only heard him get off one shot. Able and me was emptying our chambers at anything that moved or made noise. We ran into several braves but we just shot at 'em and kept runnin'. We didn't stop 'til we was spent. That's when we saw Tillman wasn't with us and figured he didn't make it."

Milum swallowed his coffee like he was catching his breath. His face expressed a look of self-loathing and futility. He proceeded.

"Well, we couldn't go back for him and we couldn't very well wait around for him; so we tried to get our bearings and then we headed out as fast as we could in the dark." Milum looked at the brothers as if he was pleading a defense. Their look back was devoid of accusation. Then he shook his head and refocused.

"It turned out to be pretty easy going, all downhill and plenty of cover to keep out of sight. Half the times we would run, and half the times walk, dependin' on the rocks and brush. Our clothes was wet at first but we wasn't that cold anymore after the runnin'. Eventually our clothes dried off and we was able to cover some ground. We kep' on 'til sunup and then we just kept goin'. We walked hard all that day and finally had to stop. There was this thick grove of cottonwoods. We laid down in a sandy dry creek bed under a grassy bank. We decided to take some rest in the grove and agreed to take turns sleepin' and keepin' watch. It wasn't much later when I saw your friend Mr. Hatch again."

CHAPTER 14

MOUNTAIN MEADOWS
COMMAND POST
UTAH TERRITORY

SEPTEMBER 11, 1857
12:50 AM

The parchment with the Prophet's orders lay on the ground next to P.K.'s right foot. The revelation and origin of the message caused a swarming in his head like a riled nest of hornets. Disorientation buzzing with disbelief, fear, and denial clouded his senses and strained his eyes. In the past he had heeded the orders of the Prophet, delivered by George Smith, that every able man must support, and belong to, the militia. He respected that directive. He could appreciate the necessity. However, he was not a military man. While taking up arms was justifiable in defense, he was at odds with offensive measures.

P.K. had a good reputation as a hard-working blacksmith. His parents had emigrated from Germany when America was still a grand and new experiment. P.K. grew to manhood working the iron mills of Pennsylvania and living near Brush Creek. His skills with iron had come to the attention of Brigham Young during their epic migration west. His know-how was critical in keeping the wagons in strong working order during the monumental trek.

The Prophet, as Brigham Young was referred to, rewarded P.K.'s contribution. He was placed in leadership of several expeditions to the southern territories. P.K.'s respect for those he directed, along with his willingness to step in for his share of the hard work, won him their respect and admiration. Cedar City grew as his most successful outpost and became his hometown. Here, the new settlers chose him to be their bishop. President Young automatically confirmed the choice.

Unlike Higbee and Lee, he was inclined only to obey orders from respected men in the church's hierarchy. In P.K.'s book, ambition had its limits. Achievement through service held much greater sway than advancement through privilege or acquaintance. Had the order in front of him been given by anyone other than the Prophet, he would have rejected it. Though disobeying a direct military order could be punishable by death, his status as bishop would carry the respect of the Cedar City militia. It was a gamble he would have taken. But going against the Prophet, that was a good way to get one's throat cut. Might not even get the benefit of a hearing.

P.K. held a deep sense of gratitude toward Brigham Young and had served the LDS president well. Only men who had achieved high standing in the church were rewarded with "plural wives." He now had three wives and eight children, status and other possessions accumulated in the past ten years—a wealthy man indeed. And this was only because of the blessings extended him by this imposing leader. This Prophet.

P.K. had made a stand weeks earlier at the church council at Cedar City. He had debated George Smith in front of the council members over the fate of the newly arrived immigrant party. He had not carried the day; otherwise he would not be here at the Meadows now. He had felt secure in arguing for a Christian response and believed he had at least retained respect from the majority of those present. Now, all he had struggled to set forth fell subject to the choices he was required to make here tonight.

P.K. sucked in his cheeks to moisten the dryness in his mouth, pursed his lips, and shot spit to the ground, almost hitting the parchment. It was an action close to mutiny, if not blasphemy. He directed his remarks exclusively to Lee. "When we were ordered here to the Meadows, it was under the pretext that we were being summoned to bury the dead; obviously a ruse. Your intentions were to get us here to help in the slaughter. You know and you knew that I was against this."

John D. Lee was being called; there could be no folding. "You're right, P.K. I admit it. And yes, I knew how you felt about it." Lee needed to move his friend a long ways. If the stakes were high for P.K. Smith, they were even higher for John D. Lee.

"If I had it to do over, I would have stood at your side at the church council meeting. There are many things I wish I had done differently. P.K., things have gone too far. Blood has been shed on all sides." Actually, the only Mormon bloodshed had occurred years prior through the predations of Gentiles against Saints in Missouri and Illinois. That is unless you count the recent murder of Parley Pratt in Arkansas.

The apostle Parley Pratt was one of the most beloved and prolific proselytizers in the history of this new religion. He'd been responsible for baptizing more brethren into the faith than almost anyone in the church. Earlier that year a jealous husband chased him down and killed him for running off with his wife. When word reached Deseret, the Saints were outraged that a Gentile, who was not even brought to trial for this brutal act, had murdered another of their principal men.

"The immigrants have made two attempts to free messengers. I can't hold the tribes here much longer. If word gets out about what's already happened, I fear for the very future of the church . . . for all we've accomplished. You and I know that we may be embroiled in an all-out war with the federal army within a few months. If that happens this will be a small start to a whole lot more killin'. An action of correction could avoid war later. There's no way out if Washington gets wind of what's been going on here these past few days." Lee let these words sink in for just a second before reinforcing them.

"Buchanan has been warned, and now he needs to know that westward migration is subject to obtaining safe passage through a territory controlled by hostile tribes. I've discussed this at length with Apostle Smith and he assures me that the Prophet intends to make this point strongly with the Gentile president through the operation being conducted here at the Meadows. However, it is absolutely necessary that when word of this gets to the federal commanders, it be laid at the feet of the Lamanites. The only way we can make sure that happens is for the brethren to be the only ones telling the story."

P.K. swallowed his disgust long enough to enter the debate satirically. "I suppose we can be sure our Lamanite brothers will go along with our version of the truth?"

"The federal agents have always used our scouts and interpreters. I expect they will continue to do so for a few more years." Lee sensed his old friend could see the futility of alternative measures. He needed to respectfully point out what he already knew.

Lee was sincere about wishing he had done things differently. As soon as Jackson's tribe had jumped the gun, things had continually gone from bad to worse. What should have been over in fifteen minutes was now past its fourth day. Lee could not remember the last time he'd been able to get a restful sleep. Over the past days, he had considered every alternative possible. He was even willing to explore ways to abort the mission he'd been sent on.

But the potential consequences in doing so were all unacceptable. At the very best he would lose his rank in the militia and the church as well as the respect of the brethren. At worst he could be facing a general court-martial and be hanged for treason. Unlike P.K., Lee felt the Gentiles in the train deserved the treatment the Saints had arranged for them. He knew the Mormon leaders, through the chain of command all the way to the Prophet himself, also felt this way as evidenced by the orders he had just handed to P.K. minutes ago.

Unlike P.K., Lee was a Danite, having been sworn into the order years prior by the stern-faced Samson Avard. "Blood atonement," the elimination of the Prophet's enemies in a manner that would not preclude their salvation, was a practice he and the others had become accustomed to.

Lee had to pin P.K. down and commit him now. He also needed to impress upon Higbee, who had been quietly standing by, the importance of the militia's work.

"The extermination of the Gentile train has been ordered. It would be treasonous to disobey such a direct order. By ordering Hatch to terminate the escapees, the order has been relayed. We all have a tough job to do. We all have a role to play. I'm counting on all the Saints here to carry out their duties. A failure to do so tomorrow, to move forward tomorrow, will result in disastrous consequences for us all. Are you willing to listen to my plan?"

The two in front of him were silent, Higbee for fear of further raising P.K.'s ire again and P.K. for needing to know just how much participation his old friend Lee was expecting from him. They were going to hear Lee out. The younger man was eager to hear of the role he would be asked to play. The older was filled with dread and despair. They would hear Lee out and let him lay the groundwork.

CHAPTER 15

LAS VEGAS SPRINGS NORTHWEST NEW MEXICO TERRITORY

SEPTEMBER 16, 1857
1:00 AM

The brothers didn't know what to make of Milum's tale. An outrageous lie or a chilling account of the worst in man? They had watched Milum, on the edge of dying, fall into their camp. They found fear in the fact that he had been with two companions but had entered their camp alone. The fate of Tillman was fairly easy to ascertain. Now what had happened to Able? They had no doubt they were also going to learn more about Ira Hatch. Henry and Cao leaned in a bit to hear what Milum would say next.

"We must have covered thirty miles gettin' to that grove of cotton-woods. We agreed to take turns at watch but we both fell asleep within minutes." Milum rubbed his eyes. "Then Able's hand over my mouth woke me up. I guess a couple of Injuns followin' our track had walked to within about ten yards of where we was sleepin'. Able heard them comin' before they saw us. We hadn't lit a campfire. He picked one of the sneaking devils off with his first shot. I took the other. Shot him right through the heart. After that's when we saw about a dozen other riders uphill from our position.

"We could see a mix of redskins and whites. A couple looked familiar, but we couldn't place any of 'em. One of 'em shouted down to us and we figured it was Ira Hatch. He said there didn't need to be any shootin'; that we could come out and they'd take us back safe. He said it was okay and that the trouble had got cleared up. Able yelled that we'd find our own way just the same. Pretty soon they all dismounted and spread out some and moved to close in."

Cao's mind was racing ahead to a note of obviousness. "They must have been trying to get an advantage." Henry's eyes rolled towards Cao and he half pointed his index finger at his little brother.

Milum continued. "The terrain worked in our favor. The canyon walls were steep, and they couldn't get around us easy without us getting some pretty good shots at 'em. It was after sundown, but there was still plenty of light. We had the best cover but they had a lot more firepower. They kept us pinned down, but we was able to keep them from gettin' too close. That's when Hatch got off a lucky shot and hit Able in the leg." Milum's head bowed down. He slowly put his hand over the wound on his opposite arm, hovering for a second before lightly placing his fingers and palm on it. "Maybe it was more than luck since his next round did this." Milum lifted his head to look at Henry and Cao again. "We returned fire and got close enough to make Hatch and his friends back off a bit. We tended best we could to our wounds. Tied off Able's leg and then my arm. Guess you can see we was in a pretty bad fix.

"Able said to leave some of my ammo with him, take some food, and make a run for it. I didn't want to leave him there but he kep' insistin'. He kep' sayin' there was no way he was goin' to be able to get away with his leg hit so bad. I had a chance if he could hold them off long enough. I couldn't out-argue him and it was no good fer both of us to get stopped from findin' help. So I went along with his idea and took off before they could get us surrounded in the dark."

Milum's torment came rushing back as he recalled the guilt of leaving his friend behind mixed with his relief of escaping another hopeless siege. This desert night had ceased to exist for Henry and Cao. The only thing they were aware of was the predicament Milum was unfolding before them. His story was taking on an import Henry could no longer ignore.

"Where do you suppose Hatch and his friends are now, Milum?"

Milum was grateful to change the topic to the danger his presence posed the brothers. "It's been over three days since I left Able there at that cottonwood grove. I been walkin' almost day an' night since then. Just restin' an' sleepin' some in the shade during the heat a the day. They had horses and I 'spect they would of caught up with me pretty easy already. That's the fear that kep' me movin'. I'm thinkin' Able was able to hold them off long enough, or that they just gave up on me. Maybe they went another way. I covered a lot of ground, so I keep hopin' Able took some of 'em down. But I can't honestly say they ain't still out there lookin' fer me."

Milum knew his presence compromised the safety of the brothers. And now they knew it too. The three of them sat, sharing the silence of answered questions as the campfire faded away.

CHAPTER 16

MOUNTAIN MEADOWS
CHIEF JACKSON'S CAMP
UTAH TERRITORY

September 11, 1857
2:30 AM

It was at Chief Jackson's camp that Ira met up with Thales Haskell. Ira led ten braves he had commissioned from the five tribes he had visited, all riding strong fresh mounts and carrying long rifles. Most of the braves had on fresh war paint. Haskell appeared greatly relieved to see Ira and the others. He had been successful commissioning two braves from Chief Youngwuds' tribe, but was having trouble with Jackson.

Chief Jackson had been having trouble with many of the braves from the other six tribes as well as some of his own. By now the finger pointing about whose fault it was that over three hundred of Southern Utah's bravest Indians had failed to defeat a hundred and forty men, women, and children while most of them were sleeping had become a regular pastime among the attackers at Mountain Meadows.

All of the whites and a majority of the Indians laid the blame at the feet of Chief Jackson. Many of the young braves agreed that it was cowardly to execute a sneak attack and therefore respected Jackson's principles to lead his men into battle in the traditional manner. However, the more veteran warriors spoke of Jackson in terms of derision. Far more braves had been killed or wounded than need be, and in their opinions, it was Jackson's fault. They should all be home by now enjoying the spoils, yet they were still here on the field pursuing the tough duty of maintaining a siege.

For chief Jackson, his status had risen among the young fools and declined among the other six chiefs in attendance and the majority of their men. He had become increasingly defensive over the debate, which was being engaged mostly behind his back. Hatch knew him to be a loose cannon on a good day. As he approached the powwow between Haskell and Jackson, it was clear that Jackson was trying to erode Haskell's authority to commandeer warriors from his tribe or any others.

None of the chiefs there at the Meadows liked the white man, but Chief Jackson despised him. He knew Hatch well enough to know that he too would have little respect for his decision-making. Hatch did not bother to dismount as the riders reined their horses to a halt in front of the chief. It was an obvious affront to the chief's status, and it had especially not gone unnoticed by Chief Jackson. Jackson was the first to speak.

"I will not send braves with you to hunt the two who got through. None of the Indians here should go with you. Your chiefs are fools to order you to follow the white leaders." He spoke directly to Haskell and to the braves lined up behind him and Ira. His animated speech and refusal to speak directly to the mounted white leader was an intentional rebuke to match Hatch's insult.

Hatch spoke directly to Thales Haskell. "Did you tell Chief Jackson about the 'big prizes' for the braves that accompany us on this mission?"

"Yes sir!" Haskell was grateful to relinquish authority to Hatch.

"Then tell Chief Jackson that we will rendezvous at Mogatsu Creek where the shootings took place earlier tonight. We will begin our pursuit in less than one hour from now. If Jackson's braves fail to join us, we will leave without them. They will not share in the prizes. However, if he chooses to send his two most trusted braves, they will be welcome."

He then spurred his mount and galloped off in the direction of James Mathew's sentry post. He had not said a word to the unpredictable chief. With only a moment's hesitation, all ten of the braves mounted behind Ira spurred their mounts as well and followed after him.

Haskell was left stranded in an awkward moment. Chief Jackson had communicated with Hatch by speaking directly to the Indian braves with him. Ira had responded to Jackson through Haskell. The only remaining participants of the verbal discussion were the two of them, now left facing one another.

For a moment Haskell contemplated repeating the directive issued to him by Hatch. Jackson, seemingly aware of Haskell's contemplation, blurted out, "I heard what your chief said. Leave us now!"

Haskell was more than willing to comply with the chief's order. As he mounted his horse, he was somewhat surprised to notice the two braves from Youngwuds' tribe followed him just as the ten braves had followed Ira's departure. He would be more surprised when three of Chief Jackson's braves showed up at the rendezvous point, an hour later, armed, mounted, and ready to join in the pursuit.

CHAPTER 17

MOUNTAIN MEADOWS
COMMAND POST
UTAH TERRITORY

SEPTEMBER 11, 1857
1:00 AM

John D. Lee took the silence of his two Mormon friends as a sign that they were ready to listen. While he collected his thoughts three members of the Cedar City militia walked into the campsite's flickering light. They were Samuel Knight, Bill Stewart, and Nephi Johnson. It was Stewart who was reported to have shot a Gentile escapee two nights ago. The three men had just finished assisting the militia with setting up a remuda to coral their horses and with herding the livestock taken from the wagon train.

Lee offered the men a seat. He would need their support too, he thought. But it was P.K. and Higbee he would be directing his remarks to. Higbee would be no problem. Captain Higbee was eager to prove his loyalty to the church and to his commanders. He needed P.K. most and he might get no other opportunity to bring the Cedar City bishop around to supporting this awful venture. He knew what the church leadership wanted, and he had to be effective.

"What we have to do about seven or eight hours from now is about the most distasteful thing I will have ever done and that any of us will ever do. I wish there was another way, but I have not been able to find it. We're going to have to make use of a stratagem to get the immigrants out of their fortress and into the open. I've spoken with Tutsegabit. He's agreed with what I am about to tell you and he will relay it to the other tribes.

"An hour or so after daybreak I will ride up to the immigrant camp and seek a conference with them. Hopefully they don't suspect the Saints are involved in all of this. I'm going to convince them that, now that the militia is here, we can provide them with a safe escort back to Cedar if they will lay down their arms and proceed in an orderly way back to the east. They will have to proceed on foot in single file with the wounded and small children in the lead wagons; the women and children second; then the men following behind."

Lee continued on, in meticulous detail, laying out what each man's role would be come sunup. Many of the participants were not present. But Lee assured those who were that he had already confirmed their part to play. He made it clear that any man's refusal to perform his duty would be reported up the chain of command as a treasonous act. The men at this meeting were to relay to the militia that a refusal to obey a direct order during a time of war was punishable by death. Lee would address all the militia at tomorrow's breakfast, at which time P.K. would be asked to lead the men in prayer.

The Cedar City bishop remained quiet throughout Lee's discourse. He was thinking his own thoughts as Lee and the others plotted. He was asking himself if there really was no other way out of this predicament. He knew that if Lee's plan could somehow be called off, the repercussions would still be dire for the church. It was difficult for P.K. to consider his life as one apart from the fortunes or failures of his church.

The immigrant train had already suffered heavy casualties. The Lamanites would not allow the return of the cattle they had been promised and had paid for with their blood. No, if the surviving immigrants were able to get back to Cedar, and eventually to Salt Lake City, and finally back to their homes in the east, there would be a great clamor of outrage against the Lamanites and anyone who had helped them. P.K. knew that the Mormon newspapers would not be able to keep the lid on the story for long. Gentile agents of the federal government, like Garland Hurt, were, and had been, operating in and around Salt Lake City for several years.

It was truly a very bad set of options. Allowing what was left of the immigrant train to go free would result in an unprecedented Gentile outrage against the church. The repercussions and likely response would reduce the Hahn's Mill Massacre and the assassination of the Prophet Smith in Carthage to mere skirmishes by comparison. News of this atrocity would shake the very foundation of the church in catastrophic and unpredictable ways. On the other hand, how long could the church hope to contain their story with so many Lamanites and Saints involved? Someone would eventually share his experience with someone not present. It was human nature.

If war between the Gentiles and the Saints did come, as Salt Lake City was expecting, then Lee was right. There would be a great deal more killing than had, or would, go on here at the Meadows. P.K. pondered what a strange irony it was that the likelihood of all-out war was one fact that made a terrible choice less terrible.

As Lee continued unveiling his detailed directive, P.K. was locked in a personal struggle between doing "what was right" and "what was best for his people." Until now he had always thought the two were the same.

CHAPTER 18

LAS VEGAS SPRINGS NORTHWEST NEW MEXICO TERRITORY

SEPTEMBER 16, 1857
1:15 PM

Once again it was Cao who could not contain himself. "So you're tellin' us that the Saints and the Injuns have teamed up to steal all your cattle and kill a whole train full o' folks. I don't ever recall hearin' o' such a thing from the Injuns around these parts, let alone from the Saints. You expect us to believe this?"

Milum himself pondered the nature of the story he was telling. "Well I sure have become convinced of exactly that over the past week or so. I don't figure I've got a right to expect anything from you boys. I know you've helped me out in a big way. But I sure as hell ain't makin' all this up."

Henry was not so eager to question the veracity of his guest as his brother was. He needed more information. "I can understand what the Injuns are after, but why Milum, do you suppose Hatch and company are involved?"

"I don't know, but I think it's more'n just Hatch and a few of his friends. A couple of days after that first attack, cap'ns Baker and Fancher sent two riders. The big Dutchman I told you about, and a fella named Will Aden, back to Cedar in hopes of getting help. Tillman owned an expensive racehorse, an' he let the Dutchman take it, since it was one of the only two mounts we had left."

"They broke through the enemy lines just before dawn. The cap'ns suspected there was some o' the whites in the region working with the Injuns, so he told 'em to avoid the Hamblin ranch house and to stay clear of the settlement at Pinto where we got some nasty glares as we passed from the people settled there.

"Those boys did what they was told. They made it through the enemy's perimeter with lead flyin' a plenty, with neither one getting hit, including their mounts. Must a surprised 'em I guess. Anyway, they rode up on three men at a campfire near a spot called Leachy Springs. The men seemed hospitable and all, until our boys told 'em of their situation. At that point one o' the men pulled his gun and shot Will Aden square in the chest. The Dutchman was able to jump on his mount and high tail it out o' there without getting shot. It was a wonder too because he said all three men emptied their pistols as he was a leavin'.

"The Dutchman made it back to the train by chargin' in the same way he charged out. Only this time they shot his mount out from under him just as he was passing our barricades. Cameron cried like a baby. I think that's why he insisted on going with Able an' me. That horse was the only thing left in the camp that he had responsibility for. After the Dutchman told us what happened, I think that's when we seriously started putting two and two together."

"And what do you mean by that?" Cao was on the horns of a dilemma. He didn't want to believe that the church he was about to join could be inhabited by men who would participate in the kind of activity Milum was describing. Yet Milum's story was compelling.

"The decision to head south, and not west, from Salt Lake wasn't made until Mormons advised it. The Mormon guides we was given kep' us clear of all the settlements we passed. If anyone had been inclined to warn us, they didn't have the chance. At Corn Creek, a band of about a dozen Injuns passed us on the trail headin' to Salt Lake City. One of Baker's men said he overheard Hamblin tellin' Hatch that they was all chiefs and that they was on their way to a meetin' with Brigham Young hisself. The fact that Hamblin invited us to graze our herd at the Meadows, which was his home, seemed overly generous. The campsite Hatch directed us to was surrounded by hills. When one of the cap'ns asked him about the potential for an Injun ambush, he told 'im the Injuns in these parts was friendly. I don't think it's too much of a stretch to figure we was set up and that Hamblin and Hatch was in on it."

It wasn't difficult for Milum to rattle off the reasons he believed the Mormons were behind it. He'd been thinking about it for several days, and the last few gave him good reason to want to do something about it. He also realized that the Young brothers provided him with the best opportunity he'd had. Milum needed the Young brothers to believe him.

"They're after you because they don't want you to bring the word of what's goin' on up there to anyone else. Is that the way you have it figured?" Henry was considering Milum's story with some skepticism like Cao was. The difference was he was willing to assess their situation in light of the fact that Milum might be telling the truth. If Milum was making it up, there certainly could be some unknown danger lurking ahead. Right now, the truth, if that is what it was, wasn't boding all that well for them either.

"That's how I've got it figured. But like I said, I don't know if they're still looking for me or not. There's still close to a hundred folk surrounded at the Meadows they have to contend with. As bad off as they are, I doubt they're gonna just give up. I don't think Abel could a held 'em off more than a half-day or so, as bad hurt as he was. A full day if he was lucky. Yet still, the further I got and the more time passed, I commenced to thinkin' that just maybe I outdistanced 'em. Or they just gave up on getting me." Milum was feeling optimistic for the first time in a while.

Henry was still assessing his options. "Well, I wonder where we go from here." He threw it out there just to see the man's reaction.

"I reckon that'd be up to you boys. My plans is to keep headin' south to San Bernardino if I can make it. All this talkin' has plumb tuckered me out. If you don't mind I think I'll see if I can catch up on my rest." Milum wasn't kidding. He leaned back on the bedroll the brothers had provided, pulled his sweat-stained hat over his eyes, and began to snore almost immediately.

Henry and Cao looked at each other. Then Henry got up and motioned for his brother to follow. The brothers walked about fifty yards out into the desert, and when they were sure they were out of earshot, began to assess the fantastic story they had just heard.

CHAPTER 19

MOUNTAIN MEADOWS
MOGATSU CREEK HEADWATERS
UTAH TERRITORY

SEPTEMBER 11, 1857
3:00 AM

When Thales Haskell arrived at the rendezvous point on Mogatsu Creek, he found Hatch and Mathews busy inventorying the weapons and examining the mounts. Ira was not one to be caught short-supplied or to have to abort a mission because someone's horse came up lame. He couldn't count on Chief Jackson to contribute to the party, so he was going to be sure the recruits he began this mission with were prepared to finish it. He checked all the actions on the long rifles and did some redistribution of ammo so that all men had roughly the same. He checked the horse's hooves for loose shoes and the shoeless horses for rock bruises. He actually had Mathews take two of the braves' animals back to the command post remuda for replacements.

One of the braves commenced to protest the exchange of his animal but was met with a look from Ira that ended his objection in mid-sentence. Ira Hatch had been given this command and he was going to command it.

By now the cloud cover had lifted and the half moon was providing enough light to cast shadows and allow some sight distance. It was actually chilly enough that the Indians had brought blankets to wrap themselves. The Mormon men wore layers of undergarments, shirts, and overshirts. All but Hatch were wondering, and hoping, that Hatch would wait until the rising sun would provide additional light to the landscape they would soon be traversing. Until then, a man lying in ambush would have all the sight advantage. All were aware of Tutsegabit's initial warning of the danger of pursuing the escapees in the dark.

They were hoping that Hatch would wait the three hours or less needed to equalize the disadvantage. Mathews and Haskell preferred the same itinerary as the Lamanites. But they knew that if Ira decided it was best to leave now, that's precisely what they were going to do.

As the hour deadline approached, the party was surprised to hear hoof beats approaching from the direction of Chief Jackson's camp. Three of Chief Jackson's most loyal braves rode up to Hatch and his party and dismounted. The largest and most severe looking one walked directly up to Hatch. This brave, known as Big Bill, was the only man present whose height matched that of the tall wiry Indian agent. He was thickly muscled and an imposing figure indeed. Just as his chief had done, he directed his comments to the Indians present, but Big Bill stared directly into the eyes of Ira as he did so.

"Chief Jackson sends three warriors to kill the two men who killed Tutsegabit's braves. I have been chosen to lead all of the warriors in this party. The white men may come and share in the prizes if they can be of help."

As the warrior made this reference about "white men," his staring eyes broke from Ira's as if to address the others. In that split second the butt of Hatch's rifle hit Big Bill high and square in the stomach, knocking the wind out of him. A split second later that same rifle butt caught him sharply along the side of his bowed head. The warrior was sent crashing to the ground. In the blink of an eye the most intimidating of Jackson's braves had been knocked near senseless. As the others looked on in stunned silence, he began gasping for air. That's when Ira began to speak.

He directed his booming comments to the fallen and humiliated warrior, but his words were mostly for all the others in attendance.

"I am in command of this party! I will be giving the orders and I will shoot anyone who does not obey! You are ordered to go back to your chief and tell him I require only his two best men! You will not be needed!"

An intense silence ensued as the eighteen standing watched the fallen warrior somewhat regain his composure and eventually remount his horse and ride off in the direction he came from. Hatch then turned his glare toward the humiliated Indian's two comrades. He did not speak a word, and they were afraid to speak or move. Hatch walked up to the closest and quickly snatched his rifle from him at the same time he was tossing his own to Haskell. Just like he had with all the others, he checked the action of the brave's weapon. He tossed the rifle back to the brave forcefully, requiring the Indian to fumble slightly to keep from dropping it. He then repeated this drill with the other of Jackson's men. This man was able to anticipate the abrupt rifle toss and deftly catch it. Not a word was spoken until Hatch concluded he had all the men present, and his own adrenaline, under control.

He walked around the men to a position where all of them could hear him equally well. For those who could not speak English he would intersperse translation for each sentence into the most common Ute dialect he knew.

"There will be danger in what we are about to undertake. The men we are after are well armed. They are probably of the strongest that the immigrants in the wagon fort had available to them. It is unlikely they will surrender even if we surround them. Even if their situation is hopeless, they will likely die first. No problem with that. Our job is to stop them from getting away and to see that they die. Their job is to kill anyone who tries to stop them."

"We have them outnumbered and we have mounts. We will catch up to them; it's only a matter of when. My guess is they'll follow the creek downhill all night. We'll fan out along both sides of the creek and keep movin' till sunup, when we should be able to pick up their track. I figure we should be able to catch up with them before sundown. Now mount up and let's get a move on. You two take the first leg of followin' the creek bed."

For this final directive Hatch pointed to the two remaining braves from Chief Jackson's tribe. Though they had just been given the most dangerous assignment, they complied without hesitation. All the others did as they were told as well. The search for the two fugitive Gentiles was on.

CHAPTER 20

MOUNTAIN MEADOWS
COMMAND POST
UTAH TERRITORY

SEPTEMBER 11, 1857
1:45 AM

As he contemplated the dismal outlook for all the choices that lay before them, P.K. knew he would soon have to commit to a course of action. His awareness of the plotting going on around him was that those in leadership positions had already made up their minds. They understood the necessity of following the chain of command. To them, the fate of all the brethren was tied to their loyalty and obedience to the interests of the church. There would be no dissent among them.

P.K. understood their point of view. He was the highest-ranking member of the church in Cedar City. He had come to know, better than most, the strength their religion brought to them collectively. Since he joined the Saints more than ten years ago, he had seen them accomplish Herculean tasks by living their religion and sticking together. Their migration west, beginning in the middle of winter, to what most would consider a desolate wasteland, was but one example. That they had begun to thrive and significantly expand their territory was another.

In spite of the knowledge he possessed and the status he held in the Church of Jesus Christ of Latter-day Saints, P.K. was keenly aware that he was not all that devout. He had seen members of his own congregation drop to their knees and yell out for forgiveness of their sins and guidance toward repentance. Emotional outbursts and leaps of faith were not part of P.K.'s makeup.

When it came down to it, P.K. was a pragmatist. He understood the utility of belonging to the structured cooperative, which was his church, and the benefit it was to each individual. A hard-working man with decent habits would, over time, thrive in such an organization. Those less disciplined would benefit less well, but would benefit still. He could not, however, reconcile that it was God's will that those in the immigrant train deserved to die. Yet would any other course lead to outcomes less dire for himself and his brethren?

"P.K., we're all in agreement. We need to hear from you. Will you stand with us?" Lee could see that P.K. was deep in thought. But he needed him to focus on the discussion at hand. Everyone around the campfire except P.K. had committed to participating in Lee's plan. Among the others there was a sense that this was payback time for all the persecutions Gentiles had levied against the Mormons. For Parley Pratt, for Hahn's Mill, for the Prophet Joseph and his apostle brother Hyrum, it was time to conclude the discussion.

"What do you want me to do, John?" P.K. had the sound of resignation in his voice. Lee wasted no time letting the council and P.K. know where he needed P.K. to be.

"When Higbee gives his command, you need to fire your piece without hesitation. Nearly all the militia is from Cedar. You are their bishop. Many eyes will be on you. If you hesitate, many will lose heart. It could result in chaos. After you've fired your piece, we need you to take charge of the children in the lead wagons and remove them to Hamblin's ranch. Will you commit to executing these duties?" Lee waited intently for the answer.

"When Higbee gives his command I will fire my piece . . . without hesitation. I will then take charge of the children in the lead wagons and remove them to Hamblin's ranch."

In the end P.K. had made it easy for Lee. His response was specific and completely without equivocation or nuance. He had done what he could to avert the looming catastrophe before him. Now he would help initiate it. All the good that he believed he, and his church, had stood for was being exchanged for his, and his church's, survival. He wondered how permanent or temporary that survival would be.

"Well, that does it then. We must rest now. We will need all of our strength in a short while. I truly believe the Lord has put us here at this time and this place. I believe we must do what the Lord asks of us. This may be our best chance to avenge the murders at Carthage of the Prophet Joseph and founder of our faith. To avenge the blood of the prophets. May the Lord be with you all." Lee needed to rest more than anyone in attendance. He also wanted to conclude the meeting before what he had accomplished started to unravel.

However, Nephi Johnson was not ready to retire and asked Lee, "Have you determined how you plan to approach and gain access to the immigrant camp?" His question reflected a valid concern for all present. Lee's success here was crucial to the overall plan. What would they do if Lee failed to convince the immigrants to allow themselves to be escorted? Or, for that matter, if he failed to gain entry into the wagon fort at all?

Lee anticipated the overall thrust of the question. "If I am unsuccessful in gaining entrance we will be in a real bad fix. I'm sending an express messenger to Cedar for orders on how to proceed if this should be the outcome. If any of the immigrants are able to make it to California, it will probably result in an army sent back from the west to attack the Saints. With the governments army on its way from the east, this could be disastrous for us all.

"Frankly I'm more concerned about convincing them to lay down their arms and leave their fortress under our escort. But I have a good plan to gain access into the wagon fort. Yesterday I was doing some reconnaissance just west of the wagon fort and I'm sure the immigrants spotted me and recognized that I was not a Lamanite. They immediately ran a white flag up a pole and sent two young boys toward me to show they meant me no harm. I left quickly because I wasn't ready to meet and discuss anything with them. When I approach the immigrants later this morning, I will approach them under a white flag."

CHAPTER 21

LAS VEGAS SPRINGS NORTHWEST NEW MEXICO TERRITORY

SEPTEMBER 16,1857
1:30 AM

Cao was charged up over what he'd been listening to for the past hour and a half. Milum's scathing indictment of the religion he intended joining was not one he could quickly reconcile.

"I can't believe my ears, Henry. This guy must be leavin' somethin' out."

"An what if what he's sayin' is true?" Henry was trying to think, and he needed Cao to think too.

Cao was still not ready to go there. "It can't be. We been through the Salt Lake Valley run two and a half times now an' we only been treated good by the Saints and the Injuns both."

"Dammit, Cao! Will you just stop worryin' about becomin' a Mormon convert long enough to think sensible for one minute. This ain't about whether or not the Injuns or the Mormons are capable of bein' killers. It's about what we might be ridin' into if what Milum says is true. If what he says is true, we could have big trouble findin' us any minute. We best be thinkin' how we intend to handle ourselves if trouble does ride right up on us. Once't we have that figured out, we can start speculatin' on what the odds are what he's sayin' is true or not." Henry was exasperated over his brother's thick headedness. He was also concerned how open Milum would continue to be if he knew what was going on in Cao's head.

"You best keep your thoughts about the Saints to yerself in our discussions with Milum. If what he's sayin' is true, he ain't likely to look kindly on your ideas about gettin' baptized." Henry hoped his brother would wise up a little and try to be of some help. After what he'd just heard, the desert trails he'd been riding the past several years didn't seem near as safe as they once did.

"Do you believe him Henry? Do you think what he's sayin' could actually be goin' on up North?" Cao could not ignore the stranger's credibility.

"I don't know for sure. Things would have to of changed a mighty lot since we last went through. But Milum sure looks like he's been through somethin' a lot like he's been describin'. That'd be a rough hundred miles on foot, even if a feller wasn't runnin' fer his life."

"Yer not thinking o' headin' back south because o' what this guy jus told us are ya?" Cao once again let his personal agenda enter the discussion.

"It's an option we should at least consider Cao. At least we can make it to San Bernardino alive. I don't think Milum could make San Bernardino without us. We can't afford to give 'im one of our mules. If we head north he's gonna have to come with us."

"I really don't like the idea of turning around." Cao knew what was coming next.

"Are you willin' to risk getting us both kilt over Molly and a religion you wouldn't even consider joinin' if she wasn't in it?" Henry figured he'd hit a nerve.

"That's not right, Henry. I can see we got a serious situation here. I'm willin' to consider all our options. And I admit I been havin' a hard time with what we been hearin'. What do you think we ought to do?"

Henry was surprised at his younger brother's moment of clarity. "I reckon we need to get some rest and be prepared to get an early start tomorrow morning. Whether we head north or south, the posse chasin' Milum could catch us if they're determined enough. There's a better chance of it if we head north, but they won't have a hard time following his track to the 'Springs.' And they won't have a hard time following our track south if we head that way. I reckon by now they've give up on ketchin' Milum. Just the same, the first thing we need to figure out is what we're gonna do if we run into 'em while Milum's with us."

"Shouldn't we consider lettin' Milum go south on his own if that's what he wants to do? That seems like the safest option . . . fer us." Cao thought he'd cleverly turned the tables on his brother.

"Like I said, I don't think he can make it out o' here on foot in any direction, and I ain't willin' to hand over to 'im one of our only two pack mules. We might as well walk over there an' shoot 'im whilst he's sleepin' as ride off without 'im. I'm not much inclined to head south neither, an' if he comes north with us, it gives us an extra gun ta match up with whoever we might run into packin' bad intentions." Henry was always the more logical.

"If we run into the crew Milum described we'd still be outnumbered about ten to three even if Able was able to whittle 'em down by a few." Cao wanted to go north, but he didn't want to die.

"My guess, an' it's only a guess, is the Injuns probly won't be a willin' to hang together with the whites over the hundred miles Milum just crossed. If the whites are more determined, there'd only be three or four of 'em. No, the question is still what we do if we run into 'em whilst Milum is with us?" Henry was struggling for the answer and hoping Cao would help him out.

"We've always been good at talking our way through stuff. We're not bad at usin' signs with the Injuns, and you know I can speak Mormon." Cao could always find a joke in the bleakest of circumstances.

Henry smiled. "Let's get some sleep. Maybe if we get a few hours we'll be able to come up with a plan that makes more sense. I'm not too concerned that posse is gonna come ridin' in here tonight. But if they're still looking for our guest over there, they'll probably get to it early in the morning. Just in case, let's not put any more wood on the campfire tonight."

The brothers crawled onto their bedrolls that night with their rifles by their sides and their pistols within easy reach.

CHAPTER 22

MOGATSU CREEK CANYON
UTAH TERRITORY

SEPTEMBER 11, 1857
3:45 AM

The early going was very slow and methodical. Jackson's braves were not eager to flush out the fugitives in this light. However, the two were less eager to elicit the wrath of Ira Hatch as their dominant comrade had done thirty minutes prior. They made a thorough search of the thickly wooded and willowed creek bed. Had either of the escapees been hiding there they would not go undetected. It was a calculated gamble on the part of the two warriors. Either the two they were looking for were laying in wait or they were moving out as fast as they could. Jackson's men were counting on the latter.

Hatch knew they were sandbagging, but he didn't care. He preferred to go slowly at this part of the search as well. Moving ahead too quickly would risk losing the track of the fugitives in case they diverged from the creek bed. For now he was satisfied just to have his troop moving in the right direction. Even though their prey was outpacing them now, come first light, they would make up that ground and then some.

Mathews rode alongside Ira as the posse descended the east bank of Mogatsu Creek; Haskell and Anderson took the high trail of the west bank. Ten warriors, five on each side of the creek, positioned themselves between the white riders and the two braves of the Jackson tribe who were risking it all slashing through the dense brush of the creek bed.

Although steep at times, the terrain was quite open and visible compared to the overgrowth at the bottom of the drainage. An occasional rock outcropping, pinion pine, or scrub cedar offered enough cover for a man to hide in or behind. Mogatsu Creek paralleled the Old Spanish Trail for a number of miles in this region. A divergence from the creek bed and its ample cover would make little sense from the escapee's viewpoint. At least this is what Ira was counting on.

His gamble was calculated, but the odds were substantially in his favor. It would be light soon. Then he would pick up their track. Then he would send fleet riders ahead in anticipation of rediscovering their track. The posse would then leapfrog and make up ground quickly on those being hunted.

Mathews had been waiting for the right time to ask: "What do you suppose Chief Jackson is gonna do about how you treated his buck brave?"

"Oh, I expect he'll make a big fuss for the benefit of his other men. Probly humiliate the buck even more'n I did just to take the onus off hisself. I'll probly have to shoot the sneakin' devil next time I see 'im." He was referring to Chief Jackson. "Either that or give 'im an old scrub horse an' smoke the peace pipe with 'im. Rather it turns out I have to shoot 'im."

"You don't think he'll pull up camp an' come after us?" Mathews was genuinely concerned about it. Chief Jackson had a reputation for impulsive behavior, and he hated to be embarrassed, even if it was through one of his men.

"I doubt it. He's already got egg on his face for jumpin' the gun last Monday. If things unravel at the Meadows he hasta know that he's gonna get most a the blame fer it. I reckon his party'll be the last one to abandon Lee an' the others, an' the most willin' to hang in there till the dirty deed is finished." Ira was always thinking ahead. "Besides, I 'spect Jackson is the kind that'll take a likin' to the killin' o' women and children."

Mathews welcomed the opportunity to change the subject to Lee's plan at the Meadows. "You think the men, who kilt the Prophet and his brother Hyrum at Carthage are in that train?"

"That's jus' rumors made up by the chain o' command to make sure the Saints in these parts get their blood up against the immigrants so we can use them up." Ira liked Mathews and he thought he could handle the truth.

"What about that steer they poisoned an' gave to the Indians up at Corn Creek. Didn't one of the young braves up their die from eatin' the poisoned meat?" Mathews wasn't sure he really wanted to know after he'd asked the question.

"I passed through Corn Creek on my way to guide the immigrants train to the Meadow, and there wasn't any poisoning that went on up there." Hatch was matter of fact.

"So you're tellin' me this group of Gentiles don't deserve what the Saints and the tribes have cooked up for 'em at the Meadows?" Mathews was careful not to place too much emphasis on the question one way or another.

"A war between the Gentiles and the Saints is about to break out that will likely result in a whole lot o' killin' on both sides. That group at the Meadows is just the first one's that's going to be kilt. Once't it gets started there'll be other trains comin' through that'll be getting the same sort a treatment. Then there's the U.S. Army regiments marchin' this way. I expect they'll be a might less easy to use up than the plain folk in these immigrant trains." Hatch was trying to elevate his student's awareness of the bigger picture.

Their horses moved forward through the night at a medium walk. Sometimes they would stop and wait for the braves doing the risky search at the creek to catch up. Then they would move ahead scouring the moon shadows cast by an occasional passing tree or rock formation, to be sure they did not allow their prey to slip past them. A long period of quiet ensued between the two men. Mathews had suspected the charges being leveled against the people in the besieged train now at the Meadows might be without solid basis. It had concerned him some that, during the hasty preparations the Saints had engaged in over the past couple of weeks, they may be rushing to a brutal judgment not fully supported by fact. Ira had confirmed just that. The charges were a trumped-up ruse.

The revelations Ira was offering increased his ambivalence and added to the gravity of the activities they were engaged in. James Mathews pondered for some time the next question he would ask Ira Hatch.

CHAPTER 23

MOUNTAIN MEADOWS
COMMAND POST
UTAH TERRITORY

SEPTEMBER 11, 1857
2:00 AM

After Lee dismissed the men assembled at the campfire they retired to their bedrolls. It had been an exhausting, long day. They knew they would need their rest later on when the tough work started. Lee himself could not sleep. One more item of preparation remained incomplete. John D. Lee needed a "white flag." He walked to his saddlebag and withdrew a small bar of lye soap. As some of the Saints began to snore, Lee stepped through the black wall at the edge of the campfire light and proceeded directly toward the chilly waters of Mogatsu Creek.

As Lee covered the ten-minute trek to the creek, he walked as a man of complete resolve. His plan had been born of necessity. It had been delivered to his men with passion and humility. All had accepted his strategy and his justification for it. He had lived his religion, and the Lord had become his guide.

John D. Lee had embraced the Church of Jesus Christ of Latter-day Saints as a young man in Illinois after his two-year-old daughter had died of scarlet fever. He had never been so low as that night when it seemed his terrible loss consumed everything. That night he began reading a copy of the Book of Mormon a friend had given him. It was more to escape from his heavy loss than to explore Joseph Smith's discoveries and revelations.

As he leafed through the pages he became captivated by its epic chronology. It was as if the book was speaking directly to him. Lee was an immediate convert. He sold everything he owned and moved what was left of his family to Far West, Missouri in June 1838. The LDS Church became his new family.

His first duties were to the Prophet Joseph as one of his personal bodyguards. He would often stand sentry as the powerful leader visited his concubines. After the assassination of Joseph Smith at Carthage, Brigham Young rewarded him for his service by advancing his station on several occasions. Lee pleased the new church leader by executing his assignments tenaciously and without delay. He lived, it seemed, to curry the favor of the patriarch. Lee's efforts did not go unnoticed by the extraordinary administrator, who himself was quite an ambitious man. He needed men like Lee to accomplish God's work. The two men became close, but not as equals.

Brigham then honored him by issuing a proclamation for Lee to become his second adopted son. To have such a rare honor bestowed upon him provided Lee with a status that would enable him to achieve in ways that would not have been possible for him otherwise.

Lee was not an easy man to like. Other Saints were not inclined to volunteer into his leadership or to sing his praises all the way up the Church hierarchy. His Danite status was widely rumored among his fellow Saints. Often referred to as the church's "Avenging Angels," well-known Danites, such as Porter Rockwell and Bill Hickman, were notorious for the number of men they killed in the service of their religion. Gentiles would describe most of it as cold-blooded murder. Rockwell was even rumored to have killed the famous writer and government agent major John Gunnison. Lee was not so notorious or suspected of such high-profile killing. At the end of this day . . . that would no longer be the case.

It had been a long journey for John D. Lee, as it had for all the Saints now present at Mountain Meadows. Thoughts of the journey he had traveled were on his mind as he approached the creek. Lee unbuttoned and removed his shirt. He then removed his undershirt . . . his sacrament garment. He was not oblivious to the significance of what he was doing. Sacrament garments served a sacred purpose for loyal Saints. They were not to be removed except during monthly bathing.

Over the past five days John D. Lee had vacillated wildly about the actions he was taking with respect to the immigrant train. It had begun with vengeance in his heart and the resolve to quench it with the immigrant's blood. This was not unlike the motives harbored by his church leadership and many Saints on down the line. Once the assault began, his emotions had begun to waver. The potential consequences of failure were too dire to contemplate. As he became aware of the horror those encircled within the wagon fort must be facing, he could not help but sympathize with their predicament, and he even began to admire their bravery.

Now, however, he had come full circle. The great challenge he and the others had been going through would soon be over. He could see the end quite clearly. The militia had arrived. Hatch would dispatch of the men who had escaped. The vengeance of Zion would soon be at hand. Lee was now convinced that the almighty Lord was guiding his hand. The immigrants were to be sacrificed to serve His purpose. The millennial prophesy of Joseph Smith was about to be fulfilled.

Lee plunged his sacrament garment into the creek and began to scrub. It was the whitest cloth he had and he was going to make it whiter. He would fashion his sacrament garment into a "white flag." It was no sacrilege to place it in the service of the Lord.

CHAPTER 24

LAS VEGAS SPRINGS
NORTHWEST NEW
MEXICO TERRITORY

SEPTEMBER 16, 1857
5:30 AM

Henry could see the first light of early dawn defining the eastern mountains of the Las Vegas Valley. Sleep had not come easy and had not lasted long, but Henry did feel rested. He began to gather wood and preparations for coffee as soon as he had his boots on.

He decided he would dip into their ample provisions and prepare to feed their guest, and themselves, a nice filling breakfast. Besides, Henry was looking for things to do so he could avoid restarting the fire until there was more light. "No sense hangin' onto the best bacon for some special occasion down the trail," he thought. He would even turn the stock loose on the volunteer melons and table grapes planted by the Mormon militia the previous year. Until this morning, the brothers had taken care to keep them out of their gardens for fear they might return and take exception to them blatantly helping themselves.

It wasn't like overland travel in the eighteen-fifties was without its risks. But Henry thought it was curious how a new threat of danger brought with it a renewed sense of living for the moment.

Henry always started his day with a goal in mind. Today's was to get himself, his brother, and their guest prepared to do some traveling. After a hearty breakfast and some considerable discussion, a decision would be made and a direction determined and they would break camp and head out.

Henry was not a dictator. But he was the older brother and believed he occupied the leader's position over Milum when it came to what needed to happen next. His preference was to continue in the direction they had planned on before Milum had stumbled into their camp. He knew Cao would favor such a choice. He expected Milum would have difficulty heading back in the direction he had been desperately trying to escape for the past five days.

Henry considered his response to Milum's strong objection should that be the case. Would he really leave this man here at the "Springs" if he refused to head north with them? It was an option as Cao had quipped. It wouldn't be murder to do so. After all he had doctored his wounds and nursed him a considerable ways back to good health. The brothers had ample food supplies they'd be willing to share with him. The man would certainly have a better chance to survive the route south than he had before.

And what was the risk to heading north? It was certainly more likely that they would run into the trouble Milum described if they did. But how likely? The posse chasing him must have given up. It would be easy to run down a man on foot, even if he was armed, if the men doing the chasing were well armed and all on horseback. That they hadn't caught up with him by now had to mean they were off Milum's trail, or on to something else altogether. Still they could be up ahead with their "something else" and probably were.

Henry and Cao had made the acquaintance of a good many Mormons along the southern route. Cao's infatuation with Molly Anderson had resulted in the brothers' invitation to church services in Cedar City and subsequently a number of stops north of there. Their first portage through Deseret two years ago had resulted in the budding romance between Cao and the pretty Mormon girl. She and her family had traveled with the train the brothers had drovered for, and there was no keeping the two young starstruck teenagers apart during the night camp gatherings. The church elders traveling with the train made it clear that Molly Anderson would not become the concubine of a Gentile. If there were to be any continued courtship between the two lovebirds, young Cao would have to make at least two commitments. And the first would have to be to the Church of Jesus Christ of Latter-day Saints.

Since then, it had been easy for Henry to talk Cao into additional cross-country contracts as long as he could guarantee their work would take them through Cedar City. Cao began studying the Book of Mormon along with the Doctrine and Covenants of the church. He missed few opportunities to display his devotion and show that he could be a worthy member.

Henry had no intention of joining the church. He wasn't even a very good Catholic by his own estimation, and he lacked the motivation possessed by his younger brother. He generally found ways to avoid religious discussions and would spend the time, when Cao engaged in such formal practices, obtaining supplies and making preparations for their continued journey. Henry, in fact, considered that his brother was behaving like a young fool. He hoped that he would eventually come to his senses.

Cao's reaction to his older brother's condescension was to work harder at proving he was serious about the Anderson girl and would complete any task necessary to prove his worthiness. Although he had committed to Henry he would return to the east one more time, his next journey back through would be to marry Molly Anderson and establish a permanent residence. He had had a number of discussions with Bishop Klingensmith about what would be expected of him from the church's point of view.

It was the relationships his younger brother had established with the Mormons of southern Deseret that entered into Henry's analysis of their current situation. It was true that the Saints had always been helpful to them as they traveled through their territory. There was a willingness to offer advice about the trail ahead, and on several occasions the Saints would provision them with more than they had bargained for.

Henry was smart enough to know that it was in the Mormon nature to convert Gentiles to their religion. This tendency made it clear to him that their generosity was merely an enticement towards this lofty goal. Still, the prospect of heading into the heart of the Mormon enclaves so feared and mistrusted by Milum was not of great concern to Henry and Cao Young.

Cao had played on their last name being the same as that of the man now referred to as the Prophet. The Saints would invariably ask if there was any familial connection between them and that of their leader. Cao would relate that they had relatives in the same general vicinity of Vermont where the Prophet Brigham was from. Henry knew of no such relatives other than those immigrants of Cornwall who had come through Ellis Island on their way to the original family homestead in Providence. He had been embarrassed and somewhat offended by Cao's naked attempt to curry favor and status with the inquiring Saints. He now thought his brother's shameless namedropping may somehow work to their benefit.

As Henry contemplated the discussion he would soon be having with his two companions, he was more resolved than ever that the three of them would be heading north if he had anything to say about it. When Cao stirred at the sound of Henry's camp tending, Henry knew he would soon be having a lot to say about it.

CHAPTER 25

MOGATSU CREEK CANYON
SOUTHERN UTAH TERRITORY

SEPTEMBER 11, 1857
4:30 AM

Ira Hatch was a man of complex character and personality. Mature for his years, few men commanded more respect; and yet Ira had few friends. He liked it that way. Ira understood that friends could be beneficial but could be even more of a liability. The respect of others was what was important, even if that respect was rooted in fear. He also believed that a man had to look out for himself and that no one else would.

When he was conferring with Lee, P.K., and Higbee a few hours earlier, he knew full well that Lee was sending him on a dangerous and difficult mission. Most of the Mormons on the field at Mountain Meadows would have balked at Lee's order. Hatch also knew that what would take place at the Meadows today was likely to turn out bad no matter which way things went for Lee and the others. Failure would most certainly result in an accountability investigation of those deemed responsible for it. After the Lamanites' performance on Monday and since, success could only mean partial success, and that would mean a partial failure. Accountability would be assigned either way.

On the trail of the fugitive immigrants, Ira Hatch was in charge. He could control the outcome, and possibly the aftermath, with respect to himself and his hand-picked comrades. Risky as his mission was, the upside potential was far better than it was for those at the Meadows. Oh, the cattle would be divided along with whatever gold and silver recovered.

There would be a thorough accounting done by the agents of the church. Rewards for extraordinary deeds would be bestowed. Ira and his cohorts would receive a share. It was the long-term consequences that concerned Hatch.

Mathews and Haskell were the only two men on the field Ira felt he could both direct and trust. Although he was of great value to the Iron military district as an interpreter and a scout, he had no military rank. He needed his handpicked comrades to understand what he understood about the events likely to unfold on this day. Rosmus Anderson was excess baggage as far as he was concerned. Rosmus would be sent home as soon as their mission was accomplished. If he could find away to send him home sooner he would do so. Right now, with Haskell and the lanky Dane on the other side of the wide meandering canyon, he would take Mathews into his confidence.

Though Haskell and Mathews had been ordered here by Jacob Hamblin, Mathew's interest in being at Mountain Meadows was more out of curiosity than in vengeance against Gentiles. However, the fervor against them in southern Deseret was so intense that he was reluctant to express reservations that an inquiring person might otherwise be inclined to. Ira's comments about the rumors of Joseph Smith's assassin and the poisoning of Indians at Corn Creek had brought him to consider pursuing answers to questions most Mormons would leave unasked.

"So where do you s'pose all this is goin' to end . . . I mean back at the Meadows?" Mathews was treading lightly.

"Lee has to find a way to use up the Gentiles or all hell will break loose. It's not goin' to be easy for him. The Lamanites have proven themselves to be pretty worthless as a fighting force. Now that he has the Cedar militia at his disposal, he might be able to get the job done. One thing's for sure, if he doesn't get it done soon, things are gonna come apart. Time is his enemy." Hatch liked the exercise of prediction.

"I would think the immigrants are the ones who are runnin' out of time. They have to be runnin' low on food and ammo. I can't imagine being in a more desperate situation than what they're in." Mathews was beginning to allow his compassion for the immigrants to surface.

"Desperate people do desperate things. Take the two we're followin' right now. The immigrants are takin' chances. They have to. They've made it out o' the wagon fort twice in the last four days. The odds are in our favor over the two we're chasin'. But they've given themselves a shot. Those at the Meadows are in a bad way too. But they're not goin' to jus' lay down an' allow us to walk up an' cut their throats."

"You really think we'll be able to catch up to 'em by sundown?" All the men including Mathews had had very little sleep over the past 24 hours.

"If we pick up their track come sunup, we should be able to get to 'em before then. I expect they were well rested. Their plan to slip past our guard was pretty well thought out. If they're young and strong they might be able to cover some ground. But they won't be outrunnin' a mounted posse on foot. We'll be coverin' ground twice as fast as they will once we pick up their track. I'm really not that concerned about catching up to 'em. The closer we get to 'em, the more we're gonna need to keep our eyes open."

"What happens if they get away? Suppose they run into someone that helps 'em out?" Mathews was speculating on the final outcome of their assignment. He wasn't looking forward to it.

"Then we've failed our mission. Failure's not an option fer us. Jus' like it's not an option for Lee and the boys back at the Meadows. I'd still rather be in our shoes, fail or not, than back at the Meadows. I done you and brother Thales a big favor pickin' you two to come with me on this." It was time Ira made clear the markers these boys owed him.

CHAPTER 26

MOUNTAIN MEADOWS COMMAND POST AND OTHER LOCATIONS ACROSS THE LAND OF THE PURPLE SAGE

SEPTEMBER 11, 1857
2:45 AM

Lee found a straight willow growing next to the creek about an inch thick and five feet long. He deftly cut the stalk near the bottom with his razor-sharp Bowie knife and trimmed the branches clean. Then, sheathing his knife, he worked the shaft through the arms of his clean damp undershirt. After rolling it carefully, he placed the makeshift flag over his shoulder and began his walk back to the command post campfire.

No one saw John D. Lee as he made the ten-minute walk back to his position. Guards, a mixture of Mormon militia and Indians, had been posted in a circled configuration facing inward toward the besieged wagon fort. Tutsegabit's camp was further downstream. Upon his arrival at the camp, Lee unfurled his banner and placed the butt of the shaft into a crevice of granite rock next to the camp. The flag would be dry an hour after sunrise. His work complete and his plan in place, Lee retired to his bedroll. He slept soundly for the first time in days.

At this place in time, Henry and Cao Young were two days' ride out of San Bernardino on their way to Las Vegas Springs. They had benefited from the same cloud cover that shielded the moon's light at the Meadows. Tonight, however, it was clear, which meant that tomorrow the desert heat would begin to soar. Other than this minor concern, they retired to their bedrolls untroubled by the uncertainties of what may lie ahead. Their contracts as drover-scouts had been profitably rewarded. They could not have anticipated the turn of events that would unfold ahead.

Warriors from the seven tribes on the field slept calmly as well. They were aware of the advancing federal army and their supposed bad intentions toward the Saints and themselves. But this information was provided entirely by their white co-conspirators. Their attendance at Mountain Meadows was motivated more by their hunger for spoils than from a dread of being invaded by a hostile force. They had already endured a ten-year incursion of the "white man"—Mormons and "gold seekers" mostly—and had tolerated the annoyance as well as could be expected. Their slumber was not disturbed by concerns beyond what gains they hoped to achieve before the end of the next day.

At least half of the militia slept uneasily knowing they would be awakened to relieve their fellow soldiers on guard duty. By now they had verified reports that they would be expected to do some killing, in advance of the burying for which they had been summoned to the Meadows. This notion did not sit well with some. However, their hard day's journey from Cedar City exhausted them sufficiently that they were able to drift off into the sleep they would need for the more taxing day they would soon face.

The riders under the control of Ira Hatch would endure a sleep-deprived night and an even more grueling day. Their incentive for reward and their desire to avoid the brewing confrontation at the Meadows was enough to sustain their spirit.

John Milum Jones and Able Baker must have been somewhat energized by the life-threatening predicament facing them. They had been allowed to rest up the day before the departure from their loved ones. But now they were running for their lives. Their detection and the shootout upstream now far behind, they expected that their desperate predicament was likely to get worse.

The commanders up and down the line from Fort Clara to Salt Lake City did not escape their own brand of sleep deprivation. By now Haslam had brought Lee's news of a botched effort and his appeal for direction. Their reply had gone back, but they would have to wait several more days for the outcome of their directive.

Daniel Wells, William H. Dame, Isaac C. Haight, Jacob Hamblin, Charles Rich, George A. Smith, and Brigham Young himself had much invested in the outcome at Mountain Meadows. Blistering oratory, secret diplomacy, calculated scheming, months of preparation, and years of autonomous power had combined in a cauldron of toxicity. Mixed with a sanctimonious zeal and a vile lust for vengeance, their orchestrations would result in an act so egregious that nearly a century and a half would pass before humanity would, once again, betray its most lofty promises on the soil of the American Republic.

For the immigrants inside the wagon fort, what would normally have been a welcome night on the open range could hardly have seemed more grim. They had most certainly heard the shots fired downstream of them when their best hope for rescue had been discovered. They could not have known if all, any, or none of their best young men had made it through. However, they must have known their chances for retrieving help had been, at best, greatly diminished.

For captains Baker and Fancher, badly wounded and facing agonizing deaths, the uncertain fate of Baker's son must have further devastated their already dismal spirits. All of them had been enduring a nightmare of increasing despair since the vicious attack levied against them the Monday prior. The men were focused on their responsibility to protect their families; the women on caring for the wounded and consoling the terribly frightened children. The wounded were focused on staying alive or preparing to meet their maker.

The arduous task of burying those dead already could not go unattended. Christians all, some more devout than others, there could never have been a time their prayers had sought more from their deity. Yet their prayers were for nothing more than what a good and sincere people should be entitled. They had already lost so much; surely a little mercy was not too much to ask. If not for themselves then surely their children should be considered. The manner in which their prayers would be answered would be known by moderately few for a very long time.

PART TWO

CHAPTER 27

TEMPLE SQUARE
SALT LAKE CITY
UTAH TERRITORY

SEPTEMBER 8, 1857
8:15 PM

It had been dark for over an hour when the Mormon leader stepped out his back door and proceeded west toward the temple bowery. "Church business" was all he said to Lucy, his third sealed wife, as he donned his overcoat and proceeded to the exit.

By now his first wife had died and Lucy had risen to the lead position of the patriarch's concubines by demonstrating her ability to handle the demanding operation of the Beehive House. There was no expectation or concern that her husband was leaving at this hour, and even if there were Lucy knew better than to voice it. "Church business" was a man's business. She knew he would not be returning to her that evening anyway.

He strode past the Lion House next door and inventoried the luminescent windows behind which eighteen of his other wives prepared themselves for bed. He knew which one he would be visiting upon his return . . . Emmeline. Little excitement stirred his loins on this occasion. It was not that Emmeline was unworthy as an object of his lust. Quite the contrary; she was presently one of his favorites. Neither could it be blamed on his advancing age. At fifty-five he was still capable of mounting considerable interest in performing his procreative duties.

The formidable leader was preoccupied with troubling news. Another express messenger had just arrived on the heels of George Smith's return from his assignment in the southern settlements. He had been receiving daily reports, sometimes twice a day.

This recent messenger had arrived in full gallop, his mount a lather of foam. A runner had been dispatched to the Beehive House immediately. At least it had been after dark. The "Southern Mission," as it was being referred to, had the potential to explode in their faces if not handled properly. He congratulated himself on having had the express riders instructed to return to the bowery stables instead of arriving directly at his front door. A man with his responsibilities must be very careful.

The bowery had served its purpose well for ten years. Plans for the new tabernacle next to it had been finalized, and now it was just a matter of raising the money. The cornerstone of the grand temple had been laid.

The bowery for which he now headed could no longer accommodate the growing number of Saints now living in Salt Lake City, the capital city of Deseret. Its rough thatched roof protected the faithful from rain and snow during only the mildest weather conditions. On the cold windy nights its open-sided walls provided little refuge. He liked the bowery for the meetings that needed to be conducted discreetly.

Only a ten-minute walk from his home, the temple bowery was the best place to conduct these meetings. With Danite guards posted at all four corners, he would meet with his war council in the center of the large covered expanse. Lanterns placed strategically illuminated the area sufficiently that the uninvited could not approach without being noticed. The distance between those in attendance and the guards themselves was adequate to ensure that only those with a need to know would be able to hear.

George A. Smith, the beloved cousin of the Prophet Joseph himself, would be there. He led the "Twelve Apostles" and held the rank of colonel in the territorial militia. Jacob Hamblin, his newly appointed president of the Southern Indian Mission, was dressed out in full leather fringe. General Daniel Wells, commander of Deseret's Nauvoo Legion, sat uncomfortably on his stool. Elder Charles C. Rich of the Quorum of Twelve sat patiently waiting. Wilford Woodruff, counselor to the First Presidency and church historian, had organized the meeting and called in the participants. James Haslam, express messenger and the man of the hour, sat nervously next to the lone empty stool that waited for their leader.

They were all seated on what appeared to be milking stools facing each other in a nearly completed circle. They all rose up in deference as Brigham Young approached to take his place on the empty stool, which would complete the circle.

"Please be seated, Brothers." He motioned with his hand palm down and the group immediately reseated themselves before they'd all even had a chance to rise. Seating himself he placed that same hand on the shoulder of the exhausted rider next to him. "Brother Haslam, you've come a long way in your service to our Lord. We must receive your report and then provide you with the comfort you've so dearly earned."

"I'm ready to go again wwww-whenever you say so sir." The stammering horseman hardly knew how to address the great Mormon leader. He'd listened to him address crowds of many hundreds of the brethren in this very place. As he handed the envelope to the Prophet Brigham, Haslam understood the adulation the Saints held for this man. He was also conscious of the tremendous power the man, this Prophet, proscribed over this vast region. He, more than most, knew well of its vastness.

Haslam was short in stature, but turned what would normally be considered a handicap in these parts to his advantage. Well known to be one of the best "express riders" in Deseret, whenever a church leader needed a message delivered quickly, especially to someone far off, he was often the man who was tapped.

His exploits over the next few days would make him legendary among the Saints. His younger brother would become a legendary rider for the Pony Express and the U.S. government. They were both capable of the kind of rides folk writers would pen songs about.

Brigham Young broke the seal and removed the parchment from its holdings. He studied the communiqué for some time before he passed it around the circle, handing it first to George Smith sitting to his immediate left. "You brought this all the way from the Meadows?" He asked Haslam, "When did you leave?"

"I left from Cedar City yesterday evening about three hours past sunset." He answered.

Young turned to Jacob Hamblin. "That's close to three hundred miles, wouldn't you say, Brother Hamblin?"

Hamblin nodded. Hamblin's summer home was at Mountain Meadows.

"That'd be about twenty-four hours! Wilford, how many mile per hour is that?" The Prophet turned his gaze to his ever-capable scribe.

Woodruff scribbled over some computations. "About twelve and a half miles per hour," stated the loyal counselor and secretary in his most proper diction.

"Why, I think you've outdone yourself, James. Has anyone among us ever heard of a distance ride to compare?" He inventoried the faces in the circle. All present either shook their heads or stared back blankly. While all present understood the accomplishment, being or having been experienced riders themselves, some were wondering why the Prophet was taking so much time with a messenger instead of dealing with the significant gravity of the message itself. None would dare express such a thought. The Prophet turned back to Haslam.

"Did you stop to sleep?" He continued, obviously aware, but seemingly unconcerned with their unspoken thoughts.

"The bishops provided me with good mounts all the way sir. I was able to catch a little shut-eye in the saddle some during the dark hours. Especially bein' I was on the way back and the mounts were headin' back to their masters' stables." Haslam's futile attempt was to downplay his accomplishment. All present were aware that Brigham appreciated modesty, especially in others.

"From now on I'd like you to address me as Brother Young, as I am honored to address you as Brother Haslam." Haslam's effort was a considerable feat. The Prophet was giving him his due. At the same time he was making sure this meeting went exactly as he wished it to.

"I want you to accompany Brother Woodruff to the Lion House where he will instruct the maids to draw you a warm bath and prepare you a hot meal." He turned his attention once again to his historian.

"Wilford, see that he gets a quiet room and make sure the maids know that he is not to be disturbed until he awakens on his own. They are then to prepare him the finest breakfast west of the Mississippi. Brother Haslam, be sure to state your preference before you retire. After you've eaten, you are to meet Brother Smith here, tomorrow morning, at the bowery stables. I'm considering taking you up on your offer to return to the Meadows with another 'express message.' Are you sure you feel up to the task?" His countenance revealed that the Mormon leader wanted an honest answer to the question.

"Yes sir . . . I mean I'm sure I can do it, Brother Young." Haslam had never felt so tired but at that moment he was sure he would be able to accomplish the task. An actual tub bath in the Lion House . . . he could only imagine. Was it possible he might even have a maid scrub his back? Wondering if the Prophet's reference to "maids" was really in reference to one or more of his plural wives, his excitement surged. He would not jeopardize such a possibility by expressing anything but complete confidence.

The Prophet motioned to Woodruff with his little finger to proceed as directed. Woodruff wasted no time. This was the end of this meeting as far as Haslam and Woodruff were concerned. The scribe also knew that his boss wanted no recorded record of the meeting that was about to take place. Woodruff never ceased to be amazed at how the Prophet could direct things. The rest of this meeting would contain discussions his boss did not want the express messenger to hear.

"Have you considered taking another wife, Brother Haslam?" The Prophet knew that Haslam had been married to the same woman for the past ten years and that she had bore him five children, but that three had died at birth. He also knew that his wife was now pregnant and due to deliver soon.

James Haslam was embarrassed by the question. "Well I have been thinking about a girl down in Salt Creek. I haven't been brave enough to speak with her about it though." Some of the others chuckled until Young cast a quick but disapproving glance their way.

"Do you have any other wives, Brother Haslam?" The Mormon Prophet placed his hand back on the shoulder of the loyal servant.

"No sir, just one sir . . . I mean Brother Young." The rider grimaced as he made the mistake a second time.

"What's the lass's name? The one down in Salt Creek."

"Miss Ann Redford. Bob and Lettice Redford's daughter." Haslam was again feeling very unsure of himself.

"The barrister's daughter. Fine choice. I'll make arrangements for some inquiries to be put in with Bishop Bryant about the girl and have him approach her parents. Bryant owes me a favor or two. If things work out as our Lord would have them, perhaps you will allow me the honor of sealing you to her sometime after your return?"

The young man was in near disbelief. He had delivered messages to high-ranking members of his church before. Some had been directed to the Prophet himself. But to be rewarded as he was being tonight was beyond anything he had previously experienced.

"I'd be very honored, Brother Young," was all he could think to say.

"Wilford, please make a note of it and place a reminder on our desk." The Prophet worked at the opposite end of the same desk from Woodruff in the tithing office attached to his home. He then rose, and simultaneously Haslam and Woodruff rose with him. "Good evening to both you gentlemen. May we always depart from one another as loyal servants to our Lord."

Woodruff placed his arm around the younger man and led him off in the direction of the Lion House.

CHAPTER 28

LAS VEGAS SPRINGS
NORTHWEST NEW
MEXICO TERRITORY

SEPTEMBER 16, 1857
5:45 AM

Henry filled two coffee tins for himself and his brother. As Milum slept soundly he began to unveil his plans to his younger brother.

"You think he'll be fit enough to do some travelin'?" He assumed his brother would understand that he meant starting out this morning.

"He looked a lot better than I thought he would during our discussion last night. I 'spect if he can hold down his breakfast he'll be O.K." Cao was eying the spread of bacon and corn batter his brother had prearranged around the pots and pans. It would do no good to feign his usual disgust at the meal his brother was preparing. They would eat well this morning.

"I say we break camp right after we eat and get headed up north." He studied his younger sibling for signs of protestation or concurrence.

"And what if we run smack into Hatch and his friends along the way?" Cao thought the brothers needed to consider contingencies.

"My guess is they aren't still following or they got sidetracked by somethin' else. But if'n we do run into 'em, we're just gonna have to play it by ear. We know Hatch is a Mormon, an' maybe we can talk our way through it. Anyway, it's not our fight, whatever it is that's goin' on between Milum and Hatch." Henry was thinking out loud and it was obvious. Milum continued to snore loudly.

"I think Milum's story last night was pretty believable. S'pose he refuses to go north. We can't very well force him." So far Cao wasn't adding much to the conversation.

"We all have choices to make and we're all free to make em. His is to ride Floppy north or walk south across a mean stretch of dry-hot desert. I don't think his shoes'd last 'im another ten miles." Henry, in assessing Milum's options, knew what his choice must be.

"S'pose you're right and we don't run into Hatch. Do we jus' take Milum all the way back to Missouri with us? Right through Salt Lake City?" Both brothers had to be wondering about the depth of anger the Saints held for this man, if not for the entire group of immigrants Milum had described.

"There's a lot we don't know. But we been treated good all up and down the trail 'tween here an' Salt Lake, an' beyond. I can't see why we'd be treated differently this time. I spect we'd be doin' Milum an' the Mormon-folk a favor by getting him to Salt Lake an' letting the church leaders sort this out." Henry looked at his younger brother as he verbalized the theory.

Cao couldn't very well disqualify that his chosen faith would not be sympathetic to Milum's plight. He was also struggling with the characterization of Ira Hatch as a bloodthirsty killer. Milum's story assumed such. But Hatch was a man of considerable reputation in these parts. "I'm sure we can talk our way through whatever we run into along the way."

The brothers just couldn't comprehend that an entire people of Christian faith could participate in such an attack as Milum had been describing to them. There had to be more to the goings-on up north than even Milum understood. There had to be those they could turn to for understanding and for justice. They had been treated decently on numerous occasions. They knew the terrain and the people better than Milum did. Milum should be safe with them.

Henry turned to tend his fire. He would need a good bed of coals upon which to begin his cooking. Cao looked off into the northeast . . . the direction of the Old Spanish Trail they would be traveling soon. Until now, he had only looked forward to making this journey. Now things were different.

Now the woman Cao longed to see seemed much further away than before, the trail not so isolated and benign but filled with unknown difficulty. He began to question his circumstance. Did he really know the people in these parts as well as he thought he did? Had he forged good relationships that would carry enough weight when and if the time came?

The brothers had experienced events before that required similar self-assessment, when an unknown group of Indians, or white folk for that matter, approached unexpectedly from out of nowhere, or when the trail ran into a swollen unfordable stream. There were times when the weather would take a quick and unexpected turn. The accompanying adrenaline rush, the need to act quickly or cautiously, was commonplace for adventurers such as they.

Milum's story had penetrated the brother's psyche in a foreboding manner. His ragged and brutalized condition bore witness to the veracity of his tale. Yet many questions remained, and the answers to them would likely lie ahead on the trail.

Henry turned back to tending his cooking. Milum's snoring was interrupted by his involuntary stretch. Soon the three men would be engaged in conversation over a campfire breakfast that would normally be the best part of the day. The gravity of the choices they would make would be heavier than any of them knew.

CHAPTER 29

MOGATSU CREEK
UTAH TERRITORY

SEPTEMBER 11, 1857
7:00 AM

The brave signaled excitedly to Ira Hatch and his companion rider Mathews. The men spurred their horses in the direction of the unknown discovery. The two braves from Jackson's tribe arrived ahead of Hatch and Mathews, as their proximity was only half the distance. After reining his mount to a halt Hatch allowed the three braves to confer and report to him their assessment.

Tutsegabit's brave had found their tracks. It was daylight now and the signs were obvious. The creek bed was mostly dry by now. They had dropped out of the mountain's higher elevations and had begun to enter the more porous high desert regions of the Great Basin. Here it was not uncommon for the land to swallow up all but the most ample of waterways. A damp depression next to the dry creek bed revealed the two sets of tracks, with one print particularly clear.

Hatch dismounted and looked up at the still-mounted Mathews. "Ride over to brothers Haskell and Anderson and have them help you circle the other men back here to me. Things are 'bout to change some."

James Mathews answered by spurring his mount off into the direction of the other two Mormons. Within five minutes the entire posse had gathered around the boot track as Ira had strategically placed his feet astraddle the telltale discovery. The others fanned out in front of him, and when the last of them arrived Ira began to speak.

"We guessed right. They've kept to the creek bed 'til now, an' my guess is they'll keep on it as far as it takes 'em. It'll be their best chance at gettin' the water they're gonna need if'n they expect to get very far. We should be able to foller their track pretty easy from here on."

"We're gonna split up inta two groups until we catch up to 'em. One group rides ahead at a slow gallop without looking for tracks but jus' stayin' next to the creek bed. Thales, you and Rosmus lead the first group up about a mile and then set your men to rediscoverin' their track. Once you've found it leave a man there for us to catch up to. Repeat that drill until you've got four men posted. I want the lead group to never have less than four men in it. Our group will start out about a quarter hour after your group leaves. We should be able to start leapfroggin' one another within the hour." Ira pulled out his stopwatch. "Anyone got any questions?"

Rosmus Anderson asked the obvious question everyone else was thinking. "What do we do if'n we run up on 'em?"

Ira translated Anderson's question so the braves would understand. Several of the braves began to snicker to one another. Rosmus Anderson exhibited none of the swagger most of the braves were inclined to exude. He was not a fighting man. Life was plenty difficult enough without asking for trouble. He'd come from Denmark a few years prior, a simple man looking for simple answers.

"You back off until the rest of us can join you. Unless you want to be heroes an' take 'em on when they have the advantage of surprise?" Ira answered Rosmus and the other brethren first, then translated the message to the Lamanite contingent. Their snickering stopped. "Thales, pick the braves you want to go with you and Rosmus and get a move on. It'd be best if we can get this wrapped up before sundown."

Thales Haskell wasted little time picking seven braves out of the pack. They left in a cloud of dust. Then, remembering the details of his orders, Haskell slowed his posse to a loping gallop.

"Check yer saddles, boys. An' make sure yer firearms are where yore gonna want 'em ta be. I reckon it'll be several hours before we catch up to 'em, but ya never know." Ira began the drill of resetting his saddle and checking his weaponry. His men followed suit. There was excitement in the air now that evidence of their prey was clearly before them. The fatigue that had beset them moments earlier was now gone. It would soon return, but for now the men were wide awake. The prospects that some had hoped for, that they would search in vain for a day or two and then give up, was now an unlikely one.

James Mathews was one who faced the more likely outcome with an increasing level of apprehension. He was fairly comfortable with the assumption that none of the Indians present could understand English, and he really didn't much care if he was wrong. It had become obvious to him that the Lamanites were in it for the plunder. No lofty doctrines at work with them. But Ira Hatch was a man he looked up to. "Are we doin' the right thing, Ira?"

Ira Hatch turned his back to Mathews and stared off in the direction of the advance party he had just dispatched. He knew this discussion the two were about to have was unavoidable. He had actually planted the seeds that had brought them to this point.

Ira Hatch was not a man who easily took others into his confidences. Perhaps it was due to his having spent so much time alone scouting the vastness of Deseret that he had somewhat grown apart from his brethren and perhaps even his faith. Certainly he was a confident man. But the independence he had developed over time would not allow him to blindly do another's bidding. He had been relieved to be dispatched from the grisly scene unfolding at the Meadows. Now only the hunting down of the two Gentiles was in question. But this too needed reconciling.

"The way I see it, James, is we're at war. George Smith made that pretty clear at the council meeting in Cedar Sunday before last. He reported that twenty five hundred federal troops are headed into Deseret to put an end to our whole way of life. I suppose what's botherin' you, and it bothers me some too, is these Gentiles we're after might not know we're at war. In the Black Hawk War it was the same. Ya start questionin' yer leaders in a time of war an' ya can get yerself shot. Shot fer treason or shot fer hesitatin', ya get shot jus' the same. All kinda bad things happen in a war. Jus' getting' through it alive can be one a the only good things ta come out a bein' in a war. We gotta do this thing. Don't let there be any question in yer mind when the time comes, Brother Mathews. You get those boys in yer sights they're likely to be havin' you in their sights too. Don't you hesitate."

CHAPTER 30

MOUNTAIN MEADOWS
WAGON FORTRESS
UTAH TERRITORY

SEPTEMBER 11, 1857
9:30 AM

Mathew Fancher completed his rounds within the immigrant compound and returned to the desperate inquiry of his own family. His countenance was what could be expected of a man who had not had any good news in some time. His cousin lay mortally wounded, having suffered a severe neck wound. Infection had obviously set in. It was just a matter of time. His sister-in-law and nephews waited quietly for their new patriarch to unveil his report.

"Cap'n Baker isn't goin' to make it another night. His wife said that after he heard the gunshots last night he hasn't said a word. The whole camp is lookin' to me now to call the shots. I'm sure glad none a our boys was in that rescue party. There sure was a lot a gunfire for a while. We can't expect that any of 'em got through. Even if they did, it's unlikely they'll get far."

Mrs. Fancher, concerned for the younger children, spoke first. "Surely an answer to our prayers will be coming. Please Matt, lead us in prayer."

Matt bowed his head and began. "Dear Lord. Please deliver us from the evil that has beset our family and friends. Give us the strength we need and the strength we will need when you show us the way. Help us to understand the nature of our enemies and the intent of their actions that we may project your will upon them in the manner they deserve. Amen."

"Amen," chorused the close-knit family of eleven.

Matt's eldest nephew Hampton was hungry for specifics. "Are there any other plans bein' discussed?" The younger man had become frustrated with the hopelessness of their situation.

"After last night's doins nobody is talkin' about any more attempts ta get through their lines. Most a the boys think our best chance will come to us in time. We have enough food to last us several weeks. Our ammo is low, but we have enough to make 'em pay dearly if they come at us here. Out in the open the advantage goes over ta them." Matt Fancher stopped short his analysis of the situation as Mrs. Fancher's glare became increasingly disapproving.

Matt motioned for the two eldest to move their discussion out of earshot of the younger ones. His efforts were for the most part in vain. For the past several days children throughout the camp had projected a grim acknowledgement of their beleaguered circumstance that was all too clear to ignore.

They walked a few paces from the family circle, knelt, and lowered their voices. Matt began again. "We have to wait and hold out for a break to come our way. When that time comes I want you to be ready. There's bound to be other trains passin' by."

William, the younger boy, spoke next. "What if no other trains come by this way? Are we goin' ta jus' set here an' wait 'til we starve? Wouldn' it be better ta jus' go out an' put up a fight at least? Take some of 'em with us?" William was ready to make them pay right now.

"An' when all the men in our party is dead, who's gonna protect the women an' children? No, we all hang together here in the fortress an' wait. Our enemies may get tired of the siege an' leave. Some of 'em might leave, an' our odds get better. Someone might see what's goin' on here an' go fer help. As time goes on our situation worsens but our chances improve that things'll shift our way." The young leader was thinking out loud. As bleak as their situation was, everyone was aware that things could get worse. After all, they had been getting worse every day for the past four days. Hope was about all they had left, and they desperately needed something to occur that would shift the odds in their favor.

At that very moment a commotion was heard, and its proximity clearly increased as it grew louder. "Matt Fancher! Someone's comin'! Two whites on horseback. One ridin' in under a white flag." The voice was Mordecai Stevenson from the Baker camp.

Excited shouting and some cheering flashed through the encampment like a bolt of lightning. Fancher and his two nephews turned immediately toward the commotion and proceeded toward it.

As the camp leader peered eastward between two overturned wagons he saw nothing at first. His rifle had been a permanent fixture in his hands for the past several days and was now at the ready, as were the weapons of all the other men present. He tempered his excitement, fearing the report he had just heard was somehow flawed. Perhaps it was only the forlorn hope of a hopeless individual playing tricks on the mind, or the lunacy of a man under stress far too long. The latter had already occurred among some of the wounded and the hysterical.

Then there it was. The riders had disappeared behind their descent into Mogatsu Creek's steep gully. Now as they rose up the side closer to them, the flag came into view first. The long pole it was attached to brought it into full view before the cowboy hats worn by its couriers became visible. Then as their mounts slowed from a trot to a slow walk the men came into full view . . . their features clearly European Caucasian . . . their dress obviously not Indian. The white flag they displayed signaled the universally understood intention that their approach contained no hostile purpose.

Some of the men started to cheer. Fancher's heart, like the others, leapt in exhilarated anticipation. But the leader would not be sidetracked. "SILENCE!!!" His shout overpowered the building cheers of his comrades and instantly stilled their expression. Questions needed to be asked. A time for celebration might be soon upon them, but for now any celebration would have to wait. After all, they had good reason to believe some whites had been working with their Indian attackers.

Five other men grabbed hold of one of the wagon bastions and pulled it open as if it were a commonplace swinging-gate. The horsemen passed through without hesitation and proceeded to the center of the wagon fortress. The immigrants did not follow. The center of their fortress had not been safe from the snipers' bullets since it was erected. For nearly five days they had preferred to stay close to the barricades and avail themselves of the fort's maximum protection. There trenches had been dug and their own marksmen positioned.

Fancher took the bold move of stepping forward a few paces toward the two newcomers. "I'm Mathew Fancher. I'm leadin' this outfit, with the help of captains John Baker and Alexander Fancher, since we started out from Fort Smith, Arkansas. Please state your names and business." Fancher's comments were as much for the benefit of the men he was leading as it was for the two strangers before him.

The man without the flag removed his hat and said. "My name is John Lee. This here is Brother William Bateman. We've come over from New Harmony, havin' heard there was a train of immigrants here under attack. It's our purpose to be of help to you if you'll allow it."

Bateman removed his hat quickly as he realized Lee had done so, and then attempted to steady his mount while crushing his hat against the makeshift flagpole. He remained silent, quite content to defer to Lee's discourse.

"Can we offer you a cup a coffee? Mr. Lee? Mr. Bateman?" Fancher was as eager as the others for the discussion to begin. But he would not sacrifice the diplomacy of proper decorum.

"That'd be right welcome. Thank you." The men proceeded to dismount as Lee accepted the hospitality for them both.

CHAPTER 31

TEMPLE SQUARE
SALT LAKE CITY
UTAH TERRITORY

SEPTEMBER 8, 1857
9:00 PM

Once out of earshot the Prophet returned his full attention to those left in the circle. "I trust you've all had time enough to read Brother Haslam's communiqué?" His demeanor now changed to match the gravity of the events at hand.

The others nodded affirmatively, but silence was their only other response.

"Sounds like your little plan has gone awry and now Brothers Lee and Higbee need some direction." The Prophet was looking back and forth at Smith and Wells as he spoke.

This time silence was their only response. Smith and Wells wanted to qualify the prophets' last statement with respect to his reference to "your little plan," but both men thought better of that idea. Young knew he had tossed them a juicy piece of bait. Ownership of the plan in operation at the Meadows belonged to all of those present. He knew that challenging them in this way would get them to thinking along the lines he wanted.

"Am I the only one among us who feels it necessary to speak to this matter?" He was now riveted on Wells. General Wells was his highest-ranking military man, and it was time he started acting like it.

"I don't think this is the time to be backing away from what we started five and a half weeks ago." Careful to not be placing emphasis on the "we,"

General Wells' short response was intended as a method of expressing a resolve to complete the plan. Neither did he have a backup plan. Backing away from what they had started conjured up scenarios that seemed intolerable to him.

Young turned his gaze to Apostle George A. Smith while barely hiding his disgust for his military commander's obvious ineptitude.

George, feeling on the spot, continued the bravado he had been feigning for more than a month. "The militia will finish off those Gentile bastards. Haight says there that the Iron County militia has been ordered in from Cedar. By God, when I was last at Cedar, Bishop Klingensmith and I debated the matter in front of the council. I gave P.K. such a thrashin' by the end of it those boys were boilin' for a fight with those Carthage braggin' buffoons."

As Young listened, he thought the man who'd just spoken was the epitome of a "bragging buffoon" himself. His brash wordy tirades had won him the admiration of the rank-and-file Saints, and his relationship to the first Prophet had elevated his popularity above what it would otherwise be. A great intellect he was not. He turned to Jacob Hamblin. "Brother Hamblin, do you believe the Lamanites will abandon Lee and Higbee completely now that it's become a siege?" The Prophet needed accurate information, not bluster and boast.

"No, Brother Young. Most of the tribes headed to the Meadows are under the firm control of Tutsegabit. Others, like Jackson's group of cutthroats, are probably the ones who have started to cut and run. The bulk of the Lamanites will stay and provide support for Lee and Higbee." Hamblin was the most knowledgeable of the goings-on in the southern settlements, and it showed. Still, he was responding more confidently than he actually felt. His assessment would turn out to be inaccurate as well.

"I agree with you, Brother Wells, that this is no time to turn back. You'd better hope the Iron County militia takes their orders seriously. It might not be a bad idea to come up with a strategy for what needs to be done in the event things continue to unravel." The Prophet was miffed, but he had to work with these people.

Charles C. Rich remained silent. He was relieved to be left out of the discussion. He was grateful his only responsibility for the plan had been to persuade the train's trail bosses to take the southern route instead of the Humboldt Trail.

"Brother Smith, winning the debate is all well and good. But if we don't win the battle, I think history will treat Bishop Klingensmith's position more kindly than it will yours. Getting the brethren into a fever pitch of anger is probably an easier task than leading them to the wholesale slaughter of over a hundred men, women, and young folk, Gentiles or not. Your commanders on the field have a very difficult job to do and I expect they'll need your best counsel at this critical juncture." By now the Prophet was directing his speech to all present.

"Brother Hamblin, whatever these sage military leaders advise, it would be wise of you not to be anywhere near your summer home at the Meadows until we know that the mission has been completed. In fact, I would suggest you head straight to Tooele and have Bishop Rowberry seal you to that Leavitt girl you've been courting. Think you can get there by this Friday?"

"Yes Brother Young." Hamblin's attention was riveted upon what the leader was telling him. He had not been that definite about his prospects with the Leavitt girl.

"I'll send an express rider on ahead with orders for Bishop Rowberry to prepare for the ceremony. It is most important that a record of the sealing be preserved at the stake. Good idea to transport a record of it back here to Salt Lake City as well." The Prophet did not need to spell it out for Hamblin. The siege was taking place on the grazing fields of his summer home. If the event that was occurring, or about to occur, was ever investigated, Hamblin would be one of the first questioned.

"I want you all to be thinking of how we might protect the First Presidency of our beloved church should things not transpire as we have intended." The Prophet paused to allow the other three to absorb this last comment.

Smith, still stinging from a perceived rebuke, showed his ignorance once again. "Aren't we going to be at war with the entire federal army very soon? When you dispatched me to the southern settlements, I thought war was imminent, the federal army on its way, with orders to hang us all. Have things changed?"

"No George. The federal army is still on its way." The Prophet waited for Smith's next questions as if he knew what they would be before he asked them.

"Then what do we care if things don't turn out? Are our backs not against the wall? Do we not fight 'til the last drop of our blood has been drained from us? Is this not the time of prophecy? The message I've been preaching for over a month had nothing to do with what happens if things don't work out. I for one won't stand for any more persecution from the hand of the Gentile. I am ready to wipe the Gentiles from the face of the earth, and that goes for their women and young folk too." Smith was getting worked up. It was time for the Prophet to take over.

"All of what you say is most likely true, George. The federal army is in the mountains headed our way. I'm sure Buchanan would like nothing better than to display those of us in the First Presidency, and a selected group of our other leaders, hanging from a government gallows right here in Temple Square."

"Yes, we are at war just as Joseph prophesied we would be. If need be we will fight 'til the last drop of blood has been drained. But this war may take a long time. Remember that Joseph also prophesied that we are going to win. The Gentile still vastly outnumbers us. It's quite possible we may need to be somewhat clever about how we go about winning." Young was losing his patience with the blustering, egotistical man.

Smith got the message and cut his intended response short.

"Hickman and Lot Smith have been sent into the mountains to engage the federal army. They will not be attacking them head on. General Wells has directed them to harass and frustrate their progress. With any luck they will have to encamp in the mountains and the Rocky Mountain winter will put an end to them.

"My point is, it would be foolish for our men to attack the federal troops head on. We will have little more than one thousand men against their twenty-five hundred. They have canons and the finest weaponry. Strategy must be employed if we are to succeed. It may turn out that the federal army will have to surrender to us and beg us for supplies. We have our agents at work in Washington right now attempting to negotiate to our benefit. I will not undermine their efforts to improve our autonomy over Deseret by acting brashly or foolishly.

"The Southern Mission always planned for the Lamanites to conduct the slaughter of the immigrant trains as they passed through our territory. It has always been our plan to portray ourselves as the only people who could control them, not the people who did the slaughtering themselves." Young sounded disgusted as he finished the sentence.

"We've come a long way together. Our church has done well by us. We've endured the Gentile's persecution for decades, and to get free from it we have subjected ourselves to the harshest wilderness, filled with savages and wild beasts. Though it may seem that the millennium is upon us, how long this will take to unfold is not clear. We came out here for good reasons. We have many advantages in Deseret that diminish the effect of our enemy's greater numbers. That does not change the fact that we must prepare ourselves for every eventuality.

"Send Haslam with orders that the militia is to do everything within its power to use up the Gentiles in that train. You'll need to come up with some plan to spare innocent life. We need to come up with a contingency plan that keeps responsibility for any failure as close to the field of battle as possible, and at the same time allows us some pretense of human decency.

"I can only imagine what my bargaining position with the federal commander will be if it is widely known that I, along with my most trusted counselors, attempted but failed to slaughter a train of American citizens, and their children, while on their way to California. You might want to think about sending someone on Haslam's heels that will see to it that our bishops and militia leaders along the way understand what's at stake here as well. A word to the wise should be sufficient.

"I do not profess to be very good. I will try to take care of number one, and if it is wicked of me to try to preserve myself, I shall persist in it; for I am intending to take care of myself."

Silence again was the response. But this time they understood clearly the Prophet's meaning. They all needed to be taking care of themselves. They all needed to make plans to protect their reputations should things not turn out at Mountain Meadows as originally proposed.

"I'll take care of it, Brother Young. Perhaps I can utilize the assistance of Brother Hamblin in that regard?" General Wells looked over at Jacob.

Hamblin nodded his willingness to assist.

Wells was eager to get this meeting over. He knew from what the Prophet had just said that the bulk of the responsibility for controlling the fallout would fall squarely on his shoulders. He also understood that his good fortune, along with that of the others present, could rest upon his ability to implement his leader's directives.

"Be sure no evidence of your orders survives the giving. Also keep your most trusted subordinates as far from the field of battle as possible. We've got our hands full to the east and to the west. By the way, what's the latest word on the Saints from Genoa and those suspected spies that were arrested outside Box Elder?"

"The reinforcements should be arriving here in Salt Lake City very soon according to our latest reports. They picked up some Gentiles, possible spies, on the other side of the Humboldt Sink. I'm having them brought in. I've sent word with our mail carriers to obtain information on them discreetly." Wells was happy to change the subject.

"When they arrive, be sure I'm notified. For now I want you all focused on how you're going to direct a successful outcome for brothers Lee and Higbee at the Meadows . . . and on how you will best serve the church if they achieve anything less than complete success." At these words Young began to rise, signifying the end of the session on this final clarifying note.

CHAPTER 32

LAS VEGAS SPRINGS
NORTHWEST NEW
MEXICO TERRITORY

SEPTEMBER 16, 1857
6:00 AM

Milum took his time getting to his feet and walked slowly and deliberately over to the campfire. The brothers observed his movements closely, assessing his capabilities with each unsteady move. As he carefully seated himself onto the stone and plank bench the brothers had positioned by the fire for that purpose, Milum still posed a troubling site.

Although the dried blood had been washed from his wounds, the wounds themselves had improved very little. His clothing was still a frightening display of the privations and violence he'd endured. The bandages applied to his arm wound had stained through and needed changing. Cao walked over to Floppy's pack and retrieved from it a shirt and pair of pants he had intended to change into once they crossed the continental divide. Handing them to Milum, both men understood that this was no small act of generosity.

Looking at the bounty of flapjacks and bacon, Milum was hit with a sensation of hunger more extreme than any he'd ever known. It was obvious the brothers were intending to share the more than ample portions being prepared. He would not forget his manners.

"I know I was damn lucky to run into you boys when I did an' I sure hope someday I'll be able to find some way to return the favor." His words did not seem to convey near the gratitude these men were due. As he searched his mind for a more fitting thank you, Henry straddled the seat next to him and looked directly into Milum's eyes.

"We're plannin' on pullin' out a here this morning, Milum, an' we want you to come with us." Henry watched his guest for signs of protest. He didn't see any.

"We're headin' north on the Old Spanish Trail until we hit Salt Lake City, an' then east from there." Henry kept his eyes locked with Milum's. Milum responded by meeting Henry's eye contact without verbalization.

"It won't do no good tryin' to talk us inta headin' back ta San Bernardi-no an' there's no way you'd be able ta make it there on your own." Henry paused again, anticipating the arguments Milum was likely to mount. Milum only politely continued his silent attentiveness.

"We figure we know quite a few of the Mormon folk along the way pretty well, havin' traveled through these parts a few times before. We think we'll be able to obtain help in sortin' out what's behind all the trouble you described to us last night." Again Henry's comment was met with no verbal response.

"Dammit Milum! I'm askin' ya ta let us know if'n you're gonna come with us er not." Henry was becoming flustered and more than a little miffed at the one-sidedness of the conversation the two were having.

Milum at once realized the rudeness of his silence and the opportunity just presented. "Why hell, I wouldn't think of lettin' you boys ride headlong into that pack a ruthless killers without my carbine to back ya up . . . after all you've done fer me. I 'spect I'd be surely dead by now if it wasn't fer the two of you. Maybe I'll get to return the favor someday sooner than I figured."

Henry and Cao looked at one another and smiled. Smiling had become a scarcity lately since Milum showed up in camp. The brothers had been expecting a tough job in persuading their guest to head right back into the direction of the nightmare from which he'd escaped. Milum had made it easy for them. And there was something in the way Milum responded that was reassuring. His company on the ride north was going to be a welcome presence. His response also had provided the brothers with significant verification that Milum's story was a truthful one.

Milum was clearly grateful for the assistance they had provided him. They had already given him his best chance of bringing help to the belea-guered wagon train. He could only hope that the brothers could somehow further assist by enlisting the help of a more Christian influence than had beset his companions so far. Until now Milum had thought only to push on to California, or until he could find a rescue force to return with.

"The people I was travelin' with in that train are in great need of help. I don't think they are gonna be able to hold out until I, or even we, could get to San Bernardino and back. I sure hope you boys know the right people." Milum's easy willingness to travel with Henry and Cao was revealed. Now that he'd survived, with their help, it was time to return to his original mission . . . to bring back help as soon as possible. Perhaps his new friends would help him find a better, faster way of accomplishing his mission.

"What do ya say we lighten our packs some an' have us a fittin' breakfast? I'd like to be campin' at the mouth of the Virgin River Gorge by sundown tomorrow. By then we ought a be plenty thirsty for water an' hungry fer shade." Henry was in a good mood for the first time since he and his brother had arrived at the Mormon fort there at the "Springs." He was a man who liked having a plan, and now he had one.

Cao immediately began assisting his brother with dishing up the meal. He too was eager to get on with the day now that things had been resolved. However, now that a potential confrontation with Ira Hatch and company was more likely than before, and likely sooner than later, Cao wanted to bring some discussion of strategy into the conversation.

"How would you recommend we play it if'n we do run into Hatch and his friends, Milum?"

Milum's mind left the hunger he was feeling while watching the breakfast plate heaping Cao administered to. "I 'spect we all need to be ready ta fight. I doubt Hatch is gonna waste much time talkin' things out once he sees me. Just the same, if you get a chance ta make yer case, ya don't want ta let on that you know anythin' about what I been tellin' ya. If he gets the drop on you boys, ya let 'em think ya jus' met me on the trail an' I was out a my head. I'll do my part ta convince 'em I still am. But I got to tell you boys, if'n I get the chance, I'm gonna do my best to kill that redskin-speakin' son of a bitch before he can kill me. I don't have no doubt that he won't pause two seconds if he gets me in his sights agin."

Cao paused momentarily as if to absorb the gravity of Milum's advice, then handed over a full plate of flapjacks, bacon, and hash. Henry delivered a full cup of camp coffee and a large slice of ripe melon. The brothers quickly filled their own plates and cups and the three men fell silent while they enjoyed their breakfast meal.

CHAPTER 33

COTTONWOOD SPRINGS UTAH TERRITORY

SEPTEMBER 11, 1857
7:45 PM

The two braves from chief Youngwuds' tribe, Spotted Marmot and Croaking Tortoise, had been assigned to flush out the thickly wooded Aspen and Cottonwood grove in their path. The thicket provided ample cover for any would-be adversary who might be lying in wait. Their posse had made good time since the discovery of the quarry's tracks, and the men had begun to temper their pursuit with an increasing degree of caution. If the men they were following were in need of a rest, and how could they not be by now, they could not find a better, more sheltered resting spot than here.

Youngwuds' braves proceeded, knowing that the others did not envy their task, but they would not shrink away from their risky assignment. Ira had been fair at assigning the lead searchers in regular rotation. By now all the men present feared Hatch more than the men they were hunting.

The braves dismounted and tied their mounts to a mesquite bush about thirty yards from the wall of trees ahead of them. From here they would proceed quietly through the thicket with their rifles at the ready. The sun had just gone behind the steep ridge of the west canyon wall, but there was still plenty of light. It would take no more than ten minutes or so to determine if anyone was concealing themselves in the lush outcroppings.

If the area proved empty Hatch would determine their prey's direction and probably make camp here before getting a fresh start in the morning.

Everyone was tired now, and they knew the men they were following would also need to bed down before too long. If a showdown didn't occur in the next ten minutes, it certainly would somewhere tomorrow between here and the Virgin River.

They proceeded quietly. Spotted Marmot took the west side of the dry creek bed, Croaking Tortoise the opposite. They stayed abreast of one another. The springs were mostly dry as well, but the grass they supported had grown high amid the quaking aspens. The braves were careful to move slowly enough that they could hear only the yellow mix of bronco and blade grass as it brushed against their deerskin leggings. Still it was disconcerting to be making any noise at all.

The grass was so high it would be difficult to see an adversary until one was within a couple of feet. The advantage would be clearly in favor of the hunted in this setting. As they progressed, Croaking Tortoise allowed himself to move further up the embankment as to avoid the noisy grass. Spotted Marmot took note and followed suit.

The two were well close enough to have a clear view of one another. But now they could not be 100 percent sure of flushing out their quarry. They would have to close ranks some on their return. For now, the intensity was plenty sufficient.

At one point Spotted Marmot dislodged a rock that rolled a couple of feet and came to a stop a few inches into the dry bushy grass. Both men froze as the sound carried well enough for Croaking Tortoise to hear. Their eyes locked momentarily with one another and then scanned the grassy expanse between them for any sign of movement. The next twenty seconds or so seemed like many long minutes as even their breathing stopped.

Restarting their respiration without making a sound was difficult but necessary before the two stealthy braves would proceed once again. Spotted Marmot would have been embarrassed by his error if this were a game like the ones he and the others of his tribe had played often as young boys. In the intensity of such a life-and-death task, embarrassment gave way to simple fear. And fear heightened the senses to a degree that even these two experienced braves had not before known.

By the time they reached the back edge of the grove, the two braves could sense that their muscles could no longer maintain the tightness that had been necessary to conduct the walk through. They knelt beside one another for a long minute while they recomposed themselves. It was not over, but both had a sense that the worst was behind them.

They must now go back through and report to Hatch and the others. Their return path would be inside the path they had just taken so they could report with accuracy that they had not missed anything. Still a dangerous maneuver, but unlikely that they had missed their prey on the first pass.

Without saying a word Croaking Tortoise nodded to his companion, and the two rose again to begin the completion of their mission. On the other side of the golden leafy grove Ira Hatch and his men had taken positions behind rock outcroppings and low-lying thickets. There was a tension among them not so far felt by the party. All were exhausted to the point of anxious discomfort that can only be achieved by having spent the past thirty-six hours awake, and the last eighteen of those in the saddle. Not a word had been spoken among them since the two braves had been dispatched toward the grove.

It was likely that all were thinking the same thing. No one wanted the day to culminate in a shootout at this late hour. The grove would be a perfect place to get some much-needed rest before continuing their pursuit next morning. Their advantage of superior numbers and fast-moving mounts would be somewhat neutralized here at Cottonwood Springs. If they were in there, their cover was quite meager compared to that of their prey.

By now they knew the two braves must have gotten through the stand of cottonwood and aspen. Perhaps they were going to catch a break. The two that were hunted must have passed through and continued. The exhaustion they must be feeling must truly be extreme. Impressive what feats "running for one's life" can motivate one to achieve.

Ira would not allow himself to speculate wishfully. He had positioned himself halfway up the west canyon wall amid an outcropping of igneous rock about the size of a church steeple. His rifle rested on a notch as he leaned over the stalk and placed the bead on Spotted Marmot as he intermittently came in and out of view. It was not the brave he would be taking aim on. Ira was looking for what was likely to happen next. There was still a good chance the men he was after were in there.

CHAPTER 34

MOUNTAIN MEADOWS
WAGON FORTRESS
UTAH TERRITORY

SEPTEMBER 11, 1857
9:45 AM

John D. Lee hunkered down toward the center of the circle of men that had now formed in the wide-open middle of the encampment. With the coffee cup in his right hand he deftly began to draw pictures with his left on the bare earth in front of Mathew Fancher and the others. Lee needed to keep their attention on something other than his pounding heart, as he could actually see it pulsing under his vest with each thump. He hoped the others did not notice and was taking measures to divert their focus.

Lee had not expected the intensity of his nervousness. He remembered having stage fright acting in the church plays in Cedar City and in Provo. However, never before had he strained so hard to maintain his composure. Lee was discovering that, in matters of life and death, it was not as easy to implement a plan as it was to devise one. Before this day was over, he would discover this truth again and again.

"You're here at what's known in these parts as Mountain Meadows." Lee drew a small X. "Brother Bateman and I live about eleven mile this way in New Harmony, which is on the other side of that big mountain behind me. It's a small ward an' I'm the bishop of it."

"The LDS militia from Cedar got here late last night, an' we been negotiatin' with the chiefs of the Piedes, the Pah'vants, and the Santa Clara tribes." Five X's were placed to represent locations for the two wards and three tribal camps from around where those here at Mountain Meadows had traveled. "This is the most Injuns I've ever seen gathered in one place, an' they're plenty stirred up too." Lee paused briefly, feeling as if he was gaining some control over himself.

Fancher took the opportunity to ask a question. "We've been told for weeks that the Indians in these parts are friendly. Why have they singled us out and attacked us so?"

"Their anger toward the white man, those in trains passin' through, has been building for some time. A number of tribes have come together, and in their greater numbers they have become emboldened. I believe it was your large herd of cattle that attracted them to your train in favor of some other." Lee was cloaking a deceit with the truth and hoping it would pass the scrutiny of those around him. Those around him couldn't have been more interested in what he had to say.

Jeremy Poteet, one of the drovers, tried to jump into the discussion. "We've seen that they've had some pale-skinned help."

Fancher immediately held up a hand toward the verbal intruder. "You'll all get a chance to ask yer own questions after I'm done." He'd get around to asking the tough questions soon enough. Right now the questioning would proceed in an orderly and systematic manner.

"How many strong are the militia you say has arrived?" The young man needed to assess the situation before he would know what was possible to accomplish. He was in a precarious position. Only being in his late twenties, there were plenty of others who might question his leadership abilities. The Fanchers were born leaders, and young Mathew was no exception.

"The Cedar militia is about sixty strong; all well armed and equipped. We arrived from New Harmony with an additional dozen men. There is some danger as the tribes have us outnumbered by about five to one, but I don't think they'll take us on as long as they feel they're getting what they want." Lee could feel himself calming with the give and take.

"What is it these devils want besides all of us dead?" Fancher didn't mind vocalizing what was on the minds of his entire camp.

"They want all your livestock for starters. And they want all your weapons." Lee thought he'd leave out the part about all of their scalps and about having fun with their women.

"Last time I took notice they had all of our cattle, and the only of our mounts they don't have are lying in and around the compound here bloated." The evidence was all around them in both sight and smell. "I 'spect we'll be rotting too if we give up our arms. You said you could help us. How would you propose to do that?"

"The militia will escort you back to Cedar. The only way we could get the chiefs to agree to allow such an escort was to agree to disarm you and to separate the men from the women and children on the walk back."

Immediately there was a stir among the other men crowded around as the details of Lee's proposal began to sink in.

"Over my dead fuckin' body . . . " Poteet from the Baker party began to curse.

Fancher raised his hand again and the crowd hushed. "How can they require such a thing from us, after the indignity they've already shown us?"

"The tribes have lost several braves, and several more are likely to die from their wounds. Many of the more hot-headed bucks are calling to revenge these losses." Lee could sense his message could easily be rejected. His heart began to pound again.

"I'd gut shoot every one o' the sneakin' devils an' leave 'em to die in the sun if I could, an' it'd be no less than every one of 'em deserves." Fancher needed to walk a fine line. He didn't want the discussion with the Mormon leader to disintegrate amidst the outraged members' objections to what they were hearing. He needed to represent their outrage to the extent that they would not disrupt the discussion with their own interruptions. Yet he dare not take such an intransigent position that the discussion ceased to progress.

"They've got us all outnumbered here, and if'n this turns into an all-out fight, I 'spect any of our chances of gettin' back to Cedar would be pretty poor." Lee needed the discussion to proceed as much as Fancher did.

"Seems to me we'd all stand a better chance in whatever action we choose if we all keep our arms in our own hands and stick together." Fancher threw this out as if it was understood that the white men would obviously stand together against the red men. It was an intentional statement he was advancing, and he intently awaited Lee's response.

Lee had no intention of allowing these Gentiles, in their severely compromised position, to dictate the standards of Christian obligation they might hold for one another. "We've worked hard for ten years to cultivate good relations with these savages, and it's about to completely unravel over this incident. I'm here on orders from my superiors to use my best efforts to diffuse this situation without placing the entire Indian nation at our throats. If you folks are lucky enough to get to California, or back to where you came from, we're happy to play a part in that. But after you're gone, our homes are still here.

"There's somewhere between three and four hundred thousand of these Lamanites here in Deseret. The stakes aren't just high for you and your group. If we line up with you folks and raise our arms against these seven tribes gathered against us, the repercussions to our brethren could be catastrophic. I can't let that happen."

Without coming right out with it, Lee had clearly communicated that there were limits beyond which the Gentiles could not expect the Mormon militia to extend.

"There's some talk in the camp that the Mormons in the region are workin' with the redskins against us." Fancher wasn't going to go into specifics with Lee, but he thought it was time to get it out in the open since he knew it was on the minds of most of the men surrounding him.

"'We took note on our arrival that Youngwuds and Jackson had some 'Freebooters' workin' with their tribes. There might be some others has some in their camps too. Any whites, highwaymen likely workin' for a share of the plunder, would have high-tailed it by now. The Saints would hunt men like that down if'n they got wind of that kind a business."

There was a long silence. The Dutchman had told them after the first unsuccessful escape attempt that he and Will Aden had run into a group of men at Leachy Springs that they had recognized in Provo as LDS. Fancher was glad none of the others took it upon themselves to point that out at this poignant moment.

"We're goin' to need to hold a council with Cap'n Baker and my cousin on this matter before we can give you an answer to your proposition. How much time do we have to decide whether or not ta go along with it?" Fancher didn't want to make this decision alone, and he didn't want it made here among some of the "hotheads."

"Sooner the better. The tribes seem to be workin' themselves into a lather over what the bucks are advocatin'." Lee was lying now. In reality his agents were having a very difficult time holding the Lamanite coalition together. Tutsegabit had allowed two of his tribal leaders and their braves to leave the field of battle already. He and Youngwuds were threatening to leave completely and immediately if their Mormon organizers didn't come up with a plan and implement it. If they did leave, it would be very difficult to keep Jackson from following suit.

Baker's drover Poteet jumped in again. "I ain't givin' up my firearms but over my dead fuckin' body . . . "

Fancher fumed, "That decision ain't been made yet, and you're not gonna be the one ta make it anyways. These men came here under a white flag an' they say they came here ta help us. God only knows how bad we need their help. We're grateful to you men for comin' here no matter what proposition you're making and no matter what we decide to do. If you can come back in an hour, we'll have an answer for you."

Poteet's face turned beet red, but he kept his mouth shut.

"I'd just as soon stay here in the middle of your camp until you make up yer minds, if ya don't mind. As long as I'm in here, I think it'd be easier for our men to convince the Lamanites to hold off makin' any rash moves. They're all waitin' for me to come back with an answer, an' I'd just as soon not go back there until I have one." Lee also wanted to be nearby in case he had to shoot down any alternative ideas before the immigrants had a chance to set their feet in one.

"We don't mind, Mr. Lee. I'll ask my boys to fetch you some more coffee whilst you wait for our decision." Fancher extended his hand to Lee and then to Bateman. Then he turned and began walking directly to the Baker wagon.

As Lee watched the tall, distinguished, and congenial man walk away, he congratulated himself on having made a good case toward influencing the camp's decision. He also felt a twinge of regret at having come face to face with the humanity of Mathew Fancher, obviously a born leader for such a young man. "Control yourself," he thought. "You must keep control of your emotions."

CHAPTER 35

TEMPLE SQUARE
SALT LAKE CITY
UTAH TERRITORY

SEPTEMBER 8, 1857
10:00 PM

The night air was crisp as the great Mormon leader strode back to the Lion House. He was used to maintaining the stride of a commanding presence wherever he went and did so even tonight in the unlikely event someone was watching. Yet he did not feel great or commanding tonight. Not only his opulent way of life, but his very life itself, was being threatened, and more so than it had ever been threatened before.

Buchanan had indeed sent federal troops into Deseret . . . strategically it made sense to do so. The Saints had run several territorial judges out of Deseret. They were even rumored to have poisoned the Honorable Leonidas Shaver by providing him with poisoned liquors at the Globe Inn Hotel. The Gunnison Massacre had also been laid at the feet of Porter Rockwell, although indictments for neither crime would ever be forthcoming.

As a result of these reports, the U.S. president declared Utah to be in a state of open rebellion. The army had intentionally advanced rumors that Brigham Young and selected others were to be arrested and placed on trial for interfering with federally appointed agents. Guilty verdicts on what amounted to treason could well result in their being hanged publicly as a way of sending a message to other like-minded dissidents.

Young and his advisors speculated correctly that Buchanan's move was a political one aimed at diluting his political opponent's advantage on the slavery issue. The elimination of polygamy and slavery would become worthy causes of John C. Freemont's opposition party. The "Twin Relics of Barbarism" (slavery and polygamy) had become a catch phrase repeated more and more often by the media of the day.

The leadership of the LDS Church had done little to dispel the negative view Gentiles increasingly held of polygamy. The Saints referred to the practice as "the Principle." The Saint's response was typically to deny any such practice in releases to the Eastern press, then to preach from the pulpit their God-given right to engage in the practice whenever they chose to. The *Deseret News* would publish these latter defiant protestations, and these would invariably find there way back to Washington and news outlets beyond . . . adding fuel to the escalating debate.

An American Moses, Brigham Young had brazenly led his people into the wilderness and put them to productive work. He was leading them toward a prosperity that would be admired by leaders all over the world, although much of the reason for his success was that he ruled his church, and its people, with complete autonomy. He had good advisors, and he listened to them. But advisors they were. When he disagreed with them, he would override them with impunity. Things were beginning to change.

The "Gold Rush" that began a few years after the Saints arrived in Deseret is what started it. The westward movement that followed had continued to grow, and the inevitable clashes increased. Young was not one who feared making bold decisions. It was Hosea Stout who was rumored to have arranged things for Judge Shavers. He along with some other Danites burned federal court papers and intimidated the government's federal judge appointees.

Young ordered Saints from the far-reaching outposts of Genoa and Las Vegas to sell or abandon their posts and return to Salt Lake City. That his people complied with such orders was a testament to the control he wielded over them, and to the loyalty they displayed to their theocratic leader. But these decisions were far from the boldest he would make.

For the better part of a year, Young had been pursuing an aggressive policy of brinksmanship with the hated Gentile nation to the east. His goal was to turn Deseret into its own nation-state . . . where he and his brethren could continue to worship their religion and its "Principles" in a manner of their own choosing.

The decision to unleash the "Battle Axe of the Lord" against the Gentiles as they passed through Deseret would have consequences far greater than some of his other directives. If the plan worked as intended, the

Gentile government would have to rely upon the Saints. The fortunes the Gentiles coveted to the west could only be had by paying the required toll and tribute to those capable of clearing the way.

However, if it became apparent that the Saints were the menace in the Gentile's way, a far more dire result would ensue. The Saints were a mere thirty thousand plus against many millions with a federal army at their disposal. Brigham Young's fear diminished as he stepped into the parlor of his favorite concubine.

"Would you like me to get you something from the pantry, President Young?" Emmeline was always one to see to the patriarch's needs. She was eternally grateful that he had convinced John D. Lee to allow him to marry her even though she and her sister had been betrothed to Lee. She still cared for Lee. She found Lee better looking than the Mormon leader, but life in the southern settlements was far harsher than was life here in the Lion House at Temple Square.

"I could use a slice of that tasty fresh bread I smelt cooking this morning, and a warm glass of milk sounds good. I can't seem to shake the chill of being out in the cool night air for the past hour." Young threw himself back on the parlor couch and lifted his feet one at a time while Emmeline removed his boots. Then, after tucking an expensive afghan blanket around him, she was off to the kitchen bakery.

Emmeline was not aware of the dire doings at Mountain Meadows, or the involvement of her former fiancé, Lee. All she knew was that she was the favorite of Young's many wives. At least she was his favorite as far as administering to his procreative duties. The usual conduct of their visits together assured she would be pregnant again soon. It was much the topic among the other wives sealed to Young.

The women of the Lion House did not work as hard as was typical of most Mormon wives and mothers. With the usual household duties divided among nineteen women, maintaining a comparatively large residential compound was significantly less demanding than it was for women of the typical Mormon family. They occupied their abundant free time with gossip and sharing the intimate details of their lives. Yes, Brigham's wives liked to talk, and Emmeline occupied the spotlight of these sessions.

As Young continued to make himself comfortable she quickly skipped down the stairs and into the kitchen. There she was surprised to see James Haslam and two of Young's more subordinate wives waiting on him hand and foot. The slightly built Haslam was already in heaven with the treatment the two buxom women were lavishing upon him. Emmeline approached the trio and began dishing up a double slice of the fresh loaf of bread. She smiled at the cowboy and politely broke into their jovial conversation. "What church business brings you to the Lion House, good sir?"

Haslam turned red in the face more as a result of the comely woman addressing him than from the quandary he now found himself in. " I jus' returned from a long ride out of Iron County an' the Prophet was kind enough ta offer me refreshment here fer the night." He felt that if he evaded the issue of tomorrow's mission he would not be guilty of divulging classified information. But now he feared he had made it sound like he was being offered more than the Prophet would ever have intended.

"I don' m . . . mean it that way exactly. I believe he only intended for me ta have a meal and a comfortable place ta sleep. I . . . I most certainly don' mean it that way either." The young cowboy was sinking fast, and the women on each side of him were enjoying his discomfort immensely. It was not uncommon for uninitiated guests to stumble over themselves during conversation when inside this sexually charged "House of Concubines." Emmeline came to the rescue.

"I'm sure you've provided an important service to the Prophet, our church and our Lord. We have a room just for hard workers like you right next to the woodshed. The girls here will draw you a private bath once you've finished your meal, and you can retire when you've finished with that. Will you be staying for breakfast?" She knew she was not stepping on the other two wives' toes. She could see that they were already heating the water, and besides, she outranked the other two in seniority.

"The Prophet did offer me breakfast . . . ma'am." He now consciously considered every word he said trying to assess whether or not he had committed some sort of inappropriateness.

"Very well, I hope we shall all be so fortunate to see you at breakfast. If not, may the Lord be with you kind sir." Smiling, Emmeline turned with the pitcher of warm milk in one hand and the ample serving of bread and butter in the other and gracefully headed back upstairs.

Haslam was grateful for the bailing out Emmeline had provided him. Somehow he knew she would soon be joining the Prophet. She was one of the most beautiful women he had ever laid eyes on. His admiration, though unspoken, was clear for all to see.

Emmeline smiled to herself. She knew she had spared the cowboy from further embarrassing himself. His expression of gratitude was obvious. Still she sensed a slight disappointment when he realized she would not be staying to assist the other two. Emmeline had been turning men's heads for some time. Her ability to do so had served her very well.

When she arrived at Nauvoo she was appalled to learn that she would have to suffer the humiliation of being a plural wife. She had resigned herself to the concept, having decided that Brother Lee was probably the best she could aspire to. She had her less-attractive sister to protect. In Nauvoo she had known Brother Lee to be a respected and high-ranking member of the church. Then her opportunity came when Brother Lee approached the Prophet for his blessing in sealing the double marriage. She charmed the Prophet appropriately and completely in a matter of a few short minutes.

As she re-entered the parlor and placed the snack in front of him on the table she wondered how many minutes it would take her to charm this man of great power again. With eighteen others to compete with here in the Lion House, and many more in other locations, she would not allow herself to get out of practice. With wives coming and going, remaining number one was not easy.

The Prophet also knew he would once again be charmed out of his socks in short order. He hoped it would have the desired effect of getting his mind off Johnston's army, western spies, and Mountain Meadows . . . if only for a short time. He wasted little time savoring his bread and milk.

CHAPTER 36

VIRGIN RIVER GORGE
NORTHWEST NEW
MEXICO TERRITORY

SEPTEMBER 18, 1857
4:30 PM

What had had been an agonizing journey for Milum to cover on foot several days earlier they were traveling in relative comfort on the return trip. The steep canyon walls rising along both sides of the giant notch gave the impression that God himself had decided this to be where one country ends and another begins. In future days this geological structure would approximate the Nevada/Utah border. For now it was the destination of a long hot ride.

They had reached the river a day earlier at the confluence of the Little Muddy and Virgin rivers. Campsites were plentiful along the Virgin, but the brothers pushed on to a favorite camp spot. The steep carved walls of sandstone offered shade from the sun. After fifty plus miles of blazing desert, and thirty more since the Little Muddy, water alone just wouldn't do.

The men had spent most of the first few hours of their journey conversing with one another about their various travels, business endeavors, and family ties or lack thereof. Milum had shared with the brothers his fear for his wife, Eloah Angeline, and their baby daughter Zabrina. He'd also told them of Abel's crush on Matilda Tackitt.

Every now and then someone would think of a good question about what they would do if they ran into Ira Hatch and Co. Milum didn't much care for the role of a complete imbecile he'd be playing if their adversaries got the drop on them. He had liked to participate in community plays and acting roles whenever he was in a cultural setting that would support such activities. But he'd always preferred to take on the role of the good guy or the love interest. Playing the "Village Idiot" was not one he'd wanted or had experience with.

The young men had a lot to talk about. However, after a few hours, Milum discovered, Cao and Henry Young were not all that talkative. Perhaps it was just what they were used to. Long treks day after day probably had brought them to the realization that by now there wasn't anything that the two brothers didn't know about each other. As time went on they just got used to passing their time with their own thoughts.

Milum respected the brothers' preferred mode and drifted off into his own thoughts. Running for his life had kept him thinking of the strategy he must employ and the determination he must have to exhort himself to push on. He welcomed the opportunity to allow his thoughts to drift. He was still sore and tired from his ordeal, and riding on Floppy's back wasn't as comfortable as other mounts he had ridden. It sure was better than how he'd been traveling the previous several days.

His thoughts took him back yet again to Mountain Meadows and then to Cottonwood Springs. He and Able Baker had given themselves the best shot they could after having blasted their way through the enemy lines. Now that their attackers knew their lines had been breached and that at least one had gotten through, it was almost certain they would dispatch some kind of tracking party against them. Their only option now would be to run as fast and as far as their legs would carry them.

All that night, and most of the next day, the two traveled further than they thought was humanly possible. They had more than doubled the distance the train had been able to make on its best day. But they also knew that the men chasing them would be on mounts. As the day progressed, the anxiety of being caught up to by men bent on their destruction continued to grow.

This anxiety grew especially strong through sections of their travel when they were out in the open for long distances and exposed to view. It was for this reason that Cottonwood Springs offered such an inviting refuge. Once inside the grove the men could see out in all directions the distance of a good rifle shot. From outside the grove, if they remained fairly still, they would be virtually undetectable.

The golden grass was two feet high in spots and afforded excellent hiding places. This was especially so along the dry creek bed where water, during more abundant times, had eroded undercuts in the bank perfectly sized for men to crawl into and completely disappear from view. It was here, under one especially secluded bank, that the two decided to hide head to head. The grass above them barely revealed the existence of the sandy creek bottom below. From this position they could see anyone coming before they would be seen.

Placing their rifles on bare roots to keep them out of the sand, the men knew any confrontation in here would start out with handguns. After getting themselves positioned, the two drifted quickly into an uncomfortable but much-needed sleep.

Milum's first recollection of trouble came with the sensation of Able Baker's hand over his mouth. Milum quickly realized it would be a bad idea to speak. Able had heard something. Milum's eyes took several seconds to focus outward. His eyes recalled something incongruous to the landscape he'd seen just before closing them a short time before. It wasn't until it began to move that he recognized it as the matted hair of a Paiute Indian. In the next second it was out of his view. Milum's heart quickened and the reaction in his look was all Able needed to know that Milum had seen what they had been worried about. The two men remained still.

A few minutes passed with Milum and Able holding their pistols at the ready. Finally Able rolled slowly onto his stomach and into the middle of the creek bed. He slowly brought himself to his knees and then raised his head so as to look upstream. Lowering himself, he motioned to Milum to replicate the same maneuver, only his view would be downstream.

As Milum slowly peered through the yellow grass his heart raced again. There they were, two Indian braves obviously searching the grove as they reached the edge of the thicket and stepped out of it.

Lowering himself he placed his face close to Able's before whispering. "There's two. They'll probably be comin' back through to make sure they didn't miss us on their first pass. Should we hide an' hope they miss us again?"

Able silently considered his partner's question. "No! If they miss us on their way back they'll jus' bring the rest of their group down on us. I 'spect they'll likely make camp in here once't they figure no one's in here. It'll be dark pretty soon. We need to drop those two braves in their tracks as they come back by and then hope we can make a stand against however many others there are out there. They won't try comin' in here after us in the dark. I'll take the first shot. You shoot the one I don't." Milum nodded. The two men cocked their handguns as quietly as they could.

It was another desperate gamble, just like the one they'd taken the night before. Just then Milum thought he'd heard a twig snap. Feeling more confident, the braves weren't being as cautious as they were their first time through. The two men steadied themselves. The braves were moving more quickly now. Their trajectory was to pass straight through the tall grass no more than a few feet each side of the streambed. Now they were a mere six yards or so away. Able nodded to Milum and the two men began to rise.

Able shot first, aiming at the bulk of the man before him. The bullet passed through the area of Spotted Marmot's sternum. Before Croaking Tortoise could swing his rifle around to the direction of the shot, Milum discharged his weapon. He didn't recall aiming for the brave's heart, but if he did his aim was true. Croaking Tortoise was dead a few seconds after he hit the ground. Spotted Marmot lay gasping for air trying to regain control of his weapon. Able was over him in seconds. His second round hit Spotted Marmot directly between the eyes. It wasn't intended to be a mercy killing, but just as effective.

"Hold yer fire boys. The trouble back at the Meadows has all been worked out. We been sent ta bring ya back safe." The voice was that of Ira Hatch.

"I reckon we'll be findin' our own way back." Able then punctuated his retort with a volley from his Winchester that he'd just retrieved from roots in the streambed.

Within seconds lead was flying into the small thicket of trees from three directions. Their movement had led to their being seen. They dove out of site into the creek bed. They could speak to each other now. "We need to get to the edges of the thicket and keep them from getting around us." Able seemed to know what his adversaries' next move was going to be. Milum didn't question as the two rose again to stake out their positions. Each man ventured outward opposite the other, to the outermost cottonwood or aspen that afforded the best cover, and began to return fire.

"Pick yer shots, Milum. They got us outnumbered and likely a lot more ammo." Able was a good marksman and picked off another brave with his first shot, one of Tutsegabit's tribe that had moved in a little too close.

That's when it happened. It wasn't as clean a shot as he would have liked, but the man had ventured just close enough to the wooded perimeter for Ira Hatch to see him. The rifle ball passed through Able's femur bone, shattering it and severing several minor arteries as well. He fell hard and rolled once again into the deep grass. Milum saw his comrade fall and felt sick in the seeing of it.

He took one more rifle shot in the direction of a member of the retreating posse and then ran to Able. Keeping low in the grass as well, Milum was surprised to see Able applying his belt as a tourniquet by the time he arrived. The pain was great enough to have drained all the color from Able's face but not the resolve from his determination. "The shot that hit me came from behind that rock outcropping just up the hill. Milum, I think he's close enough you might be able to get a shot at the son-of-a-bitch."

Milum crawled slowly to the edge of the thicket, keeping the trunk of a large aspen between him and the rock outcropping. He started by poking the barrel of his rifle over a low protruding branch. As he focused on the rocks he could see the eyes of Ira Hatch peering over the sights of his repeater rifle. Hatch was waiting for movement, and it was clear he hadn't yet seen any, or Milum would be dead by now. This time it was Ira's turn to feel the pain of a rifle ball. Milum rose to his knees to get a better angle. It was then that Hatch noticed the movement. The two fired almost simultaneously at one another.

It seemed the lava rock exploded in Ira's face. He had seen the muzzle flash of light but had blinked from the firing of his own weapon just in time. Still the shattered rock stung his face. Ira was unconcerned about the pain, which was overshadowed by the fear of losing his vision. Ira was used to controlling men as much with his eyes as with his voice, his fists, or his guns. When he opened his eyes and could still see, the hunter exhaled in relief.

Crouched securely behind the rocks Hatch signaled to his men to stay put. Once the darkness was upon them he would make his way back to his men. They would make camp, post guards around the grove, and pursue their prey again in the morning. He knew he'd wounded both men. Tomorrow he'd figure out how to finish them off.

Milum recoiled from his position like he'd been struck by a rattler. The rifle ball tore through the triceps of his left arm just below the bone. He knew his shot had missed but the searing pain was more than he could contend with. He retreated back to Able and began tending his arm by tearing off his sleeve and applying it in a tight wrap. "How you doin', Able?" Somehow the question felt inappropriate. He immediately wished he hadn't asked it.

"I'd be doin' jus' fine if you could tell me ya shot the son-of-a-bitch that did this ta me." Able grimaced with nearly every word.

"It was Hatch. Ira Hatch, the bastard that led us to the Meadows. I came close enough ta spray a good amount of rock in his eyes, but I know

I missed. I've half a mind ta head right up there an' finish him off." Milum was trying to build the courage to do just that. One word of encouragement from Able and he'd be on his way.

"I guess that confirms our suspicions that them beloved Saints was behind this whole thing from the start. That doesn't bode well for the folks back at the Meadows." Able had finally tightened his belt around his thigh enough to significantly slow the flow of blood.

"I'm pretty sure the rest of his party has backed off far enough that I could get up there an' go at it one on one with the lyin' sneakin' bastard." Milum was still getting himself worked up.

"No, Milum. I know what we gotta do now an' you goin' one on one with Hatch ain't part of the plan. It'll be dark enough soon an' yer gonna head downhill again toward San Bernardino. I'm gonna stay here an' hold 'em off as long as I can." Able had that certain tone in his voice, but mixed in a measure of resignation that Milum didn't much care for.

"What was that a little bit ago about us makin' a stand here together in the trees?" Milum pretty much figured their luck had flat run out here at Cottonwood Springs. Time to take as many of these murdering thieves with them as they could.

"We still got a chance, Milum. At least you do . . . of gettin' help and bringin' it back. There's no way I'm goin' any further on this leg. But now the fact that I'll be stayin' behind actually improves our odds of you gettin' through." Able was making sense and Milum had to be smart enough to see it.

"I can't leave ya here, man. Don't ask me to do that. I'm wounded too. I say we fight it out together and make 'em pay as much as we can." Milum was befuddled by the gravity of the situation. The prospect of heading out alone was a daunting one. As bleak as their prospects had been, the men had drawn strength from each other. Milum was sure that he had drawn more from Able than Able had from him.

Able chuckled. "Ya gotta do it. It's the train's only hope. Leave me half yer ammo and you take half my food. Bring the rifles an' any ammo those two braves were packin'. If I can hold out long enough an' make 'em think we're both in here, you might be able to get a good enough head start on 'em to get you beyond their reach."

Milum complied with Able's instructions. By the time he had Able set up as well and as comfortably as he could make him, it was pretty much dark.

"I'm havin' a real hard time with the thought of leavin' ya here alone, Able."

"I know ya are, Milum. But this is the way it's gotta be. Ya gotta play the hand yer dealt. My last stand is here in these trees. We all have ta die somewhere. We still got family back at the Meadows. Think of Eloah Angeline an' yer baby girl. They're countin' on us ta bring back help. I can't do it, so you have to. Now get goin' an' try not to leave a track, at least for the first few hundred yards."

Able reached out his hand and Milum took hold of it. Their eyes locked. No more words were spoken. Then Milum stood and walked briskly to the south edge of the thicket and paused momentarily. He could not bring himself to look back at his friend. Tears were streaming down his face by the time he stepped out into the open desert beyond.

The rest of the arduous journey was uneventful except for the increasing hardship of it. He hadn't seen another human being since that night until he had stumbled into the brothers' camp in a desperate condition. He was no longer afraid for himself now. Perhaps having come so close to death, and at times wishing for it, had changed his soul.

He had struggled with his decision to leave Able behind, and at times he was overwhelmed with guilt for having done so. At others times he forgave himself in light of the obvious sense it made. He was at peace now that he was with the brothers. Able's plan had worked. They had made the right choice. Even if things didn't turn out, they had each done their best in pursuit of a most worthy cause.

Who knows, things were starting to look up. They had traveled over eighty miles back in the direction he had run away from. Surely Hatch and Co. must have given up the chase. Here they were, riding up the Virgin River where they would soon make camp for the night. They were already nearly half the way back to Mountain Meadows, and the brothers had informed him there were settlements between here and there where they might be able to enlist help.

The shot rang out from a rock ledge about ten feet above them and forty yards away. The force of the blast blew Milum off his mount, and all the animals reared in fright. As Henry and Cao fought to get there animals under control, nearly a dozen armed men, most of them Indians, stepped from behind several positions with their weapons trained squarely on the two remaining men. Surrounded, they had no chance to raise their weapons in response. To do so would be suicide.

Henry and Cao looked down on Milum as he lay on the sandy riverbed. Life was draining from him fast as Henry's and Milum's eyes met. Milum was thinking how it would not now be necessary to engage in the undignified pretense of acting like a man out of his head. Then his thoughts faded into the vision of his beautiful wife and daughter.

Henry had guessed Milum's thoughts fairly accurately as Ira Hatch, the man with the smoking rifle, stepped lightly down from his rock perch and strode briskly toward the surrounded men.

CHAPTER 37

MOUNTAIN MEADOWS
WAGON FORTRESS
UTAH TERRITORY

SEPTEMBER 11, 1857
10:00 AM

The coffee was fresh brewed and good. By revelation, hot drinks had been forbidden by the Prophet Joseph Smith. Since then, John D. Lee had forgone the pleasure of the drink to prove his obedience to the religion he'd become a leader of. It was a pleasure he missed . . . most of the time. None of his wives would abide having the vice on their premises. The only time Lee had been free to indulge in it had been those few occasions he'd chanced upon some Gentile traveler around breakfast time . . . or when visiting his friend P.K. Smith. P.K. was one of the few Saints he knew, and the only one of status, who defiantly partook of the habit.

For Lee, it was a chink in the otherwise devout discipline he imposed upon himself. For the most part, he kept it hidden from his brethren to protect his image for those to whom he preached. He recalled chastising the bishop from Cedar, asking how he could so openly violate the Prophet's edict. He now remembered how P.K. had simply smiled and filled two mugs, delivering one to him and stating, "It's a shame what they did to the Prophet at Carthage jail. He did mankind a lot of good in his short life, and even when he was wrong he meant well." As P.K. raised his mug to toast, Lee raised his in response. From then on Lee knew where he could get a good cup of coffee without being regarded a hypocrite.

P.K. had been a good friend. Life in the southern settlements had been hard. He was as hard working as Lee was ambitious. Lee admired the bishop. Lee had achieved higher rank, but P.K. was better liked among the brethren. P.K. had always celebrated Lee's successes and encouraged him to seek more. There was no competition between the men. At least there was none directed from P.K. toward Lee.

As he sat in the immigrant camp accepting their hospitality, he realized that his friend was the better man. P.K. would not have found himself in this predicament. Not if he'd had his say. It was because of Lee, and the devout ones up the line, that P.K. was now at this troubling crossroads. Just like his coffee indulgence, his friend would have been willing to break with his more zealous brethren and walk a more tolerant path . . . come what may. The two had forged an alliance over the years, scratching out a living from the rocks of this rugged desert topography and supporting each other when it counted. Lee hoped his friend would not abandon him now.

Lee began to rise as the wagon leader approached. His heart began to race once again. "Need to get back into character." Lee thought to himself, "No time to wallow in thoughts of self-deprecation. Get that heart to stop pounding and get the agreement you came here to get."

Lee was acutely aware that he needed the immigrants more than they needed him. A failure on his part to achieve this objective would very likely lead to an unraveling of the plan that had been agreed on weeks prior. It would lead to the complete failure of a mission he had been assigned to complete. The consequences of failure were unimaginable to Lee. He quickly forced the unthinkable from his mind.

"There's no way I'm gonna convince any of my men to hand over their weapons to those redskin devils. We've lost too many good men, and a few of our women, to those murderin' savages. I wish there was some way we could work this out. Cedar City sounds a lot more hospitable than it did the last time we passed through there, given the fix we find ourselves in here." Mathew Fancher was hoping to appeal to the humanity of his guests and strike a definitive "No!" on the disarmament plank of Lee's proposal.

It was the opening Lee was waiting for. "What if we made a show of it and loaded all your weapons in one of the wagons an' set that wagon on up ahead guarded by part of the militia? We could put the wagon up at the lead an' your men single file toward the back. I think we could explain that the arms had to go back to Cedar as evidence at the trial. Once we get back there we could return them."

"Trial? What's this talk of a trial?" Fancher knew if he didn't ask, the men surrounding them would likely step into the discussion. He needed to keep control of this.

"The chiefs know we handle disputes by holdin' trials. We tried and convicted some of the Piedes over the murder of Captain Gunnison a few years ago an' they've seen us try some of our own. We told Tutsegabit we'd put you on trial for the braves they've lost here at the Meadows and for the members of the tribe they think members of your party poisoned back at Corn Creek." Lee waited for it to sink in.

"What's this about us poisoning at Corn Creek?" Fancher patience was beginning to fray. "We gave a cow to a tribe at Corn Creek that looked like they'd starve if we didn't. There wasn't anything wrong with it."

"Well, a few of the tribe got sick on it and they're sayin' one of 'em died. Look, it's probably made up to give a pretense for attackin' you folks here at the Meadows. If they can't prove it, it ain't gonna come to nothin'." Lee was mixing lies with truth again.

It was in fact the Mormons at Corn Creek, with George A. Smith, who planted the poisoned-meat story as a pretense to give motive to Indians they intended to blame for the attack they enlisted them to participate in. Lee also knew the truth about Gunnison and was counting on the Gentiles not knowing.

Young Fancher had just gone through a difficult negotiation with Captain Baker and his cousin Captain Alexander Fancher. In their misery, they had emphatically opposed the idea of handing over the arms to anyone. Both these men knew they weren't going to make it back home even if they could make it to Cedar City. Still their judgment was not to give their Indian attackers any such advantage and to trust the Mormons only as much as necessary. It was very unlikely either would have approved of Lee's modification. His cousin, delirious with infection and fever, had struggled to speak, getting out what sounded like a garbled, "God no, Matt!"

Mathew Fancher was desperate not to let the only opportunity he'd seen in days slip past. He was confident that his people would be exonerated in the face of any such accusation as Lee described. On the other hand, he sensed that Lee meant what he'd said about not putting his brethren at risk by siding with the Gentiles in a running battle with the red man. He could feel the eyes of the men surrounding them. He knew they were waiting for his decision and that some were not going to like his decision, whatever it was.

Just then Adj. Daniel Macfarlane could be heard galloping up to the wagon gate. Several immigrants began to open the gate. Stopping short of it he shouted, "Tell Major Lee that a couple of the tribe leaders are getting impatient. I'm not sure we're going to be able to hold 'em back much longer." He then abruptly spun his mount around and galloped back in the direction he'd come from.

Like his cousin, Mathew Fancher was a decision maker. It was not his nature to do nothing when faced with a tough choice. It was time for him to make a decision. Turning to Lee he said, "Go back to your militia and tell them to join us here in the encampment. We'll pull out a couple of the wagons and start loadin' the injured in one and the children in another. How many teams can you muster to pull wagons?"

Poteet scowled but remained silent. All the others near enough to have heard young Fancher remained silent as well. As frightening a prospect as was Lee's arms condition, the excitement of actually being able to escape their dire situation was overwhelming. Now, at least there was hope. They needed hope desperately, for they were bone tired of living in fear.

Lee wasted little time. He knew what Macfarlane was really referring to was more Lamanite defections. He turned to Bateman. "Go to where the militia is camped and ask Higbee how many animals they can spare to come in here and hook up to these wagons. We're gonna need a minimum of three teams. I'll meet with the bishop and the others and inform them of how we intend to proceed. We'll meet you with Higbee and proceed back here with the whole group. Let him know to get the company ready to go forthwith."

Bateman and Lee mounted up and turned their animals to leave. Just then young Fancher snatched the reigns from under the head of Lee's mount. In a split second, Lee's heart began to pound as hard as ever. Then the nausea caused by too much adrenaline hit his stomach. The two representatives of their various parties locked eyes.

For a fleeting moment Mathew Fancher could see fear in Lee's eyes. Then the Mormon bishop recovered. Fancher stored the information and pretended not to notice. "We've been in a pretty sorry fix here these past few days. You're not seein' us at our best." The captain nodded toward the drover who still carried his scowl. "If we get out of this mess we're in, it's my hope to be able to give you an' your men a proper thank you for what yer doin' for us."

Lee nodded toward the impressive young leader and said nothing. He was both relieved and shamed by what the grateful man said. He was mostly relieved when Mathew Fancher released his grip on the reigns of his mount and allowed him to proceed on his way. As he and Bateman descended the steep bank of Mogatsu Creek and dropped from the view of the besieged party, he could feel the beads of sweat on his forehead. He resolved that he would, as much as possible, avoid further contact with the honorable young man whose fate he'd nearly sealed.

CHAPTER 38

TEMPLE SQUARE
SALT LAKE CITY
UTAH TERRITORY

SEPTEMBER 9, 1857
6:30 AM

Emmeline floated to the side of the bed with a full breakfast tray and softly placed it in the optimum position. The Prophet stretched, smiled, and proceeded to dig in. He'd had a fine night's sleep, just what he was hoping Emmeline would help him accomplish.

She did not run the Beehive House or occupy the role of number one sealed wife. But there was something special about Emmeline. It wasn't just that he was at ease in her presence. He was intimidated by no woman, or man, anywhere in the vast territory he controlled. The difference between Emmeline and most of the others was that he enjoyed her company. The others, for the most part, provided him with the variety any man needed to be kept interested. He also found her to be the most attractive of any of his wives so far.

Though this was not the first time, it was not customary for the Prophet to spend the entire night with one of his subordinate brides. Typically he would return to the Beehive House next door after administering to his procreative duties. He liked to sleep in his own bed, unless he was sleeping with Emmeline.

He expected he'd have to pay for the minor indiscretion of not returning to Lucy, who held rank over all the others. Not that Lucy wasn't used to the Prophet dallying with just about any woman he wanted to dally with.

Jealousy was not an option to be expressed openly by any plural wife . . . even number one.

His absence would cause her to check with her sister Clarissa, Brigham's sixth wife and the one in charge of the Lion House after hours. The wives kept track of where the Prophet was at all times. She would inform Lucy that the Prophet was properly located and Lucy would then return home, her sleep having been sufficiently interrupted. There were complexities to living in a polygamous household.

Emmeline leaned back on the parlor couch while her husband indulged in an ample meal of bread, butter, and warm milk. The Prophet was a man of simple tastes and advocated that the brethren be the same.

"So what's going on in the southern settlements that you have an express rider racing to and fro?" Unlike Brigham's other wives, who would not dare to query into a man's business, in the past she had found the Prophet to be quite forthcoming to her expressed interests.

This time he hesitated before answering. "You wouldn't be inquiring about one Mr. Lee, would you?" A raised eyebrow acknowledged the old love triangle that existed between the three. They had often cajoled each other about the competing interests of her two would-be suitors and the circumstances that ultimately brought about their marriage.

But this time Brigham was buying time. He had known instantly that Emmeline had come up with something surrounding Haslam's presence downstairs during one of her bread and milk runs. But the information she was asking for was of a far more sensitive nature than she could imagine.

They had married just over twelve years ago. She was his twentieth wife, and he'd married twenty-nine others since marrying her. But she had given him more children than any of the others, an obvious by-product of the "more than her fair share" time the two had been able to arrange with one another. It was also a fact that had not escaped the notice of the others.

With a slight smirk on her face Emmeline replied. "Am I not to be concerned with the welfare of our brethren in any part of the land of our inheritance?"

He knew she wanted information. All the women in Salt Lake City were starved for information. It was only women like Emmeline who had the moxie to ask for it. Normally, it was his custom to indulge her. What he usually had to say wasn't much more than advice he was giving on what to plant where or the appointment of a new bishop. The information surrounding his communications with officials in Iron and Washington counties was of a much more serious nature.

"Just some difficulty with the Lamanites and an immigrant party passing through. Damn Gentiles get them stirred up, and they always look to us to help settle things down. Shouldn't amount to much as long as they mind their manners."

She sensed he was holding something back. Time to take a different tack. She slid off the couch and sashayed over to the bed, where she snuggled up next to him. "You know I've never regretted, for even one day, marrying the man I married. It's just that sometimes I worry about my friend Rachel Andora."

Her motive sounded plausible enough. Young was hoping he could get off this easy. "Would you like me to ask Haslam to make an inquiry and report back?"

Rachel Andora Woolsey had been her best friend and had married Lee only a couple of weeks after he had married Emmeline's sister Louisa.

"That would be just wonderful. Can I give him the message?" her excitement sealing the deal.

It was more than he'd wanted to concede, but it was too late. He would just have to talk to Haslam, after Emmeline, and make sure he had his priorities straight. "Go ahead and talk to him now. Tell him I'll be down with final instructions shortly."

Emmeline kissed him on the cheek and rushed out of the room.

As the Prophet finished his breakfast, he was once again preoccupied with the situation to the south. He was not all that concerned that Emmeline was going to ascertain something she shouldn't, or even with the message she would be sending along to her friend. He was more concerned with the actual message Haslam would be carrying to the southern chain of command, and who would know about it.

He finished his sumptuous meal and proceeded to get dressed. He decided to forgo his usual morning shave so that Emmeline wouldn't have too much time with Haslam. By the time he arrived downstairs in the kitchen, the express rider was ignoring his breakfast and practically eating out of her hand. "I trust you've been given your instructions and are prepared to ride like the wind in the discharge of your duties?" The Prophet would make light of Haslam's responsibilities as long as Emmeline was present.

"You can count on me sir . . . I . . . I . . . mean, Brother Young." Haslam had taken the jest seriously, mostly due to his not wanting to diminish the importance of Emmeline's request of him. Her only request had been for him to inquire directly of John D. Lee as to her friend's health, as she had been reported to be once again with child, and report back upon his re-arrival at Temple Square. She had also handed him an envelope he was to ask Lee to deliver to Rachel Andora.

It was unlikely Haslam would get any glimpse of Emmeline's friend residing in New Harmony at the Lee compound. She had no way of knowing that this location would not be on the route Haslam would follow. But a verbal report from Lee would do just as well until a return letter could be received. Lee was likely to send some response of his own. After more than a dozen years since losing her to the most powerful man in the region, Lee was still much smitten by Emmeline and she knew it.

"You remembered. Good man, Brother Haslam. Now finish your breakfast and then accompany me to the bowery stables." The Prophet wanted to get on with the important business he had in store for the young rider. Haslam immediately focused on devouring the last of the bounty on his plate.

"Do take care of yourself, Brother Haslam. Be ever so watchful for the hazards and perils in your path. We hear so much about the dangers of the wilderness to the south." Emmeline made it sound like Haslam must be the bravest of men. It was her irresistible way of guaranteeing her instructions would receive the highest priority. Haslam would work extra hard to please the Prophet. He would risk life and limb to curry the favor of the most beautiful woman of Deseret.

Haslam's chest swelled with pride. "Don't worry, ma'am. Bein' on top of the fastest mounts in the territory cuts down on the danger considerable." He wolfed down the last of his apple pie, arose, and bowed to Emmeline and then to the other women working the kitchen.

Satisfied that she had accomplished all she could and would now have to wait, Emmeline smiled, arose, and proceeded back to her room. She would be on the alert for any new information she could acquire coming out of the southern settlements. She knew that the Prophet had been holding something back. Aside from tending to their children, she had not much else to do but discover what orchestrations the powerful Mormon leader was engaged in.

As Brigham placed his arm around Haslam's shoulder and began to guide him out of the Lion House, he observed Clarissa completing her shift.

"Clarissa dear, be a good girl and inform Lucy that I'll be attending church business over at the bowery this morning and will return shortly thereafter." He preferred not to have to deal with Lucy right now . . . and any attitude she might have about his overnight stay. Clarissa nodded without uttering a sound and headed next door.

CHAPTER 39

VIRGIN RIVER GORGE
NORTHWEST NEW
MEXICO TERRITORY

SEPTEMBER 18, 1857
4:45 PM

Milum was gone by the time Ira Hatch reached his lifeless body. He looked down at the quarry he'd been tracking but took no time for self-congratulation. The mission he'd been sent on was only partially complete. Now there were two more variables that needed to be dealt with. He needed to know what the two mounted horsemen knew, and if they were the only two who knew it. He began with the assumption he was going to have to kill them both.

As he scanned over Milum's body he took note of the rough condition of the man's face, hands, and semi-bootclad feet. Someone using two hands had applied a field dressing. The pants and shirt he was wearing, though somewhat worn, were fairly clean. Too clean for a man who'd been running, on foot, night and day, for the past week. He did not look at the two who had obviously been responsible for the doctoring and the fresh clothing. He spoke first to his men and then to Cao and Henry.

"These two make any false moves I want ya to do to them what I jus' done to this here dead feller. Now you boys slowly get off yer mounts an' sit over there on that rock yonder." Hatch pointed the barrel of his rifle to a large flat rock perched on the edge of the sandy riverbed and flowing emerald-green stream.

Henry and Cao exchanged worried glances and in complete silence did as they were told. Hatch continued to study the body. Hoof beats could be heard as two braves from Jackson's Santa Clara tribe galloped by along the other side of the stream and gave chase after Floppy, who'd scampered off downstream immediately after Milum had been shot. Haskell and Anderson took charge of the other three animals that had made up the threesome's transportation mode while Mathews and a Piede brave disarmed the brothers of their side arms.

Having ascertained enough to know that Milum had spent some time in the company of his two captives, it was time to determine how much they knew. Hatch turned and walked over to the rock upon which the brothers were seated. Placing the butt of his rifle in the sand in front of him, he hunkered down into a balanced squat eye level with them.

"I need to ask you boys some questions. I expect you to answer truthfully. Before we start you need to know that I'm gonna know if yer tellin' the truth or not. You also need to know yer very lives will depend on whether or not I believe you're tellin' me the truth.

"Seems like you're the law, the jury, an' the judge in these parts. Sure you don't want to jus' tell us what you want us ta say?" Cao hated for anyone to tell him what to do, and he was foolish enough to let it show to a proven killer when the killer had the drop on him.

"Shut up, Cao." Henry's hope was to stop Cao before his mouth got them both killed.

"Get this straight, young fella. I'm gonna be asking the questions an' you an' yer partner here are gonna be answerin' 'em. I got good cause to cut both you boys down right now jus' fer bein' caught in the company of that one lyin' in the sand over there. It'd be a might simpler on me ta finish it right now. If you cooperate with me, ya might get the opportunity to get some of yer own questions answered. Think of me any way ya want. Fer now ya better think of me as the man who's gonna put an end to yer lives if ya don't cooperate."

The brothers said nothing in response. They just waited for Ira's next question.

Ira looked at Henry. "What's yer name?"

"Henry T. Young."

"What's his?" Pointing the barrel of his rifle at Cao.

"That's my brother Cao." Henry took his time answering, but not too much time. He knew the questions would become more difficult. For now he had no intention of being truthful with all of his answers. But he also intended to do his best to convince Ira he was.

Hatch continued with Henry while staring directly into Cao's eyes. "Where you boys from, Henry?"

"We left Lancaster, Pennsylvania, several months ago. My brother and I grew up in Rhode Island near Providence." It was Henry's hope to keep Hatch talking as long as possible. He was sure he and his brother's lives were in considerable danger.

Now it was Cao's turn. "What brought you out to these parts, young fella?" It was Hatch's intention to thoroughly question the brothers before deciding what was to be done.

"We been droverin' and scoutin' for the Mathews and Tanner Company, and fer other outfits, these past few years." Cao decided to follow his older brother's tone and tempo when answering Hatch's questions. Hatch's comment about putting an' end to their lives had registered with Cao, as did the visual of Milum lying in the sand behind the interrogator.

"When was the last time you worked for Matthews and Tanner?" Hatch was quite familiar with this company of Mormon freighters. He needed to pursue the relationship.

"The first time we came out this way was about two years ago. Mathews and Tanner was over by Philly hiring drovers to foller a herd west, an' they needed hands. We worked for 'em again startin' out last year as scouts fer a train headin' to San Bernardino."

"Why would Matthews and Tanner need scouts to San Bernardino?" Hatch knew that Matthews and Tanner knew this trail better than any white men alive. The brother's veracity was now in question.

"They sent us ahead with a freight line they had a contract with out of Salt Lake City. We drovered that trail with them before so I guess they figured we knew the way." So far the answers had been easy for Cao and Henry.

Hatch returned his penetrating eyes back to Henry. It wasn't all that uncommon for the Mormon traders to hire Gentiles at the terminus of their trips to and from. Plausible so far. "When and where did you run into the fella behind me?"

Henry was grateful it was he who would be fielding this question and not Cao. By now he knew what Hatch was attempting to determine. He would do his best to keep Milum's dream alive if he could.

"He stumbled into our camp at the Mormon Fort over at the Vegas Springs three mornings ago and collapsed. It was just after sunup."

Ira stared at the man being interrogated for a prolonged moment. "And neither of you'd never had any acquaintance with him before that?"

"No sir." Henry knew he was in a critical phase of the questioning.

"Looks like he was in pretty bad shape?" Hatch backed off a bit.

"Yes sir, he was." Henry wasn't going to give up more than he had too. He knew the answers he was providing might cost him and Cao their lives.

Hatch turned to Haskell. "Go through all the saddlebags. And check out all the pockets on the corpse. I'll need a complete inventory of everything you find. You find anything in writing I want to see it immediately." Hatch then turned back to Henry.

"So what'd this fellow tell you about himself once he came to?" Hatch scanned back and forth between his two prisoners.

There it was, Henry thought. These were the questions whose answers could determine their fate. "He was in and out of consciousness the first day he was with us. We spent it providin' shade and tendin' his wounds as best we could. He'd say things from time to time, but none of it made any sense. Then two nights ago he came to and commenced to tellin' us he'd been with a group of immigrants out of Arkansas that had been attacked by Indians this side of Cedar City.

"He and two others were able to go fer help, but he was the only one to make it as far as he did. He wasn't completely sure what happened to his friends, but he figured they didn't make it. He had the feelin' he was being pursued. Reckon he had that part right."

Henry had surprised himself. Call it a hunch. Somehow he decided sticking to the truth was going to give he and Cao their best chance. Cao suddenly hoped Hatch wouldn't ask him any more questions. Even still, he wasn't sure why his older brother was being so honest.

"Since you left the fort at Vegas Springs yesterday morning, have you boys crossed paths with anyone else?" Hatch was still sizing up the situation. Had the breech gone any further or was this as far as it went?

Henry hesitated. Then he thought he was hesitating too long. A lie here could lead to questions not so easy to answer later. "No. The only folks we've come across since we left San Bernardino was him yonder and your party." Henry knew it was risky to let Hatch know he could put an end to his dirty little secret right here and now by giving him and Cao the "Milum treatment." He had the feeling that he was speaking to a man with a keen sense of when he was being lied to. Still he wished he could have answered this last question differently.

Thales Haskell came running over to Hatch. He'd found something in Milum's pocket. It was a piece of parchment with a great deal of writing on it. He handed it to Ira, who paused long enough to read its contents.

"That fella behind me happen to give you a name?" Suddenly Hatch was preoccupied with the parchment.

"Milum Jones was the only name he gave us." Henry wasn't going to turn over everything. He was still primarily concerned with not saying anything that could get him and his brother killed. The violent death of the man he'd recently saved hadn't fully sunk in, but it was starting to.

The parchment read as follows:

> To all Masons, Christians, Americans, Citizens, and Fellow Members of Man Kind,
>
> A hostile force surrounds us. We have been under siege for nearly four days. Thirteen of our party has been killed. Another dozen are severely wounded. Our attackers are made up of mostly Indians of the region. However, we fear that they are being assisted by more than one White man. Our location is in a high mountain meadow near Jacob Hamblin's ranch about 35 miles west of Cedar City. We pray to Almighty God, in the name of Jesus Christ, for help to be sent us forthwith. We pray that if help cannot find its' way to us in time to deliver us from this horrible plight, justice shall be meted out to those savages responsible for our demise.

God Speed,

Captain Alexander Fancher-wounded	Captain John T. Baker-wounded
Eliza Ingram Fancher	Manerva A. Baker
Hampton Fancher	Mary Levina Baker
William Fancher	Melissa Ann Beller
Mary Fancher	David W. Beller
Thomas Fancher	George W. Baker
Martha Fancher	Abel Baker
Sarah G. Fancher	Mary E. Baker

Christopher C. Fancher

Triphenia D. Fancher

Margaret A. Fancher

Talitha Emmeline

Marion Tackitt-wounded

Sebron Tackitt-killed by attackers

Matilda Tackitt

James M. Tackitt

Jones M. Tackitt

Pleasant Tackitt-killed by attackers

Armilda Miller Tackitt

E. Milan Tackitt-killed by attackers

William Henry Tackitt

Cynthia Tackitt

Mary W. Dunlap

Ellender Dunlap-killed by attackers

Nancy M. Dunlap

James D. Dunlap

Lucinda Dunlap

Susannah Dunlap

Margerette Dunlap

Mary Ann Dunlap

Rebbecca J. Dunlap

Louisa Dunlap

Sarah Ann Dunlap

Lorenzo Dow Dunlap

Nancy Dunlap-wounded

Thomas J. Dunlap-wounded

John H. Dunlap

Mary Ann Dunlap

Jesse Dunlap, Jr.

Nancy Dunlap

America Jane Dunlap

Prudence Angeline Dunlap

Georgia Ann Dunlap

Sarah F. Baker

William T. Baker

Mordecai Stevenson-wounded

David Hudson-killed by attackers

James C. Haydon

Thomas Hamilton

Tom Farmer-killed by attackers

George D. Basham

John P. Reed

Alf Smith-killed by attackers

Jeremy Poteet

Jeffrey Poteet

Charles H. Morton

William Wood-wounded

Solomon R. Wood

Richard Wilson-wounded

Charles Stallcup

Milum L. Rush-killed by attackers

William Prewit

John Prewit-killed by attakers

Lawson A. McEntire

Silas Edwards

William M. Eaton

Allen P. Deshazo

John Beach

William Cameron

Martha Cameron-wounded

Tillman Cameron

Isom Cameron

Henry Cameron

James Cameron

Martha Cameron

Larkin Cameron

Saladia Ann Brown Huff

William Huff

John Milum Jones

Eloah Angeline Tackitt Jones

Zabrina M. Jones

Newton Jones-wounded

Felix Marion Jones

Charles R. Mitchell

Sarah C. Baker Mitchell

John Mitchell

James Mathew Fancher

Frances Fulfer Fancher

Robert Fancher

J.D. Mitchell-killed by attackers

Dale H. Mathis

Philip L. Mathis

Jeffrey Logan-wounded

Kay Lee Logan

Kara K. Logan

William Allen Aden-killed by attackers

Elisha Huff-killed by attackers

Levi Huff

Joshua Huff

Nancy Saphrona Huff

Josiah Miller

Matilda Cameron Miller

James William Miller

Adelia Cameron Fitzgerald

John Calvin Miller

Mary Miller-wounded

Joseph Miller

Zacharia Poteet-killed by attackers

Patrick Mathews

Mariellen Hobbs

Katherine Hobbs

Violet Fitzgerald-killed by attackers

Lilburn Hobbs-wounded

Pondering Henry's last response, Hatch turned the page around and showed it to the two men on the rock. He was far enough away from them that they could not read its contents. But they could see that it was some kind of message followed by a long list of names or some other kind of inventory. As Henry and Cao strained their eyes to see, Ira concluded they had never seen the document before. He folded the parchment and stuffed it in his shirt pocket, making sure to fasten the button to lock it in. The interrogation was over. The parchment contained the last piece of information Hatch needed to determine what he must now do.

CHAPTER 40

MOUNTAIN MEADOWS
COMMAND POST
UTAH TERRITORY

SEPTEMBER 11, 1857
10:15 AM

As the two riders galloped eastward from the wagon fortress ascending the trail toward the rock outcropping that concealed their command post, Lee peeled off left, which allowed Bateman to pursue his destination alone. Knight and Johnson turned with anticipation toward Lee as he reined his mount to a halt. P.K. sat staring into the campfire, seemingly oblivious of the arrival of his friend and to the gravity of the message he was soon to reveal.

Lee dismounted, handing his reigns to Nephi, but otherwise ignoring him and Sam Knight. He walked over to the opposite side of the fire pit facing P.K. "The plan is set. We need to proceed forthwith to the militia and march with them to the Gentile position. Higbee will command the maneuver."

P.K. looked up to Lee as if he was about to say something. But he did not. P.K. simply placed his feet under himself and raised himself from his seated position, dusted his hat, and fastened it snugly atop his tall muscular frame. He walked directly to where his mount was tied followed closely by Lee and the others.

"Will you have a prayer for the men this morning, P.K.?" Lee was again worried about how supportive his old friend was going to be. The air was thick with the unspoken understanding of how important P.K.'s leadership was going to be in front of the militia.

"I'll have a prayer," was all P.K. said.

It was enough for Lee. P.K.'s silence to this point had been disconcerting. Any reassurance that he was still on board, no matter how small, was better than the cold silence he'd been projecting.

"Mind lettin' me know what chapter and verse?" Lee couldn't resist, but this was too much for P.K.

"Yes I do mind," was his only response.

Lee would have to accept it. The two had always shared a rivalry over the Book. P.K., with his deep booming voice, was a natural from behind the pulpit. He'd been invited to preach in front of the Salt Lake congregation in the bowery. Lee had been envious. He thought he knew the Book better than did P.K.

They had frequently jousted over the appropriateness of passages used to punctuate specific themes for the benefit of their flocks. But Lee knew better than to ask his old friend to provide inspirational guidance to the men, and then to also tell him what he should say. He would just have to hear it along with the others.

The four men untied and mounted their horses. The three-minute ride to the militia's encampment was done without further discussion.

* * *

Upon their arrival they observed Higbee directing the formation of three ox teams. The others were milling about, securing their gear and tending the stock in the temporary remuda that had been thrown together over the past several days. Most of the men had been told they would be conducting this operation on foot. Much of the activity centered around oiling and loading their handguns and rifles.

Lee spurred his mount into the lead and headed for Higbee. The young captain observed the approach of the leadership and immediately turned to Bateman. "Call the men to formation," he shouted.

Not knowing what exactly to do, but feeling the need to do something, Bateman charged toward the men milling about and began shouting. "Line up in formation! Line up in formation!"

Higbee, embarrassed, turned back to his effort directed at organizing the ox-teams as Lee and the others dismounted. Higbee turned to Lee and nodded his understanding that the plan they'd discussed last night was unfolding as it should.

As awkward as it was, Bateman's call to muster was effective. The men were lined up in formation within two minutes. Higbee, the highest-ranking officer over the Iron County militia, was always eager to display his authority. True to form he was first to speak.

"Men, we are about to proceed with a military operation under orders from our leaders in Salt Lake City. The blood of our prophets Joseph Smith and Parley Pratt is about to be avenged. That's right, Mrs. Pratt identified two of the Gentiles in the train as having been at the scene of the crime. I got it by express messenger two days ago from Salt Lake City." Higbee decided to omit the additional news about the killers of Prophet Smith and his brother Hyrum at Carthage also being present on the train. P.K.'s rebuke the night before had given him cause to think better of it. But P.K. hadn't been told of the evidence involving the murder of Pratt.

"We have the honor of representing our people in this long overdue and first act of retaliation for the persecutions perpetrated upon us by the eastern Gentiles. As your major it has been my honor to lead the Iron County militia to this point. However, Major Lee is the highest-ranking officer here on the field of Washington County. Being that we have crossed over the county line, I am going to turn the command over to Major Lee, who will address you at this time." Higbee saluted the formation and took one pace backward.

Lee stepped forward. Without saluting, and in his most commanding voice, he addressed the seventy plus men whose attention was riveted upon him. "Loyal members of the Iron and Washington county militias, fellow Saints, brethren. You are now acting for the reorganized Nauvoo Legion by recent order of General Wells. We have arrived here today under orders signed by Major Isaac Haight, as directed by Colonel William Dame and drafted by the war council in Salt Lake City. Brother Haslam embarked from there with the written orders just two mornings ago."

Lee paused briefly, and then reinforced the point. "We are all under orders to be here. These orders of the military chain of command are from the very head of the chain. Failure to carry out these orders will be viewed as an act of treason and shall be punished accordingly."

Some of the men shuffled their feet and looked about to the faces immediately around them. All remained silent awaiting Lee's further comments.

"Those of you that have been ordered to commence this operation on foot will be required to march in formation to the Gentile fortress. Once we proceed out from there, each man is to line up single file alongside one of the Gentile men. Major Higbee will command the orderly march from this position and upon his command to 'Halt' and 'Do your duty'; you are to discharge your weapon targeting the Gentile next to you. If there are any of you who are too big a coward to carry out this order, you are still ordered to discharge your piece into the air and leave the hard work to those of us who know how to fight our enemies."

The color drained from the faces of several of the men listening.

"You men to whom I speak have the easiest job. You're not being asked to kill women and children. Others will carry out that bloody work. Only the small children are to be spared. This operation must be completed today. We are at war with the Gentiles. You all know the Gentile army is approaching the leadership of our church in Salt Lake City. Today we fight for our families, for Deseret, for our church, and for the freedom to worship in our own way. Bishop Klingensmith will now lead us in prayer."

Lee stepped backward a pace and looked at his old friend. He was relieved to see the bishop holding a copy of the Book of Mormon. Immediately he wondered what words in that book his friend would rely upon to address the men. Even more, he worried what message those words would support.

P.K. looked down at the book as he opened it to the passage selected. He slowly took several paces forward until he was closer than Lee or Higbee to the men he was about to address. He stopped and slowly raised his head. Before he began his eyes met those of some men he'd known for years. Almost all of them recognized him as their neighbor in Cedar City and as their bishop.

"Two Nephi, Chapter Twenty Six: Paragraph Three . . . And after the Messiah shall come there shall be signs given unto my people of his birth, and also of his death and resurrection; and great and terrible shall that day be unto the wicked, for they shall perish; and they perish because they cast out the prophets, and the saints, and stone them, and slay them; wherefore the cry of the blood of the saints shall ascend up to God from the ground against them.

"D&C Eighty Five: Paragraph Five . . . And it shall come to pass also that the remnants who are left on the land will marshal themselves, and shall become exceedingly angry, and shall vex the Gentiles with a sore vexation.

"Alma, Chapter Forty Three: Paragraph Thirty . . . And he also knowing that it was the only desire of the Nephites to preserve their lands, and their liberty, and their church, therefore he thought it no sin that he should defend them by stratagem . . .

"All the forgoing passages were written from revelation by the Prophet Joseph Smith. Many of us here knew Brother Joseph. He was a great inspiration to us . . . and to me. We have a new Prophet now. He directs us to be here today. The following revelation comes to us through him.

"D&C One Hundred Thirty Six: Paragraphs Seventeen, Eighteen and Thirty . . . Go thy way and do as I have told you, and fear not thine enemies; for they shall not have power to stop my work . . . Zion shall be redeemed in mine own due time . . . Fear not thine enemies for they are in my hands and I will do my pleasure with them."

P.K. took one pace back, lowering his gaze once again. Satisfied that P.K. had kept his end of the bargain, Lee looked to Higbee and simply nodded. Higbee stepped forward and once again took charge.

"Alright men, we're going to march out from here in double file. Once we get to the Gentile camp, on my command, we'll line up along their rank, one Saint to one Gentile with one backup. Forward march!"

Lee, P.K., Johnson, and Knight mounted up, as did another half dozen members of the militia. Those mounted also lined up two by two to the left and downwind of the column as to minimize the effect of dust from their animal's hooves. A light breeze had kicked up. Higbee had a reputation for being a stickler drill instructor during training sessions with the militia. Some viewed his rigidity with amusement. Others disdained Higbee as a shameless brown-noser, unworthy of their respect. All present took his commands seriously this morning.

In less than ten minutes from Higbee's command, those in the immigrant camp got their first glimpse of the Nauvoo Legion as it rounded the hill behind which Lee's command headquarters had been concealed from them for the past five days.

CHAPTER 41

TEMPLE SQUARE
SALT LAKE CITY
UTAH TERRITORY

SEPTEMBER 9, 1857
7:00 AM

James Haslam walked stride for stride with the man good Saints believed to be the highest authority of God on earth. James was a true believer. The mission he would be sent on this morning was, he sensed, of enormous importance. War hysteria had gripped Salt Lake City since the July 24 celebration at Little Cottonwood Canyon when word had arrived from O.P. Rockwell of the approaching federal army. This same hysteria had radiated outward to all the settlements in all directions. But something big was happening in the south, and he had been asked to be a part of it.

"I want you to spare no horseflesh in bringing General Smith's message to Colonel Dame." Young was not going to elaborate any further than necessary. He could sense the seriousness the young man was placing on his responsibilities, and he would do nothing to dispel his enthusiasm. Still, he must be careful about the extent of any particulars he might reveal. Unlike the buffoon George A. Smith, Brigham was not one to show anyone his hand until it was time to collect his winnings.

"There's good mounts at all the settlements 'tween here and the Meadows, Brother Young. The weather looks to be holdin' too. With any luck, I should be there by tomorrow night." Haslam's statement was made with confidence and a little pride. Its notice did not escape the Prophet.

"That would be a ride to recall for some time, Brother Haslam. I'll be sure to attach a voucher to your satchel asking the bishops to expedite the transfers. Once you've accomplished your run, go to Hamblin's ranch house for rest and refreshment. I'll attach a voucher for you to give to his wife Rachel. Jacob won't be there so she should have plenty of room and sustenance to accommodate you. I'd like you to remain there under Major Higbee's command until Jacob returns. Bring back to me any message either Lee or Hamblin submit. And don't dally too long in Salt Creek with that Redford girl on your way back." With that, the Prophet gave a wry wink, which served to diffuse the gravity of the conversation to that point.

"Should I swing through Harmony on my way back, sir . . . I mean, Brother Young?" Haslam grimaced as he made the mistake again.

"No, Brother Haslam." Overlooking the slip the Prophet continued. "Major Lee will deliver Emmeline's communiqué to her girlfriend. Your work is far too important these days to be sent out of the way to deliver messages that can wait. I say, young man. We're going to have to confer upon you some kind of rank in our fledgling army. I must speak with General Wells about it."

Again Haslam's head was spinning with the importance of it all. He'd never done anything but take orders all of his life. Was it possible the Prophet was about to make him an order giver? He became speechless. The awkward silence that ensued did not seem to concern the powerful leader walking next to him. He seemed preoccupied with his own thoughts now. The silence continued the rest of the way to the bowery stables.

* * *

George A. Smith and General Wells were in deep conversation as the two approached from the east. They did not notice their arrival until they were about twenty paces off. Once observed, the two high-ranking Mormons ceased their conversation and smiled at the approaching brethren. A fine-looking sorrel stud stood saddled and ready to mount. Smith reached for the satchel, which would undoubtedly contain the communiqués to be delivered.

Smith immediately began the conversation as if he was going to take charge of directing the young rider as to the specifics of his mission. "We have here four sealed communiqués . . . "

"Your directions can wait till my presence is no longer required here. I deliver to you Brother James Haslam, who to my knowledge holds no rank on our militia. I trust, General Wells, that you will remedy that situation before Brother Haslam departs." Young communicated just enough aggravation that Haslam was the only man present that didn't notice.

At once Smith realized that he had nearly failed to maintain some distance between the First Presidency and the specific details of the operation at hand. "Of course," he almost whispered as he placed the contents back in the satchel.

General Wells began to write something on an official-looking piece of parchment. "I'll resolve the issue of rank right now. Brother Haslam, I hereby appoint you Special Emissary to the General Command in Salt Lake City . . . signed General Daniel H. Wells. I'm writing this on the voucher we discussed last night after you left the meeting. Present this to the bishops or stable masters at the various settlements along the way. It requires them to provide you with their best mounts in the most expedited manner they can muster. If any fail to comply with that, you are to report them to me upon your return. I don't think you'll be needing to make out any reports. This is a special voucher we only use for our highest priority, and I made sure they all knew about it on my last pass through. Apostle Smith here reinforced the issue more recently. Here is a second voucher that will allow you to prevail upon Rachel Hamblin to provide you with accommodation and sustenance at Jacob's summer home."

"There you go. A genuine field promotion if I ever saw one." Young winked again as he knew Haslam would be surprised that the vouchers he'd spoken to him of during their walk over had already been taken care of. "I'll be sending inquiry through Brother Hamblin, or some other messenger, who will be following your track some days behind you, to speak with Bishop Bryant about that Redford girl. Upon your return, you may inquire with the bishop about your prospects with the young woman. But do not dally . . . there will be time for that later. Remember the most important thing is for you to spare no horseflesh between here and Mountain Meadows. I'll look forward to seeing you again, and to hear the particulars of your historic ride. God speed, Brother Haslam." With that the Prophet turned and left.

* * *

Finally Smith could commence his instruction as he once again began removing the communiqués from the satchel. "These first two are addressed to Colonel Dame in Parowan. The one labeled #1 is merely his instructions on what he needs to do with the one labeled #2. He will reseal #2 and place it back in the satchel for you to deliver to Commander Haight in Cedar City. The one addressed to Haight and labeled #3 will provide him instructions as to what to do with this one now addressed to him and labeled #2. It shall be resealed and placed back in the envelope for your delivery to major's Higbee and Lee at Mountain Meadows.

"These communiqués are highly classified. You are not to look inside these directives. You are to protect their seals and the integrity of what is inside them with your very life. Do you understand?"

Haslam was quite impressed with the level of sophistication he was being entrusted. He had the distinct feeling that Smith and Wells had stayed up half the night putting the package together that he was about to carry in the satchel. Possibly Hamblin had his hand in it as well. He would have been surprised at the amount of input Wilfred Woodruff had contributed. "I understand. The directions seem straightforward enough. I don't think I'll have any trouble following the instructions."

"Of course you won't." Smith slapped the young man on the back. "Now, before you depart do you have any questions of either of us?"

"Well, I was wonderin', General Wells, if it would be possible for me to be appointed regiment band leader of the Nauvoo Legion? It seems like it would be a good idea if the legion had a marching band like other regiments." Haslam was completely serious.

Wells and Smith were completely derailed by Haslam's question. Finally Wells recovered enough to respond. "Of course. It's something I've always wanted myself. But we have higher priorities to deal with now. We're about to be engaged in a war. Once we obtain our military objectives east of here, I think we can look into establishing a regimental band."

The two superiors looked toward the readied horse, and it became clear that it was time for Haslam to mount up and ride out.

The young man took the satchel from Smith's outstretched hand and securely fashioned it behind the saddle. There was an eerie silence as he prepared his departure. The two older men were as unaccustomed to spending so much time in the presence of someone of Haslam's status as he was in theirs.

Once mounted, Wells stood to attention and saluted. Smith awkwardly followed suit. Haslam returned the courtesy and then nodded as the number two and number three highest-ranking military men in the territory smiled toothy grins.

Without further delay, the most respected express messenger in all of Deseret spurred his mount to a full gallop. As he rounded the turn pulling away from Temple Square, he allowed his animal to relax into a comfort-able lope.

This was going to be a test of endurance for him and all the other fifteen animals he would be riding over the next twenty-four hours or so. Haslam was looking forward to it. It was the nicest time of the year to be riding horseback along the western slope of the Wasatch Range. James Haslam believed God put him on this earth to ride. This was going to be a ride to remember.

CHAPTER 42

VIRGIN RIVER GORGE
NORTHWEST NEW
MEXICO TERRITORY

SEPTEMBER 18, 1857
5:15 PM

Ira Hatch stood up and strolled away from the brothers. Once out of their range of hearing, he motioned to Haskell and Mathews to approach his position. As they approached, his thoughts returned to Henry and Cao Young. Though he could not be sure what Milum had told them, there was still a good chance the brothers knew more than they had so far let on. It was possible they knew too much.

Hatch had not given up on tracking Milum Jones. Able had made a good stand in the cottonwoods and had given his partner a good thirty-six-hour lead before he'd bled to death. After burying him at Cottonwood Springs, they'd followed Milum's track to the confluence of the Santa Clara and the Virgin Rivers. From there they couldn't be sure if Milum had gone upstream or down. They'd guessed wrong in deciding to eliminate the upstream option first.

Hamblin, Lee, Haight, Dame, and George A. Smith would certainly advise that these brothers should be put out of the way. Ira was subject to the same military chain of command as all the others and was outranked by all these men. His status as Indian agent and interpreter offered him an insular role in the Nauvoo Legion compared to the other militia members.

Jacob Hamblin, recently appointed president of the Southern Utah Indian Mission, and Ira's immediate supervisor, also kept his subordinates

away from the grunt work. Thales Haskell and James Mathews were subordinate to Ira. Because of Hamblin's recent promotion, the status of all
three had been elevated.

But Ira Hatch was a leader, not a follower. Though he had just hunted
down and killed two men as the result of a direct order, his taste for killing
was beginning to sour. The list of people he'd just viewed had had an effect
on Ira. It was very likely that all the people on that list were now dead.
The brothers posed no immediate danger. If his two captives were going
to present problems for the chain of command, he may well be expected
to kill them too. But now, here at the gorge, he was in command. Perhaps
he should put the problem into the hands of his superiors and let them
deal with it.

"Thales, I'm thinkin' of having you, Dudley, and Rosmus escort these
men up the Virgin River as far as the Narrows. Then camp there for a day or
two to be sure they don't double back. I don't want those boys over yonder
findin' out more'n they already know. If they continue on up the Spanish
Trail, it's likely they'll run into the immigrant camp, whatever's left of it.
After keepin' company with that fella we been chasin', they just might get
too good at piecin' things together."

"Rosmus claims he thinks he knows these two. Says the younger fella
is sweet on one of his daughters and has been studying with the bishop at
Cedar to convert to the Saints." James Mathews had seen enough killing
this past week. He thought the new information might make a difference
to Ira.

Ira pondered this new information briefly. He would have liked to send
Anderson. But he couldn't take the chance that Rosmus might reveal too
much to the brothers, being that they may be old acquaintances.

"In that case it's probably best that Rosmus stays with me. I'll send
Jackson's braves with you. I need ya ta make damned sure those two don't
double back on you."

"I'd rather ride with Rosmus than Jackson's Santa Claras." Thales didn't
see the danger Ira did. But Ira always looked further ahead than most.

"Look at it this way. You'll have an opportunity to practice the Santa
Clara tongue. You be sure you don't let those two boys over there in on
what's been goin' on up north. Listen to everything they have to say. But
don't you say anything about that immigrant train up north. After a couple
of days guarding the Narrows, head back to Fort Clara. I'll be there waitin'
for Jacob's return. Anything you find out from them boys, we're gonna
need to know it. We need to know how much that dead feller told 'em

before he died." Ira modified his last sentence as he nearly said ". . . before I shot him."

Ira was taking a risk by not killing the two brothers while in his grasp, and he knew it. But he still intended on meeting his responsibilities should he determine definitively that the brothers possessed information damaging to his brethren. He didn't have enough information yet to order the destruction of two more lives. Neither did he relish killing people just because they happened to be in the way.

James Mathews understood where Ira was headed. "Do you want us to send Rosmus over?"

"No. I'll need to find out what he knows of those two, but I'll go to him. You two stay here and watch 'em until I've had a chance to talk to him. I'm not sure I want there to be any reunion 'tween Rosmus and those boys." Ira was finished with the conversation and proceeded forthwith to where Rosmus Anderson was tending to the stock.

* * *

Haskell and Mathews watched Ira leave, then began to walk in the direction of Henry and Cao. Better get started finding out what the two Gentiles knew. The sentries stopped about ten yards from the seated men. Both thought it best to maintain their dominance over the two unarmed captives, at least for the time being, by keeping their rifles at the ready. Their intention was to eventually turn the men loose, but it would have to be done in an orderly way, and on their terms.

Henry and Cao studied the approach of the two new riflemen. Were they approaching with bad intent? Had Ira Hatch just given the order to execute them? Every new overture was one of uncertainty and trepidation. Cao sensed only fear. Henry was more analytical, but could sense his brother's concern. "They could have kilt us a dozen times by now, Cao. Don't make any fast moves."

Cao just remained silent and looked at the rifles and the hands holding them. His body was taut and ready to go. But his big brothers advice kept him in check.

James spoke first. "Camp'll be set up soon an' we can rustle you boys up some grub." Then Thales made the mistake of looking over at Milum's lifeless body. All eyes focused on the corpse, and the offer of dinner seemed totally inappropriate.

"Don't worry 'bout him. Ira'll bury him proper. That's just the way he is." Haskell's attempt to right the indiscretion was only partly successful.

"Why'd he shoot him in the first place?" Henry could sense they were in the company of subordinates who would not be determining their fate.

"We been chasin' that one for a week. He kilt some Injuns up north, an' ever since we been tryin' ta keep the lid on a powder keg. The Injuns from here ta Fort Bridger are threatnin' ta kill every Gentile that wanders into Deseret." Haskell's revelation was measured. Ira's admonition was fresh in his mind. He didn't want to reveal too much, but he needed to break the ice.

"Was it murder, or did he kill them in self defense?" Henry had lots of questions. He was going to keep asking them as long as they would answer.

"Oh, it was murder all right. The first one was anyway." Haskell didn't want to leave any doubt that Milum got what was coming to him.

"You saw the murder?" Henry was not going to abandon Milum so easily.

"I saw the Injun he kilt. He was unarmed." Haskell did not like the direction of the conversation.

"How can you be sure if you didn't see the murder? Someone else could have removed the gun. Milum could have took it hisself." Cao couldn't resist following up on what his brother started.

"Is that what he told you? That he took the Injun's gun after he kilt him in a fair fight?" Haskell was taken aback some but welcomed the entrance of the younger more impulsive brother.

"Yes he did." Cao lied. "He also said that the Injuns kilt one of his friends." Cao wanted to discredit his captors.

Henry could see that his brother was going to drive the conversation into a standoff if he let him. In any standoff they would be at a severe disadvantage. "What my little brother is trying to tell you is, until Mr. Hatch shot Mr. Milum, we had no idea he was wanted for any kind of crime, let alone murder. If'n you folks say he's a murderer, we're in no position to argue about it with ya. We were just tryin' ta help out a stranger that appeared to be in serious need."

Haskell now welcomed the cooler-headed discourse of the older brother. Just then the approach of Ira Hatch with a shovel and the brothers' pack mules pleased him even more. It gave him the opportunity to bring a temporary end to the troubling conversation.

"We'll have plenty of time to help you boys sort all this out. We been assigned to escort you to a safe route north." With that Haskell turned and began to walk toward Hatch.

Mathews was content to stand there and keep his mouth shut. He resolved not to respond to any questions the brothers might direct his way. Fortunately for him, no more questions came.

Ira stopped briefly to confer with Haskell before both then proceeded back to the rock upon which the brothers remained seated. Hatch walked up to Henry and handed him the reigns of the two mules. "You boys will be stayin' in camp with us tonight. Tomorrow you'll be escorted north a ways so we can be sure you'll avoid the trouble goin' on between here and Cedar."

Not wanting to engage in further conversation with the brothers, he turned and walked over to Milum and began to dig a grave in the sandy creek bed next to his pale lifeless body.

CHAPTER 43

MOUNTAIN MEADOWS
WAGON FORTRESS
UTAH TERRITORY

SEPTEMBER 11, 1857
11:00 AM

All was bustling with excitement and optimism around the immigrant camp. Some could not restrain the urge to cheer. Others were too busy to interrupt their activities. And still some maintained a foreboding sense of doom.

The breeze that had kicked up was light, and the temperature had cooled significantly from a few days before. But it was a sunny day in the high mountain meadow and they couldn't have asked for nicer weather.

Jeffrey Poteet and some of his friends had been discussing staging a protest about giving up their weapons. As the Nauvoo Legion snaked its way down to the steep draw cut by Mogatsu Creek, all but three of his party drifted away and began making their own preparations to move out.

"I got a real bad feelin' about this," Jeffrey said to the two that remained.

"Looks like all but us are fixin' ta go along with young Fancher and that Mormon bastard." John Beach had been a Mormon hater since his family had been driven out of Missouri. A Mormon raiding party had torched his family farm near Independence. It was retaliation for an earlier raid on one of their settlements. But Beach's family had only been minding their own business.

Jeremy Poteet, Jeffrey's younger brother, could see that things were about to get worse. "Here comes Fancher now."

Mathew Fancher had just come from a difficult negotiation with an agonized Captain Baker and his cousin Captain Alexander Fancher. The health of both men had deteriorated greatly, and they stood almost no chance of surviving much longer. Baker had argued as forcefully as he could that the younger Fancher not agree to give up their arms. Unable to formulate an alternative, Mathew Fancher prevailed over his objection.

Fancher knew that the three scowling men were all that was left of any opposition he might encounter. The way they clutched their rifles told him they were trying to set their heels in support of one another. Fancher was going to settle this right now. "If you three think you're gonna put the whole deal in jeopardy fer all the rest of us by refusin' ta give up yer arms, yer gonna have a fight on yer hands an' it's gonna end bad fer ya'll real soon."

"Do you realize what kind a chance yer takin' by lettin' these backstabbin' polygamists take control of our arms? We know it's been Mormons helpin' out these redskin devils. Don't be a fool!" Poteet knew he wasn't going to be able to win his argument by force so trying to be reasonable was his only alternative. That's when Fancher knew he'd won the argument.

"Dammit, Jeff, a chance is all we got. What chance we got surrounded by four or five hundred bloodthirsty, well-armed redskins? We got wounded dyin' off every day. All our horses and cattle are dead or gone. We're runnin' out of ammo, not ta mention food. Every day things have been gettin' more an' more hopeless fer all of us. Now we got seventy-five well-armed Christian soldiers who say they're gonna give us an escort out a here, but only if we make a show of layin' down our arms. Do you really think they're gonna double-cross us? I suppose there's a chance of it, but given our alternatives don't it seem like a chance we oughta take?" The young leader had made his point.

The desire to get out of their appalling circumstance was too much even for the dissenters. "All right, Matt. We'll go along. But it's a hell of a gamble." Jeff wasn't going to wait for his last two confederates to desert him, and he knew they both were going to if he didn't throw in the towel.

"Don't worry boys. I gotta feelin' things are going ta work out fer us after all. We just gotta keep our heads an' stick together. Gettin' back ta Cedar City is just the first leg. We're still gonna be a long way from home for a long time yet." Fancher was not unconcerned about Mormon complicity with their bleak circumstance. In fact, he was being more optimistic than he actually felt.

Much like Milum had described to the Young brothers at Las Vegas Springs, the entire immigrant camp had had a chance to put two and two together. He didn't have as much evidence against the Saints as did Milum; but as one of the train's leaders, he had some foreboding encounters with Mormon leaders from Salt Lake City. A setup was a possibility. However, Fancher could not fathom that the entire Mormon organization could be complicit with such an action.

The "White Flag of Truce" was encouraging. Lee had been convincing. The sight of seventy-five white men marching toward them in formation with no obvious hostile intent came very close to being the miracle they needed and had been praying for. It was natural for him to believe that this many of his own color would not conspire toward his, and his peoples' destruction. His mind truly was thinking of Cedar City and points beyond. It was only natural for a trail boss to do so.

* * *

Higbee brought the formation up the other side of the draw and into the wagon fortress as the appointed sentries opened the swinging gate formed by the swiveling wagon tongues. Lee and P.K. entered the compound on horseback. Knight and the other riders remained outside the fortification. Nephi Johnson, the best Indian interpreter left at the Meadows, had gone to notify the chiefs that their plan was in motion. Once inside, Higbee gave the infantrymen the commands, "Halt!" followed by an immediate, "At ease!"

The immigrants couldn't help but stare at the military contingent in their midst. As far as a military unit, they were a pretty rag-tag-looking bunch of men. Unlike the uniformed and spit-polished regiments they had seen back in the East, this was a group of un-uniformed and unkempt men who appeared to have been thrown together on quite short notice. However, they marched and held formation well, having been mustering for drill training for several weeks now on an almost daily basis.

Lee rode over to young Fancher. P.K. dismounted and stood scanning the crowd of people who'd gathered about. He could not bring himself to make eye contact with any of them. Like Lee on his first visit into the encampment, he was struggling to maintain his focus. Lee and Higbee, by contrast, appeared to be in complete control: Lee with implementing the orderly exodus of the immigrants; Higbee with positioning his men.

"These the three wagons?" Lee wanted to keep things moving.

"Yep. Wounded and the little ones already loaded inta these two here. We'll have the men place their weapons in this one as they pass by it if you think that'll satisfy the red demons up yonder." Fancher motioned toward the Indians that had gathered on horseback in several locations in the surrounding hills. They were still out of rifle range, but Fancher, Poteet, and the others were wondering how long that would last once the immigrants surrendered their armaments.

Lee seemed to understand Fancher's thought. "I reckon it'll satisfy 'em well enough. I got their chiefs to agree to keep their distance. I expect they'll follow us for a ways an' then most of 'em will probly head back to their camps."

With a motion of his arm, Lee signaled the three teamsters, led by Sam Knight, to enter the compound with their oxen. Sam McMurdy and Carl Shirts, the other two, followed Knight's example. As the animals were backed into place and harnessed to the doubletrees, Lee gave final instructions to Fancher.

"The wagon with the children will leave first, followed by the one carryin' the wounded. Then the women and older children followin' on foot. The men go next escorted by the militia. We have ta make it look like the men are under arrest ta satisfy the Lamanites. That's the name our religion gives to the red man. Last out will be the wagon carryin' all your arms. Don't worry, those militia that don't escort the men will be positioned at various points along the procession guarding the wounded, the women and children, and a sufficient number to make sure the arms are secure at all times."

"I believe all our people are ready. I'll explain it to the folks and get the women started." Fancher wasted no time. For very different reasons he was eager to get things moving as well.

P.K. and Sam Knight tied their horses to the two lead wagons: P.K.'s to the first wagon carrying most of the small children; Knight's to the one carrying a few more children and all of the wounded. Lee noted that some of the kids had climbed in with the wounded. He decided to let pass the deviation from his stated protocol.

From here P.K. walked over to the militia and took his place at the end of the formation. He would proceed from here on foot. Knight climbed up to the wagon seat and took the reigns. McMurdy and Shirts took similar charge of their wagons.

The women and children kissed and hugged their husbands and then proceeded toward the exit gates. Ahead of them the teamsters started their teams. As the procession began there was still an air of excitement throughout the camp. There was also awareness that there was a long journey on foot ahead of them.

Uneasiness came over the men as they watched their families leave ahead of them. Their concerns not to let them get too far ahead made it a little easier to place their guns and rifles in the third wagon so they could proceed after them. Lee and Fancher helped with this task by taking the weapons as they were handed them and placing them as gently as time would allow on the floorboards of the wagon.

The Poteet brothers and John Beach fell into line. Fancher and a couple of others close by noticed Jeremy give a little tug on his carbine before surrendering it to Fancher. Fancher nodded, acknowledging Jeremy's simultaneous protest and compliance. Lee observed the nonverbal communication without response.

While the men passed through the gates one at a time, an armed Mormon sentry and his backup took their positions alongside their Gentile. Mathew Fancher was the last of the immigrants to vacate. The immigrants who had traveled so far with dreams of a new and fruitful life were separated from all possessions except what they could carry in their hands or on their backs. They knew that the savages overlooking their departure would soon plunder all they could not carry.

Lee mounted up and followed Carl Shirts' armament wagon, leaving the wagon fortress deserted along the meandering creek in the grassy meadow.

As the procession wound its way along Mogatsu Creek and headed north to the Old Spanish Trail, everyone looked back, if only for a short glance, at the sight of the carnage they were leaving behind. A dozen of the immigrants were buried inside the compound. A good number of the horses and oxen lie bloating in the sun. Close to forty wagons had been tipped over or sunken in wheel trenches dug to provide protection from the snipers that had positioned themselves behind the rock outcroppings they now strolled past.

The scene was an obvious testament to the immigrants' struggle for survival. Leaving the protection the bulwarks had provided was disconcerting, but this was overcome by the anticipation of having possibly succeeded in their effort. The Mormons were tangled in anticipation as well, but of a much different kind.

CHAPTER 44

TEMPLE SQUARE
SALT LAKE CITY
UTAH TERRITORY

SEPTEMBER 9, 1857
7:30 AM

The Prophet had been up well over an hour by the time he reached the front porch of Hosea Stout's house. Although his wives were awake, Hosea was not. His fifth plural wife Lucretia answered the door graciously, welcoming Brigham Young into the home, and led him to a comfortable chair at the kitchen table.

"Can I offer you some breakfast, President Young?" the coy young woman asked. She was barely sixteen years old and showing with child. Her full, firm breasts did not escape the notice of the patriarch, who already had children her senior. She threw her shoulders back, not willing to miss an opportunity to reveal her womanhood. There is a saying among polygamist wives, "Would you rather have 100 percent of a 10-percent man, or 10 percent of a 100-percent man?" Lucretia was standing in front of a 100-percent man, and she knew it.

"No thank you, dear. I've already had breakfast. I'm so sorry to trouble you so early, but I have a pressing need to speak with Brother Stout." The Prophet liked pregnant women. He found them especially attractive early on, and this one was quite comely.

"Well of course you've already eaten. A man with your responsibilities must be served his morning meal whenever he desires it." With an admiring and unintimidated smile, she turned to leave the room to notify her husband that the Prophet himself was waiting to speak with him.

The Prophet was impressed with the young woman's easy banter. Many of the young ones became overly shy upon first meeting him, especially when receiving little or no notice. As the shapely young brunette sashayed from the room, he wondered how Hosea had managed to sneak this one past him. Looking back before disappearing from the doorway, she caught his admiring gaze and didn't seem to be at all surprised or displeased by it. "He'll be with you shortly, President Young."

Young had routinely greeted the new church converts as they arrived in Salt Lake City from their long and arduous journey. Aside from providing a well-deserved and climactic reception to their weary pilgrimage, he obtained the side benefit of getting the pick of the litter when it came to plural wives. Heber Kimball and he had shared this responsibility since the first year of the Saints' settling in the Salt Lake Valley. Young had been sealed to forty-seven plural wives in the past fifteen years, many in this manner. Kimball had more wives, but Young was more discerning and prideful when it came to assessing and securing prime female stock.

The majority of these unions had not worked out for one reason or another. The Prophet was never able to keep more than nineteen of them under one roof at a time. That wasn't going to keep him from trying again, however. There were always other roofs in other locations for housing them.

Within moments it was obvious Lucretia had sounded the alarm, as several of Hosea's other wives began to scurry about in an obvious attempt to assist their husband in preparing himself for an impromptu but very important meeting. The Prophet liked the deference and special attention women extended him. Even though he apologized for causing them to deviate from their normal routines, he actually reveled in the benefits that came with his most exalted position.

But Young especially liked to sneak up and embarrass his subordinates, as he had done this morning with Stout. For any man in this country it would be a given that normal wakeup was a good hour before sunrise. Stout would be embarrassed being caught in bed at this late hour of the morning, especially to be caught lazy by the Prophet.

When Hosea Stout stepped into the kitchen to greet his most important client, he could see that Lucretia had the president well entertained. She had coaxed him into having a slice of apple pie she had just taken out of the oven. The Prophet rarely deviated from a boring diet of bread and milk. A stickler for routine and self-discipline, women were the only indulgence he just couldn't resist.

"Why here's the lucky man right now." Young was eager to commence his business with the Mormon attorney. But he would not forget his manners toward such a fetching young lady.

Stout blushed as he entered his kitchen and saw the Mormon leader seated in the chair routinely assigned to him. The obviousness of his having slept in was apparent to everyone in the room. "I hope the women offered you some breakfast." He launched into quick recovery mode hoping to render his tardiness forgotten.

"I'm sorry to intrude on your morning, Brother Stout, but I have some important business to discuss with you and I was hoping you would walk and chat with me while I head over to the tithing office." Young was not really sorry, just maintaining his mannerly disposition for the observing women, especially for Lucretia.

"Why certainly, President Young. It would be my honor." Stout was laying it on a bit now.

"Dear Hosea, it's Brother Young to you. And please ask your lovely wives to address me in that manner as well." He included the others out of politeness, but it was really Lucretia he was offering the privilege.

As Young placed his hand on Stout's back and began to follow him out the back door from the kitchen, he smiled and winked at Lucretia much like a father would a daughter. The young radiant woman blushed as she smiled back, but eye contact remained unbroken for a second or two longer than would have been normally appropriate.

The amply experienced womanizer had not misinterpreted the message, obvious only to the two of them. He'd fielded such nonverbal communiqués many times before from many other women.

The Prophet couldn't help but think of a tactic his predecessor used to employ when confronted with similar situations. "Surely there must be some far-off mission I could send Stout off to."

Joseph Smith, the church founder, had employed such maneuvers before the Saints emigrated from Nauvoo. Then Young remembered another of Smith's teachings to him and the other apostles. "Whenever I see a beautiful woman, I pray for grace."

He quickly wiped from his mind the thought of sending Stout on a mission. "Hosea's too important a counselor. Right now I need him here." The Prophet closed the door behind them and proceeded with the Mormon lawyer toward the tithing house. As a man of grace, Young was no match for the original Prophet of the LDS Church. Pragmatics, not grace, was the strength Brigham Young brought as the leader of his people.

Once in the middle of the street, the Prophet turned around and looked Stout square in the face. He was in plain view of passersby who were using the boardwalks along the side. But he was far enough from them they would not be able to hear what he and Stout were discussing.

"As you may be aware, Brother Hyde has recently returned from Carson Valley ahead of his contingent of Saints from that settlement. He believes a spy by the name of Yates has been working with the Gentile army and procuring supplies for Johnston's troops. I'd like you to meet with Brother Hyde to determine a course of action." Young was all business now that he was out of proximity of the buxom Lucretia.

"Are you thinking you'd like me to handle him like I did Bill Hibbard back in Nauvoo?" Stout knew the Prophet would remember how he had knocked the suspected mobocrat spy senseless with a rock while holding the position of chief of police. The incident happened some ten years prior, and the action had encouraged Hibbard, upon his recovery, to relocate to an area more tolerable to both himself and the Saints.

"Actually I was thinking of something even more permanent than what you offered Mr. Hibbard." The Prophet looked around to be sure no one was in range of hearing.

Stout fell into silence. He had always been a loyal servant to the church and especially to its prophets. However, he'd worked hard over the years to elevate his status by engaging in challenging academic study aimed at practicing more diplomatic negotiations on their behalf.

Young could see the look of concern on the younger man's face. "Look, I certainly don't expect you to be the one bouncing the rocks off this double-dealer's head. Get Brother Hickman on it. You've become far too valuable and sophisticated to be getting your hands dirty with this man's ilk." The Prophet was good at reading people.

Hosea breathed a sigh of relief. "I'll talk to Brother Hyde immediately and assist him in any way possible."

"That's a good man. Be sure to give me any report on your progress. Things have been happening fast lately. Information is power, you know." Young patted Hosea on the back as the two men parted ways.

CHAPTER 45

VIRGIN RIVER GORGE
NORTHWEST NEW
MEXICO TERRITORY

SEPTEMBER 18, 1857
6:00 PM

Thales Haskell and James Mathews escorted Henry and Cao upstream a ways and began helping them unpack and stake out areas for their bed-rolls. Mathews tried to shift the conversation to small talk in hopes of postponing a more discomforting dialogue.

"It won't do no good to offer ta help Ira with the buryin'. He jus' won't have it. When he kills a man, he's the one who's gonna do the buryin'. It's like a matter of pride or respect or somethin'." As his voice trailed off he looked at Haskell and could tell his partner was unimpressed with his effort to engage in small talk.

"What James is tryin' ta say, is Ira is a man of the Lord an' he believes in bein' respectful to the lives of all men on earth." Haskell wasn't entirely comfortable with his explanation, but he felt it was an improvement over Mathews'.

"Did he bury Able Baker too?" Cao just couldn't resist. He'd already made up his mind that Milum was the truth teller and that Ira Hatch and his comrades were most likely up to something unimaginably wrong. Like Henry, Cao didn't think he had anything to fear from these two.

Meanwhile Henry was drilling Cao with his eyes. Letting these two know too much of what Milum had told them was a dangerous path.

One glance from his big brother and Cao knew it was time to shut his big mouth.

"Was that the name of the fella at Cottonwood Springs? Able Baker?" Haskell was good at knowing when to open the door for more information.

Henry jumped into damage-control mode. "He said he'd been travelin' with two fellas, one named Cameron and the other he kept referring to as Able. Cameron got picked off early on by some Injuns. Able and Milum were wounded at the same time up the trail from here. He claimed he had to leave Able behind. Bad leg wound. Seemed to bother him quite a bit, havin' ta leave his friend behind. Gave him some trouble ta talk about it."

Henry, like Cao, was giving up more information than was prudent, and he knew it. The difference was he wasn't going to put it out there in an antagonizing manner. Like his younger brother, he was pretty certain he was in the custody of men who had killed both of Milum's friends, and possibly a good many others. He wanted to see how Haskell and Mathews would respond to the information he was serving up.

"There was three, as far as we could tell. An' the Lamanites did kill the fella early on. The Gentiles kilt a couple of the Injuns too. An' then there was the poisoning of the Lamanites up at Corn Creek. That's what got it started I s'pose. Hopefully, when the word gets back about that one Ira's diggin' for, it will put a stop to all the killin' for a while." Haskell felt guilty promoting a story he knew was a lie. But the conversation was getting sticky again and he needed a reasonable way to bring it to an end.

Like Hatch, Haskell had joined the Fancher train at Corn Creek, but posing as an apostate Mormon seeking to leave the territory. His purpose was to determine the Gentile defense capabilities and any personal information about their attitude toward the Saints. Because of this he knew the rumors of the Gentiles making threats aimed at the Saints were in fact . . . rumors.

"So you boys is joinin' up with the Injuns agin the white man now?" Cao could see where his brother was headed and wanted to help out. He just wasn't as good at this type of thing as Henry was. He could also sense that Haskell was trying to bring the conversation to a close, and Cao wasn't ready for that to happen.

"We have to live amongst the Lamanites here in this territory. There's settlements scattered across Deseret here for three hundred miles in four directions. All of 'em LDS. Every farm and ranch run by Mormon families exposed an' out in the open. Any one of 'em no match for the savage tribes. We've worked hard for ten years to be on good terms with these Lamanites. If we have to join up with 'em once in a while to take care of some murderin' Gentiles to keep them from turnin' on us, then that's what I expect we'll do." Thales was fired up. He'd gone farther than either he or James wanted to go with the conversation. But he was getting close to the truth, and it made him feel a little better about the situation they found themselves in.

Cao and Henry didn't say any more. They just resumed preparations for the night's camp by continuing to unpack and lay out their things. Both men had heard enough to chew on for some time. Perhaps it was best to keep the remainder of their thoughts to themselves for a while. Haskell and Mathews were thinking the same thing.

CHAPTER 46

MOUNTAIN MEADOWS
UTAH TERRITORY

SEPTEMBER 11, 1857
11:45 AM

As the convoy proceeded northward along the Old Spanish Trail, several of the immigrants unsurprisingly turned to their would-be rescuers and attempted to strike up conversations. For some of the militiamen, this proved to present a more awkward situation than it did for others.

Those on horseback kept themselves busy directing the evacuation. The women had no pedestrian escort and were intent on keeping up with the wounded and small children riding in wagons ahead of them. The wagon teamsters had a similar justification for not engaging in small talk with their human cargo. The majority of their passengers were not in a very talkative mood, being in such pain and discomfort at having to be jostled about.

The immigrant men, having each to walk side by side with at least two militiamen, began a natural effort to establish a rapport with those now presumably guarding their well-being.

Though Mathew Fancher was the last to take his position at the end of the procession, he was the first to endeavor to bridge the divide with his escorts . . . the bishop of Cedar City backed up by Pvt. James Pearce.

"I'd generally say it's a nice day for a long walk. How long do you think it'll take us to get to Cedar City?" He knew they'd not be able to complete the trek until sometime the next day and was in reality wondering where they'd be camping out and how susceptible they'd be to attack.

"I reckon we'll be in Cedar sometime around mid-day tomorrow if we can keep everyone movin'." P.K. was still having a difficult time making eye contact with his charge and knew his dilemma might arouse doubts. Though he sensed where Fancher was headed, he thought it best to keep his answers short until he could gain some composure.

"You think these redskins trailin' us will leave us alone tonight?" He figured the man next to him would understand his worry.

"They'll have to come through us to get at you and your folks. Once't we settle in for the night I 'spect the major will return your arms to you." Listening to himself lie, P.K. found it more difficult to converse, instead of easier as he'd hoped. He was also conscious of the men within earshot of their discourse. James Pearce was right next to him; Joseph F. Smith and William Edwards were both near enough to hear the exchange between the Gentile leader and their bishop.

It was one thing to speak in support of treachery, but a more difficult one to actually perform it in front of the very men who respected you. Was it his imagination, or could P.K. feel their high regard of him sinking like a stone?

"You appear to hold some rank amongst your people." Fancher was satisfied, so far, with the answers he'd been receiving. Time to test the authenticity of his escort.

"I hold no rank in the militia here, but I'm the bishop of Cedar City stake."

"I expect that still makes you a leader. We've been in big need of a Christian influence lately. We're sure obliged for whatever sway you've had in helping us out here." Fancher was watching P.K.'s reaction closely.

P.K. let this last commentary fall flat. He could not think of a suitable response that would not prove to the others how duplicitous he'd actually become. Lying was something P.K. was not used to doing. This was a bad time to find out he was not very good at it.

"We'll do our best to repay you for the peril and sacrifice you and yer men have undertaken on our account. In spite of all we've lost, the folks in our outfit are well known for paying their markers." Fancher sensed a discomfort in P.K. and interpreted it as a possible aggravation . . . or was it alarm?

Again P.K. could not find words with which to respond, and still he could not bring himself to look at the man.

"When we get back to Arkansas, I'm gonna have ta tell all the folks I see that you Latter-day Saints is as fine a group of Christians as I've ever run across. I've known plenty of fair-weather Christians who would have just stayed home rather than to risk comin' out into a dog-fight like this one we got ourselves into here."

Pearce and Edwards glanced around at the bishop, curious of his reaction to the Gentile's observation and commentary. They quickly looked away. P.K. continued walking. He was wondering how much longer it would be before Higbee would sound his order. He deeply dreaded and longed for the signal at the same time.

"Was there some kind of council gathering held at Cedar City before the militia was ordered to come out here and help us?" Fancher was beginning to feel uncomfortable with the one-sidedness of the exchange he was having with the bishop.

"There was a council meeting." That was as far as P.K. could go. It was an awkward terseness that ended his reply. The council meeting was held more than a week ago, and the vast majority of those in attendance had voted for the annihilation of the entire immigrant party. These facts were particulars P.K. could not allow Fancher to hear. "Higbee's command better come soon," he thought.

"Is there anything you can tell me? My people are gonna need to know something of where they stand with your folks once they get back to Cedar." Fancher was looking intently at the bishop now. He was acutely aware of the man's unwillingness or incapacity to look him in the eye. Something wasn't right.

Pearce, Edwards, and Smith were each glancing back at the two leaders sporadically and thereby escalating the intensity of the uneasiness. P.K. continued to put one foot in front of the other, looking at the even ground in front of him as if he needed to be cautious not to stumble on God knows what.

Finally Fancher had had enough. He took two steps forward and one to his right as if to insert himself in front of his escort. The action brought P.K., Pearce, and Edwards to a halt as the four men stopped, facing one another. A few steps more and Smith and a couple of men ahead of him noticed the change and turned to look back as well.

Mathew Fancher recalled the fleeting look of fear on Major Lee's face earlier that morning when he'd grabbed the reigns of his horse to thank him. Now he was staring intently into P.K.'s face as if to dare him to look him in the eye. "You're not going to help us, are you? What Mr. Lee told us about providin' safe passage isn't true, is it?"

P.K. had no alternative but to look up into the man's eyes. He could see that any additional deception was not going to work with this man. Panic and dread gripped his soul for several very long seconds. His lie was exposed as if he'd confessed the details of his complicity before God himself . . . without having to say a word. Then he heard the call.

"Halt! Do your duty to Israel." It was Higbee's signal.

As Fancher glanced up the line with a look of enraged betrayal in his eyes, P.K. swiftly raised his handgun and fired directly into the man's torso. The explosion cracked like a nearby bolt of lightning and was followed by the deafening roar of at least forty other rounds letting loose almost simultaneously.

As the smoke from his weapon cleared from before his vision, all he could perceive was that the man no longer stood before him. He had fallen, but the man of God could not glance down at what he'd done. Making eye contact with the man alive had been difficult. Looking down at his lifeless body was not now possible.

CHAPTER 47

SALT LAKE CITY
UTAH TERRITORY

SEPTEMBER 10, 1857
10:00 AM

Hosea Stout liked dealing with the stern-faced Orson Hyde even less than he did the Prophet when Brigham Young was in a bad mood. Hyde was always in a bad mood, it seemed. There was always someone in need of a good thrashing, and it didn't matter if it was an apostate or a Gentile. He seemed to think the majority of the Saints were perpetually on the verge of apostasy and therefore in constant need of being whipped back into line. The Gentiles deserved one just because the Saints were going to have to undertake the unpleasant task of cutting all their throats someday anyway. Orson Hyde hated Gentiles.

Hyde reminded Stout of "Brigham's Sledge Hammer," Jedediah Grant. Grant had led the Saints in the Reformation movement initiated by Young earlier in 1856. He had railed from the pulpit against the Saints' sinfulness and filthiness for six months, until in December of the previous year when he'd abruptly died. Typhoid fever was the official reported cause. However, some tended to whisper that Grant had succumbed to the administering of an offended Saint of high status who also possessed the skills of an apothecary.

Stout was not sorry to see him go either. There were some who suspected that Hosea had done the poisoning. He didn't mind when the church's religious leaders chastised the brethren as long as they didn't include him in the mix. He'd been around long enough that he felt deserving of more respectful treatment.

Hyde was one of those who was aware of his seniority over others and was going to make sure they were aware of it too. It was with this mindset that Hosea stepped up to the apostle's door and gently rapped.

The stern-faced religious leader opened the door and said, "Come in. We've got an unpleasant task to perform." He turned and walked into his foyer expecting Elder Stout to follow, which he did.

True to form Hyde offered no refreshments or hospitality of any kind. He forbade any of his wives to show their faces whenever any visitor crossed over their threshold. The only exception he would make to this rule was for Heber Kimball or the Prophet himself.

Hyde had had an unpleasant experience once when, on a mission to Israel, the Prophet Joseph Smith Jr. had used his wife as his own while Hyde was away. Referred to as the "American Mohammed" by the Gentile press, Smith had made no apologies for the indiscretion. He simply handed Marinda Hyde back to her sealed husband upon his return to Zion. No record of any further discussion of the matter would ever be revealed.

"I suppose the Prophet told you about that Gentile scoundrel Yates. Supplyin' beef cattle, ammunition, and horses to our enemies, who'd hang us if they could. Then he rides in to our religious refuge, big as life, and commences to throw his money around looking for drink and company like we was the bordello capital of the West."

Stout could sense that Hyde was in a particularly bad mood. What he didn't know was that Hyde had recently been swindled by a Gentile in the Carson Valley when he'd complied with Young's order to "sell all" and return to Salt Lake City. Hyde had taken a meager down payment in his haste to leave the area, and it was beginning to look like his remaining proceeds would not now be forthcoming. Stout sensed he'd need to tread lightly. "What evidence do we have against this Yates fellow that he's been spying?"

"Why he isn't makin' any pretense that he's not. He's been down at the Globe Inn the past three days braggin' about makin' a big sale to Johnston's army. He sure isn't a Saint, the way he uses profanity even in the company of the sisters that do the serving over there. I think you're takin' your law-yerin' studies a little too seriously if you're gonna start asking me to produce evidence." Hyde looked at Hosea as if perhaps he might be the wrong man for what he intended.

"What course of action do you propose we take with respect to this Mr. Yates?" Stout had learned over the years that it was usually best to let his superiors suggest courses of action rather than offer his own.

"The man needs to be put out of the way, Hosea. My proposal is that you find out when he intends to head back General Johnston's way so we can make the proper arrangements to get that done." Hyde locked into Hosea's eyes as if he would not be letting go until he received a satisfactory response.

"I'll head over to the Globe Inn and see what I can find out. I'll let you know as soon as I have something." Stout nodded his complicity to go along.

"That's a boy. We'll teach these Gentiles to be a little more respectful when they think to tread upon our Zion." Hyde got up and proceeded to walk Stout to the door.

Stout thought he might have seen a brief smile purse the grizzled man's lips as he finished his statement about Zion. But then he realized it was no such thing.

As he was about to be ushered out the door Stout remembered to ask Hyde about the third man engaged with their "unpleasant task." "The Prophet mentioned something about Brother Hickman getting involved?"

"Ah yes, our shepherd dog with sharp teeth. He's been working with Lot Smith in our attempt to frustrate and delay Johnston's army from entering the valley. It's very likely Mr. Yates will be heading in their direction once he leaves town. Brother Hickman is very good at taking care of this kind of business. He will be involved if the Lord delivers Mr. Yates into our power at the right place and time." Hyde actually did smile this time, though it was very brief.

As Hosea Stout passed through the door and back onto the street, he did so with a very mixed set of feelings. He was relieved to be parting ways with the contentious apostle. However, Bill Hickman was one of the few men in the territory he actually feared. For years he'd been diligent about avoiding contact with the notorious Danite. Though Stout had committed his own list of less-than-civil services on behalf of the church, his exploits could not, and would never, match Hickman's.

CHAPTER 48

VIRGIN RIVER GORGE
NORTHWEST NEW
MEXICO TERRITORY

SEPTEMBER 17, 1857
5:30 AM

The brothers had slept poorly, each taking turns keeping watch over the other throughout the night. They'd been allowed to go off far enough from their captors that they could whisper to one another freely without fear of being overheard. Milum's abrupt execution continued to flood their thoughts. Henry tried to keep their discussion focused on the challenges that lay ahead.

"If they were going to kill us I think they would have just plugged us both and buried us here in the soft sand long side of Milum. What I don't understand is why they want us to alter our route north and put us on a trail we're not familiar with." Henry had some ideas why, but he was looking for some corroboration from his little brother.

"It's either because they don't want us to see what's goin' on up north, or they plan on killin' us up ahead somewhere . . . maybe makin' it look like an accident." Cao had begun to think the worst about the Saints.

"I 'spect yer right about not wantin' us ta see what's goin' on up north. If they route us all the way up to the headwaters of the Sevier River like they're sayin', we'll get back onto the Spanish Trail well north of Cedar City. That'd be at least fifty or sixty miles north a where Milum said his folks was surrounded." Henry waited for Cao's protest.

"I say we give 'em the slip first chance we get an' go in a direction that suits what's best fer us." Cao waited for Henry to expose his motive.

"Now don't be lettin' yer wish ta see that Anderson girl cloud yer thinkin'. We could wind up like Milum over there real easy if we don't watch out." Henry wasn't as negative as Cao might have expected him to be.

"I'd like ta talk to the bishop about all this, Henry. We got a lot of unanswered questions an' he's the only Saint I know that I believe might be able to give us the answers." Getting close to Molly Anderson was working on Cao too. He just wasn't conscious of how much he wanted to see her.

Molly Anderson was invading Cao's mind more and more persistently of late. Though his desire to pursue the Mormon priesthood was gone, his desire for Molly had only increased. He needed to see her and find out if his change of heart was going to be a factor in her future desire for him.

"How do you know Bishop Klingensmith isn't gonna line up with Hatch an' his boys?" They needed a friend, but where in this hard land, almost completely controlled by Mormons and Indians, were they going to find one?

"I don't know. But if these fellas aren't gonna kill us, I doubt the bishop will want to be givin' that order."

Just then they heard Thales Haskell call out, "We'll have somethin' fer you boys ta eat in a few minutes. Coffee's ready now."

As the brothers slipped on their boots, Henry said to Cao, "Let's not be takin' any chances by tryin' ta give 'em the slip. I think we're safe as long as they see us as cooperatin' with 'em."

* * *

Only whites were assembled around the campfire. The Indians were stationed at various locations upstream and down from their position. They were engaged in their own morning rituals. Ira had sent Rosmus Anderson downstream quite some distance with orders to signal the advance of any traveler in their direction. Ira still did not want the brothers and Rosmus to have anything to do with each other. During the trauma of Milum's killing, the brothers had not noticed Anderson's presence, as he had theirs.

The brothers strode into camp and each accepted a tin of coffee from Thales Haskell. Ira Hatch motioned for the brothers to sit on the only empty log available.

"I 'spect you boys have some questions. Now's the time ta ask em." Hatch was all business. This was his usual whenever he assumed to speak, which was seldom.

"My brother and I was wonderin' why we just couldn't head north with yer party instead of havin' ta foller a route we're not familiar with?" Henry chose to pose the question before his brother posed it in a more demanding sort of way.

"There's a number of good reasons. One of 'em is that I'm not gonna be headin' north from here fer some time. My home is just a mile or so up the Santa Clara from here and my intentions is ta go there an' stay fer a spell. Once Thales an' James complete their escort of you boys to the Narrows, they'll be doin' the same as me since they live near where I do. So you'd be on yer own passin' through a hostile area. I don't like yer odds in makin' it through."

"As far as the trail goes, once you start up the Narrows, you won't have any trouble followin' the trail. You'll see soon enough that there ain't no other way to go. You just follow the Virgin to its headwaters; go over a hump and yer in the headwaters that drain into the Sevier. You just foller it down until you reconnect with the Spanish Trail. Any other questions?"

"Suppose we decide we want ta take our chances an' just head north from here and go up the way we're used to?" Cao just couldn't help himself.

Hatch looked at Cao and paused. Since Hatch meant what he was about to say, he leaned forward a bit and took his time saying it.

"I'm only gonna say this once. It ain't somethin' I'm willin' ta argue with you boys about. Thales and James here are gonna escort you boys up the Virgin to the start of the Narrows. Two of the Santa Clara tribe will be goin' along. Their people have a camp there, and there is usually anywhere between twenty and thirty braves there this time of year. I'm sendin' a message along with 'em to tell their chief that if he sees the two of you come out of the Narrows once you've gone in, to bring me both yer scalps.

"Now every one of these braves here with us wants to kill you because they know yer Gentiles. Once you get into the Narrows they won't follow. A bunch of there people was washed away in a flood years ago. Since then it's 'bad medicine' to go into the Narrows as far as they're concerned.

"Now you boys have a choice to make. an' that choice is to accept the escort I'm providin', or I'll turn these Lamanite savages loose on you right here and now." The conversation was over as far as Ira Hatch was concerned. A long silent pause ensued.

"I reckon my brother and I will be takin' you up on that offer of an escort." Henry looked at Cao with a look that told him he was speaking for both of them and he better not add anything to it.

CHAPTER 49

MOUNTAIN MEADOWS
UTAH TERRITORY

SEPTEMBER 11, 1857
11:55 AM

In an instant the Mormon bishop knew he'd made a terrible mistake. The panic and anguish he'd felt only moments before were replaced by a despair more trenchant than any he'd ever known. How would he ever tolerate himself, now that he'd committed treacherous murder?

Momentarily he thought of looking down at the object of his shame. He spun to his right to avoid the truth of it. His eyes met those of Pvt. Pearce.

Though shaken, the young man looked back at P.K. with wide frightened eyes. He had not fired his weapon. He had not had to. P.K. had completed the order for both of them. He began to stagger and then sat quickly on the ground. Pearce buried his face in his hands and began to cry.

P.K. had not taken a breath for what seemed an eternity, but was in reality only about ten seconds. The suffocation was more than he could bear. Nausea overcame him as he knelt to expel the contents of his stomach. He needed relief but it was not forthcoming. The nausea remained.

Then he remembered the children. He still had a job to do. It was a job that was not steeped in treachery, but that held some possibility of recovery. It was the lifeline his soul was in need of. He needed to find a path away from the horror he'd made. P.K. began to walk forward again, up the trail.

As he proceeded, his eyes were met with new horrors worse than he could imagine. He passed Joseph F. Smith, who didn't seem at all affected as P.K. had been. Joseph examined the body of the man that lay before him for signs of life, and then began checking his pockets. His ambitious detachment in the face of the grisly scene would serve him well in the years to come.

Capt. Joel White, Commander of Co. D. of the Cedar City militia, was busy barking orders to his men. "Check their breathing. Be sure the job is finished. Save yer ammunition. Use yer knives."

A few of Captain White's men had reacted like young Pvt. Pearce and were sitting down looking at the carnage with disbelief. But most were staying busy completing their bloody work. Capt. John Higbee had dismounted and was closing on a wounded man who seemed to recognize him. He was apparently an apostate who had tried to escape the territory by hitching a ride with this ill-fated company.

"I wouldn't do this to you, Higbee," the man struggled to shout. He was kneeling in severe pain, having been gut-shot.

"You would have done the same to me or just as bad!" was Higbee's cold retort. He then grabbed the man by his hair and cut his throat. For years Higbee's action here at Mountain Meadows would be debated among the brethren. Some would defend his work as humane, and as an act of "blood atonement" by which the apostate would be eligible for salvation in the hereafter. Others would vilify his action as one of the most brutal deeds committed at Mountain Meadows. It would not come close to being that.

When Nephi Johnson heard the volley of weapons fire, he'd given the command for the Indians and a few of his brethren to attack the women and children. It was his job to make sure the Lamanites spared the "Innocent Blood"; that being those children deemed too young to talk. He would only be partly successful.

As P.K. approached Nephi's position, the carnage was still taking place. Enos, the notorious "Free Booter," seemed engaged in his work with a relish Lucifer himself would find tasteless. With a look of excited glee this mercenary's tomahawk came crashing down on one skull after another. The age of the victim seemed of little importance to him. After striking down two or three in proximity, he would quickly remove their scalps. After rubbing their bloody naps on his chest while issuing curdling war hoops, he would proceed again in search of his next set of trophies.

One of Enos' victims began to regain consciousness after the blood-thirsty savage had moved on. William C. Stewart rode up to her and dismounted. He grabbed her by the neck as she struggled to her feet. He looked into her dazed eyes before he plunged his bowie knife deep into her chest. From P.K.'s viewpoint it did not look anything like an act of mercy. Nothing he was seeing looked like anything he'd ever seen before.

The other mounted riders were busy now too. Dudley Leavitt chased down some of the faster runners. Those he could not hack down with his sword, due to their cowering low to the ground, he would dispatch with his revolver. Adjutant Daniel Macfarlane was equally proficient and much more cool about it. His expressionless demeanor was one P.K. would not forget.

Lt. Oscar Hamblin was one in Nephi's group. His brother owned the rights to these meadows, and perhaps he felt somewhat more justified in defending them from these Gentile intruders. Wearing war paint like his Indian friends and with only his knife as a weapon, one after another he tore at the younger women's clothing, ripping them mostly from their bodies before mercifully dispatching the women with his knife across their throats.

P.K. was drawn to an infant that was still being clutched in the dying arms of its mother. He gently pried loose the mother's hands as she faded into an unconsciousness caused by wounds from which she could never recover. He proceeded to the lead wagons where he knew the other small children would be. P.K. would never know that the child was Zabrina Jones, the daughter of Eloah Angeline and John Milum Jones.

As he approached another scene of mayhem, he heard the bleating screams of anguish from mostly young children. Lee, McMurdy, and Knight were completing the dispatch of the wounded captains Fancher and Baker and several of the other wounded adults who had been mixed in with five or so children. They used rifles to shoot their victims through the open backs of the wagons until only children remained alive. P.K. heard McMurdy shout, "Oh Lord, my God, receive their spirits, for it is for thy kingdom that I do this."

By the time P.K. arrived with the infant in his arms, the three were dragging the bodies from the wagon and checking for signs of life in full view of the children. Their horrified little faces looked on, and they were overcome with hysteria over the ghoulish scene unfolding before them. P.K. tried to place himself in front of the terrified children so as to block their view of the indignity and the horror. He was suddenly furious at the blatant insensitivity, but his fury went unnoticed by his Mormon brethren. Then he remembered his own dealing with young Matt Fancher.

One of the older girls, with tears streaming down her cheeks, reached out to take the infant from P.K.'s arms. He allowed the kindness. He didn't know it, but the sadness evident on his face told the girl he was not to be feared. For the first time since he'd arrived inside the immigrant wagon fortress, he felt almost human. Though the feeling would be short-lived, it gave him the strength he needed to remain focused on doing what needed to be done.

Lt. Carl Shirts, the third teamster carrying the weapons, pulled his team into position behind the other wagons. P.K. quickly motioned him to pull his wagon around the one being unloaded by Lee and the other two teamsters, and into a position to block the view of the children. Shirts was puzzled and oblivious to what P.K. was trying to accomplish, but he quickly complied with the bishop's hand signals.

P.K. then saw Pvt. James Pearce step from behind Shirts' wagon. He could see that Pearce had only partly recovered. His bewildered look belied his having viewed some of the same ghastly scenes P.K. had just walked past. He motioned for the young man to approach. Grabbing him by the shoulder he shouted, "Do you think you can handle this team?"

The private nodded.

"Then get up there and grab the reigns, and when I tell you, you head this team on up the road to Hamblin's place." P.K. was intent on improving this ugly situation as quickly as possible.

Pearce did as he was told and was somewhat relieved to have something constructive to do. P.K. immediately turned to the other children, one of whom had suffered an ugly arm wound, and began to usher them into the wagon containing the majority of the children. Once he had the twenty tearstained faces assembled as best he could, he intended to mount his horse and order Pearce to proceed. But he would not be quick enough.

By now almost all the firing had ceased. The men of the immigrant party had all been dispatched early on. There had been less than thirty of them that had survived the initial attack and subsequent siege several days prior. Today, these remaining unarmed men stood no chance against the well-trained and equipped sixty-odd-man militia.

The thirty-five or so mature women, and the forty-five or so boys and girls, were the target of Nephi's men and the Lamanites. Only about forty or so Indians, mostly from Chief Jackson's tribe, remained at the Meadows by the time Higbee gave his "Halt" order. Nephi and his war-painted

men were only about ten in number. Though their blood lust propelled
them, the fifty-odd attackers had their hands full chasing down eighty-odd
women and children who were literally running for their lives.

The mounted riders performed their duties soundly as their terrified
prey scattered west, south, and north. They had the south and west sides
well covered. Some of the older kids, and most of the mothers of the young
children in the wagons, chose to run north. Some of these made it the far-
thest. Now several began to approach the area of the wagons and the men
struggling with the disposition of the wounded.

Nephi's contingent of painted Saints and Lamanites had dispatched
the older women and the boys most quickly. The younger, more attractive women were not all so fortunate. William Stewart and Pvt. William
Edwards had caught up with two young girls, Lucinda and Susannah
Dunlap, obvious twins who looked to be about fifteen. The men positioned
themselves so that the girls knew there was no longer any chance of escape.
They immediately began to beg for their lives.

"Please, we'll do anything," cried Lucinda, her hands clasped in front
of her as she faced Stewart as if praying to God himself. The gesture only
encouraged the wicked Saint with the blood-stained hands.

"Then take off yer clothes," shouted Stewart, with an eager sneering
grin on his face.

The terrified sisters looked at one another with desperation. As Lucinda
began to disrobe, Susannah followed suit. She had had a good upbringing
and she wasn't going to allow her twin to suffer the humiliation alone.

Several members of the Pinto and Fort Clara contingents of legion-
naires (Nephi's men) began to gather around. William Slade, John W.
Clark, Richard Robinson, and Prime Coleman positioned themselves so
as to form somewhat of a circle around the girls to get a better view. Amos
Thornton, Albert Hamlin, William Slade Sr., and Oscar Hamblin soon
joined the gallery of spectators. Most of these men sported menacing
bloodstains on their hands and clothing.

"Now dance!" demanded Stewart.

Their dignity having been literally stripped from them, the girls began
to perform a rudimentary form of prancing about with the hope of spar-
ing what was left of their shattered lives. Just then Nephi Johnson stormed
into the circle and looked directly at Stewart. Somehow he had known that
Stewart was the instigator behind the macabre ritual being forced onto the
two teens.

"Did we come here for this purpose? Is this the duty our Lord calls us to?" Johnson was furious with all the men surrounding him. He was furious with himself. But he focused his fury on Stewart.

Stewart simply shrugged, walked up to Susannah, the girl closest to him, grabbed her by the hair, and cut her throat. Lucinda screamed and ran over to her sister's naked, blood-streaked body as it crumpled into the dirt.

"You said you'd spare us if we . . . ."

Her pathetic blubbering protest was cut short as Stewart straddled over the naked, kneeling girl. He grabbed a handful or her hair, yanked back her head, and cut her throat from ear to ear.

P.K. and the others had been unable to see much of this horrific spectacle due to the crowd of men encircling the exploit. They could only get a sense that something quite wrong was taking place. What occurred next, however, only a stone's throw to west of this episode, was plainly observable and quite another story.

Chief Jackson and his swollen-faced buck brave "Big Bill" ran down a beautiful, young, dark-haired girl of about sixteen years within fifty yards of the parked wagons. It was sixteen-year-old Matilda Tackitt, the young beauty Able Baker had been so smitten by. Big Bill roughly grabbed her from behind, holding her arms. He turned her to face his depraved Chief. Jackson gave her a leering grin before ripping her dress downward in one violent motion, exposing her nakedness for all to see. Oblivious to their audience, Big Bill dragged the bewildered hysterical Tackitt girl to the ground on her back, pinning her arms to the dirt up over her head.

The sneering chief looked toward the men manning the wagons. There was no shame evident on his face. His face held a sinister smile, as if he was going to show these weak-stomached white men how it's done. In one brutal motion, he dropped his knees roughly between her legs, forcing them to spread apart. When he began to untie his leather leggings, the outrage he was about to perform became apparent to P.K. and the others uphill from them.

P.K. reached for the reigns of his horse, hoping he could intervene before any more of the humiliation being forced upon the young woman could transpire. But Lee beat him to it. Covering the distance in the lightning swiftness of about six seconds, he arrived before the brazen chief could obtain his pleasure.

"No!" he shouted, drawing his handgun and pulling back the hammer. He took turns aiming it directly at the chief and then at Big Bill, taunting them as to who would get it first.

The two savages let go of their captive, jumped up, and stepped back from her. Matilda lay there trembling and bewildered. The possibility that she might be spared had not yet begun to sink in. Both Indians had feral looks of surprise and fear in their eyes.

Satisfied that the two were sufficiently cowed for the moment, Lee lowered his pistol and coolly squeezed off one round that entered Miss Tackitt squarely between the eyes.

CHAPTER 50

TEMPLE SQUARE
SALT LAKE CITY
UTAH TERRITORY

SEPTEMBER 15, 1857
7:30 PM

Hosea Stout had made several discreet forays into determining the identity and whereabouts of Mr. Yates. He was ever mindful of not allowing himself to be connected with the marked man. It wasn't difficult. He'd stopped by the Globe Inn a couple of times and generally let his friends tell him what new patrons had shown themselves lately, if any.

The atmosphere had been charged with discussions of General Johnston's army marching on Zion and what the Nauvoo Legion was going to do about it. "Mobocracy" was a term all too familiar to the lexicon of the Saints. It always seemed to lead to their persecution, whether it be in Palmyra, Kirtland, Independence, or Nauvoo. They'd come to Deseret to escape it and had done so for ten years. But mobocracy was on the march again.

There had been mention of the Gentile stock trader who was known to frequent the establishment during the later hours. Richard Yates had seemed oblivious to the concern the Saints might have with him aiding and abetting the enemy.

Like most Gentiles, Yates wasn't taking serious the rumors of Johnston's army actually engaging in a military campaign against U.S. citizens. Nor did he think the Mormons would be foolish enough to provoke them into one. Mormons tended to remain discreet when discussing their concerns with Gentiles. He was content to pass his time in one of the few taverns Brigham Young allowed to exist on the streets of Salt Lake City.

The Globe Inn was owned and operated by David Candland, a Mormon eager to provide information to those he suspected to be in the know. Hosea Stout was one such person. Stout didn't even have to ask Candland for information. He would automatically tell him the latest whenever he frequented his establishment.

Candland liked serving the Gentile patrons of his establishment. They usually had more money to spend than did their Mormon counterparts. He especially liked to report on Gentiles who might express a superior attitude after having had a few beers or glasses of wine. He equated attitudes of superiority with persecutory behavior, and that could only mean one thing: Mobocrats were infiltrating Deseret.

There was a reason Brigham Young allowed such an establishment to exist. The Prophet Smith had revelated against strong drink, and for the most part, Young had perpetuated that doctrine. Brigham Young would boast publicly that he controlled an extraordinarily effective intelligence network throughout Deseret. "Do you know that I have my threads strung all through the territory that I may know what individuals do?" It was often said that "a sparrow could not fall from a tree in all of Deseret without the Prophet knowing about it." Hosea Stout was part of this network. David Candland was as well, although he couldn't be sure.

As Stout took his seat, Candland made his way to his table carrying a mug of Stout's favorite brew. "That Gentile arms dealer I told ya about is in again tonight, shootin' his mouth off about how the Gentiles is gonna civilize us Saints." He whispered as he wiped the table and placed Stout's beverage on it.

Stout looked about as if the intruder were sneaking up.

"He's over in the corner with a couple of other Gentiles new in town. They're throwin' some money around. Especially Yates. He's the tall one with the dark moustache." Candland left as if no words had been exchanged.

"That was easy," thought Stout. He waited a minute and then picked up his glass and began to walk in the direction of the Gentiles. As he passed the innkeeper he said, "I think I'll like the light better over at this table." And he proceeded to the only vacant table near Yates and his friends.

Stout could hear what Yates and his companions were saying without difficulty. It was early in the Globe Inn and quiet. Yates wasn't trying to be discreet.

"I love dealing with the government. Anytime you negotiate with people who are spendin' someone else's money, you're gonna cut a good deal. I pretty much tell 'em what I want, and they hand it over. Oh, sometimes they try to make a show of it. Tell me they can get cattle cheaper from the locals or some such bluff. But they've never let me walk away empty-handed yet. And once the transaction is completed, they ask when I can get back with more and how many. I swear this is the easiest money I've ever made."

Yates had had a few and was enjoying the company of a couple of adventurers from the east who'd entered the territory for the purpose of negotiating a mail contract with the Saints. They'd shared a meal together and feigned interest in what Yates was saying. He appeared to be ready to buy them all another round of drinks.

The Gentiles he was sitting with would negotiate in vain for the mail contract they were seeking. A man named Kimball had purchased it earlier that year. Kimball was actually a "down-on-his-luck" Saint who'd been acting as a shill. They didn't know it but the mail contract they were competing for was already owned. The owners happened to be Brigham Young, Bill Hickman, and Orrin Porter Rockwell. This was a contract the Prophet had every intention of hanging onto.

"When will you be headin' back to Johnston's army?" asked one of diners.

"I have one more delivery to make before the end of the year. I'll probably try to meet up with 'em middle of October somewhere around Bridger or Black's Fork. They're movin' slow on account of all their rolling stock and the road over South Pass bein' so bad. But they should be able to get that far by then." Yates raised his hand to get Candland's attention.

"Barkeep! One more round over here for me an' my friends!" he shouted.

Candland complied immediately and showed no sign of having been offended. But that was only because he didn't want Yates to know.

Stout nursed his beer. Now he would know when to begin his surveillance of Mr. Yates in earnest. In about three weeks he would begin frequenting the Globe Inn consistently. First he would find out where Yates was stabling his horse. Then he would learn how long he had advanced his payments for room and board, and where. If he were doing any banking locally, he would know the extent of it. He would also have a look at any mail Mr. Yates was sending or receiving while in Deseret.

CHAPTER 51

THE NARROWS
UTAH TERRITORY

SEPTEMBER 19, 1857
7:00 PM

They arrived at the mouth of the Narrows near dusk after having traveled through some of the most remarkable country the two brothers had ever seen. After leaving the confluence of the Santa Clara and Virgin rivers the scenery had grown increasingly more dramatic. The first day's ride had been through expansive sweeping valleys bordered distantly by tall vertical cliffs painted in hues of orange and red. The meandering river seized the focal point of this portrait and was lush with large stands of cottonwoods and an array of other foliage. Some of the leaves were presenting the first signs of autumn as they began to alter their color. Areas of meadow grass were plentiful and a welcome change from the infertile desert they had crossed their first hundred miles out of Las Vegas Springs. Casey and Floppy, the two gluttons, demanded frequent stops to fill their hungry bellies.

Henry had passed through the extraordinary rock crevice of the Virgin River Gorge several times and had never ceased to be impressed by it. As their journey progressed through unchartered territory, the gorge would lose its rank as the incomparable geographic phenomenon it had always been for him. They were soon in the midst of what would eventually become one of America's most popular national parks. The brothers were two of only a handful of white men ever to have seen it.

It seemed with every turn of the river trail for the past fifty plus miles the trail narrowed while the cliffs grew steeper and taller. The colors continued to change from red to orange and back, only now with an occasional chalk-white thrown in. Long before the usual sunset occurred for the region, they were immersed in shadows from the labyrinth of immense canyon walls. The bright sun made the multicolored formations more luminous as they towered above, and in front of, their entrancing view.

As they approached the summer camp of Chief Jackson's tribe, the scene took on an almost surreal image. Teepees were spread out in an orderly manner in the sheltered natural amphitheater out of which the Virgin River seemed to appear. Smoke from the fires spread in strata just above the tent poles, but well below the rim of the towering cliffs. They'd heard drumbeats for several miles before reaching the enchanting compound. An air of festivity, or was it something more ominous than that, filled their ears and eyes as they approached the encampment.

Thales Haskell and James Mathews had quieted noticeably since they began hearing the drumbeat. Haskell was especially knowledgeable about Jackson's people. Whether they be for celebration or the drumbeats of war, he could only be sure they meant Jackson and his men had returned from Mountain Meadows. The brothers were not aware of the scene that had ensued near the headwaters of Mogatsu Creek between Big Bill and Ira Hatch. They were all about to find out how Chief Jackson would handle the humiliation Ira had visited upon his thickly muscled brave. Only Haskell and Mathews knew enough to be concerned.

"Was Hatch serious about these redskins wantin' to kill us back at the Santa Clara?" Cao thought he'd break the ice that seemed to be forming around their two Mormon escorts.

"Yep," replied Haskell. Lost in his own contemplations, he failed to elaborate. As much as he and Haskell dreaded another confrontation with Chief Jackson and his buck brave, they were understandably wondering about the outcome of the standoff at Mountain Meadows.

"Well then, why should we figure they won't just get right down to business killin' us? Maybe it's not such a good idea fer us ta be ridin' on in there." They were about a hundred and fifty yards from the nearest teepees now, and Cao was in need of reassurance. However Haskell and Mathews were too preoccupied with their own concerns to be of much comfort. Finally Cao and Henry instinctively reined their mounts to a halt.

Haskell was first to take notice. The four whites had come to a stop now. But the two braves kicked their animals to a gallop and within seconds were whooping their arrival in greeting their people. "Look," said Haskell, "it's too late fer us to turn back now. We got good reason ta be headin' in there. And besides, once we tell 'em you two will be headin' inta the Narrows, they'll figure yer as good as dead anyhow."

Cao was not much reassured.

"Look boys. We're not all that eager ta be ridin' inta this camp either. The last time we had any dealing with their chief, we parted on none too friendly terms. Now all four of us are well armed, and they know better than to come right out an' attack us. Let's jus' go on in an' have a little powwow. Usually if'n ya go in an' act like yer not afraid, like ya got every reason ta be there, things work out jus' fine." Mathews and Haskell had seen Ira Hatch and Jacob Hamblin ride into tense situations like this a dozen times and employ the same technique Haskell just described. They were all still alive.

"I hope you boys know what yer talkin' about." Henry gently spurred his mount, and the four men proceeded to cover the last segment separating them from their fate.

The four palefaces did their best to mask any signs of fear. It was just the pounding of their hearts clearly visible through their shirts that would have been a dead giveaway had the tribesmen thought to take a slightly closer look. As they slowly rode their mounts into the camp all the members of the tribe including the women and children soon had them surrounded. The presence of women and children should have settled their nerves some, but somehow it didn't. One of the braves they had arrived with approached with a smile on his face. This was their first encouraging sign.

"Your people, my people, victorious at Mogatsu Meadows. All Mericats have been killed. Tonight celebrate with feast. We kill beef taken from Mericats." The brave spoke as if it was understood that the men on horseback would be joining in with the festivities.

The brothers each registered the brave's words as they attempted to suppress making any sign of recognition. Haskell, though interested in hearing the brave's report, was conscious of what Henry and Cao must be thinking. He quickly changed the subject to another more innocuous concern. "I do not see Chief Jackson or Chief Jackson's horse."

The brave, suddenly aware of Haskell's concern, smiled as if he had more good news. "Chief Jackson go north tell great white chief of victory over Mericats. He not come back to summer camp. We meet him winter camp after leave here."

Still not completely relieved, and still concerned for what the Gentiles must think, Haskell asked, "What about Big Bill?"

The brave smiled again. "Big Bill in teepee. Face black where Hatch hit with rifle. He shame. He not come out while face black."

Haskell sighed in relief and turned to his companions. "Looks like we caught a break boys. The mean ones around here are either gone or gone inta hidin'. The rest a these Lamanites are in a playful mood. We'll eat well tonight."

The men dismounted and walked their animals through the camp to an area near what must have been the entrance to the Narrows. There was no visible passageway as far as they could see. Just towering rock walls blocking their way. The reminiscent flow of the meandering Virgin River, and no evident waterfall nearby, was the only telltale sign that a passageway of some sort must exist somewhere ahead. Or could it be that such a flow just bubbled up out of the rocks somewhere nearby?

The two Gentiles would be parting company with their Mormon escorts tomorrow morning here at this site. Henry and Cao were looking forward to being on their own again. However the sense of the unknown that lay before them had never been laden with more uncertainty and trepidation.

As they began loosening supplies from their pack animals, a ruckus ensued as six braves on ponies raced after a thousand-pound long-horned steer. They had already managed to place two arrows into its side and were making a sport of placing more. Finally the wounded beast turned to put up a defense. After withstanding additional abuse for about ten minutes, and ten additional arrows, the suffering beast collapsed. Whooping and yipping, the braves descended upon the animal with their knives.

The four whites looked upon the celebratory scene with varying degrees of revulsion. All four were familiar with proper techniques for slaughtering large animals. It was common knowledge that it was best to kill the animal when it was calm, and to do it quickly. Aside from being the more humane practice, the meat would dress out more tender and would taste better. The fear-induced adrenaline pulsing through the meat of the braves' kill would produce the opposite result. However, the revulsion they held for the scene was a result of more than the quality of the steaks they would be offered tonight.

CHAPTER 52

MOUNTAIN MEADOWS
UTAH TERRITORY

SEPTEMBER 11, 1857
12:15 PM

Chief Jackson looked down at the young woman of whose virtue he'd just been deprived and then looked up at Lee. He surveyed his surroundings, seeing the men and children at the wagons and then those in Nephi Johnson's group. Looking back at Lee he projected a scornful sneer and spat at the ground near Lee's feet. He then turned and walked easily back in the direction of his campsite. Big Bill followed dutifully behind, trying his best but failing to emulate the scoffing persona his chief had just displayed.

Lee stood alone looking down at the beautiful young woman he'd just executed. She was more beautiful than any of his wives. More beautiful than Emmeline Free or even Lucretia Stout, the young new wife his friend Hosea had recently taken. He thought she was more beautiful than any women he'd ever known. He hated Chief Jackson and felt justification in stopping him from committing an outrage upon her. He would need to look to his faith to somehow justify what he had not stopped himself from doing. It was a justification that would not come so easily.

The men gathered around Nephi Johnson began to disperse in different directions. Most headed back in the direction of the wagon fortress. The plan had always been to assist the Cedar militia with securing whatever treasures existed there, and some of these men were eager to get on with it.

Nephi Johnson continued to stare directly into the eyes of William Stewart. Stewart stared back as if to say, "I'm not going to take on any shame from you." Finally, Stewart turned and walked off with George Adair toward P.K. and the wagons. He figured correctly that Nephi would be heading the other way.

P.K. turned to James Pearce, Sam McCurdy, and Sam Knight. "Get these kids up to Hamblin's. Rachel and Caroline will have their hands full. Help them out as best you can. I'm going to check if there are any other children alive back down the trail."

P.K. wanted to get his charges as far away from the grisly scene as possible. He also wanted to be sure he hadn't missed any other small children who may have been carried in their mother's arms. With great trepidation he began walking back in the direction of the victims.

He had just witnessed the difficult choices of Nephi Johnson and John D. Lee. Their execution slaying of the three women was a logical outcome of the plan they'd set in motion. All three were obviously old enough to talk. They could not have been spared. However, seeing it done had been an ugly reality none could have fully contemplated.

He dreaded the possibility of finding older ones still alive as he once again began his descent through the killing fields. He no longer thought he could manage an action such logic would require.

Before young James Pearce could proceed with his wagonload of hysterical children, he saw Lee heading his way. McMurdy climbed up onto the wagon seat next to him and took the reigns from his hands. "You might be of more help trying to calm down those in the back."

As Lee approached, George Adair and Bill Stewart closed in on the wagons as well. Adair was sticking close to Lee. He and Stewart had arrived at the Meadows with Lee several days prior. Captain Harrison Pearce had followed after his son, having seen him walking dazed behind P.K. Captain Pearce had been a hotheaded advocate out of Santa Clara preaching for the destruction of all Gentiles in Deseret. For now, he was mostly concerned that his son had not displayed a sufficient degree of bravery on the field of battle.

As the grouping of men arrived in the vicinity of the wagons, a discussion ensued at the behest of Capt. Pearce. "Some of these kids are too old." His comment was directed at Major Lee.

"I can't do any more killin'." Lee responded, downcast.

"So who's too big a coward now?" Pearce responded as he reached for the girl holding the infant P.K. had given her. As Pearce dragged her from the wagon the girl seemed to understand what was happening. She handed the infant to another one of the girls to hold. Placing one hand firmly around the back of her neck, Pearce roughly walked the youngster around the wagon out of view of the screaming children and then gave her a shove. She took a few steps to catch her balance and then wheeled around, looking at her attacker square in the face. "Your religion is evil! You're all evil!" she shouted.

Pearce raised his handgun, pointing at her face. Just then his son James rushed toward his father shouting "No!" Captain Pearce sidestepped the maneuver, shoving his son to the ground. He raised his gun again and immediately fired, dropping the young girl like a stone.

Turning to face his son he could see his hatred and another anticipated attempt to tackle him coming. Captain Pearce took what looked like deadly aim and fired. The bullet grazed the side of James face and head, leaving more than one ugly scar he would carry for the rest of his life.

Most of the others were shocked by what they had just witnessed. The girl Pearce had just killed could not have been more than ten years old. For a father to make such a serious attempt on his son's life was almost as shocking. The others stood in silence too stunned to move or speak.

For George Adair the episode had a more unexpected effect. He immediately grabbed one of the larger children from the wagon, a young boy of no more than six or seven years. Pulling him from the wagon by his ankles, he swung the boy in a looping motion with all the force he could muster and brought the boys head crashing down on the iron rim of the wagon wheel. The crunching sound of his skull collapsing against the iron left little doubt of the boy's prognosis. For years to come, when drinking to excess, Adair would brag to his friends about what he had done to the Gentile boy and how the crushing of his skull had sounded. His imprudence would earn him an indictment for murder in later years, but he would never be brought to trial.

Lee had seen enough. Amid the screams and pleas of the eighteen remaining children, he knew it was time to regain control of his men. "Let us not argue and fight among ourselves. We've all done some pretty awful things today. These were things that had to be done. Now let's get the rest of these little ones up to Hamblin's where we've got some women who can help us tend to them."

Somewhat shaken himself, Capt. Pearce holstered his gun and, with as much vocal authority as he could bring forth, said, "I'm gonna head over to where they was holed up an' see if I can find me some Gentile plunder."

With that he turned and strode away, hardly acknowledging his bleeding son as he passed by. Adair and Stewart followed him closely as if he was the only one present making any sense.

James Pearce, holding his hand to the side of his head, turned his back to his father and the other two as they left. Lee and the others proceeded to man the wagons and move them up the trail. For some of the men, heading away from the scene of the past hour's slaughter was a more welcome proposition than heading back into it. Others did not seem to mind.

PART THREE

CHAPTER 53

WHISKEY STREET
SALT LAKE CITY
UTAH TERRITORY

SEPTEMBER 27, 1857
8:00 PM

"Barkeep! Bring me and Mr. Stout here another brew!" shouted Yates to Candland as he continued to enjoy the atmosphere and the evening at the Globe Inn. He'd been loyally patronizing the place for several weeks now and had no idea how much the manager hated him.

"Don't mind if I do." Stout knew but didn't care what Candland thought of the Gentile trader. He was having an equally good time and had gotten to know the stranger better than anyone else in Salt Lake City had. Yates was living the kind of life Stout had always dreamed of. There was a vicarious attraction to getting to know him. Both men were about the same age, in their forties and in the prime of life. Where Stout had chosen the stifling rigors of sacrificing for the Lord, Yates had embarked on the more exciting life of a merchant marine.

"I'll be headin' up towards Black's Fork in a few days. Part of the shipment I'll be deliverin' includes some fine Kentucky whiskey Johnston likes to pour for the dignitaries he entertains. Why don't you kiss your wives goodbye for a week or two and ride up there with me?" Yates had taken a genuine liking to Stout. He found him to be much less guarded than most of the Saints he'd met so far. And Stout had been willing to engage in gregarious discussion with him regarding his favorite interest . . . polygamy.

"Ya know it's been ten years since I've passed through that country an' I think I'd enjoy seein' it again." It really hadn't been that long. He had another reason for wanting to go along.

"Now tell me, Hosea, which one of yer wives are you gonna miss the most? There ain't gonna be any female company fer either of us 'til we get back." Yates fancied himself a ladies' man and had coaxed more than one Mormon plural wife into flirtatious dialogue on the streets of Salt Lake City. He'd obtained an irreverent reputation among the Mormon men with regard to the proper conduct one should display when conversing with someone else's chattel. Especially among those who were having a difficult enough time maintaining harmony in their harems.

"Why, I suppose that would be the one I'd been apart from the longest." Stout found the Gentile's curiosity amusing. He was also lying again. Lucretia was always the one he missed the most. She was also considerably more alluring. Now that she was six months along, getting away from the others for a few weeks might provide him with a plausible excuse for not having to fulfill his procreative duties with those he found less tempting.

Yates slapped his leg and laughed out loud. "I must say. You Mormon folk sure seem to have it figured out. But tell me, don't yer wives ever get jealous a one another?"

"Well, I did get a bucket of cold water dumped on me and my latest wife for spendin' too much time together after we were first sealed." Stout was relaying a true story to Yates this time.

"I swear! So the feathers do fly when ya get one too many hens in the coop." Yates was about to roll off his chair. He thought nothing of the scene he created when he roared with laughter. This especially irked Candland as he could not help but overhear and was looking for any reason to take offense anyway. Candland was a practicing polygamist as well. Unlike Stout, as far as Candland was concerned the subject of plural marriage was off-limits to Gentiles.

"It only lasted a day. The discord, that is. A couple of the elders sat her down and schooled her in the ways of a dutiful plural wife. I haven't had a problem with that one since." Stout was back to making things up as he went along. The stresses polygamy brought to a family were always present and close to the surface. This was especially true for those families of men who held a lesser station in the church. Fortunately for Hosea he had risen to a higher level than most men his age. His prestige allowed him to exert more control over his women. The majority of Mormon men, even in its heyday, did not engage in the practice, or "the Principle," as it was referred to.

"By God! You're killin' me!" roared Yates. "If I keep listenin' to you, I'm gonna have to become a Saint myself. Either that or become an elder. How does an elder school a plural wife to be dutiful anyway?" Yates roared again.

Candland's eyes glared in the direction of the two patrons. The impropriety of their more than audible conversation was catching the attention of some of the others. For anyone of a lesser rank than Stout, Candland would not have hesitated to intervene. It would not have been the first time he would have lectured an ill-mannered Gentile in the defense of Zion.

Stout could see that Candland was about to come charging out from behind his service bar and plow into the raucous Gentile he was humoring. He had only to raise his hand slightly for Candland to rethink his next move.

Candland wondered why Stout just didn't let him serve Yates some of Hosea's special brew like he had done for Judge Shaver. But Stout had developed a genuine liking for Yates. Besides, the Prophet had told him to have Hickman dirty his hands with this particular Gentile.

"Well, it's settled then. As soon as I get mail confirmation that the arrival of my goods is imminent, I'll let you know when I'm leavin'. It shouldn't be more than a couple of days before I get word. We'll be leavin' a few days after that." Yates liked Stout but would have asked him along anyway, just so he could engage in more conversations about plural wives.

"Let me know," responded Stout. But Stout already knew. The dispatch Yates awaited had already arrived. Stout had already read it. It would be resealed and would arrive as Yates expected. Stout would now proceed to Orson Hyde's residence and inform him that he had gotten an invite to travel with the target. If Hyde had been in contact with Bill Hickman, their plan would be near set.

CHAPTER 54

THE NARROWS
UTAH TERRITORY

SEPTEMBER 20, 1857
6:15 AM

Henry and Cao were up early. Henry had little trouble waking his usually lazy brother. He walked over to Thales and James to let them know they were preparing themselves to leave. An uneasy truce had evolved between the four white men. Camping in close proximity to a tribe of noisy Indians celebrating the recent slaughter of over a hundred white folks is enough to result in a reevaluation of who best to ally with.

The Indians had been up half the night, dancing, feasting on the beef they'd butchered, and engaging in victory rituals. They had a rather large display of fresh scalps to dance around since they'd been the largest tribe remaining on the field of Mountain Meadows at the time of the massacre. The women and children joined in with the revelry right along with the braves and older men.

Sleep had not come easy for the brothers since they'd witnessed Milum's killing three nights prior. As they watched the Native Americans perform their ghastly ritual an uncomfortable silence surrounded them and their white companions. Several times Haskell had to feign politeness toward their hosts' attempts to entice them to join in with the festivity and merriment. Though appreciative of this effort, the brothers could not wait to get off by themselves where they could begin to sort things out.

"Aren't ya gonna stay fer some breakfast?" Thales wasn't keen on him and James having their morning meal with Jackson's braves. As grateful as they were that Jackson wasn't there and that Big Bill was in hiding, they too had found the braves' celebratory victory behavior unnerving.

"I reckon we'd just as soon get movin'. We'll stop an' eat somewhere up the trail. Speakin' of which, is it really gonna be that easy to get to the Sevier this way?" It was obvious in the manner he continued his packing that Henry had made his mind up whether his hosts were willing to help with directions or not.

Thales smiled. "There's one fork. The right fork takes you up Orderville Canyon. The straight fork puts you on her North Fork. Either one ya take, as long as ya keep headin' upstream, is gonna get ya to the Sevier. The trail might be a little friendlier on the North Fork, but both trails are good once ya get through the Narrows."

"Are we likely to be runnin' into any more of yer Lamanite friends up ahead?" Cao was being practical for a change.

Stewart decided to throw his two cents worth in. "No chance of it until you start headin' down the Sevier. Kanosh has a couple of summer camps along up there. But there's a good chance his people will be pullin' out for the winter by the time you pass through. Your biggest concern, in my opinion, is not gettin' caught in an early storm. It's high country the Sevier runs through fer a long ways, an' snow can come early up there."

"Much appreciate the advice." Henry was sincere. They'd gotten off to a rocky start with the Hatch subordinates. Neither of the brothers felt what happened to Milum was finished and forgotten as far as they were concerned. But they knew that neither man was responsible for Milum's death. Haskell and Stewart had been helpful and to some degree understanding of what the brothers must be thinking about the killing . . . or killings.

The men shook hands before Henry and Cao mounted Casey and Doc and headed upstream.

* * *

And upstream it was. Within a minute their horses were forced into the middle of the Virgin River. The canyon walls narrowed so much that the river was wall to wall in most places and for long distances. Its winding pattern had not changed nor had the height of the walls. It was spooky, and the horses didn't like it either. At times the walls narrowed so closely that the depth of the river rose to compensate for the diminished stream capacity. Had the brothers not been atop their horses they would have been forced to swim.

"If it weren't for that band of bloodthirsty redskins back at the mouth, I'd be inclined to think twice about pushin' mounts up this way. It could hardly be called a trail." They could talk now as Henry had to dismount for the purpose of leading the animals through a particularly unique passage. Overhead the walls, if they could be seen at all, rose in a roughly perpendicular manner. But here at the bottom, where the river was doing its work, it had eroded the bottom of its bed into more or less a tunnel.

"Do you think the Mormons helped wipe out that train that Milum was tryin' ta bring help to?" Cao was still struggling some with his ecclesiastical future and needed help.

"I think they killed Milum without so much as givin' him the benefit of a trial. That pretty much sizes it up fer me, Cao." Henry looked at Cao when he said it. He knew what Cao was thinking.

"You think there's any truth to what they said about that party poisoning the Indians along their way?" Cao was trying to place himself in Thales' and James' shoes. They did live here among some fairly primitive inhabitants. He was thinking how vulnerable they were, even where they had just parted ways. As eerie as it was here in the Narrows, he did not feel as insecure as he would have if he were back there with Big Bill and his friends. Haskell and Stewart had told them how lucky they all were that the big Indian had been too humiliated to show his face. It was even luckier that Chief Jackson hadn't yet returned.

"I think Milum was tellin' the truth and he didn't say anything about any poisonin'. And though I don't think Hatch was lyin', I think there was a lot he wasn't tellin'. We can't even be sure that the people in that train have been wiped out. But I think we're gonna find out before we get out a this country."

The going was slow as the horses struggled to find their footing under the silty water. The bottom of the stream was covered with rounded fist-sized stones, perfect for grinding away the canyon floor but difficult for obtaining a stable foothold even for a sure-footed animal like Casey. The mules seemed to mind the least.

After about seven miles or so the brothers started to become worried that they'd never escape the towering walls and punishing river trail. Henry was concerned that the horse's hooves were starting to soften from having spent so much time immersed in the grinding rock and water channel.

They'd come to, and passed, Orderville Canyon, choosing to take Haskell's advice. Now they were beginning to hit a few areas where the direct sun warmed their backs and some good stretches of dry ground, which they took their time passing over. They'd been steadily climbing uphill and had gained a good deal of altitude. Finally they came to a spot that seemed to be perfect for a meal stop—a good width of dry ground on the east side of the river and a gushing spring with a number of artesian outlets on the west.

"I don't think we have to worry about Jackson's braves anymore." Cao expressed the concern for both men. It was easy to see why the Indians would have avoided this trail. Aside from being an eerie stretch of difficult travel, any amount of thunderstorm activity, or substantial rain upstream from here, could easily result in an inescapable wall of water. No sign of a well-defined trail was apparent anywhere since they'd left Jackson's camp. Telltale evidence of frequent washouts suggested that the route was being scoured over and over. No wonder the Indians believed it was bad medicine to enter the Narrows. Making frequent use of this trail was a risky game of chance.

"No, I think we're done, for the time being, with Mr. Hatch and Company and their Lamanite friends. I'm gonna check out that spring over there and see if it's tasty enough to fill our bags." Upstream from the gushing artesian the Virgin River was almost narrow enough to jump over. Henry hopped rocks to the other side and proceeded to climb through the lush foliage surrounding the cascading water feature. It was still steep enough he only had to lean forward and brace his hands on the rocks to immerse his face in a crystal clear fountain of ice cold water.

"Oh that's good!" shouted Henry. Cao wasted little time hopping over the river and climbing the bank for his turn.

"Mercy! I say we fill our bags and hope for a hot day ahead." Cao was enjoying himself. It was good for both brothers to have something to think about other than the life and death considerations that had been confronting them the past several days. The weather had cooled. The relentless approach of autumn and the increase in elevation were forces of nature that would not often be denied, even in this grand and unique country.

"I think we're almost out of here. If this is still the Virgin River we have ta be getting near her headwaters. We probably won't make it over the top today. I say we get as close as we can and build a fire in some high mountain meadow where we can rest the animals' feet."

"Stewart made it sound like we won't have any more contact with the red man until we get over the hump and onto the Sevier. I'd just as soon not have any more of that kind of company for a while." Henry knew he was speaking for both of them after last's night's annoying sleep.

"Amen!" Cao was not about to argue.

CHAPTER 55

MOUNTAIN MEADOWS
UTAH TERRITORY

SEPTEMBER 11, 1857
1:30 PM

P.K. walked through the meadow of death looking for signs of life as the Indians were stripping the bodies of every bit of clothing they had on. The whites had already checked all their pockets and lifted all their packs. Most of the plunder of coin and gems were obtained through this effort.

It was a loathsome and ghastly scene. The brethren and their Lamanite allies had done a good job of making sure that no life was left among their targets. Most of them had sustained head wounds from bullets or tomahawk blows. Throat cutting seemed to be a popular method of dispatching their prey as well. Many of the victims had sustained both.

Only one infant was to be found—a baby girl deceased in her father's arms; a bullet having passed through the infant's abdomen and into her father's breast had ensured the demise of both. Why had it been necessary to take his scalp and then cut his throat? Was the throat cutting to hasten his death? Had the scalp been removed afterward? Numerous such examples were scattered over the meadow. For the rest of his life he would strive to console himself by hoping that their deaths had been somehow made more merciful, and not less.

After arriving at the wagon fortress the immigrants should never have agreed to leave, P.K. saw that a number of the Lamanites, and a few of the brethren, were overcome with the lust of treasure seeking. The Indians tore into the bedding and clothing like children at the climax of a pillow fight.

Their interest was mostly for the clothes and any tools that had been left behind. The brethren were searching for jewelry and coin.

"You fools! Let the Lamanites take the clothing and leave! I command you men of the Cedar militia to guard any valuables you find so they can be turned over to the tithing office in Cedar City! There will be an accounting and a full reporting to the first presidency in Salt Lake City of how we dispose of the property of these Gentiles! DO YOU UNDERSTAND?" P.K.'s tirade caught the attention of the men present, and some of them started to encourage the Lamanites to take what they held and be on their way.

Joel White, not wanting to allow the bishop to usurp rank over him, shoved Elliot Wilden and a man named Jukes out of the wagon they all three had been plundering. "Come on, boys. The bishop is right. Let's see if we can get things under some degree of order around here."

Wilden and Jukes began to coax the Indians away from the wagons. Enos was not about to be coaxed. He turned and flung Wildens' arm away. "What right have you to deny us these prizes? Have we not done our share?"

Wilden was taken aback. Enos' chest was blood smeared and he was still excited with blood lust. He shoved past the surprised Wilden and proceeded to stuff his pillowcase with additional supplies.

A number of Indians mounted for travel began to arrive on the scene. Among them were chiefs Tutsegabit and Jackson. A few of the braves began to complain to their chiefs in their native tongue. It was a developing scene that had all the makings of a nasty confrontation.

"Company D! Secure all wagons. Allow the Lamanite to have all items of bedding and clothing. Any items of jewelry or coin are to remain secure in the wagons." Joel White commanded enough men that two Saints were soon atop each wagon and ready to defend them with weaponry if need be. As an act of conciliation, they began to hand items of clothing and bedding to the Indians. From then on the plunder of what remained of the immigrants' property proceeded in a somewhat orderly fashion.

Higbee rode in at a full gallop. He ordered John Urie and William Edwards to proceed forthwith to Leachy Springs where a sizeable number of the immigrant's cattle were being gathered for a drive into the Harmony Valley. The chiefs could see that the Mormons, through superior organization, were soon to commandeer the lion's share of the booty. Barking a few orders to subchiefs present, Tutsegabit and Jackson rode off in a gallop to the north. The remaining Indians fell into line with the other militia working the wagons in seeming compliance with the white men's orders.

It would be their job to report to the chiefs, upon their return, of the disposition of the spoils.

Satisfied that things were in order at the wagons, P.K. began his return to the children. First he would retrieve his camp gear from behind the hill where Lee had unveiled his plan the night before. How repulsed P.K. had been. Yet he had agreed to do his part. Oh, if he could only go back. He would have railed against his old friend. He would have single-handedly turned the others against such a diabolical scheme, or he would have died trying. It was too late for that now. Now he could only do what he could for the children.

P.K. shouldered his pack and began to walk in the direction of Hamblin's. When he approached the site where he'd left Lee and the others, he saw two more naked bodies lying on the ground. He'd seen so much already he prepared himself to be resistant to the sight of it. Then it hit him. One of the bodies was of the young girl he'd handed the infant to as Lee and the others were dispatching the wounded in the other wagon.

He remembered how her look had brought him out of his state of perpetual self-loathing. Unlike the other children lost in their hysteria and fear, she had been able to see the despair in someone else and extend her compassion. Was it because she was older than the others that she had the capacity to reach out to him when he was himself so lost? Now was she dead because of that capacity?

Again he was sinking into that depth he had been in before this wonderful child had pulled him from it. What had he become? What had his people become? He looked at the boy. He could only tell he was a boy by his exposure anatomically, his skull crushed to a degree that would have rendered his appearance unrecognizable. Then he had been stripped naked for the small value of his clothing. This child had been significantly smaller than the girl. Why was he so brutally destroyed? Would others fall prey to the same brutality? He could not allow that. He still had work to do. No time now to descend into that crater of self-pity.

P.K. arrived at Hamblin's shanty within fifteen minutes. He could see that the wagons he'd left the children in were now unloaded. Several men stood around outside, apparently with nothing to do. He hoped the women were attending to the children. Lee, McMurdy, Knight, and young Pearce saw P.K. coming.

Anticipating his question, Lee said, "The children are inside being tended to by the women." As if this was going to satisfy his friend that all was well now. All could see the anger flow back into P.K.'s face.

"I can see how those two young ones were tended to after I left." P.K. was almost too distraught to put up a fight. What was the use in it now? But there were still the other children to stick up for. Someone had better start.

"My father shot her, Bishop Smith. And then he tried to kill me." Pearce turned his head only slightly to reveal the ugly gash along his cheekbone and continuing back just above his ear. Then he looked down as if to be ashamed.

"It was Adair who killed the boy. He jus' seemed to go berserk." Mc-Murdy chimed in.

Sam Knight, sporting a white shirt, was nearly soaked from head to toe with blood. He'd come by his gruesome look by having hauled several of the wounded adults out of the wagon after he, Lee, and McMurdy had finished them off. He must have made for his wife a pretty site, showing up with eighteen shrieking children and the obviously complicit appearance. "Rachel's tendin' to two of the young'uns that's wounded. Says they won't be able to travel 'til mornin'. My wife is inside an' I think she's so upset with me I doubt she'll ever speak to me again."

P.K. had nowhere to go with his anger. It was obvious to him for the first time that all of them were not even remotely prepared to deal with the disturbing ramifications of what they'd just done. "Well, aren't we just one fine set of Saints. Promise me one thing, that you'll do everything in your power to help me take care of the children that remains. They're young and maybe with time they'll be able to forget that any of this dreadfulness ever happened."

The four men facing P.K. seemed to be more than eager to nod their acquiescence to his request.

CHAPTER 56

ECHO CANYON
NEAR BLACK'S FORK
UTAH TERRITORY

OCTOBER 18, 1857
10:30 PM

It had been a pleasant ride from General Johnston's outpost. Fortunately, the weather had held and the conversation had been jovial. They had traveled just far enough from Black's Fork that Orson Hyde had passed them going the other way, ostensibly on his way to a sit-down with the general and anyone else who might listen to his church's plea for moderation. In reality it was all a show for Yates to encourage him to maintain his belief that nothing significant was ever going to come from Buchanan's forcing democracy upon them at the point of a bayonet. Hyde would actually only be riding a short ways farther to meet with someone who had already been ordered to track Stout and Yates.

Hyde's real purpose was to provide Bill Hickman with an authoritative authentication, from a high-ranking church authority, that Hosea Stout was indeed traveling with a man that Brigham Young wanted put out of the way. This order had already been delivered to Hickman by Stout and Joseph A. Young, one of the Prophet's sons. This occurred the day before at Fort Bridger during Johnston's exodus from that burned-out position.

Hyde would not risk actually going into the Gentile army compound. He and all the other ranking members of the church believed they would be hanged without trial if they ever fell into the hands of their enemies. Tonight their mission required no mistakes and few witnesses.

"I'll be sending Brother Hickman your way when I see him. I'll tell him to look for your camp. It never hurts to have an extra man along with what the Lamanites have been up to lately. Look for him sometime well after you've made camp." The look in Hyde's eyes as he said it left no doubt that their plan was being implemented as scheduled. Stout had nodded his understanding as Yates had continued on his way down the trail ahead of him. Yates seemed unconcerned with the conversation Stout and Hyde were having. Just as well.

A few miles further they came upon Major Lot Smith and General Daniel Wells posing as emissaries for the church also on their way to meet with the army. The two commanders cordially invited the two to camp with them for the evening since they already had a good fire going. Stout accepted for both men. After that the four sat around the fire swapping stories and doing a little drinking of some of the Kentucky whiskey Yates had procured.

The Mormons drank a little just to be hospitable, and it was much to Yates glee that he was able to get all four of his Mormon companions to indulge in the sinful practice at all. The Mormon contingent insisted on singing religious songs and saying a prayer or two as well. This combination of drink and heads bowing only made Yates sleepy, so he excused himself to his bedroll early.

Since none of the others knew when Hickman would be arriving, Stout had offered to take the first watch while the others retired to their bedrolls. He allowed his thoughts to drift as he sat on the plank atop two blocks near the flickering campfire. It had been dark for several hours when Stout began to wonder if Hickman would ever arrive. He'd begun to think the jovial Yates might live another day when he suddenly realized the presence of someone sitting right next to him.

Stout nearly died of fright when he realized it was the burley Hickman astraddle the plank looking right at him. Fortunately he was able to squelch any verbal utterance when he saw the Danite's single finger raised perpendicular to his lips signaling him that it would be imprudent to sound his arrival.

As quietly as Hickman had arrived, he rose and beckoned Stout to follow him away from the other sleepers of the camp. Once sufficiently out of earshot he whispered, "The one lying off to himself is Yates?"

"That's him. I swear, I don't know how you were able to get so close without me havin' heard you make a sound." A somewhat embarrassed

Stout had followed Hickman to where he'd tied his horse and pack animal. Hickman began to dig through the packs assembled atop the mule.

"I larned a long time ago that when I don't want to get snuck up on, to not be making my camp within earshot of a running stream. It gives the sneaker all the cover he needs after dark to get right up next to ya." Hickman smiled at Hosea as he whispered this tidbit of wisdom.

"You gonna take care of Yates now?" Stout knew better than to advocate in the Gentile's defense. The time for that had long since passed.

"Yer plannin' on heppin' me out, ain't you?" Hickman maintained the same grin he seemed to have kept in place since the two men had walked away from the fire.

"If it's all the same to you, Brother Hickman, I'd just as soon wait here 'til it's over." Stout was hoping his complicity would end here, at least somewhat like the Prophet and he had agreed. He could tell by Hickman's grin and the emphasis on the "ain't you?" that his request was not likely to be granted.

"That won't do, Brother Stout. You see we're ALL here to put Mr. Yates out of the way. Now if I was alone it'd be no problem. But the one thing that ain't gonna happen is three Saints witness to one Saint doing all the dirty work. It's kinda like not sleepin' next to a noisy stream if ya don't want to get snuck up on, or somethin' like that." The grin and jovial nature remained the only constant of Hickman's demeanor as he handed Stout a lantern.

Stout looked over toward the campsite where a high-ranking major and the commanding general of the Nauvoo Legion lay sleeping. His sense of dread only increased exponentially as he tried to imagine what awful duty Hickman was about to ask him to perform in front of them. Hickman seemed to read his thought.

"Don't you worry 'bout them. I'll make sure they have a part in this too. It don't matter how much they outrank us." Hickman reached across the mule and untied an ax and a shovel. His smile seemed to lesson some. "Now you light the lamp and walk around to the Gentile's feet and shine it right in his face. Don't you worry if he wakes up. It ain't gonna matter. That's all you gotta do. I'll be doin' the heavy liftin' at that point."

Stout knelt down and began to struggle with the complex set of steps involved with starting a kerosene lantern in the dark. His hands were shaking some, but he wasn't going to let the legendary assassin know how afraid he was if he could help it. Once the lantern was lit the two proceeded in the direction of their prey.

Hosea covered a circuitous route to arrive at Yates' feet while shielding the lantern's light as much as possible until arriving at his destination. Hickman had no trouble covering the shorter distance to about three feet from where Yates' head lay on his folded coat. From the still flickering campfire light Stout could see Hickman's face nod that he was ready to receive the lantern's light. Stout unveiled its full luminescence in the direction of the man he could have called his friend. Yates began to stir. Before he could bring an arm up to shield his eyes enough to see his polygamous hero the blunt end of the ax came crashing down on his forehead. The sound of his skull crunching inward from the force of the blow was one Stout would be unable to forget for the rest of his life.

* * *

The sound must have been incongruent enough to wake Wells and Smith from their slumber. The two slipped on their boots and staggered over to investigate Yates' lifeless body. By that time Hickman had finished rifling through his clothing and bedroll and was now busy counting a significant quantity of gold coins he had found. They all knew Johnston would have paid Yates for the delivery of more cattle from his connection back in Nebraska. The nine hundred dollars was no surprise.

"I expect the one who makes the report to the Prophet should be the one who delivers this sack of coins. Would you agree, Brothers Wells?" Hickman had a way of taking charge even when he was outranked, as in this situation. By referring to him as brother and not general, he diminished Wells' higher military rank. Like Rockwell, Hickman loved the way religious theocracies worked.

"That makes sense. And that's the way it's going to be." Wells didn't want to sound too passive when accepting another man's suggestion. A silence ensued in the wake of the realization that nobody really wanted to be the one to make such a report. The reason the four of them were here was to keep the knowledge of Yates' demise as close to the church's collective vest as was possible. Young had discussed the mission only with his son, Hyde, and Stout, and then only briefly with Hyde and Stout. Hyde had brought Wells and Smith in for logistical reasons.

The only logical choice was Hosea Stout since he was the only man present that Young knew to be involved in the planning of it. Before Stout could resolve Wells' dilemma for him by volunteering to make the report and deliver the gold, Hickman spoke up.

"All right, I'll do it. Brother Stout, If you won't mind countin' it up so's we all know how much I'm obligated to deliver, I'll get started on the first turn a diggin' Mr. Yates a final restin' place. You brothers won't mind takin' a turn with the diggin' would ya? I don't want to work up too much of a sweat in the chill of this October night air." Hickman's inquiry was directed to Wells and Lot Smith.

"No, Brother Hickman. We'll take our turn with the diggin'." The general was well aware that Smith and Stout were stunned at the impertinence of the request. By any reasonable analysis, the confident Hickman was subordinate to Wells, who sat high atop the military chain of command. Wells answered quickly so as to keep the others from dwelling too long on it. Hickman had been so cool in his demeanor, so matter of fact in his response to calculated murder of the Gentile, that Wells had not had time enough to adopt a commanding presence over the discussion.

"Well that settles it then." Hickman tossed the bag of gold over to Stout and proceeded to the shovel he'd laid aside for its very purpose.

Hickman had ulterior motives for delivering the report to Brigham Young. First, he intended on asking the Prophet, and his business partner, to split some of Yates' money with him. Since he, Rockwell, and Young had gone into the mail delivery business, Young had been slow to share the profits of the enterprise with his two mainstays. Young had been siphoning off most of it to the pending war effort. Second, he liked to know, and he liked Young to know he knew, who the Prophet could most depend on when it came to the kind of Lord's work most of his Saints didn't like to do.

Within an hour Mr. Yates was buried beneath about three feet of rock and dirt next to the campfire that illuminated the worksite. Once the site was packed down and smoothed out, the campfire was moved over the few feet necessary to eliminate any sign that a fresh excavation had been made. Afterward, the four Mormon loyalists retired to their bedrolls. Hickman chose the site where Yates had recently slept. The others wondered how the Avenging Angel could sleep soundly on such a location. As it turned out, on this night he was the only one who did.

CHAPTER 57

NAVAJO LAKE
UTAH TERRITORY

SEPTEMBER 22, 1857
7:00 AM

It was frosty for the first time since the brothers had left Pennsylvania earlier that year. The scorching hot days between San Bernardino and the Virgin River Gorge were now remote memories. Henry stoked the campfire and positioned the coffee pot for their morning wakeup. Cao stirred but showed no signs of rising. The brothers were accustomed to hard traveling, but the tension of late had added to their exhaustion. They had arrived at Navajo Lake early the day before, and their animals were much in need of rest.

Henry had not been eager to descend into the Sevier River drainage basin where they might run into more Indians. Regardless of what Haskell and Mathews had said about Kanosh leading one of the more peaceful tribes of the region, Henry had seen enough of the war-painted red man for a while. As he and his brother were enjoying their rest in the mountains near the nine thousand foot level, a time for decision was coming fast upon them.

"Wake up, Cao. We've need to talk."

"Any coffee yet?" For Cao, this was about as responsive as he could be at this hour of the morning.

"It'll be ready to drink before yer ready ta drink it." Henry knew Cao would be over shortly.

Cao slipped on his boots and staggered over to the campfire. Henry handed him his cup and then poured one for himself.

"I'm thinkin' if we head due west from this little lake here, we'll be likely to tie inta the Spanish Trail somewhere's around Cedar City." Henry knew that would get Cao going.

"I expect we'd come out five or ten miles south a there. May have to cross over a draw or two. You thinkin' maybe it ain't such a bad idea to talk with the bishop after all?" The prospect of seeing Molly had caught his attention. He just didn't want to be obvious about it.

"Actually I was thinkin' a checkin' out fer ourselves that train Milum was tellin' us about. It's not the safest idea I've ever come up with, but I know it's gonna eat at us all the way back ta Pennsylvania if we don't get straight what happened to those folks." Henry was looking at his younger brother as if he was hoping he would at least try to talk him out of such a dangerous course.

Cao was silent for some time before he replied.

"It gives me some satisfaction that we won't be doin' as we were told by Hatch. It's still a risky move ta be headin' in there if all of them folks were murdered like that redskin at Jackson's camp said." Cao was usually not averse to risk, as long as he was doing what he wanted.

"If you don't want ta do it, I won't force the issue. We could just hit Cedar City an' head north from there." Henry was opening the door for the discussion they'd needed to have for some time.

"I don't plan on joinin' up with the Mormons any longer if that's what yer getting' to." Cao was annoyed at having to broach the personal issue.

"What you plan to do about Molly?" Now that it was out there, Henry might as well dive into it.

"I figure she'll just have ta come with us. If these people have done what we both expect, we can't very well leave her behind with folks that would conduct themselves in that way." Cao was cornered so he just went for it. These thoughts had crossed his mind for days, but he still hadn't figured out what he was going to do or how he would tell Henry.

"Whoa! Talk about contemplatin' a risky move. We don't even know what happened with the folks in that train and you've already convicted the whole Mormon Church. And how do you propose to kidnap one of their young women and smuggle her out of a country as big as Canada?" Henry knew that sometimes Cao had to be shocked into his senses.

"I haven't got it all figured out yet, O.K.?" Cao had begun to miss Molly so much lately that she was all he could think about. She might really need him.

"Look. We been able to wind our way through some pretty intense situations lately. But so far, the only killin' we seen done has been done to Milum. The people who kilt him could a kilt us easy any number a chances. We still don't know enough to go off half-cocked rescuin' damsels in distress. Hell, she might not be so hell bent on getting' out a the country. Have you thought of that?" Henry was coming on strong.

Cao was silent for a minute. Henry let him stew.

"All right. Let's go find out what happened to them folks and make our minds up then." Cao knew that his brother would not object to this.

"Let's eat and then get the animals ready to do some cross country." Henry was content to have a plan that would get them through the next few days. Still he wondered what unforeseen events lay ahead.

Cao was comforted but frustrated that he would be passing so close to Molly Anderson without being able to see her for several days. He'd just have to be satisfied that he was getting closer. He would figure out what to do with her later.

CHAPTER 58

MOUNTAIN MEADOWS
UTAH TERRITORY

SEPTEMBER 12,1857
10:00 AM

Sleep had been fitful throughout the night for P.K., as it most surely had been for the others. They'd heard the children inside Hamblin's shanty wail and sob all night long. Lee and McMurdy had picked up their bedrolls and moved far enough away from the mournful episode to escape the torment. P.K. and Pearce stayed nearby to prevent any Saints from deciding other children should be permanently silenced, as had been done earlier.

About midmorning a contingent of ranking members of the Iron County Nauvoo Legion arrived at Hamblins'. Among the dignitaries were Colonel William H. Dame of the Nauvoo Legion and Major Isaac C. Haight of the Cedar City militia. Probate Judge James Lewis of Parowan accompanied them.

P.K. watched their demeanor closely as they surveyed the pathetic sight of forlorn children being cared for by Rachel Hamblin and Caroline Knight. At his own personal risk, P.K. planned to challenge these men should they decide more children were old enough to warrant being put out of the way. Fortunately for him, they seemed to be silenced by the solemnity of the spectacle and the prospect of what they might be seeing in a mile or so.

"P.K., you'll see that these children are provided good caring homes in and about Cedar City?" Haight wanted a stake in the only decent task available surrounding this entire sorry affair.

P.K. looked at the stake president and simply nodded his agreement with the question.

"Well, let's get on with it," was all Dame had to say as he and the entourage left the shanty and headed towards their mounts. All of the men, including P.K., Lee, and Higbee, proceeded back to the Meadows. Captain Joel White had been dispatched earlier that morning to command Company D. in the burying of the bodies. Lee and Higbee were hoping, beyond hope, that he would somehow have been able to get the job completed prior to them having to view the macabre scene in the presence of their superior officers. P.K. dreaded the sight of it, but he wanted Dame and Haight to see the product of their orders to the militia.

It was a short ride to the Meadows, done mostly in silence. Dame tried to sound officious as they walked their horses forward by asking peripheral questions: "How many of the wagons will remain in a usable condition?" "What has been done with the cattle?" "Have all the valuables of the train been secured?"

Higbee jumped for the chance to answer. Lee and P.K. didn't seem all that eager to assist with the information. The closer they got to the scene, however, even Higbee found it increasingly difficult to keep his train of thought. As they approached the depression where Captain Pearce and George Adair had dispatched of the last two children, P.K. noticed that their bodies had been moved away. Grateful at not having to see the evidence of their molestation again, his stomach still churned at having to pass over the site.

Finally, they ascended out of the natural depression and into full view of the field of slaughter. To Lee's and Higbee's disappointment, Captain White's men had only completed the piling up of about half of the men's bodies. Most of White's men were making slow progress excavating enough of the hardpan earth to bury more than a hundred bodies. To make matters worse, their first up-close views were of the tormented and mutilated bodies of the women and children.

The sight hit Dame and Haight like a punch to the solar plexus. Dame dismounted and knelt as if he was going to become ill. Haight sighed deeply but remained mounted, the color draining from his face. Judge Lewis simply had the look of a man who wished he could be any place other than here. Unlike his two friends, he was not here in any official capacity. He was deeply regretting his decision to ride along to satisfy his curiosity.

The ghoulish vision was unlike anything they'd ever seen. The predations of Lucifer, as depicted by the finest biblical artists, could not match the vileness of what lie before them. The butchery of some the women's disfigured bodies was an especially disturbing sight.

"Horrible! Horrible! This must be reported to the Prophet immediately." Dame said, at a loss for more helpful words. He grabbed his saddle horn as if he was going to remount.

"Horrible enough! What do you mean by reporting it immediately, Colonel Dame?" asked Haight. Haight's signature was on the written order to commence the killing. An order he'd received from Dame.

"I mean I must report the matter to the authorities immediately." Dame said more forcefully as if it was a matter of utmost urgency that his superiors be informed of the great tragedy laying before them.

Haight who was also visibly shaken by the carnage did not like Dame's tone for some reason. "How will you report it?"

"I will report it just as it is," Dame replied somewhat defensively.

"Yes, I suppose so, and implicate yourself with the rest?" Haight was looking with disgust at Dame.

"No! I will not implicate myself, for I had nothing to do with it. I did not think there were so many of them, women and children, or I would not have had anything to do with it." Dame let go of the saddle horn and sank to his knees once again.

"That will not do, for you know a damned sight better. You ordered it done. Nothing has been done except by your orders. And it is too late in the day to order things done and then go back on it, and go back on the men who have carried out your orders. You cannot sow pig on me, and I will be damned if I will stand it. You are as much to blame as anyone, and you know that we have done nothing except by what you ordered done, and by God I will not be lied on." Haight's rant had increased in volume to the point where all within fifty yards were beginning to take notice.

In a subdued tone and pitch, Dame responded so that only the men close by could hear. "I only said if I had known there were so many, I would have had nothing to do with it."

Dame was making a weak attempt to hold his ground. His station was a precarious one. He knew that the orders had come from up on high, but he also knew that there was a conscious effort made by his superiors to keep the written orders close to the field of battle. For his own benefit, he needed to see that the debate Haight was waging ended.

Lee knew it was time to intervene. It was obvious by now that it would be necessary to secure an oath of secrecy among all Saints present at the

Meadows. This kind of argument between the highest leadership of the region would only undermine that effort.

"We're going to need to gather the men around and instruct them on how we will all proceed from here on. The men need to know we are all together in this." Lee stopped his near whisper for a moment to make sure Dame and Haight acknowledged this last statement and that he had their attention.

"Higbee will call the men together. Colonel Dame, I think it best that you swear the men to the oath as we discussed. Major Haight, it's important that you back Colonel Dame."

"I'll back him as long as he backs me, an' all the rest of us." Haight looked back toward Dame. "If you sow pig on me, you can bet I'll put the saddle on the right horse." He was referring to Apostle George A. Smith as he punctuated his comment by jabbing his finger in Dame's direction.

"P.K., when they're done, I think the men could all benefit from another prayer." Lee looked at his old friend, still unsure of his resolve.

"Couldn't we all, Brother Lee? But first I think the men could use a hand with a mighty unpleasant task," was all that P.K. said before he rode over to a nearby tool wagon and removed a shovel from its bed. The others followed suit for, paltry as it was, they dared not miss out on the only opportunity available to humble themselves.

CHAPTER 59

TEMPLE SQUARE
SALT LAKE CITY
UTAH TERRITORY

OCTOBER 20, 1857
1:00 PM

Hosea Stout would breath a sigh of relief upon saying goodbye to Bill Hickman. He'd just finished traveling with the well-known assassin for the past day and a half. General Daniel Wells and Captain Lot Smith had remained in Echo Canyon to see to the Saint's military harassment of Johnston's army as it attempted to pass through the mountains on its trek to Salt Lake City. Stout wished he'd had as legitimate an excuse to part ways with the notorious Danite.

It wasn't that Hickman wasn't jovial, or even an interesting traveling companion. He was all of that. Stout even shared his tendency to engage in strong drink from time to time, something Hickman had indulged himself in during the ride back now that he had possession of all of Yates' possessions. However, Stout preferred beer and wine and was not comfortable when it came to imbibing with Hickman. It seemed far too easy for this man to kill people.

Hosea himself had carried out brutal justice in his service to the Lord and was prepared to do so again if asked. He'd nearly killed the man Hibbard who Brigham Young had expected of being a spy. He felt justified in the doing of it and comfortable with the result. After being knocked senseless the man recovered sufficiently to relocate to safer quarters, leaving the church alone after that. Stout took relief in knowing he'd not have to wrestle his conscious over this man's death as the years passed.

His only other purported activity of a somewhat lethal sort was the persistent rumor that he poisoned people. Joseph Smith's brother, Samuel, a fierce antipolygamist and front-runner for ascension to Prophet, Seer, and Revelator was the case most often whispered about. Brigham benefited by Samuel's death. He attained the position after the original Prophet's assassination. Brigham had been in Boston at the time of Joseph's death. Samuel's poisoning provided Brigham the time needed to return to the competition.

Stout handled such rumors by, for the most part, ignoring them. After all, he was the chief of police, and a response wasn't necessary. However, Hosea was not inclined to act impulsively with respect to these matters. He took pride in taking actions that were well thought out and carefully calculated. It was also important to Stout that any action contemplated along these lines, against any man, be well deserved.

Hickman, though his technique was no less deliberate, seemed unconcerned about his target's culpability. If the Prophet said the man should be put out of the way, that was all he needed to know. He exhibited no concern about killing Yates whatsoever. The more time he and Hosea spent together, the clearer it became that Hickman spent no time at all dwelling on the right or wrong of any action he took. In future days "Wild Bill Hickman" could have become a poster boy for the definition of a psychopath.

"Take care, Brother Hickman," said Hosea, peeling away as they passed by the Lion House. Hickman could report to Young on his own and allow Woodruff to account for Yates' $900 in coin. He would also deliver Yates' horse over to the bowery stables for the proper disposition. The fine Kentucky whiskey and his other personal belongings, which were of equally fine quality, would wind up at the home of one of Hickman's ten wives.

"I'm sure our paths will cross once more in our service to the Lord." Hickman laughed out loud as if he'd just shouted something very funny.

Stout smiled politely and tried not to noticeably cringe as he spurred his mount to a trot. He was really hoping no one would notice his return to Salt Lake City. He just wanted to get home and get out of sight.

Hickman dismounted and tied the horses to the hitching post outside the Beehive House. He took his time all the while looking into the unshaded windows of the Lion House. Heaven knows what one might see gazing through those windows if one gazed long enough. Hickman loved being a Saint.

Finally he walked up the steps and rapped on the door. Brother Wood-ruff appeared a few seconds later as expected.

"Come in, Brother Hickman. We've been expecting you." Wilford projected his usual demeanor regardless of who it was he was welcoming into the Beehive House.

Hickman removed his hat and followed Wilford into their office.

"I might need to speak to the Prophet in private for a bit, Brother Woodruff." Hickman had no idea that Wilford Woodruff was destined to become the fourth Prophet of the LDS Church. Neither did he know that Wilford hated everything about Brother Hickman.

"Of course, Brother Hickman. The Prophet will be with you short-ly."

A few minutes passed before the Prophet entered the room.

"Brother Hickman. How is my business partner? Are we making money hand over fist?" The Prophet was in a jovial mood.

Hickman tossed the heavy bag of coins onto the Prophet's desk. It landed with a telltale metallic thud.

"I wish I could say it was from the mail contract, but I haven't seen half that amount from our partnership since it started." Hickman figured he might as well get right to the issue that had been eating at him for months.

"Now you know we've been preparing for war, Brother Hickman. And the report I've been getting from General Wells is that things have been heating up over at Fort Bridger way. It is a time when all good Saints have to sacrifice." Young looked steadily at the bag of coins while he spoke. He would be careful not to speculate as to its origin, though he had a pretty good idea.

"It's from the spy Yates, Brother Young. General Wells and the Nauvoo Legion won't have to worry about him any more. I got word from him, Lot Smith, Brother Hyde, Brother Stout, and your son that you wanted him put out of the way. That's a might many Saints who know about somethin' that could of just as easily be handled 'tween jus' me an' you." Hickman wasn't trying to chastise the Prophet. He was just letting him know that he had undergone some risk in getting Yates' contract proceeds consecrated to the church, and for that risk he was entitled to something.

"That was good, Brother Hickman. It's a good thing that that man is out of the way. How would you feel if I had Brother Woodruff divide this bounty into three equal shares? Let's say there will be one share for the war effort, one share for you, and one share for me. Once we get this war business behind us, I'm sure our mail contract will yield great profits."

Hickman knew he was being offered a two-to-one split in the Prophet's favor. He also knew that once the Prophet put a percentage on a proposal, his mind was made up.

"That sounds right generous, Brother Young. And please remember, if you want me to do anything just let me know it. I'll be there, and there will be no tale left behind . . . I am on hand." Hickman knew better than to try for more. His relationship with Brigham Young was the only one of any value to him.

CHAPTER 60

HARMONY RANGE
UTAH TERRITORY

SEPTEMBER 24, 1857
8:00 AM

Henry and Cao had enjoyed traveling over the scenic mountains east of Navajo Lake. It had been downhill most of the way with plenty of water and grass to pacify the hungry animals laboring beneath them. On crossing Kanarra Creek they were in the heart of the Harmony Range on the border separating Iron and Washington counties.

After avoiding several of the homesteads dotting the southern end of Cedar Valley they found themselves skirting several hundred head of cattle that did not appear as commonplace as they should. The cattle were Texas longhorn, the first of such breed of cattle that the brothers had ever seen this side of the Rocky Mountains.

"You thinkin' what I'm thinkin'?" Cao scanned the length of the meadowy landscape for any sign of mounted cowboys tending the herd.

"It don't prove much yet, but it sure does remind me of that first night we spent at the Vegas Springs when Milum told us about the train he was with and the breed of cattle they was trailin'." Henry was on the watch as well. If these were cattle stolen from the immigrants the thieves might still be watching over them.

"Milum told us there was over a thousand head. Wonder where all the rest of 'em are." Cao stood on his stirrups to gain a few more inches on his view of the terrain.

"Let's give this herd a wide berth and try to stay in the tree line as much as we can 'til we can get over to the rim of the basin where Milum told us they was attacked. Somethin' tells me that if we want to get ourselves into a position where we can see things fer ourselves, we don't want to be runnin' into the folks responsible for tendin' to these cattle."

Henry knew it wouldn't be easy to travel thirty miles of the Spanish Trail undetected, especially while leading pack animals. Fortunately, most of the trail was thickly lined with scrub cedar that made it possible for them to disappear almost instantly if they could detect oncoming riders before being detected themselves.

As it turned out, they only had to conceal themselves twice as wagons passed by headed from Little Pinto toward Cedar City. Most of the time they were able to stick to the trail, leapfrogging each other and keeping a lookout for one another. They made good time, and within several hours they were overlooking the little shack of Hamblin's Ranch.

"From what I recall, The Meadows Milum described ain't more'n a mile or so beyond the cabin over there. There was a pretty good watering hole toward the lower end. That's the place it seemed he described and I figure to be where they circled the wagons." Cao was looking at Henry to see if he was in agreement.

"O.K. Let's swing over to the south an' hope the folks in that cabin don't notice us." Henry's recollection was the same as his younger brother's.

They were in open country now. Their observance of Hamblin's shack was that only a couple of women were present. They waited until everyone was inside and began the final leg of their day's journey by sweeping around the residence in a southwesterly direction. The brothers had little to say to one another as they kept their animals moving at a brisk trot. They were close enough now that even if they were detected, they would not be turned back before being able to get a clear view of the dramatic site Milum had described.

As they rode in from the east they passed the very campsite used by Lee and the others as an observation headquarters for the days leading up to the massacre. They began to scan the landscape for any signs of a scuffle. Aside from a couple of coyotes loping out in the distance, the area appeared vacant of life or death.

The anticipation continued to grow about what may lie behind the outcropping of rock. Behind it was the watering hole Cao had mentioned and the likely spot the immigrant train had been holed up behind their breastworks. When they rounded the rocks and came into plain view of the spot they had been looking for, nothing much of an unusual nature confronted them.

There were the telltale fire pits and some other earthen disturbances one would expect from over a thousand head of cattle and forty covered wagons passing through. There were no bloating animal carcasses or bullet-ridden wagons scattered about.

Cao wondered if Milum had been missing out on important facts the day he'd stumbled into their camp. "You think maybe things did get settled and the immigrants were allowed to move on like Hatch was trying to tell Milum at that cottonwood grove shootout they had?"

Henry just shook his head and began to breath a sigh of relief. He could not now describe, even for himself, what he had expected to see here on the expanse of Mountain Meadows, but he had not been looking forward to it. It appeared that perhaps the killing of Milum had been an isolated occurrence involving no one but the deceased, Hatch, and the men that Hatch led.

Then something caught his eye. It was more coyotes, this time several in a pack. And it was a large pack with several digging and with several others trying to get into a position to dig. Others were working in concert attempting to pull something from the loosened earth.

Henry began to point at the spectacle for his brother to see, but Cao was engrossed with a similar scene about four hundred yards to the north of the spot where Henry was looking. Here another twenty or thirty coyotes were working in a similar fashion. Every now and then one of the coyotes would run away from one of the packs with something in his jaws. One or two would give chase for a few yards, then stop and go back to the pack.

The brothers had seen wolves and coyotes working the carcass of a dead animal on many an occasion. It was not the behavior of the animal activity that was so unusual to them. The packs were unusually large, with as many as fifty or sixty animals concentrated between the two locations. Suddenly their foreboding feelings came rushing back.

"I think we're gonna have ta go down there and see what those coyotes is after, Cao."

"I reckon so, Henry."

The brothers drew their pistols and proceeded to walk their already nervous animals down to Mogatsu Creek, and toward the pack closest to them.

CHAPTER 61

MOUNTAIN MEADOWS
UTAH TERRITORY

SEPTEMBER 12, 1857
11:45 AM

The men worked side by side with their religious and military leaders preparing the place of internment for the many lives they had taken. Theirs would not be a proper burial by any standard. The graves would be shallow. The men were piled in first, as they were in closest proximity to the trenches they'd dug for themselves inside the wagon fort. The rest of the digging was confined mostly to the natural drainage of the terrain where it would be easier to effect cover . . . and easier for the winter rains and spring runoff to uncover them later.

As the sun rose overhead and the heat of the day fell upon them, the hard work began to take its toll. It was obvious that Col. Dame and Judge Lewis were no longer accustomed to hard work as a result of the lifestyles of their elevated positions. Higbee could see that his superiors were not going to be able to hold out much longer. The contrast between their effort and that of their subordinates was growing more and more conspicuous. He approached Lee. He didn't think Major Haight or P.K. were inclined to give a respectful reprieve to their superiors.

"The men need to break for lunch, Major Lee. This might be as good a time as any to call the men together for the swearing of the oath." Higbee glanced at P.K. to be sure the insolent bishop wasn't about to chastise him with some new rebuke. Dame and Lewis overheard him and immediately stopped their digging.

"Will you have a prayer?" Lee looked at P.K.

P.K. nodded. "Go ahead, John. Call the men together."

Higbee immediately began shouting for the men to muster forth. He turned to Bateman and said. "Mount up and ride up to Hamblin's and tell any men who might be there to get down here double time."

Bateman dropped his shovel where he was standing and ran to where his horse was tied. Within ten minutes Bateman was back and the men were called to attention. Apparently no one but the two women and the still-petrified children remained at Hamblin's cheerless dwelling.

"Men! Colonel Dame has asked to address you. Please give him your full attention." Lee was doing his best to sound as authoritive as he had the day before. Still he thought it best to keep his remarks concise.

Stepping forward Dame puffed out his chest and began with the intention of equaling his major's tone and tenor.

"It is a grim task that we now ask you to perform one day after having carried out the orders of your commanding officers. You have executed your orders well and proven yourselves worthy soldiers in the service of the Lord."

"The result of the federal army's march on Salt Lake City is unclear to us hear in the southern region. We must keep all details of the operation here at Mountain Meadows a highly classified secret. This maneuver was always contemplated to be reported as an Indian attack, and a warning to the Gentiles in the east that traversing through our Deseret is a risk that cannot be undertaken without serious consequence. Knowledge that the legion participated in assisting the Lamanites by use of stratagem could severely jeopardize the commander in chief's ability to negotiate a favorable settlement with those who would seek to persecute us.

"I will ask your bishop to lead us in prayer, after which I will swear all of us here today to an oath of secrecy. Bishop Klingensmith?" Colonel Dame was going to be sure that the last words spoken here on the field were his. He was only going to speak them after he knew what the others had said.

P.K. stepped forward without hesitation. He had known for several hours that he would be leading the prayer. Now that the horrible deed was done there was nothing he could say that would undo it. He wanted to find some way to bring comfort to the men he expected to live amongst for the rest of his life.

"From the words of our first Prophet, Seer, and Revelator, Joseph Smith Jr., it is my hope that we can obtain solace in the face of so grim a task as we have been asked to perform here at the Mountain Meadows.

"Doctrine and Covenant One Thirty Two: Paragraph Fifty Nine . . . Verily, if a man be called of my Father, as was Aaron, by mine own voice, and by the voice of him that sent me, and I have endowed him with the keys of the power of this priesthood, if he do anything in my name, and according to my law and by my word, he will not commit sin, and I will justify him.

"Doctrine and Covenant One Thirty Three: Paragraph Twenty Eight . . . Their enemies shall become a prey unto them.

"Doctrine and Covenant One Thirty Three: Paragraph Fifty One . . . And I have trampled them into my fury, and I did tread upon them in mine anger, and their blood I have sprinkled upon my garments, and stained all my raiment; for this was the day of vengeance which was in my heart.

"May God bless you all. Amen." P.K. backed into formation with the other leaders assembled, closed his book, and looked straight ahead.

Satisfied that an appropriate prayer had been provided, Dame stepped forward again. Looking behind him at Haight and Lee in particular, he began again by asking a question.

"Would any of our other leaders here like to address the men?"

Unlike the day before, none of the others betrayed any sign of wanting to accept his invitation to speak. Satisfied that he was now free to bring this meeting to its termination, Dame puffed his chest out once more.

"Those of us within the presence of my voice do hereby solemnly swear upon our very souls, and the souls of our families, and upon the souls of our descendants unto the fourth generation, that we shall never speak of the events that took place here at Mountain Meadows on the eleventh day of September in the year of our Lord eighteen hundred and fifty seven. We do further swear, under penalty of death, that we shall not speak of events prior, or subsequent, to this day in any way. We do hereby swear that this is a 'blood oath' and that anyone who violates said oath shall be subject to being put out of the way for having done so. Those who affirm to abide by said oath shall signify now by saying 'AYE.'"

At chorus of ayes broke forth to the satisfaction of all present. Regardless of what each man was thinking or holding in his heart, no one present on the grim field of death looked forward to being associated with the operation.

"If you men are smart, you won't even speak of this to your wives." Dame then whirled around and spoke directly to Haight in a voice loud enough for all to hear.

"I expect you, Isaac, to make a full report to the Prophet in Salt Lake City. I expect it will be a complete and factual report. The Prophet is the only man on this earth who may be told of this affair and it shall not be considered a violation of the oath we have taken here today." Dame then turned again, walked briskly to his horse. He untied the big black stallion, mounted up, and proceeded off in the direction from which he had arrived. Judge Lewis followed his lead, leaving Haight and the other leaders behind to assist in completing the grim burial.

Feeling would be strained over the abrupt departure of the two high-ranking Saints, and over Haight's tiff with Dame earlier, for some time to come. For now, those remaining on the field only wanted to finish the dreary task and go home.

Animal carcasses were dragged out of sight of the trail and left to rot or be eaten by the scavenging animals. The wagons had been righted and hitched to teams that had arrived from Fort Harmony and Fort Clara. By dusk all of the bodies had been covered adequately from view if nothing more. The men could not delude themselves into believing that the bodies would not become exposed through the scavenging animals and erosions caused by winds and water. At least for now the Mountain Meadows looked, once again, like the peaceful sanctuary it had always been.

The last of the teamsters was pulling out of the Meadows with his load. None of the Indians remained, most bands having gathered as many articles of clothing and blankets as they could carry while at the same time driving one or two head of cattle back to their camps. Before saddling his horse and leaving the scene, Haight approached Lee and P.K. for a final conference.

"John, I'll be submitting my written report of what happened here to the Prophet as soon as I can. I'm gonna do my best to see that our weak-kneed colonel doesn't try to make it out that this was somehow all our idea. Since you were here when it happened and I wasn't, I think it best that you make a report to the Prophet as well. I want you to meet with the Prophet in person. You have a good relationship with him and that should help limit any shenanigans Dame may try to engage in.

"I know you and the bishop have a lot of property to secure. We found a lot of gold here today and there's likely to be a lot more hidden in the hounds of those wagons. Be sure to check 'em good. Whatever you find, make sure you choose some good men to accompany you to Salt Lake City. If we wind up in an all-out war with the federal army, that gold will go a good way to buyin' the supplies were gonna need for the fight."

"We'll take care to see that a full accounting is made and received, Major Haight." Lee was tired and looking forward to getting away from the Meadows for a good long while. Nearly twenty years would pass before he would find himself on this field once again.

As the years passed by, Isaac C. Haight would become increasingly fearful that the events he'd authorized at Mountain Meadows would catch up to him. Though his church would always protect him and uphold his ecclesiastical status, he would never stop in his effort to foil the work of Gentile investigators. It would result in disastrous consequences for at least three men.

As Haight began to mount his horse, he said, "I liked your words of prayer, P.K. I would have had a difficult time finding even one appropriate passage for the men under these circumstances."

P.K. looked at Major Haight as the major looked back at him. "I had hoped I could find an appropriate passage for the people we just buried."

CHAPTER 62

TEMPLE SQUARE
SALT LAKE CITY
UTAH TERRITORY

OCTOBER 21, 1857
7:00 AM

The Prophet rapped firmly on the door and then readied himself to be greeted. He'd retired early the night before, having administered his procreative duties with Lucy's sister Clarissa. She was younger, still in her twenties, and fairer than her older sister, but the experience had left the Prophet wanting. Shortly after completing his part he'd fallen fast asleep. Clarissa was the only other of the Prophet's wives who was allowed to sleep in the Beehive House. When the Prophet awoke Clarissa would be working in the kitchen preparing his ample breakfast.

After devouring a second helping of his usual fare (Clarissa was a good cook), the Prophet was eager to get about the business of the day. It was a busy time. After all there were spies to deal with, gamblers and whoremongers to roust, and Gentile trains to plunder. Elder Stout's residence would be a good place to begin his work. Once again, and much to the Prophet's liking, it was the lovely Lucretia who answered the door.

"Why President Young, what a pleasant surprise. We've been hoping we'd get another visit from you. Please do come in." Lucretia couldn't have been more gracious.

"You have such an uplifting manner in the way you greet your guests, young lady. I'm going to have to require the other sister Saints to take lessons from you. But please, it would be my privilege if you would address me by 'Brother Young.'" The Prophet reached out for her hand and gave it a chivalrous kiss.

"I really do have a bone to pick with you, though." Leading him to his favorite chair, she glanced back at the Prophet as she spoke with a look of mild perturb.

"Really? Have I done something to curry your disfavor? Heaven forbid." Young enjoyed bantering with young women, especially this one.

"Yes, Brother Young. I'm afraid the assignments you've been giving our husband are having a troubling effect on our happy home. You see, with seven wives he's been required to spread his attentions rather thin of late." As she spoke Lucretia looked at the Prophet in a way that nearly brought him to a rare loss of words. She was showing slightly more than she had during his last visit, but he still found her radiantly attractive.

"Now, now, my dear Lucretia, we must all make sacrifices. We mustn't be expecting to receive our paradise here on earth. We live in troubled times. But surely you must know that the full resources of the Beehive House are at your disposal whenever Hosea is away." The Prophet's thoughts were coming dangerously close to leading him astray when, just in time, Hosea entered the room.

"President Young, I'd planned on calling on you today. Would you care to join us for breakfast?" Hosea was more relaxed in the company of the Prophet than last time. He'd just finished tidying himself up after having had a wild night of pleasure with the voluptuous Lucretia. He would have been surprised to know she had initiated such a provocative discussion with the Prophet.

"No, no, Brother Stout, I've already eaten. I do have business to discuss with you however. Would you care to take a short walk with me while you work up an appetite for whatever your lovely young wife here is cooking?" The Prophet winked at Lucretia.

Lucretia struck a rather sensual and inviting pose as the two men exited out onto the street. As they looked back, both men thought the pose was meant for them and not the other. They were both wrong. It had been meant for both of them.

* * *

"Do you have any new information on those six spies detained at Box Elder?" Young was all business now that he was out of proximity of the buxom Lucretia.

"They arrived last night and have been placed under guard over at old man Dalton's house. There's plenty of room for 'em, him not havin' a family and all. Their arms and valuables were brought in, inventoried, and secured as well. They were carrying a lot of wealth and some equipment that looked like they were fixin' to set up a house of chance. Cards, dice, some kind a wheel they called a roolett." Stout had just obtained the information the night before.

"Don't sound like spies, just another ruthless group of Gentiles looking to defile the hearts and minds of the weaker souls among us. Can't be sure which is worse. How much wealth would you say?" The Prophet didn't want to overlook an aspect so important as money.

Times were tough in Deseret. The Saints had to import most everything but the food they produced. The Prophet had been a promoter of self-sufficiency, but one result of such a policy was to severely restrict cash flow. The Saints knew how to survive, but until they could develop the unlimited potential of their economy, they could not flourish. Now that an attack upon them was imminent, the Prophet considered every dollar that passed through Deseret to be subject to consecration.

"One man was carrying about $8,000 in gold coin. Others held less than that, but still substantial. They're decked out in the finest of practical riding leathers, saddles, and tack. Their riding stock is about as fine as any I've ever seen. Add it all up and Huntington says they're worth an easy $25,000. Still, Dimick thinks the money could be for bribes, and the gaming equipment just a cover. They don't appear to be low-life types, though one did tell Dimick they came by the money from selling a tavern over on the Merced River in California." War hysteria had gripped Hosea Stout, and all the Saints, especially those with any proximity to the war council. And $25,000 was more than a small fortune in 1857.

The six detainees was only one of the Prophet's pressing situations during these troubling days. On behalf of General Johnston, Captain Van Vliet had been conducting negotiations with Young regarding the federal army that was presently camped in the mountains near Fort Bridger. Johnston's stated intentions, according to Van Vliet, were to march into Salt Lake City and establish a fort somewhere in the vicinity. Only God knew what else they might have in mind.

The complex operation surrounding the immigrant train to the south was occupying more and more of Brigham's time. But the prospect of spies from California had entered his psyche in a manner that heightened his paranoia in a new and foreboding manner.

Earlier that year, Young had issued a general recall of all Saints that had settled far off or outside the Utah Territory. Mormons (militiamen and colonizers) from San Bernardino and the forts in Las Vegas and Genoa were ordered to sell their farms for what they could get, buy ammunition or lead and powder, and return to Deseret at once. Some did so grudgingly but all did so obediently.

The Mormon contingent from Genoa, a small settlement on the western fringe of Deseret at the foot of the Sierra Nevada Range, had crossed paths with six men from Mariposa County, California, at a spot near the present-day Truckee River. The men were in the prime of life, well armed, and riding prime stock. They were so friendly the wagon master invited them to accompany the train through the wilderness along the Humboldt Trail towards the Great Salt Lake Valley. The men agreed, welcoming the additional numbers that might be necessary to hold off a large band of predacious Indians.

After reaching the salt flats of what was to become known as Bonneville, where land speed records would someday be set, the Gentile contingent decided they would speed ahead of the slow-moving train toward their Salt Lake City destination. Many days prior, riders from the Saints' rank, including Orson Hyde, had made the same decision. Unbeknownst to the Gentiles, their decision was initiated with intent to warn General Wells that a contingent of six possible spies were headed in from California.

It had been rumored and feared for several weeks that a second Gentile army would advance upon them from the west to attack in a military pincer movement, or to merely prevent the escape of Saints fleeing the advancing army out of the east. Could this be an advance party sent in to obtain reconnaissance?

"The one carrying the fattest money belt is named John Aiken. His brother is also with him, and the other four are claiming to be business partners. Whatever they are, we don't have enough evidence to convict them of spying against the Saints even in one of our courts." As counsel for the First Presidency, Stout was looking to see what action Young wanted him to pursue. However, he knew quite well that if Brigham wanted a conviction he could have one in any court in Deseret.

The Prophet stroked his chin whiskers for several seconds before responding. "Keep them under guard for the time being until we can figure out what to do with them. Under no circumstances do we want them meeting up with the Gentile army over near Fort Bridger. It's looking more and more like we're going to be able to keep Buchanan's army bogged down in the mountains until next spring. Keep me apprised of any new information you obtain from them. We have plenty of time to come up with a plan for these six." Young finished his sentence with a noticeable tone of disdain for the captives.

Upon hearing the inflection in the Prophet's voice, Stout thought the six men were not going to fare well in Deseret whether the Prophet thought they were spies or not.

CHAPTER 63

MOUNTAIN MEADOWS
UTAH TERRITORY

SEPTEMBER 24,1857
5:00 PM

As they pushed their animals down the hill toward the scavenging coyotes the brothers were aware of the setting sun over the western ridge. In another hour they would not have enough light to see much of anything. Normally they would be zeroing in on a good campsite for the night, something they generally liked to do. The task now in front of them might not be so rewarding.

The mules strained at their bridles. Doc and Casey's eyes were wide with excitement. Coyotes were common even to the animals. But this pack was uncommonly large. And there was a scent in the air. As they got closer the coyotes backed away, but not very far. Their number and the reward they were seeking had emboldened them. Henry drew his rifle out of its sheath and they instinctively scattered away to a much greater distance.

Doc and Casey moved forward more easily, now towing the stubborn pack animals at will. They were within about thirty yards of the excavation site when the scent hit them again. No mistaking it this time, it was the unmistakable scent of moldering death. The brothers pulled up their kerchiefs, which helped very little. Their mounts just had to bear it. Henry headed in a direction that would put him alongside and upwind of the site. The breeze was slight but it was enough to provide some relief.

The first thing he saw was the bottom half of what may have been a man. He appeared to have been disemboweled. Most of his buttocks and all of his genitalia had also been chewed away. As they rode along, the brothers saw evidence of several other victims, mostly the exposure of chewed limbs of what they could only guess to be men, but certainly human.

Henry saw enough of this first set of scavenged remains to be satisfied as to what he was seeing. He did not attempt to stop and dismount for a closer examination. Cao followed his example as they continued to spur their mounts and drag the pack animals along at a brisk pace in the direction of where they'd seen the other large pack of coyotes at work. By now both men had the plummeting sensation that what they were likely to find was going to be more of what they had already seen.

Henry waved his rifle in the air as he sensed the predator's notice of their approach. This set reacted in much the same way as the others had. At first it appeared to be the same grisly scene, but it was worse. Several children had been yanked fully from beneath the soil and were in various stages of having been consumed. Two had long hair matted with blood and dirt, obviously young girls. One woman was also exposed, her naked body having been savaged by the animals after her death in grotesque ways, but more obvious ways than what may have occurred before.

Henry could not bring himself to stop. The intermittent whiffs of death could not be avoided, and the sight was too upsetting for him to continue to gaze upon it. He proceeded to a location upwind and far enough away that the specific site of what lay there was no longer clearly evident. Cao followed, his face pale and his body shuddering. They stopped to look back. The coyotes were already back at work on the men; the others were on their way back in to continue with the women and children. The brothers looked at one another but said nothing.

"It won't do no good to pick off them coyotes. We don't have enough ammo to get 'em all. All it'd do is signal the folks over in that shack we passed that we're here." Henry was just thinking out loud, and actually he was trying not to think. Milum had told them there had been well over a hundred people still alive in the train when he left them two weeks prior. He'd seen evidence of only twenty or twenty-five, but it was obvious the covered trenches he and Cao had just ridden past concealed a great many more that the coyotes hadn't yet gotten to.

"You think maybe the Indians did the killin' and then Mormons did the burying?' Cao was still having trouble with the gravity of what it all meant.

"I don't expect the Indians would go to the trouble of buryin', so Mormons probably are responsible for that. They did a might poor job of it if you ask me." Henry was angry. He didn't have all the facts yet, but someone should be made to pay for what happened to these people. Most likely a good many "some ones" should be made to pay.

"I wonder where all their wagons are. Milum said there was about forty wagons in this train." It was helpful for both Cao and Henry to keep their minds on reconstructing the crime and off what they had just seen. It was a difficult mental exercise in that the first task required a certain amount of the latter.

"Don't think there's any doubt that those longhorns we passed used to belong to these folk." Henry surveyed the ground below him in observance of the many thousands of hoof-prints.

"I expect those women we saw over at that shack up the road might be able to shed some light on what went on here." Cao, like his brother, wanted answers.

"Looks like there's been a whole lot of wagon traffic up and down the road over there. That probly explains the whereabouts a the wagons. Someone's hauled 'em all away." Henry was back to thinking about those "some ones" again.

"What do ya say we ride on up to that shack where we saw those women an' ask 'em what they know?" Cao knew it could be risky and wanted his brother's take.

"I think we best find some out-a-the-way spot to camp fer the night an' give ourselves a little time to think about what our next move should be. I'm talkin' some spot out-a sight an' with no campfire. I'm not sure we oughta be runnin' into the people who did to those folks over there what they done." Henry was pretty set on not looking for any more trouble on this day.

"There was a pretty secluded hollow a couple a hills to the east a that hill we came down. I think we can get far enough off the trail that we won't be runnin' inta anyone." Cao wasn't going to argue with Henry. Neither of the brothers felt very safe right now.

"Let's get ourselves off a this wide-open field an' over where you jus' said. Maybe by mornin' we can figure out what's best." Henry spurred his mount and headed south, giving the trenches and coyote packs a wide berth. The brothers had seen enough.

CHAPTER 64

TEMPLE SQUARE
SALT LAKE CITY
UTAH TERRITORY

SEPTEMBER 28, 1857
7:30 AM

John D. Lee arrived at the front door of the Beehive House at the appointed time. He'd arrived the day before and had stayed the night at the home of his longtime friend Hosea Stout. Lucretia, Emmeline, and his own wives Sarah Caroline and Rachel Andora had been girlhood friends in Nauvoo. Lucretia was thrilled to see Lee and eager to obtain as much information about her friends as possible. Though treated most cordially, Lee had been preoccupied with his thoughts for more than a few weeks of late.

As the Prophet's gatekeeper Wilford Woodruff opened the door, Lee removed his hat. Though these men had known each other for a long time, this was a very formal and very much anticipated meeting for all three of them. "Come in, Brother Lee. We've been expecting you."

"Thank you, Brother Woodruff." Lee followed the church historian into the office of the Prophet. The room had been doubling as a mailroom, and it was strewn with papers. Brigham Young rose from the seat behind his desk and greeted Lee warmly.

"Brother Lee, how have you been? I understand the product of our troubled times has fallen upon those of you in the Southern Mission as weightily as it has upon the rest of us."

"I hope not, Brother Young. I most certainly hope things are not as bleak here as they have been in our neighborhood." Lee wasn't eager to get down to brass tacks, and neither was the Prophet.

"We're not out of the woods yet, I'm afraid. Johnston's army still approaches and our negotiations continue. It's still possible that we'll be able to postpone all-out war until next spring, if that's any consolation." Young knew how news hungry all of his subordinates were about the approaching federal troops. He'd tossed Lee a bone that he'd lately become quite used to tossing.

"I believe the brethren are prepared to do their part in the south, if it comes to that." Lee postponed the inevitable once again, but knew he wouldn't be able to avoid the topic much longer.

"Please sit, Brother Lee, and tell us what transpired with respect to the immigrant train that passed through here a couple of months ago. We're hearing disturbing tales from dubious sources I'm afraid. I need to know the details of what happened from a loyal Saint before the Gentile press starts to whip up another batch of hatred against us." Young was choosing his words very carefully now.

He had little intention of revealing what he already knew, which was substantial. Chief Jackson and Chief Tutsegabit had already visited him almost two weeks ago. Isaac Haight had sent in a full written report. Lee had no way of knowing about the Indian chiefs. Young already had many very accurate details. Now he wanted Lee's.

"As I'm sure you're aware, the initial attack did not go as well as planned. Chief Jackson's had his braves attacked ahead of my comm . . . " Lee was cut off.

"Please, Brother Lee, don't assume that I have been aware of anything with respect to the fate of the immigrants. I'm interested in hearing as much of your details as you can provide." Young was not going to make this easy.

"All right. Let me start with the night before the attack. Will that be acceptable?" Lee had been rehearsing for days the report he intended to give to the Prophet. Once he got started he did not want to be interrupted and lose his track.

"That will do for starters, but I may want to go back to some point before that before we're done. I'll let you know." Young had little intention of divulging anything of what he knew of the massacre to anyone. When it came to knowing how to keep from getting one's tail caught, the Prophet was much more savvy than was Lee, or most others for that matter.

"Well, we'd assembled braves from about seven of the southern tribes and hid them out at various camps between Pinto and Hamblin's ranch house the night of September 6. Jake Hamblin told me that five of the chiefs you met with earlier didn't show. Tutsegabit, Youngwuds, Chickeroo, Toshob, Moquetas, Jackson, and Noucopin all brought good bands of braves. Arapeen, Kanosh, Quanara, and the Pahvants didn't show. We'd hoped to have a few more of the regional tribes present, but with three hundred plus well-armed braves on the field, and contingents of the Nauvoo Legion from Santa Clara, Harmony, and Pinto there as well, we felt we had enough to complete the maneuver if everyone played his part.

"Next morning, ahead of my signal, Chief Jackson has his braves attack. Once I hear the rifle firing commence I did my best to get the rest of us in a position to join in, but the damage had been done. Jackson's braves extracted some casualties from the immigrants, but all they really accomplished was to give 'em an early warning and a chance to circle their wagons. By the time I got the rest of the tribes and our men into a position to actually join in the fight, they were dug in. Then the best we could do was encircle 'em and make sure they couldn't get free."

Lee paused shortly as if to offer Young an opportunity to interrupt. Young listened attentively but said nothing. Woodruff scribbled on his notepad as if he was transcribing every word Lee was saying. It was an uncomfortable pause for Lee. Finally Young nodded for Lee to continue.

"Keepin' 'em in the trap wasn't as easy as you might think. We had 'em well out numbered an' during the daytime it was easy. Come nightfall we had to increase the guard and rotate 'em in shifts. Many of the Lamanites tired of sentry duty quickly, and it became clear that within another day or two we wouldn't have any of 'em left. That's why we sent for the militia at Cedar and for direction from the war council here in Salt Lake."

"On the second night of the siege, the immigrants sent two men out on horses. There was a hail of gunfire, but they made a clean break. I reckon they hit our line so fast it just sort of surprised us. We sure thought we was in a bad fix at that point. Fortunately fer us they run into Sam Knight, Nephi Johnson, and some more of our boys camped at Leachy Springs on their way to join forces with us. I believe it was Sam Knight or Bill Stewart who shot the fella referred to as Will Aden. Thales Haskell referred to him by that name. Thales had been travelin' with the train posing as an apostate since Corn Creek. Thanks to Thales we knew a lot about their capability."

Lee was throwing out more than he needed to and was studying the Prophet's demeanor for any signs of acknowledgement. He assumed Young would have known about Thales posing as an apostate, possibly even ordering it. The cagey Mormon Prophet betrayed no acknowledgment of any kind.

Lee continued. "The other fella, a big brute of a Dutchman, was able to get away and fled back to the wagon fort. We cut his mount out from under him after he broke back through our perimeter. He got up an' ran back into the ring of wagons. Things were contained again, but we had to figure they were onto some of the Saints bein' involved." Lee paused again. Young only looked on attentively.

"On the fourth night of the siege, I believe it was the 10th, our force was joined by the Cedar militia, and we received your order from Salt Lake as delivered by James Haslam. We were all amazed he could have covered that much ground in such a short time. He was plenty tired so I told him to head on up to . . . "

"Who signed the order you say Haslam delivered?" Young wanted to see how Wells' and Smith's "express message" plan had worked.

"It was Haight's signature but Haslam said the orders came from Salt Lake City." Lee was puzzled for a moment as he was not sure what Young's question preordained. Young shrugged as if it didn't matter, and again Lee continued.

"Later that night three of the immigrants made it out under cover of darkness by floating down the creek past our guards. Lucky fer us they were detected before they got much past our perimeter. One of 'em was kilt right there. I was informed just before I left for here that Ira Hatch and a posse we sent with him were successful in tracking down the other two and putting them out of the way.

"Next morning we implemented the plan to decoy the immigrants out of their fortress. The militia had the responsibility of dispatching the men. Nephi Johnson's group, together with what was left of our Lamanite friends, dispatched the women and older children." At this point Lee was doing his best to stay away from the details of the operation.

"You're telling me that some of the Saints were involved with the killing of women and children?" Young was feigning surprise. He'd already heard of the slaughter of the women and children from Haight and from chiefs Jackson and Tutsegabit. Haight had defended the Saints saying " . . . if they had killed every man, woman, and child in the outfit, there would not have been a drop of innocent blood shed by the brethren." Jackson had even scoffed about how some of the white men had behaved like squaws and how Lee had ruined a perfectly marketable female who could have brought big wampum in trade.

"Our orders were to kill everyone old enough to talk. Were you not aware of the contents of that order?" By now Lee was feeling cornered. He was mostly concerned for himself but also for all the men on the field who had participated.

Young ignored the question and continued to get himself worked up. "This was supposed to have been carried out by the Lamanites. Killing of women and children for the sins of the men? This whole thing stands before me like a horrid vision. I must have time to reflect upon it."

"We did everything in our power to spare the youngest children. Seventeen of them we now have placed in the care of good families around Cedar City. We were following orders. We were acting for the good of the church, and in strict conformity with the oaths we've all taken to avenge the blood of the prophets." Lee was starting to fight back. He sensed there might be a movement afoot to assign blame. This was always a possibility ever since Jackson placed the mission in jeopardy by jumping the gun.

"You must talk to no one about these doings. Not even to Heber Kimball. This is the most unfortunate affair to ever befall the church." Young was up and pacing back and forth.

"You must sustain these people for what they have done, or they must be released from their oaths." Lee wasn't backing down. He knew the Prophet could trust him. Now he needed to know if he could trust the Prophet. For a very long ten seconds or so the room was silent. Even the scribbling of Woodruff's pen had ceased.

"I must consider the problem overnight. Please return tomorrow morning, Brother Lee. If you have any word for Emmeline of Sarah Caroline or Rachel Andora's well-being, I told her I would send you over with it. She awaits you in the parlor of the Lion House." Young seemed to have backed off a bit. He was once again speaking to Lee as the longtime friends they were.

Lee stood and shook hands with Young and Woodruff. His knees felt weak as he turned and walked out of the Beehive House. The meeting had not gone well. He'd been dreading it for days and now he knew why.

CHAPTER 65

SALT LAKE CITY
UTAH TERRITORY

OCTOBER 21, 1857
9:00 AM

By the time Hosea Stout had eaten his breakfast, saddled his mare, and trotted her the three miles to the Dalton house, the October sun had succeeded in comfortably warming the day. It was the most stunning time of the year in the multihued capitol city. Most of the native cottonwoods had turned golden, and an abundant assortment of deciduous and fruit trees planted by the brethren over the past ten years had begun to contrast brilliantly with the much larger originals. The swift-rising poplars had started to outpace the fruits in stature. However, the fruits would not be outmatched by any in the bounty of their yield, which was now in full maturity.

In general, Stout would have been fairly smitten by this scene of visual radiance amid the mild autumn air. Today, he was not thinking of such pleasantries. As he approached the old man's residence, he thought only of the interrogation method he would employ.

Armed guards had been placed at the front and back of the building. There would be at least two guards inside. Replacements had been arriving at four-hour intervals. The arrival of the six men from California had caused quite a stir amongst a people who had been worried about the approaching Gentile army.

Hosea dismounted and tied his mare to the hitching post. Sylvanus Collett, the lanky front-door guard, nodded his greeting as if Stout was well expected and walked the twenty paces or so to open the front gate.

"Any new revelations from our well-heeled guests?" Hosea might as well get right to collecting the information he came for.

"No. They just been makin' small talk mostly. Showing the boys card tricks and whatnot. Entertainin' set of fellas. Not at all what I'd expect ta be spyin' for Uncle Sam." The seedy-looking Collett had taken somewhat of a liking to the detainees. They'd been quite generous in sharing their knowledge of card tricks. They also doled out a better grade of chewing tobacco than he'd ever before known.

"Don't be getting' too fond of 'em, Sylvanus. The Prophet don't think much more of Gentile gamblers than he thinks of Gentile spies." Stout wasn't kidding. He had hoped the report he'd given to the Prophet earlier that morning would have been enough to end the matter of what to do with the six men. He knew why Young had recently been trying to revive the Doctrine of Consecration among the brethren.

Deseret needed money. This was especially so if they were going to be waging war. Joseph Smith had prophesied the consecration of the property of Gentiles unto the church. An opportunity to apply this doctrine to Gentiles of questionable repute was as strong a temptation as was the capture and elimination of Gentile spies.

Walking past Collett he arrived at the front door, knocked, and then announced, as he entered, "Hosea here!"

Seated around the main table sat four men. Four others busied themselves in the kitchen area working up a mid-morning snack. The Gentiles at the table included a man who went by the moniker of "Honesty Jones" and another called Tuck Wright. The two Mormon guards were Joe Hunt and Joseph Harker. John Aiken and his brother Tom were most involved with the food preparation. John was carving on a ham and a large roasted turkey. Supervising this effort were the other two of their traveling companions, Colonel Eichard and John Chapman.

Simon Dalton sat at the other end of the large room with a big grin on his face, seeming happy to have so much company. The cholera had come through a few years back and wiped out both of his wives and all seven of his children. He'd lived alone in the big house ever since. The first year he spent pretty much in quarantine. The brethren brought him provisions to his front gate. When they were clear he would come out to retrieve the goods and shout a "thank you." Everyone had thought it was remarkable that a disease would afflict a family and wipe out all but the feeblest member of it. They all said that he survived because he'd always been one of the most devout of all the Saints.

"Well, I'm glad I won't be missin' out on the picnic." Stout had interviewed these men once already and had taken a genuine liking to them.

"I'm sorry ta say this here ain't our first confinement, Mr. Stout. But we're sure hopin' it won't be our least pleasant." John Aiken was always looking for an opportunity to express the humor of any situation.

Honesty Jones, the more serious of the six companions, got right to the point. "Well, what does President Young prophesy for our future?"

Jones had no way of knowing that Hosea had just come from a discussion with Brigham Young about him and his friends. Stout wasn't going to tell them either.

"No final decisions have been made yet, but I don't think you're going to be allowed to develop any kind of gaming establishment anywhere in Salt Lake City." He might as well start feeding them some of the reality they'd ridden themselves into.

All of the men focused their attention on what Stout was saying. They'd just crossed more than five hundred miles of desolate wilderness to establish an entertainment hall that would be serving at least twenty-five hundred federal troops.

Jones charged in. "I expect the federal marshall will have something to say about that. Last time I checked this territory belonged to the United States of America. Sure looks like there's a lot of vacant land that's still waitin' for someone ta make a private claim of it. Or does Brigham Young think he owns it all?" His comments were measured in comparison to what he wanted to say. Jones had been a constable back in Mariposa County and knew a thing or two about the law.

"He's territorial governor, last time I checked, and I suppose that gives him more rights to makin' the rules of this territory than anyone else in this room." Stout's response was also measured. Jones had no idea how close he'd just come to summarizing Brigham Young's definition of ownership rights in the state of Deseret.

"Did you happen to find out how far out the federal army is from enterin' Salt Lake City?" John Aiken was cooler headed than was the self-assured Jones. It was a fact that he and his brother had sold a pub in the county seat in Snelling, California. He asked his question as he set a platter of meat in front of those seated at the table and handed other, smaller ones to Hosea and old man Dalton.

"They're a good distance this side of Devil's Gate fixin' ta push over South Pass sometime in the next few weeks. But it's startin' to look like they won't be arrivin' in Salt Lake 'til sometime next spring." Stout had to be careful. So far, the fact that a war may be imminent between the Saints and the federal troops had not been shared with these men. He knew there was a chance some kind of settlement would be in the offing during the weeks and months to come.

He was also becoming more and more sure that these men were not spies, but were nothing more or less than they had consistently represented themselves to be: "speculators in the entertainment and establishment business" is how they put it. They seemed oblivious to the reaction their plans would elicit from the blue-nosed Saints. If they were spies they had been much too obvious in their desire to meet up with the Gentile troops.

"Well boys, that'll teach us to be in such a fired-up hurry ta rendezvous with any government-led expedition. I can just see how good our tavern's gonna do over the winter with nothin' but Mormons fer customers and a modern-day Prophet settin' all our odds." Tom's quick wit summarized their situation. Possessors of obvious resources, these six capable men had come by their prosperity honorably and methodically. They could afford to see the irony and the humor of their situation.

"We'd sure appreciate it, Mr. Stout, if you could find out how the church authorities are gonna handle our situation so we can commence with whatever changes we're gonna have ta make with our plans." John Aiken had always been a problem solver. He spoke as if this was only another problem that he would soon find a way through. He had no problem with staying outside Salt Lake City, as long as he could set up near the federal army. They certainly had the means to withstand a stay in Salt Lake City through the winter, that is, provided the Saints returned what they had confiscated. It might be just a matter of waiting to see when and where the army set up.

Hosea Stout nodded his willingness to obtain the answer these men sought of him. He could tell that although they were frustrated with the revelations unfolding before them, they were not at all worried for their safety. Under other circumstances he would be warning them that they should be very worried. Self-doubt crept in as he chose to go along with the pretense that these men were only being temporarily inconvenienced.

CHAPTER 66

CEDAR CITY
UTAH TERRITORY

SEPTEMBER 25, 1857
8:00 PM

Henry had agreed with Cao that their next move would be to meet with Bishop Klingensmith. It was a risky move in light of the strong possibility of Mormon involvement with the massacre of the immigrant train. His younger brother seemed to have a great deal of confidence in the bishop with whom he'd studied Mormonism. Besides, it was dark and his household was one of only two they were familiar with in all of Cedar City.

From Mountain Meadows they had traveled undetected back up the Spanish Trail. The brothers were even more careful on the trip back than they had been the day before. Unnerved by what they'd seen at the Meadows, it seemed clear to both that they needed to ally with someone if they expected to get through the territory.

They knocked lightly on the door, aware that at this late hour they were likely to alarm the inhabitants inside. P.K.'s first wife Hannah came to the door.

"Who is it?"

"It's Cao Young and his brother Henry. We was wonderin' if it might be possible to speak with the bishop." Cao knew he had the best chance of having his voice recognized by the woman.

The door opened with the light of a kerosene lantern. "Come in, Cao. Henry, I don't believe we've met but you're very welcome in our home."

The brothers entered to see a house full of children. There were six in the main room of the two-room house, and it was obvious from Hannah's condition that another would soon be arriving. All the children were quite interested in the two large men walking into the room. They kept quiet. It was clear that Hannah ruled the humble home with an iron fist.

"Sorry to trouble you, ma'am, especially at this late hour. We really need to talk to the bishop." Cao wasn't all that comfortable around children, especially when being the focus of their stare.

"I'm afraid that won't be possible young man. You see the bishop is on his way to Salt Lake City."

"He's going to meet with the Prophet." Keziah, the six-year-old, couldn't resist interjecting the big news.

"Won't you join us for some berry pie? Sarah Ann here just baked two, and Moroni just finished straining tonight's milking." Sarah Anne was fifteen years old and looked at Cao the way a housecat looks at a mouse. She was quite attractive, favoring her mother, who was an attractive woman still, though older in appearance than her thirty-one years would have indicated. Hannah had already borne eight children. Though two had died, she would bear seven more before her childbearing days were through.

Immediately, without waiting for their acceptance of her invitation, Hannah started making preparations for her guests.

"Hannah Henry, help Nancy with setting the table. Keziah, run to the barn and bring back two milking stools. Lavina, keep Triphenia entertained while we tend to our guests." The children sprang to attention and did as they were told.

"We really shouldn't be . . . " Cao started to look for a quick exit when Henry ruined it for him.

"We can stay for one piece of pie, Cao, and we'd be much obliged, Mrs. Klingensmith." Henry had taken an immediate liking to the warm hospitable scene inside the modest abode. Though a little confining considering what he and his brother were used to, it reminded him of days gone by when he was a young boy back in Lancaster. After the events of the past ten days, and especially the past day and a half, the homespun hospitality they were being offered was a bit of humanity in stark contrast to what they had recently been exposed.

As the brothers sat at the large table and enjoyed their milk and pie, the children could barely contain themselves. Giggles turned to snickers and then to kicks under the table. A stern look from Hannah brought things quickly under control.

"Could you tell us for what business the bishop was traveling to Salt Lake City, Mrs. Klingensmith?" Henry thought there'd be no harm in the asking.

"Please call me Mrs. K. It's so much easier to pronounce. Where have you boys come in to Cedar from, the north or the south?" Neither Henry nor Cao had missed her obvious evasion of the question.

"We been through the Virgin River to the headwaters just east of here. Before that we rode through a canyon the likes we never seen before. Then we rode over to the Mountain Meadows an' we jus' came back from there."

Henry figured they'd come here to see if they could find an ally. Hannah's expression changed only slightly.

"Keziah, please clear the table." By now Keziah knew her mother was displeased with her interruption about her father's trip to Salt Lake City.

"Moroni, take the stools back to the barn. Sarah Ann, put the dishes in to soak and then take the kerosene lantern into the bedroom and read the younger ones a story." With some slight grumbling, the children sprang obediently to action.

Looking at Henry amid the organized chaos of her home she said in a normal tone of voice, "Once I've got the children settled, we'll talk some more."

It took all of five minutes for the children to complete their assignments and retire to the one and only bedroom. They usually slept in the other room, which was the room they also ate their meals in and played in during the day. P.K.'s other two wives and families occupied separate homes nearby. Once they were tucked in for a long story, Hannah was ready to resume the conversation.

"Did you see what happened to that immigrant train that passed through here about three weeks ago?" Hannah was all business now. She knew the presence of the two Gentiles in her home could only mean trouble.

"We sure did, ma'am. We'd sure like to know who was responsible for it. And we'd like to know if it's safe fer us to even be here in Cedar City, or even in Deseret for that matter." Henry wasn't one to beat around the bush. Neither was Hannah Creamer Klingensmith.

"I don't know. I'd like to say you boys are safe. But I suspect you're not. Rosmus Anderson passed through the Mountain Meadows a few days ago. He claimed he saw you boys down by the Virgin River Gorge. He's been tellin' everyone who'll listen that Ira Hatch killed a man you boys had been traveling with. He's tellin' that everyone in that wagon train of Gentiles that went through has been put out of the way." She paused briefly.

"The way the men around here have been reacting to what Rosmus has been saying has led me to believe that it's not safe for him to be in Deseret anymore. I don't want you boys to think I don't love my religion. It's my love for my religion that tells me to tell you that I think you boys need to be very careful. And maybe you should look for a way to get out of Deseret as fast as you can." There was a long pause as the brothers digested their pie along with what Hannah had just told them.

"We're much obliged, ma'am. We best be leavin' you in peace now. And thank you very much fer yer hospitality, and fer yer kind words of advice. When the bishop returns, let him know we think he has a right fine family." Henry meant what he said to the gracious woman. It was obvious that she had risked much in her forthrightness. The brothers walked to the door, donned their hats and left.

Hannah was one of many strong Mormon women who believed that nothing but the truth was good enough for her religion. Still she felt relief in that she had not had to divulge the reason P.K. had embarked on a journey to meet with the Prophet.

CHAPTER 67

TEMPLE SQUARE
SALT LAKE CITY
UTAH TERRITORY

SEPTEMBER 28, 1857
8:00 AM

It was a very mixed set of feelings John D. Lee carried in his heart as he stepped up to the front door of the Lion House. His meeting with the Prophet had confirmed his worst fears with respect to how the aftermath of the Mountain Meadows Massacre was going to play out. He and his compatriots had done the bidding of their commanders, and now responsibility would be assigned to what was in their commanders' best interests. He had hoped the visit with the woman he was about to greet would be a happy reunion between two kindred spirits. Now he knew his anticipation would be dampened down at best.

He wondered if she had changed much as he lightly knocked at the front door. He tried to clear his thoughts of the disturbing meeting he'd just finished while he waited for a response. It was Clarissa Decker who opened the door.

"What a wonderful surprise it is to see you, Brother Lee. I suppose you're here to visit with Emmeline. I think she's been awaiting your arrival. Please do come in." Clarissa knew quite well that Emmeline was expecting him. She and the others had known since an hour after he'd arrived in town the night before that he would be visiting Emmeline this morning. The history of the Prophet, Lee, Emmeline, and her sister had been bandied about incessantly since . . . all behind Emmeline's back.

"Thank you, Clarissa." After removing his hat, Lee followed her into the ornately decorated parlor.

"I'll let her know you're here." Clarissa was almost giddy. Emmeline was one of her least favorites.

A few minutes passed . . . a virtual eternity. Just now, time alone with his thoughts was not a good thing for Lee. Suddenly he realized that Emmeline was in the room, having entered from a direction he had not anticipated.

"Has something terrible happened? John, you look so sad." Standing in the room's side entry near a display of lace curtains, he had not detected her. She had been able to observe him unnoticed for some time.

"Why Emmeline, you surprised me." Quickly brightening his expression he hoped to ignore her comment and hoped she would as well.

"Has something happened to Sarah Caroline? Is it the child?" Her first concern was for her friend.

"No, Emmeline. She and the child are both fine. Margaret Ann is a happy, healthy little girl." Lee was relieved to have so easily directed the conversation away from his sad demeanor.

"And Rachel Andora, I hear she is once again with child. Please tell me she hasn't lost it." Emmeline had reason to be concerned. Childbirth had already taken the lives of a number of her young friends.

"Rachel Andora is doing just fine." Lee responded.

"Thank goodness. But please tell me, John, why are you in such a state of dejection? I've never seen you look so forlorn." Emmeline was not the kind to get easily sidetracked.

"I suppose I have let things get into my mind that are best kept out. You certainly look as beautiful as ever." It was a feeble attempt to move the discussion in a more cheerful direction.

"We've known each other a long time John. You know that flattery is wasted on a woman like me. What's wrong?" She walked over to the sofa and sat down, placing his hand between hers.

"I never was very good at hiding my feelings from you, was I? Please understand that there are certain things I simply cannot discuss right now." Lee was in a dangerous position. He probably loved Emmeline more than he loved any of the sixteen women he'd married so far. But he knew he dare not trust her completely. After all she was married to the man who might be planning to swear away his life.

"John, if there is ever anything I can do to help you, please find a way to ask me. I'm not going to pry. My marriage to the Prophet has not changed the way I feel about you. If you need me, I will help you if I can. Now tell me how Rachel Andora, Sarah Caroline, and the children are doing."

"Thank you, Emmeline. If it comes to it, I will ask for your help. But let us talk about more pleasant things for now. Rachel, Sarah Caroline, and the children are doing quite well. Here, I've brought you a letter Sarah Caroline has written. It is a comfort to me that the three of you have remained such close friends. I hope that will always be the case." He handed her the sealed envelope. The remainder of their time together was spent pleasantly catching up on how their lives had prospered since their last visit.

CHAPTER 68

TEMPLE SQUARE
SALT LAKE CITY
UTAH TERRITORY

OCTOBER 22, 1857
9:00 AM

It had begun to cloud up somewhat as Hosea Stout made the short stroll to the Beehive House. As he passed in front of the Lion House, he couldn't help but think of Emmeline Free. Both he and John D. Lee had been smitten by the beautiful woman back in Nauvoo. They had actually competed for her attention with one another. Lee, the older and more experienced of the two, had let Hosea know he would not relinquish his claim on the young woman and that he was prepared to appeal to the Prophet if need be.

He was quite familiar with the story of how Brigham had coerced Lee into giving her up to him. Lee had been a close friend of Stout's, and he had dined in Lee's home on many an occasion. In his eyes, Emmeline was the only woman he'd ever met who could rival the seductive Lucretia. He wondered if he would have handled the loss the same way Lee had, had he been put to the test.

Striding past the Lion house he fantasized about proposing a swap, Lucretia for Emmeline, for a period of time. Hosea smiled at himself as he arrived at the front steps. He would never actually suggest such a thing. It was just fun to think about it. He knocked on the door of the ornate residence and waited for it to open.

Wilford Woodruff answered with his usual propriety. "Do come in, Brother Stout. We've been expecting you."

"Thank you, Brother Woodruff." He always felt like he had to concentrate on his enunciation when speaking to Woodruff. He proceeded to follow Wilford into the office where the Prophet was seated.

"Well tell me, Brother Stout, what new information have you with respect to our supposed spies?" Brigham Young was the poster boy for efficient expediency when dealing with his subordinates. But then everyone was his subordinate. He was the only man on earth who enjoyed the privilege of speaking to his one and only superior, the Lord himself.

"I really haven't come up with anything new other than to have become more convinced that they are not spies. I do believe they had every intention of establishing a 'House of Lady Luck' specifically for the purpose of exploiting the soldiers heading this way in Johnston's Army." Hosea wouldn't dare withhold information from the Prophet. But he'd just given the Aiken party its best chance of surviving their business venture into Deseret.

The Prophet frowned. He would liked to have known if the men were in fact spies even though he was hoping they were not. "So, just another set of Gentile gamblers and whoremongers come to suck the decency out of a decent community?"

Stout remained silent. He knew better than to defend these men further after the Prophet posed such a question.

"Just as well. Spies for the Gentile army could have made things right sticky. If they're spies, I don't dare let them go. I don't dare put them on trial, and I don't dare execute them until all hell breaks loose." Young was thinking out loud. It was something he would only do in front of men he'd known a long time and trusted.

Stout honed in on the part about execution. He wanted to know if his report had placed the Aiken party in even more jeopardy than if he had continued to support the possibility of them being spies. "They're asking me to ascertain whether the church council has made a determination of when they can be released."

"I'll be the one who determines 'IF' they'll be released or not. There'll be no council making that decision. These are very difficult times, and we're not going to be allowing any of the weak-kneed brethren to have their two-cents worth." Young looked at Hosea to check his reaction.

Hosea went silent again. Woodruff leaned back in his chair, but he too said nothing. A weighty silence filled the room.

"Tell them that the council has met and decided to release them. They can retrieve their possessions over at the Townsend House. However, they will not be permitted to proceed to Johnston's army under any circumstances. Other than that they are welcome to leave the territory or stay and be welcome. And tell them there will never be any 'Houses of Lady Luck' allowed to exist in Deseret as long as the Saints have anything to say about it. That should convince them to get a move on. Tell them if they choose to leave, we'll provide them with safe passage out the Southern Trail."

Turning to Woodruff, he said, "Send word to Port Rockwell that I have a job for him to do."

Woodruff nodded, rose from his chair, and left the room.

Hosea did the same. The conversation was over, and it was obvious to him that the Aiken party was doomed.

* * *

As Hosea descended the steps from the Beehive House he no longer amused himself with thoughts of the "House of Concubines." His thoughts were filled with the fate of the men with whom he had shared food and laughs the day before. Back in Nauvoo, Hosea had often frequented drinking establishments owned by Gentiles. It was one of the things he missed.

As far as Gentiles go, they'd been a pleasant lot. They'd treated him and their guards with respect. They'd even respected the Saints' decision to detain them without too much complaining. He was troubled with the decision to involve Orrin Porter Rockwell. He knew what that meant.

Just then he heard, "Wait up." It was Wilford Woodruff quickly striding toward him after having just stepped out a side door of the Beehive House.

Hosea waited for the loyal Saint to catch up. Woodruff spent more time around Brigham Young than all of his wives combined. Should Hosea express his concerns to the ultimate insider?

"Don't be troubled, young man. Much worse things are afoot than the fate that befalls men of chance. Mind if I walk with you for a spell?" Woodruff was attempting to comfort Stout by speaking down to Stout's level.

"Is it that obvious?" Stout would open up a little.

"It's only natural to be concerned for the mortality of men you've sat across the table from and shared conversation with. It's easier to make the hard decisions a leader must make when you haven't done that. Perhaps that's why you were asked to interrogate those men." Woodruff was genuinely trying to be of comfort.

"I appreciate what you're saying, Wilford. But I've had to make hard decisions myself from time to time. Remember, I'm a Danite." It wasn't anything Wilford didn't already know about Hosea.

"Yes indeed. A good soldier you've been for that daunting group. Can you imagine where the Saints would be if we hadn't had men like you in the service of our Lord? You haven't forgotten that O.P. Rockwell is a Danite as well?" Woodruff was attempting to reconcile his own acquiescence as much as he was attempting to assuage the younger man's conscience.

"I was hoping that here in Deseret, we would be able to leave all that behind. I was hoping we would be able to attain a more civilized existence." Stout was being sincere. He was also still struggling with his conscience.

"If you believe in our Prophet Joseph, civilization will never come on earth until the Gentiles submit to Zion, and the redemption of Zion shall only come by power." Woodruff waited for the younger man's reply.

"Doctrines and Covenants One Hundred and Three. I'm quite familiar with that passage, Brother Woodruff. It's just that I've tried to be of service in a different way. For Rockwell there was always, and still is, only one way."

"Also . . . D and C One Hundred and Four. The poor shall be exalted in that the rich are made low." Woodruff was fond of quoting the words of Joseph Smith Jr.

Both men resented the fact that the Prophet was so close to Rockwell and Hickman. They knew that killing was a necessary part of managing power at the Prophet's level. That's why it was necessary for him to have bodyguards around the clock.

Neither Woodruff nor Stout was above having a man put out of the way. It was the methods Rockwell and Hickman employed they found troubling. Their killings were brutal, usually employing the use of guns or knives; sometimes the blunt end of an axe. They were both muscular brutes. Their very presence was intimidating, a persona they both seemed to enjoy. They had no respect for the chain of command. They worked directly for the Prophet and would sneer at anyone, even the second in command of this powerful organization.

The two reached the middle of the intersection where they would be parting ways. Woodruff spun half around and stopped in the middle of the temporarily empty street. Looking up he said, "Seems to be a storm brewing out of the south. Time to gather in our harvest and make preparations to protect what we've worked so hard to build. It appears winter may arrive early this year. Good day, Brother Stout."

"Good day, Brother Woodruff." But Hosea Stout didn't really feel like it had been a very good day.

CHAPTER 69

COAL CREEK
UTAH TERRITORY

SEPTEMBER 25, 1857
10:00 PM

It was plenty dark as the brothers walked their horses and pack animals to the outskirts of the small town of Cedar City. They kept their voices low as they pondered the conversation they'd just had with the bishop's wife. There was little danger of their presence causing a stir at this late hour. However, they both knew they would not feel that way if they were traversing these same streets during the light of day. Then there was the apprehension regarding their destination. Just how safe would they be at the home of Rosmus Anderson?

"Ya know it might not be the smartest thing we could do ta be showin' up at the Anderson home after what Mrs. K. just said." Henry knew it was futile to change course now. He just wanted to be sure his brother would be going in with his eyes open.

"If you'd rather not go I understand. I'll meet ya at the north end of town at about midnight." Cao wasn't about to be dissuaded.

"Should I expect to see you then, or you and the Anderson girl?" Henry thought he should have something to say about any addition to their party his little brother might be inclined to make.

"If she's willin' to come with me, Henry, how can I just leave her there?"

"Maybe if'n you believed it was in her best interest?" Henry hadn't had much luck reasoning with Cao, but he had to try.

"You saw what they done to those women back at Mountain Meadows. How can you ask me to leave her here amongst people who could do a thing like that?" Cao's mind was made up.

"First of all, we can't be sure exactly who did that to those folks at the Meadows. Second, even if it was the folks around here, you got no reason to think that Molly is in danger of bein' treated that way." Henry was not looking forward to the baggage this particular young woman was likely to bring along.

Cao wanted Henry to see it his way. "You heard Mrs. K. Molly's step-dad has been shootin' his mouth in a way these folks don't like. I wouldn't put it past 'em to do the same as what they done to those folks planted over at Hamblin's ranch." He knew Molly was likely to be a burden but would be better protected by the two of them than if it were just he and Molly.

"Can we at least wait 'til we've had a chance to talk to Molly and her parents before we set our purpose on smuggling a Mormon teenager out a the country under the noses of the Mormons? We just might be puttin' her, and us, in a whole lot more danger than any of us er in already."

Just then the sound of hoof beats coming from the direction of Coal Creak could be heard. Henry quickly steered his animals off the well-worn trail into a thicket of fruit trees. Within a few seconds four riders sped past their position in full gallop. They were close enough now to the Anderson farm that it was likely these men had just left there. Henry had to grab hold of Cao's reigns to prevent his dash back out onto the trail.

"Hold on, Cao. There might be more. Let's just walk our mounts up there an' tie 'em off some distance from the house. We need to keep our wits about us if we're gonna manage to do any good."

Cao dismounted immediately and began to walk his animals deeper into the fruit orchard. He wasn't going to argue with his brother, but he was intent now on getting to the Anderson home as soon as possible.

They tied their animals to the branches of an apple tree a good hundred yards from the Anderson home. They could see the light of kerosene lanterns coming from inside the farmhouse. A dog barked continuously but did not seem to be barking at them. It sounded more like a mournful wail than the bark of a dog warning of intruders. They assumed it was a response to the four horsemen who'd just left. The brothers began their walk to the front door of the second home in Cedar City where they might expect a welcome.

As they approached the front gate, the dog continued to bark, only now at them. But interspersed between barking, the dog would whimper and stare at the ground as if it was looking at an invisible rabbit. He made no attempt to challenge the strangers entering the gate of the fenced yard. The brothers walked quietly up to the door, and Cao gently gave it a rap.

At first silence was their only response. Cao knocked again. Then he heard a frightened voice he barely recognized. It called out as if it was coming from one of the back rooms.

"What more do you want from us? Haven't you taken enough?" It was Molly's mother in near hysterics.

"Mrs. Anderson. It's me, Cao Young! Are you all right?"

Footsteps ran to the door, and within seconds the door flung open and Molly was hugging Cao more tightly than she ever had. "Thank God it's you. We are so frightened. It was so awful." Molly was distraught as was evident from her tear-stained cheeks.

Mrs. Anderson had quickly composed herself and was now doing her best to usher the young men into the house. "Henry, Cao, please come inside. You of all people must not be seen."

The brothers quickly stepped inside removing their hats. Cao wasted no time. "Who were those four riders that just left in a such a hurry?"

"They're terrible men, Cao. They mustn't have seen you. Please tell me they didn't see you." Molly stepped back a bit to observe Cao's response.

"They didn't see us, so don't worry 'bout that. Why have you been crying so? What did those men do to you?" Cao was a bundle of questions.

"Where's Rosmus, Mrs. Anderson?" It seemed it was only Henry who was thinking clearly.

Now Molly was having a difficult time keeping her composure. "I think we'd all better take a seat. You have a lot of questions, and we have a lot to tell."

At that Mrs. Anderson burst into tears and ran from the room.

CHAPTER 70

TEMPLE SQUARE
SALT LAKE CITY
UTAH TERRITORY

SEPTEMBER 29, 1857
8:00AM

Storm clouds were unusual for this time of year. But the sky was dark and the scent of a cold rain was in the air as John D. Lee stepped up to the front door of the Beehive House. He'd resigned himself to the feeling of dread he'd taken away from yesterday's meeting. Wilford Woodruff appeared only seconds after he lightly rapped on the door.

"Welcome, Brother Lee. Please do come in." The proper gentleman turned and walked toward the Prophet's office. Lee followed dutifully.

"Brother Lee. Pleased to see you here so promptly as usual. I do hope your visit with Emmeline was a pleasant one and that you were able to catch up sufficiently with one another." Young was almost effusive in his demeanor.

"It was very nice, Brother Young. We had much to catch up on. She is always so pleasant to spend time with." Lee wasn't going to let on that there were any lingering resentments resting in his heart.

"I'm so glad to see you this morning, Brother Lee. I went to bed last night with a heavy heart, as I'm sure you know. Thought I'd take the matter of the fate of that immigrant train straight to the Lord. John, I feel first rate. I asked the Lord if it was all right for the deed to be done, to take away the vision of the deed from my mind, and the Lord did so, and I feel first rate. It is all right. The only fear I have is from traitors." Young turned and walked behind his desk.

Lee didn't quite know how to respond. He was being hit with an entirely different atmosphere than what he'd encountered the day before. He knew he should be pleased, but somehow he just couldn't react so positively in so short a time frame.

"Now, is my understanding correct that Haight swore the men to a blood oath of secrecy there on the field the day after the massacre?" Young was all business now.

"That's correct. All the men were in league with one another in the swearing of it. It was a solemn proceeding." Lee, for the first time, had verification that Young had received word of the massacre. Haight must have made good on his pledge to report it. Lee was starting to feel better.

"That's good. Now John, I need you to provide me with all the names of all the Saints who were involved in any way there at Mountain Meadows. I want to know of everyone who was there even if they weren't there during the massacre. Anyone that knows anything about the goings-on there, we need to know about him. Brother Woodruff here is going to write down everything you tell us. Try not to leave anyone out. That oath that everyone swore to is going to be enforced. Anyone who wasn't there to swear to it is going to get his chance. We already have a good man working towards that as we speak. We must keep this whole thing a sacred secret.

"Once you and Wilford are finished, I'll need you to get to work on writing a report of the massacre that lays all the blame to the Lamanites. When you've finished, and I've had a chance to review it, file it with Wilford here, our church historian.

"I've sent for Major Higbee and bishop Klingensmith. When they arrive we'll decide how to dispose of the property that was taken. It would be good for you to stick around for a few days at least until they arrive. I understand you met a young lady down in Provo on your way up here. Is that true?"

"Why yes, yes it is." Lee was somewhat derailed by the sudden change of topic, although it wasn't much of a surprise that the Prophet would know of such a personal matter that had only begun to transpire a few days prior.

"Well, Brother Lee, if it's more than a passing dalliance, might I not be privileged to the honor of presiding over the sealing of my adopted son to his next wife?"

"The honor would be all mine, Brother Young." Lee had recovered enough by now to know that he would not be hung out to dry. The Prophet would know all there was to know about the massacre. Another wife would be Lee's reward for the work he'd done.

CHAPTER 71

TEMPLE SQUARE
SALT LAKE CITY
UTAH TERRITORY

NOVEMBER 18, 1857
10:00 AM

It was a brisk November morning, the kind of morning good for taking care of business. Wilford Woodruff led the two Danites into the tithing office where generals George Grant and William Kimball waited.

"The Prophet will join you shortly, gentlemen. Please make yourselves comfortable." Woodruff turned and left the room. He didn't know how to be anything other than polite, even when the people he addressed were not at all to his liking. Back in England he would have made an excellent butler. He would eventually become the fourth man to occupy the coveted position of the first presidency known as Prophet, Seer, and Revelator of the Church of Jesus Christ of Latter-day Saints.

He could tolerate the generals well enough. It was the two men he'd just led into the room he despised. It was apparent that they had not bathed in months. They wore their weapons openly for all to see, and fear.

Grant was the first to attempt a cordial remark. "Brother Rockwell, Brother Collett, welcome to Salt Lake City."

The two men being addressed each grabbed a chair and sat. Rockwell offered Grant nothing in return. Collett, detecting the slight, followed with his own silence.

"No use tryin' ta make small talk with O.P. Rockwell, George. O.P. don't bother bein' nice to anyone he doesn't feel like bein' nice to." General

Kimball had known Rockwell longer than had Grant. Neither man cared for Rockwell, but they had to put up with him. Collett was just his latest sidekick. Collett would have to look out for himself.

The two generals began to make small talk with each other. Rockwell had made his point. He would be subordinate to no one but the Prophet. Men like him and Hickman stalked the earth with an immunity that comes only with swearing allegiance to the highest authority anywhere and then making his will their purpose.

Men like this were not more devout than other devout followers—quite the contrary. When the Prophet needed to instruct, to comfort, to lead, or to inspire his flock, he was more than capable of doing all those things from his pulpit. When he needed to smite his enemies, or those of the church, Danites did the smiting. Much of the time it involved cold-blooded murder.

* * *

"They're waiting for you now. May the Lord be with you." Woodruff shuffled through the office of the Beehive House past his boss as if he could do no more to protect him.

"May he be with me indeed, Brother Woodruff. It's times like this that I need him to be near the most." Young was not looking forward to this meeting. He'd been having far too many of them lately. He much preferred meetings that involved making money. But Brigham Young was the kind of man who never hesitated in "taking the bull by the horns." His empire was being more and more frequently threatened, and bold action was required.

"I look forward to the day when we shall not need to employ the services of such men, Brother Young. There is such an unsavory aspect in dealing with the likes of brothers Rockwell and Collett." Woodruff had made no secret of his dislike for such notorious Danites. At least not to his boss.

"That day will come, Brother Woodruff. If not while I walk the earth, then perhaps in your day." He'd been grooming the younger Woodruff to be his successor. Young would have to find a way to outlive Heber Kimball, John Taylor, Orson Hyde, and a host of other aspiring contenders first.

"You'd better get over there. I suspect brothers Grant and Kimball are writhing in agony by now. I certainly would be." Woodruff silently wondered if he himself would be up to the task of dealing with such grave circumstances and with such unsavory men.

"It never hurts to let your subordinates twist a while before you commence a meeting. It usually makes them more amenable to your suggestions once you do arrive." Young liked imparting these pearls of wisdom to his protégé.

"I'll remember that the next time you keep me waiting."

Young winked at his loyal counselor and stepped out the door.

* * *

Young walked briskly across the street. He did not maintain his usual deliberate stride. He truly hoped no one was watching. The less he became publicly associated with the likes of O.P. Rockwell and Sylvanus Collett, the better. He was through the front door of the tithing house and into the meeting room within a minute of having left the Beehive House.

Grant and Kimball almost leapt from their chairs in deference to the great Prophet. Rockwell and Collett rose also, only more slowly and more unsure of the mannerly protocol expected in such settings.

"Please be seated gentlemen. Thank you for coming. I'm sure you want to get right down to business. General Grant, why don't you bring us current on our situation in the south?" Young seated himself as he spoke and watched the others do so as well.

"We're still looking for the Gentiles Brother Hatch let slip through his fingers down near Fort Clara. We have reports that they've been sighted in or around Cedar City. Hamblin and Dame are doing what they can to apprehend them." Grant's information was nothing new, at least not to Young.

"Seems they already was apprehended once. Maybe apprehendin' ain't the right approach we ought ta be takin' with them two Gentiles." Rockwell wasted no time making a case for the superiority of his methodology.

"None of us have had the opportunity to hear why Hatch let them go. It could well be he determined that the Gentiles did not pose a threat." Kimball had attained his station by acting reasonably and responsibly. He also felt his rank should command more respect than Rockwell had been inclined to bestow.

Rockwell took the challenge. "Maybe determinin' how much of a threat a Gentile poses ought to be somethin' that gets determined by someone more experienced than an Indian interpreter."

"He did get the men Brother Lee sent him to get. Had to go quite some distance to get them too." Grant did not want to allow this meeting to transpire without an acknowledgement of some of the successes the chain of command had achieved.

"And now we have two more men out there that could do damage to the Saints." Rockwell wasn't going to let go. Collett wasn't going to say anything.

"What about the Anderson fellow who's been reported to have broken the blood oath the Saints took at the Meadows?" Young didn't worry about successes, only loose ends.

"You won't have to worry bout Brother Anderson shootin' his mouth off no more. I expect the brethren around Cedar City will be keepin' their oath a little better from now on." Rockwell had had some successes of his own.

"I have to agree with Brother Rockwell. In hindsight Hatch should not have allowed the two Gentiles to go free. Now how are we going to take care of the situation?" Young wanted to conclude the debate and get on with the primary subject of the meeting.

"Brother Collett and I'll take care of it. I'm told we're goin' ta be headin' back down that way anyhow. We'll see to it." Rockwell lived to show up those who would sit in superiority to him.

"Tell me what you plan to do about the 'Sporting Men' from California." Young had just settled the debate over the two Gentiles; now it was time to tackle the six Gentiles. Fires seemed to be breaking out all over Deseret these days.

"Stout has informed them that they will be provided an escort out the Old Spanish Trail if they choose to leave. They've also been told that brothels and gambling halls will never be allowed in Deseret. Four have expressed a desire to leave. They also know that Johnston's army won't be here 'til spring at the soonest, if they ever get here at all. Two want to stick around to see how Johnston fares." Grant had promoted the Prophet's suggestion to have Rockwell lead the escort south. Both he and Kimball, and many others in the church hierarchy, looked forward to getting the unsavory Danite out of the city.

"Brother Rockwell, do you have enough good men to handle the six of them should they all decide to avail themselves of your escort?" Young knew better than to micromanage. But things hadn't gone all that smoothly at Mountain Meadows and he wanted to be sure future operations did not result in a looming public relations nightmare.

"Sylvanus and I have two other good men we can trust. If all six of 'em decide to go, we might have our hands full." Rockwell usually presented himself as fearless. The Gentiles he'd be escorting were purported to be large, well-armed, experienced men. He'd planned enough of these jobs to appreciate the danger of being underprepared.

Grant saw an opportunity. "I can assign some good men to help you out, Port. How many you think you're gonna need? Ten, fifteen?"

Rockwell glared back at Grant, letting him know he didn't appreciate his offer.

The Prophet intervened. "That won't be necessary. Hamblin's back in town and planning to leave in the morning. I'll have him take another message, ahead of your escort, to Bishop Bryant in Salt Creek. He will have a sufficient contingent to help you depending on how many of the Gentiles stay with your escort. Brother Grant, you keep your scouts on the lookout for any of the six that depart Brother Rockwell's escort between here and Salt Creek. We may need to plan another operation to deal with them."

Grant and Kimball nodded their acceptance of the terms.

"May the Lord be with us all as we carry out his will." The meeting was over.

CHAPTER 72

COAL CREEK
UTAH TERRITORY

SEPTEMBER 25, 1857
10:30 PM

"Rosmus Anderson. What have they done with him?" Henry had an idea the answer had something to do with the dog that was still barking and whimpering outside.

Molly Anderson hung her head. Rosmus was only her stepfather, but he had taken good care of her, her mother, and her four sisters.

"He's outside under that fresh pile of dirt the dog is guarding, isn't he?" Henry couldn't help think that the nightmare just kept getting worse.

"They came just after we'd finished dinner. They said Mr. Anderson had violated an oath to the Lord for which he must atone. That he had said terrible things about the Saints and what they had done at the Meadows." Molly looked up to see if anything she was saying made any sense to the brothers. Their look assured her to continue.

"He tried to argue with them at first. He said he wasn't at the Meadows when the oath was taken. But they just kept silent and kept staring at him. Finally he said if they would just let his wife and girls be, he would not object.

"They said they would see that the Lord would provide for us and that we could all be together in heaven as long as he went behind the veil with the right intention." Molly started to cry again.

Henry wasn't quite sure what she was referring to now. He looked to his brother for understanding.

Cao wasn't ready to interpret. "Was the bishop with them?"

"No! It was Daniel McFarland, John Higbee, James Haslam, and that horrible Mr. Rockwell. It was because of Rockwell that Mr. Anderson agreed to do it. He kept pleading with the others while he was looking at Rockwell, and the way he smirked and looked at me . . . " Molly burst into tears once again.

"Tell us what they did, Molly. I know it's hard, but we gotta know what happened." Henry was having trouble assessing the degree of the danger he and his brother were in. Molly seemed to pull herself together.

"Mr. Higbee stayed with Mr. Anderson while they read passages together. Mr. McFarland, Mr. Haslam, and Mr. Rockwell dug the grave." She almost broke again but shook it off.

"When they were finished, Mr. Higbee led Mr. Anderson out and had him kneel at the edge of the grave. That's when Mr. Rockwell used his knife to cut his throat. We all watched it. They held him while his blood drained into the grave. Then they dropped him in and covered him. They told us to tell any Gentiles that he ran away to California." Molly's affect had become emotionless.

Just then Mrs. Anderson returned to the room. "You were not supposed to tell, Molly. What is to become of us now? You boys are in danger just being here. If they knew you were here they would kill you. If they know you've been here they will hunt you down."

"Mother! Cao and Henry are our friends. How can we not tell them?"

"You must leave at once. It's not safe for you to be here. It's not safe for us having you here." Mrs. Anderson wrung her hands as she spoke.

"No one knows we're here, ma'am. We didn't even tell the bishop's wife we were coming. Do you think those men will be coming back here tonight?" Henry needed time to think. This was probably the only safe place where he and his brother might be able to find out more of what they needed to know.

"They won't be coming back here tonight. If that Mr. Rockwell ever comes back here, I'm going to take my life." Molly was looking at her mother as she spoke. Mrs. Anderson burst into tears and ran from the room again.

"You're gonna have to come with us, Molly." Cao looked at his brother Henry. He had that look that said he would not back down on this.

"Can we all just calm down a bit? I don't think any of us is thinkin' clear enough to be makin' any big plans right now. Molly, what was Rosmus saying went on over at the 'Mountain Meadows'?" Henry knew what he was likely to hear, but he and his brother still needed to hear it.

Mrs. Anderson burst back into the room. It was obvious she had been listening to the conversation. "Molly, the more you tell these boys, the more their lives will be in danger. Can't you see? The brethren are enforcing a blood oath. Rosmus has already been sacrificed for it."

"They have a right to know. Because their lives are in danger, we have an obligation to tell them. What kind of a Christian people have we become? Cao was studying with our own bishop to become one of us. Would you have him thrown to the wolves because he has not yet been baptized? I have had enough of being told the Gentiles are our enemies!" Molly knew her mother would never have the courage to stand up to the authorities of the church. Molly was not like her mother. It was Mrs. Anderson's turn to hang her head.

"They killed almost all of them. More than one hundred men, women, and children. They took all of their livestock and all of their possessions and then buried them in shallow graves. They spared only a dozen or so of the smallest children. Most of them have been placed in homes here in Cedar City. The bishop and others have gone to Salt Lake City to turn over their valuables and to report the slaughter to the Prophet. The Lamanites helped, but it was the brethren who caused it." Molly's tone left no doubt that her faith in her religion had been shattered.

"Was the bishop involved?" Cao now feared that the man he trusted most to provide him with the truth might be complicit in the horrendous crime they'd become aware of.

"Yes. Bishop Klingensmith was there. He's the one who placed the children with families here in town. And they know that you were with the Gentile that Ira Hatch killed. Some people are questioning his judgment in allowing you and Henry to go free. I wouldn't know any of this if Mr. Anderson hadn't told us. And now because he told these things, he has been sacrificed." Molly was near tears again.

"I can't believe the bishop could condone such an action. I can't believe anyone could." Cao shook his head in disbelief.

"Did Rosmus seem to know why the folks here would do such a thing?" Henry needed as much information as he could get.

"He told us that orders had come from Salt Lake City just before he left with Elder Hatch to chase down those that escaped. A few weeks before the immigrants passed through, Apostle Smith came through alerting the brethren of their expected arrival." Molly was earnestly trying to be of help now.

"Did Rosmus happen to mention anything about Jacob Hamblin bein' involved in this?" Cao was following his brother's lead.

"He and brothers Lee, Johnson, and Knight were involved in working with the Lamanites. Mr. Anderson said Brother Hamblin was not at the Meadows when a sacrifice was made of those people. But the entire militia was called out. Almost none of the men in this town were not involved in it. You and Henry should not let yourselves be seen. I'm afraid it won't be safe for either of you as long as you're anywhere in Deseret."

"We've rode hard all day, Mrs. Anderson. If we could spend the night in your barn an' maybe leave tomorrow night, we'd be much obliged." Henry was speaking directly to Molly's mother. He figured if she weren't willing, they'd need to start making other plans now.

"Of course you're welcome. But you must know that if they find you they will kill you. You'll have to keep your animals in the barn and out of sight." Rosmus had been dead only a short time, and already Mrs. Anderson knew how deeply she would miss the security of a man in the house.

Though he had been no match for the four church elders who'd carried out his atonement, he had begged for the safety of his bride and stepchildren. The solemnity with which they'd carried out the ceremony led her to believe they would keep their word. At least she was confident three of them would. Higbee, McFarland, and Haslam were well known to her. Mr. Rockwell was of great concern. She had not missed the leering desire he'd displayed toward Molly. Clearly his intent had been to intimidate Rosmus.

Rockwell was seldom seen this far south, and chances are he would not be returning any time soon. Mrs. Anderson would continue to cast her lot with the Saints. Her choices were quite limited. Her eldest daughter looked at things differently.

"When you leave, I'm going with you." Molly had made up her mind. It was now just a matter of the other three adults in the room making up theirs.

CHAPTER 73

TEMPLE SQUARE
SALT LAKE CITY
UTAH TERRITORY

SEPTEMBER 30,1857
7:30 AM

His animals were the finest in all the territory and the best cared for. He had swine, sheep, and cows. His chicken coops were raked daily. The nearby gardens grew the best produce in the city. The production was more than adequate to supply the substantial needs of all seventy-five inhabitants associated with the Lion and Beehive houses. The excess was distributed to the less fortunate through the administration of the tithing office.

Schoolchildren, and the Prophet's children, were given chores here in the morning before and after lessons. Their morning chores completed, they were now nowhere to be seen. The cauldron used to cook the pig slop was cooling as the four men strolled past. Milk cans from the morning's milking sat in the creek awaiting the dairyman's pickup.

Everywhere they looked they saw signs of perfection. The carpentry of the corrals, coops, stanchions, shelters, and pens were of a level far superior to what Lee and the others had become accustomed. Charlie Hopkins was in awe of all he saw. P.K. was also impressed with the industriousness of the Prophet's stockyard. He chided himself for the envy he felt in his heart, then dismissed the thought and accepted the necessity for the Prophet to project such a display. The brethren must be provided with inspiration, and who better to provide it than the Prophet himself. He still wanted to believe that inspiration was always good.

He and Charlie Hopkins had just delivered a substantial load of gold and silver coin and other valuables. The full wagonload of plunder represented a fortune by any standard in all of Deseret. P.K. had questions, but knew better than to be too direct in his questioning.

"You men have benefited the church enormously with the delivery of the property yesterday. We will make the most of it I assure you. With respect to the cattle and wagons that remain in Iron and Washington counties, dispose of that property; let Brother Lee take charge of it. He and Brother Hamblin will determine the beneficial use of that property." Young looked at P.K. as he was speaking. It was the Prophet's first acknowledgement so far with respect to the massacre since the morning's activities began.

"What about the children?" P.K. had been curious as to the level of involvement the Prophet had engaged with respect to the planning of the attack.

The Prophet frowned as if he was not happy with the question. He responded slowly. "They're innocent blood, and we are obligated to care for them as if they were our own. I trust they've all been placed with the most capable families you can find among the brethren?"

"They have, indeed, Brother Young. I was thinking more about the long term." P.K. had been impressed with the lack of planning, with respect to the aftermath, which was becoming evident. If the orders "Kill everyone old enough to speak!" had originated in Salt Lake City, as he and the others had been led to believe, would there not at least be a plan for the care and disposition of the children?

The Prophet seemed to read his thought. "You must forgive me, Brother Klingensmith, I have been so preoccupied with General Wells of late, and the specter of Johnston's army, I haven't given enough thought to matters of childcare. I'm sure I'll be entering negotiations with the Gentiles soon over the matter. When I have a clear vision of what is to be done with them, I will send you word. Until then, I advise all of you to refrain from discussing the matter of the immigrant party with anyone. Neither do I want those children showing up here and causing a stir. It is most important that the oath be kept at all hazards." Appearing a bit perturbed, it was becoming clear to Lee and P.K. that the Prophet was trying to wrap up the meeting.

"We sure could put a few of those long-horned cattle to good use. Some of the brethren who marched with the militia to the Meadows put me up to askin' ya about the possibility." Charlie Hopkins had missed the subtle clues that Lee and P.K. had not. Now his two companions waited for the rebuke they were sure would come his way.

"Brother Hopkins, it was the Lord that brought the Gentiles under our control and it is he who will continue to do so. All the property is to be consecrated unto the church. That is the only way it can be placed to the benefit of all the brethren. Brothers Lee and Hamblin will also need to exercise a judicious hand in settling up with the Lamanites." The Prophet's words had let Hopkins off easy. His tone, however, was laced with warning.

"I understand, Brother Young. I had ta ask. Hope ya don't mind." Hopkins' method of addressing the Prophet embarrassed Lee and P.K. All three of them knew that many of the brethren had made off with considerable more plunder than what had been delivered to the Prophet. The immigrants had been transporting considerable wealth. In later years historians would document estimates from $50,000 to $100,000 in 1857 dollars.

"Brother Hopkins, please tell the brethren to keep living their religion and the Lord will be sure to provide for them and their families."

Young knew that he needed to be diplomatic with those who'd carried out the church's dirty work in the south. He also knew quite well that Lee and Hamblin would distribute the cattle in a manner that would reward the right people, themselves not to be excluded.

"I suspect the three of you are as hungry as I am by now. Brother Lee has informed me that the two of you plan on heading back to Cedar today. I've instructed the women to have a fine breakfast ready for us upon our return to the Lion House. Shall we go?" The Prophet was finished with the conversation, and the four men proceeded as suggested.

CHAPTER 74

SEVIER RIVER
UTAH TERRITORY

NOVEMBER 21, 1857
9:30 PM

Winter had offered up its first cold blast of the season as the party moved one day south of the little town of Salt Creek. A light dusting of snow continued to fall as the four men met to discuss their strategy. Earlier that evening they'd been approached by the four men Bishop Bryant had assigned to help them. They'd asked politely enough to share camp for a night. In light of the weather it seemed a reasonable request. The Gentiles did not seem to expect any form of treachery to be in play.

"The Colonel and the Aiken brothers are sleepin' under the freight wagon near the fire. Tuck Wright is under the spring wagon next to 'em. Our boys that Bishop Bryant sent is fakin' sleep under the other freighter closest to the river. They each slipped a king bolt up their sleeve before they bedded down. They're ready to go." Sylvanus Collett had done a good job of assessing the party's preparation. Everyone knew it would be O.P. Rockwell who would signal the start.

John Lott and Joseph Harker were nervous. Ordinarily this kind of work was not their cup of tea. Their commander, Lot Smith, had only recently pressed them into service to the unpredictable Rockwell.

"I don't understand why we need to use clubs and king bolts. Wouldn't our side arms be more effective?" Lott knew it was risky to express an opinion contrary to Rockwell's. But Collett, who didn't command the same respect, had laid out the plan. Clubbing the Gentiles to death was a little too "up close and personal" for John Lott.

Collett was offended at Lott's challenge but looked to Rockwell to respond.

When Rockwell remained silent and just kept looking at him, he knew he'd have to defend himself.

"What's the matter? Ain't got the guts to take 'em on man ta man?" It was a poor display of leadership. But then Sylvanus Collett had never been much of a leader.

"Clubbin' a man ta death while he's asleep don't sound like such a brave act neither. I say John's got a point." Harker had spent considerable more time around Collett than Lott had. He knew that underneath his swagger he was a coward. Sylvanus shrank from the discussion. All eyes were on Rockwell now.

"We save our ammo. Too easy for a firearm to misfire and then one a those Gentiles will be wide awake from the shots that let off. You know they be sleepin' with at least one a their own side arms and a rifle to boot. There's also the chance someone's camped closer than any of us think. With this snow we had no visibility before we made camp. Any gunplay would likely alert 'em to come snoopin'. We stick to the plan and only use our side arms if'n we have to." The discussion would be inaudible to their intended targets. The light snowfall provided a helpful muffling of the treacherous preparation in process.

Lott nodded his acquiescence and Rockwell continued. "I'll take the one in the middle under the freighter. John and Joseph will line up on either side of me. Sylvanus, you take Tuck Wright under the spring wagon. We'll be watchin' you and timin' our swings along with yours. Make sure you take good aim."

Rockwell waited until the other three acknowledged his instruction with a nod and they were off.

Their first stop was to signal their backups. Jacob Bigler was to back up Rockwell. John Kink, Parley Pitchforth, and Samuel Pickton had been assigned to Collett, Lott, and Harker respectively. The first stunning blow was to come from the unwieldy clubs with the backups jumping in with the more damaging and maneuverable kingbolts.

The eight men walked together as a well-choreographed unit. The silence was as absolute as any could have experienced, but the pounding of their hearts pulsing inside their heads was deafening. Any doubt produced by the indecency of their action was subordinated to completing the tactical complexity of the maneuver.

Sylvanus raised his club, hesitated momentarily, and then brought it crashing down with all his might. His aim would have been perfect if it had not been for the edge rail on the springboard wagon above. Tuck Wight spun to his knees instantly. The sound of the rail shattering having almost the same effect as the discharge of a gun, he looked up at the stricken Collett. John Kink leapt into the fray before Wright could get his bearing and came crashing down on Wright's head twice in quick succession with the king bolt. Kink then jumped back to survey his work, but to his dismay his blows did not have the desired effect. Only slightly stunned, Tuck Wright charged into Sylvanus' midsection, driving him backwards into a thick stand of rabbit brush.

Back at the freight wagon, Rockwell and his men were having slightly better success. The clubbing had stunned all three of the sleeping men sufficiently enough to give the backups a clean headshot at their man with the king bolts. Jacob Bigler's aim was off enough that his blow only served to put a nasty gash in John Aiken's head, arousing him from a momentary stupor and spurring him to anger. Like his friend Tuck, he dove at the man closest to him and commenced to give Jacob Bigler a thrashing he would never forget. Collett was getting a similar beating from Wright. The flickering firelight illuminated the intermittent blows.

While the melee ensued, Orrin Porter Rockwell coolly stepped over to the scene of the beating being administered to Bigler and with a heavy swing clubbed John Aiken over the head. As Aiken's body slumped lifelessly astraddle Bigler, Rockwell drew his side arm and took aim at the bare back of Tuck Wright. The round of his Navy Colt revolver entered shoulder high as Wright lurched forward from the blast. At first it appeared he would fall. Then he seemed to right himself as he ran off into the darkness of the night.

"Are the damned Gentiles all dead, Port?" Jacob Bigler was shouting as he pushed John Aiken's body away.

"All but one! The son-of-a-bitch ran!"

Collett came staggering out of the brush spitting blood and teeth. Both he and Bigler were an awful sight. Bigler had one eye swollen shut and was bleeding profusely from the nose and mouth. Both his upper and lower lips had been badly split. John Aiken and Tuck Wright had only had a short time with them but they'd made it count. None of Rockwell's men had any appetite for giving chase.

"Snow seems to be lettin' up. Tomorrow mornin' we'll pick up his track and ketch up to what's left of him. We're at least 25 miles out a Salt Creek. I know I put one in him. I doubt he'll get too far. Let's get these three into the river before anyone who might have heard my shot decides to come nosin' around." Rockwell and Collett watched while the other six grabbed wrists and ankles. Within a short minute they'd tossed Colonel Eichard and the Aiken brothers into the swift cold waters of the Sevier River.

CHAPTER 75

CEDAR CITY
UTAH TERRITORY

NOVEMBER 15, 1857
6:15 PM

More than six weeks had passed since the brothers had arrived at Coal Creek where Rosmus Anderson had been "blood atoned." Molly Anderson's announcement that she intended on leaving with them had set off an intense negotiation between Mrs. Anderson, the brothers, and Molly. She was the eldest of five daughters, and Mrs. Anderson could not bear to lose the only other family member capable of providing her with some support.

Cao could not bear to leave without Molly. Henry was struggling with the thought of leaving his little brother behind. He tended to side with Mrs. Anderson regarding the efficacy of taking the fifteen-year-old on a very dangerous journey through Deseret. She would slow them down and make it more difficult to talk their way out of any "tight spot" they might stumble into.

The brothers were a welcome asset, filling in for the vacancy left by Rosmus. The feeding of the animals, the milking, the wood chopping, etc., were ancillary to the protection they provided the family of women against the feared return of Rockwell. Then again, there was the mother's fear of what her religious leaders would think of her for harboring the hunted Gentiles.

Cao had argued for more time to pursue a confrontation with Bishop Klingensmith. The events surrounding the murders at Mountain Meadows and that of the children's stepfather had destroyed his confidence in the religion he had intended to make his own. The faith of his true love was just as challenged.

Mrs. Anderson was in a state of denial, clinging to the doctrines of her church as if it could somehow be satisfactorily explained in the next life, if not in this one. Overwhelmed with grief and fear, she could only agree that somehow the bishop might be able to provide the young people with the guidance and understanding she could not.

As soon as word had come that the bishop was back in town, and it had grown dark enough to travel undetected, Cao insisted on making the short ride to the bishop's house. Henry went along just to be sure that some form of religious fervor would not decide their future. His view of Mormonism had never been encouraging. By now he found it to be plainly revolting. Without protest, Mrs. Anderson assented to Molly accompanying the boys.

Cao rapped lightly on the door as not to startle the inhabitants. He knew that the bishop had only just arrived. It would normally be impolite to intrude so early, but their circumstance was pressing.

Hannah Creamer Klingensmith answered the door as graciously as she would for a set of dear friends. The three of them knew she must have grave feelings about their presence on her threshold. She would not allow her personal feelings to override her sense of propriety when greeting innocent young folk, even though their appearance could only mean that she and her husband would become more conflicted.

"Welcome, Cao, Henry. Molly, it's so nice to see you. Please come in and tell me how your mother is doing." Her concern was genuine. It was obvious she had heard about the atonement of Rosmus Anderson.

"We're here to speak with the bishop, Mrs. K. I know this must be an inconvenient time, but our purpose in coming is of great importance." Cao had waited a long time. He hoped she would understand.

"Of course. I'll send Sarah Anne to get him. He's over at the barn tending to a sick calf. I'm sure he'll be very pleased that you've come. Until he arrives, may I offer you some apricot pie? We've just finished dinner and were about to enjoy some ourselves." It would have been impolite to refuse such a hospitable offer.

The three guests seated themselves around the table and began to engage in an awkward session of small talk. Mrs. K. was very careful to be sure her children were kept busy and out of the room. Soon the discussion would become much too sensitive for them to overhear. Mrs. K. seemed capable of diffusing the tension surrounding them. By the time P.K. entered the room, the others felt like they were exactly where they should be.

"Cao, Henry, it's good to see that you boys are in good health. Molly, I'm so sorry to have heard what happened to Rosmus. He was a good man, and such a thing as was done to him should never have occurred." P.K. had been doing a lot of thinking lately. The events of the past month had changed him. Always a man of deep resolve, his confidence of late had been severely shaken. He was determined to get it back, but it would need to take a different form.

"Should those folks up at the Mountain Meadows have had done what was done to them?" Cao figured he'd get right to it. P.K. was going to get his new sense of resolve tested. The little room suddenly became very quiet.

P.K. looked at his young student more deeply than he had ever done before. "No, Cao. They most certainly did not deserve that which was done to them."

"I hear you were a part of what was done. Is that so?" Cao wasn't going to back down now. A big part of him was hoping that P.K. would set the record straight. He wanted to believe there was something in this country that was still worth believing in. Was there someone who had the authority to rectify the terrible wrongs that had obviously been committed?

"I'm so very sorry that I have to say that I was a part of it. I wish I could tell you that I did everything I could do to prevent it from happening. But I stand before you ashamed to admit that I was part of the cause of it." It was both difficult and liberating for him to admit this to his houseguests. It had been more difficult for him to admit it to Hannah. His new resolve would be to honestly face the truth and the future. This would be one of his first tests.

Henry wasn't sure if he should leave the room or draw his side arm and commence firing. All he could muster of himself was a muffled shout, "Why?"

P.K. sighed deeply as he searched his soul for an honest answer. "It's a difficult question to answer, but I'll try. I did it because I was afraid of what would happen to my family and me if I refused. I wish I could say I did it because I believed it was what God himself wanted. But I did not, and I suppose I shall be condemned to eternal hell because of it. I do believe that some of my brethren did act in faith, and I hope that they shall somehow be forgiven before they are sent beyond the veil. But I knew better. For me it was a terrible act of fear and selfishness."

Hannah remained silent as her husband spoke. She tried to look lovingly at the three young people sitting at her table. All the while tears were streaming down her cheeks.

"So I expect you'll be turnin' yerself in to the authorities?" Henry was still without a clue as to where the discussion was headed. His was a question he just needed to ask.

"And what authority would it be that you are referring to young man?" P.K. was more than twenty years Henry's senior. He also knew his remaining time on earth was less precarious than was Henry's and Cao's.

"I expect that'd be the authorities in Salt Lake City. I know there's judges working in Salt Lake. I had to post bail for Cao once when he got drunk in last year's pass through. You don't suppose you can admit to participatin' in a mass murder an' not have to answer fer it?" Henry was carrying the discussion for Cao and Molly. They were too stunned and speechless at what they'd heard to continue with their questions.

"I expect I'll be answering for what I've done every minute of every day for the rest of my life. But I won't be answering to the authorities in Salt Lake City. At least not yet. I expect those authorities are going to be much more concerned about what to do about you and your brother than they are about me.

"You boys had best be figurin' out how to get out of this country without bein' seen. That's not going to be very easy. They know that you saw one of the young men that got away get shot. The man that did the shootin' is bein' strongly criticized for not doin' the same to you. I expect there's going to be some pretty tough hombres lookin' for you." P.K. was sincerely showing concern for the brothers, and his sincerity was compelling.

"Molly's comin' with us." Cao didn't know what else to say. He just wanted to let everyone, including Henry, know here and now that he would not consider any other course. Molly grabbed his hand and looked at the others as if she too could not be dissuaded. The time the two had spent together these past weeks had brought them to an inseparable state of mind. They would face any hardship their love for each other would bring them to.

P.K. sought to express that her presence on the brothers' journey would only jeopardize their chances. He wanted to appeal to her mother's need for her to stay. As he looked at their resolve he knew his effort would be a wasted one. "I will do my best to see that your mother and sisters are looked after. Be especially careful whom you trust."

"I don't expect I'll be pursuin' my baptism any further, Bishop. Molly an' I have been talking about getting' married by a Catholic priest once't we get back to Pennsylvania." Cao needed to bring the subject of his religious studies with P.K. to some degree of closure.

"I certainly understand, young man. Best of luck to you and Molly, and best of luck to you Henry. I fear you're all going to need a great deal of it."

CHAPTER 76

SALT CREEK
(NEPHI)
UTAH TERRITORY

NOVEMBER 22,1857
6:45 AM

For the past three hours the pain and agony he'd been feeling had become a dull numb torment. It was necessary for him to separate his spirit from the wretched, battered vehicle that carried it. Thoughts of whether his severely damaged body could ever feel normal again would enter his mind, but he would quickly push them aside.

The bullet lodged in Tuck Wright's back had continued to throb throughout the night. The two deep gashes on top of his head had finally stopped bleeding, and the cold night air had actually helped minimize the pain. His bare feet had ceased all feeling early on. It was the incessant bone-chilling cold that had kept him moving.

Apart from knowing that to stop walking meant sure death, the shivering discomfort was only partly tolerable if he kept moving. There was also the requirement to do whatever it took to inform someone of what had happened to him and his friends last night at camp on Sevier River. He was alone in a hostile environment on his last legs. Showing his enemies they had not yet succeeded was enough to push him forward.

Tuck Wright was an experienced outdoorsman, as were the men he rode with. He knew how to survive amidst the elements of nature when properly attired and prepared. As a gambling man, he would not have taken a long-odds bet on himself under these circumstances. But he had pushed on despite his hopeless condition.

By the time he had covered the twenty plus miles over the snow-covered trail and was stumbling back into the little town of Salt Creek, he held no resemblance to the man who had passed through that hamlet only one day earlier. He and his three companions had projected an impressive appearance of manhood. He now staggered forth hunched over, arms folded and his hair and leggings matted with his own dried blood.

They had all been in the prime of life, well dressed and well equipped. They had been the envy of all who had the opportunity to gaze upon the striking portrait they'd made in the town square. How could they have known some would covet their good fortune enough to inflict such a hateful suffering?

It was young Guy Foote who was first to see the pathetic pale figure stumbling forward through the entrance of South Main Street. He was in the town square the day before when the impressive group of frontiersmen left town with their notorious escort. At first he did not recognize the figure heading for him as one of the same. Then he noticed him wearing the expensive leggings seldom seen in these parts.

The fifteen-year-old Foote stepped off the boardwalk in front of his father's hotel and began to approach the figure. For a moment he was repulsed by the man's ghoulish appearance. Then, recognizing his desperate need, he approached with the intent of offering the observably needed assistance.

Wright and his friends had stayed in his father's hotel the night before. Wright and John Aiken had each offered him a generous tip for tending to their horses and pack animals. The man was now at the last of his strength. The simple exercise of ascending the two steps to the establishment seemed more than he could have accomplished without young Foote's assistance.

Once inside, Guy's father and mother were shocked at what their son had just brought through the door. They stood agape for several seconds while Guy's best friend Reuben Down arose to provide additional assistance. Finally Mr. Timothy Foote recovered sufficiently to direct the threesome into a main-level room off the parlor where they could attend the man without disturbing any paying customers who might soon descend into their midst.

Mrs. Nancy Foote wore a stricken frown as her husband ordered her to fetch a pale of hot water and cloth. She turned and left, shaking her head.

Mr. Foote could see that Wright was going to need medical attention. "Reuben, run down to Bishop Bryant's and tell him he needs to get over here at once."

Upon Mrs. Foote's return, Timothy cleaned the back wound and two deep scalp wounds at the top of Wright's head. By the time Reuben returned with Bishop Bryant in tow, he was preparing to extract the ball from Wright's shoulder. He had not summoned the bishop to do the doctoring.

Wright grimaced and contorted while Foote washed his wounds with a splash of whiskey. He cried out when Foote probed the bullet wound with a pair of "clamp tweezers" in search of the ball. Fortunately, Tuck Wright, a large strapping blacksmith a day before, did not have the strength to resist Foote's efforts. The innkeeper was finally able to extract the ball of a Navy Colt revolver.

Bishop Bryant looked on in near horror while Wright passed out under the stress of the pain. The father told his son to keep an eye on the patient while he visited with the bishop. Nancy Foote was still shaking her head in obvious disapproval when the two men entered the kitchen. She clearly wanted to express her opinion of the circumstance before them. Her nonverbal demeanor displeased her husband, and he was not going to have any of it.

"Leave us, woman! The bishop and I will discuss this matter in private. The less you concern yourself with this matter the better."

Mrs. Foote lowered her gaze and left. Defeat was a common experience among plural wives in Deseret. They had to accept it.

Earlier that year Timothy Foote had taken a plural wife after ten years of monogamous fidelity with Nancy. It had been a bitter pill for the formerly proud woman. Elizabeth was seven years her junior, and her husband seemed to prefer showering all his attention on his new bride. So many of the men were taking plural wives these days, especially those who were the most inclined to live their religion. She would have to obtain her paradise in heaven. It could not be had in this life.

Bryant whispered, "Why are you trying to save the Gentile? You were part of the meeting when we decided to send Bigler and the others ahead to help Rockwell." They had received explicit instructions from Salt Lake City, through Jacob Hamblin, that the Prophet wanted them to provide whatever assistance necessary to help Rockwell accomplish his mission.

"I agreed to comply with the directive Hamblin delivered, but I was not ever selected to be an active participant in putting them out of the way.

That is the duty of Rockwell and the others, not mine." Foote was way ahead of Bryant. He knew that too many of the town's people were already aware of the strange turn of events transpiring in the room on the other side of the hotel parlor. Although this was an almost entirely Mormon enclave, appearances still might mean something to some of the brethren.

Just then Guy Foote entered the kitchen. "Mr. Tuck Wright is awake, and one of the Aiken brothers has just stumbled into the hotel. You better come. The two of them are talkin' together right now."

Mr. Foote and Bishop Bryant looked at one another and immediately headed for the room where the two Gentiles were now located. Upon entering they were both shocked to see a second man, John Aiken, appearing to be in a similar condition as Tuck Wright had been when he was assisted into the hotel.

Tuck Wright was sitting on the edge of the cot, and Aiken was kneeling on the floor in front of him. The two men were sobbing and embracing one another as only men could who had somehow managed to pass through a violent near-death experience. The sight brought tears to the eyes of the usually stoic Nancy Foote. The bishop and Mr. Foote looked on with a new sense of alarm. Guy Foote watched with amazement at the drama unfolding before his eyes. He was seeing things this day that he would testify to twenty years later.

John Aiken had shown up in a crumpled bloody heap on the doorstep of Mrs. Frances Cazier. She already knew about the other man being assisted at Foote's hotel and said, "Why, another of you got away from the robbers and is at Brother Foote's."

"Thank God! It is my brother," he said. Mrs. Cazier and a handful of others now littering the main street had watched as he ran the whole distance from her home to Foote's Hotel. Reeling like a drunk, his hair and shirt clotted with his own blood, he'd burst into the parlor of the hotel as if he were a demon possessed. When Reuben Down led him to where Tuck Wright was being cared for, he realized his brother was dead and only he and Tuck had survived.

Bryant looked at Foote, and without saying a word the two knew what each of them needed to do. Foote approached the two men and started to tend the head wounds of John Aiken. Bishop Bryant backed out of the room and began the process of determining the implications of what had gone so terribly wrong on the banks of the Sevier River . . . and what needed to be done about it.

CHAPTER 77

SEVIER RIVER
UTAH TERRITORY

NOVEMBER 22,1857
1:00 PM

The signs of a scuffle were everywhere. The light dusting of snow the night before had not melted off, and the blood-stained contrast made the investigation much easier than it would have been otherwise. Henry found a couple of Sylvanus Collett's teeth lying near the smoldering campfire.

"Looks like there was a hell of a fight here. By the amount of blood around, my guess is some of 'em didn't fare too well." Henry continued to conduct his investigation while Cao and Molly tied the animals to some stands of mesquite brush.

"Whoever it was came down here from the direction a Salt Creek, had one hell of a row, then headed back the way they came. Hard ta tell how many there were. I see at least five separate kind a boot tracks, but it could be double that. And at least two of 'em took off in their bare feet. Must a been three or four wagons and lots a stock." Henry was calling out his facts and assumptions in hopes his starry-eyed companions were of a mind to help him decipher the puzzle.

"What do ya think the chances whoever it was'll be headin' back this way?" From his question, Henry could see that Cao and Molly weren't going to be of much help to him. Cao had become much more concerned about security now that he had assumed the burden of Molly's protection.

"I expect if they were comin' back they wouldn't have took the wagons. From the ruts it looks like they was pretty well loaded down. But I'm just guessin'." Henry was standing on the bank of the river now trying to make sense of the signs left from the dousing given to Colonel Eichard and Tom and John Aiken.

"What do ya think of using this same spot to camp fer the night? It looks to be a good spot, so close to the water an' all." Cao wanted to get started setting up the tents before they lost the day's sunlight.

"Too close to the trail. An' I don't think this weather's gonna hold. There's another snowstorm comin' I'm sure, an' I'd hate fer us to get caught in a blizzard. Looks like at least one fella got thrown in the river. Probly happened up near where you two are standin'. There's a bare set of footprints downstream here where he crawled out of the river." Henry was wondering if what happened here recently could be more than just a fight.

Now he had Cao's interest. Cao began following the bare tracks Henry had discovered earlier. "The two sets of bare tracks come together over here." He walked a little further up the trail. "They get covered by the teams right here. Whoever struck out barefoot left first. The rest of the party follered."

"We can make it ta Salt Creek if we keep movin'. That'll put us in there well after nightfall but then we don't want ta be seen ridin' inta town in broad daylight anyhow." Henry was conscious of the hardship the young woman would experience traveling through this country in winter. He and Cao were well prepared to suffer the elements and had done so many times. Things were different now.

Henry wanted to get away from the crime scene. Molly had friends in Salt Creek: the Redfords. Friendly Saints represented a premium to the brothers at this juncture. Since leaving Bishop P.K.'s home, having to assess the danger ahead had become a tricky exercise. He would get no argument from his brother. Molly wanted to set next to a warm indoor fire again, and Cao knew it.

CHAPTER 78

SALT CREEK
(NEPHI)
UTAH TERRITORY

NOVEMBER 22, 1857
6:30 PM

The Salt Creek tithing office often doubled as a post office, and sometimes as a general meetinghouse. The men assembled inside were mostly a mix of Mormon personalities often seen in this sleepy hamlet of Saints. Bishop Bryant, Timothy Foote, and James Woolf prepared themselves to represent the best interests of their town. Jacob Bigler and John Kink were there to explain what had gone wrong. Collett and the others had been asked to stay clear, to guard the plunder, and to keep a low profile at the bishop's corrals. James Haslam sat quietly next to Rockwell, but Rockwell alone would represent the interests of Salt Lake City.

Bishop Bryant began, "Boys, you made a bad job of it; two got away. Salt Creek won't be trusted with another job any time soon."

The other men in the room avoided making eye contact with Rockwell. He was well known for being reluctant to accept criticism. Bigler's face attracted the most attention. He took the bait and responded to it.

"If that fool Collett hadn't missed his mark things would a come off as planned. The thought that the Gentile who did this ta me might be in yer hotel is enough ta make my skin crawl." Jacob Bigler had endured a poor night's sleep and a cold ride home, which included plenty of time to think about vengeance.

"It had to of been John Aiken. He said he heard one of you say 'One of the son-of-a-bitchin' Gentiles ran.' He was fakin' bein' knocked out so's you wouldn't finish him off. Then, after you tossed him in the river, he hoofed it back here an started tellin' the colonel, and anyone else who'd listen. He and the colonel have been over at Foote's Hotel piecin' things together. I reckon by now they have things pretty well sorted out. I expect Timothy an' his family are the only ones who have their confidence, if anyone in this town does." Bryant wanted to be sure all present knew how damaging the Gentiles in their midst could be to the cause. A long uncomfortable silence ensued.

"Well boys, if ya ask me we're all just wastin' our time jawin' about it. Collett screwed up all right an' he paid fer it with a face worse than Jacob's here. Now I still got two of their party to take care of up north. If it ain't clear to you boys that we still got some work ta do, may the good Lord have mercy on ya." Rockwell had little patience for decision making by committee.

"Well, what're you suggestin' we do, Port? Walk in ta Foote's Hotel and slit their throats?" John Kink was not used to these kinds of operations and he sincerely wanted Rockwell's instruction.

"That'd suit me fine. Get the work over with an' get me on down the trail soze I can complete what I started. I'll walk inta the room with my side arm an' my knife drawn. Anyone here willin' ta back me up?" Rockwell meant it.

"Now let's hold on a minute. Some of the Saints in town might not be so eager for doin' the Lord's work as we are. What about sendin' an express rider to Salt Lake City an' see what they say? We're lucky to have Haslam here courtin' the Redford girl. Might we be able to press you into service over somethin' this big?" Timothy had his patrons to think about, not to mention his wife and son who'd been spending considerable time attending to the two wounded Gentiles.

"I'll do whatever you folks here decide is best. Whatever you think the Prophet would want us to do, I'm yer man." Haslam was a bit embarrassed by the disclosure of his intentions with the Redford girl. Still, he knew better than to take a position of strength on any issue with a man like Port Rockwell in the room.

"Ah hell! We know what has ta be done. I say we do it. If you boys is worried about Salt Creek ever bein' trusted again with more work, then let the next message Salt Lake City gets be word that these Gentiles has been put out a the way. I'm sure they got enough ta think about with regard to

Johnston's army an' would most appreciate it if we handled this ourselves." Rockwell knew he was the only one in the room making any sense.

"I'm not sayin' we shouldn't put them out of the way, Port. I just don't think we ought to be doin' it here in town." Foote could see that Rockwell wasn't going to back down to anyone in the room. The best he could accomplish would be to prevent throat cutting in his hotel. Now he surveyed the room for support. It was James Woolf who saved the day.

"There's a little place called Willow Creek about eight miles north on the Old Spanish Trail. There's a spring near a small abandoned cabin. I hear they're in no condition to travel for another day or so. I reckon when they are, they'll want to go back that way to link up with their two friends that stayed behind. If you'll give me one of the stake wagons, I'll offer to drive 'em back that way. You an' yer men can leave ahead of us an' be waitin' in that cabin fer us to come along."

James Woolf was slightly more than twenty years old. He sensed this was his opportunity to strike a blow for his church. He had begun to see how the church rewarded those who took on the risk of doing the Lord's "dirty work." Two living examples, Rockwell and Haslam, were sitting right in front of him.

CHAPTER 79

SALT CREEK
(NEPHI)
UTAH TERRITORY

NOVEMBER 22, 1857
7:00 PM

They were careful to bypass the main entrance of the little town by heading in an easterly direction until they could approach the Redford residence from behind. The snow had picked up again, as Henry had expected, but it was not the blizzard he'd feared. It was coming down heavy enough, however, to provide them with more than adequate cover as they skirted past the other homesteads along the way.

The Redfords had a small farm on the outskirts. They were able to approach the dwelling unnoticed. Molly's family of six had stayed with the Redfords after her paternal father had died from black canker.

Mr. Redford, having left a successful law practice in England to pursue a new life and religion in America, was more well-to-do than most of the Saints in Salt Creek. With the help of the Stake, he had been able to provide for the Hansons for almost a year. About a year ago, a widower, Rosmus Anderson, had arrived with a contingent of new Saints sponsored by the Perpetual Immigration Fund. Bishop Bryant had arranged the marriage, seeing that it was more proper for a widowed mother of five daughters to be supported by someone other than the tithing office or the goodwill of a tithing Saint.

During the year that Molly Anderson, then Molly Hanson, had lived with the Redfords, she and Ann Redford had become the best of friends.

Ann's parents had treated her and her siblings like their own. Ann, being the same age, had become very close to Molly. After leaving her family back at the Coal Creek farm, and striking out on her own with her Gentile fiancé, the anticipation of seeing Ann filled Molly's thoughts with memories of a better time.

The Redfords were strong on education, and it was here that the thought of becoming a nurse had been planted in Molly's outlook. Ann's mother had gone to school for midwifery in England, and in Mormon communities her expertise was in constant need. Ann and Molly had accompanied her on many late-night deliveries as her dutiful assistants. This and doctoring the variety of animals on the Redford farm had instilled an ambition in her that few Mormon women were allowed to pursue. She'd shared her dream with Cao, who found this rather unique feature in her attractive.

The three decided that Molly would approach the home and the brothers would wait for her "all is safe'" signal. Fortunately the Redford's kept their dogs inside during the snowfall. Molly knocked the same way she always used to. It was Ann who showed up at the entry-door window.

"Ann, it's me, Molly Hanson!" she shouted through the closed door, knowing Ann would more readily recognize the Hanson name.

The door flung open, and the two young women embraced each other. Ann's parents, Bob and Lettice, were soon participating in the happy reunion. Finally, Molly stepped back a bit to announce her purpose.

"Ann, Mr. and Mrs. Redford, I'm running away. My fiancé and his brother are out by the barn. I know this must be a terrible imposition, but would you please just meet with us for a while. There isn't anyone else we can turn to."

Ann turned to her somewhat stunned parents with a pleading look. Lettice was first to break the silence. "Why, of course we'd be delighted to meet your fiancé and his brother. Please call for them to come inside."

"Oh, thank you, thank you." Molly turned and signaled for the brothers to advance. Introductions were made and the unexpected guests were ushered inside and made comfortable around the dining room table. The Redford's other five children crowded the small room until Lettice ushered them off to attend to their chores. Berry pie and warmed milk were provided for desert.

"So tell us, Ann, why have you decided to leave? Have you considered your mother and the younger children? And what about the church?" Mr. Redford thought it his duty to inquire into matters so important to a young woman's future. Ready to engage in a serious interrogation, he also cast a disapproving eye in the direction of the purported fiancé, Cao Young.

"Because they killed Mr. Anderson. It was to atone for having broken 'an oath of silence' about the terrible massacre of those poor people on their way to California. And poor Mr. Anderson hadn't even taken the oath. He wasn't even there when it was took." Molly had to stop to regain her composure. The memory of having watched it was bringing back the emotions she'd experienced as Mr. Anderson was being murdered.

The Redfords, indeed all the people of Salt Creek, had heard conflicting stories of the massacre. Some rumors had the tragedy as an entirely Lamanite operation. Others, from those more in the know, had it closer to the truth. The Redfords had heard reports from both sources. They had not yet heard about the "blood atoning" of Rosmus Anderson.

"Dear child! Who could have participated in such an act? And how can you be sure the church was behind it?" Mr. Redford found Molly's words quite alarming. He and Lettice had stood for Rosmus and the widow Hanson at their wedding.

"I saw it with my own eyes. Mr. McFarland, Mr. Higbee, Mr. Haslam, and that terrible Mr. Rockwell did it. Mr. Anderson went willingly only after they promised him no harm would come to Mother and us kids." Molly had overcome her emotions and was determined to provide the Redfords with a convincing account of what had happened. If she could not elicit their help, then she must at least obtain their neutrality.

Molly's statements were followed by another period of stunned silence. She could not have known that her mention of Mr. Haslam would be the cause of it.

It was Ann who broke the silence this time. "Molly, I have become betrothed to James Haslam. The directive was delivered to Bishop Bryant and was signed by the Prophet himself. My parents think it is such a great honor."

She turned to her parents. "Maybe now you'll listen to me. If he could do such a thing to Mr. Anderson, how could you want me to marry such a man?"

"Please! Please! We must all take a moment and sort all this out. Things are afoot that are very troubling indeed. James Haslam is at the tithing office right now meeting with the authorities regarding two Gentiles who wandered into town badly beaten and near death. One of them had a bullet in his back that Brother Foote removed." Bob Redford was no longer on the offensive.

"I guess that explains the two bare-footed sets a tracks we follered in here for more'n twenty miles where we saw signs of a scuffle back at the Sevier River." Cao looked at his brother Henry. The brothers had been quite silent up to now.

"Mr. Redford, are any of those other men Molly just mentioned here in town or at that meeting with Mr. Haslam?" Henry figured it was time to see how forthcoming Mr. Redford was going to be.

"I don't know. But I do know that Port Rockwell was here yesterday, and he left with four Gentiles, two of whom I just spoke about." It was not in Mr. Redford's nature to lie, and he was still trying to make sense of things himself.

Was it just him and the four Gentiles, or did he have some others with him that might be inclined to side with him?" Henry wasn't going to stop asking questions as long as he was making progress.

"He had three other men with him, but Brother Haslam wasn't one of them. The whole town is in an uproar about it. The four Gentiles were all pretty well heeled. The speculation is that they got robbed by a group of bandits or renegade Lamanites. There's been a lot of that kind of trouble around these parts lately." Mr. Redford was thinking out loud, and he began to realize that could be dangerous.

"We know. We saw where some folks decided to bury, in shallow graves, a hundred or so California-bound travelers over near Mountain Meadows. It didn't appear to us it would be somethin' the Injuns, I mean the Lamanites, might do." Henry thought he'd let Mr. Redford chew on that for a second. Mr. Redford was momentarily stumped. Henry decided to press it a little more. "You happen to know a fella named Ira Hatch?"

"Of course. Everyone in these parts has heard of Ira Hatch. I know of him. I've met him more than once. But I can't say I know him. He's not an easy man to get to know. What is it that makes you inquire about him?" Redford was beginning to feel more and more defensive, but he still wanted to put things together more than he wanted to clamp down on the discussion. Cao and the women had become mere spectators to the conversation.

"My brother and I saw him kill a man that escaped from that same group of travelers I just told you about. He didn't even so much as take the time to ask the man a question. He just shot him off our mule he was ridin'. Now we've heard he might be in some kind of trouble with the church fer not doin' the same to Cao an' me." Henry could see that Mr. Redford was shaken.

"Where did this happen, young man?" As disturbing as the revelations were to him, Redford was not going to shrink away from it.

"Down on the Virgin River, in the Gorge."

"May I ask, what are your plans?" Redford placed a high premium on what was best for his family. Now that Ann's future was uncertain, he focused on the future of the three young people who had arrived at his home with these horrible revelations.

"We're going to do all we can to get out of this forsaken Deseret and get back to Pennsylvania where decent folks can lead decent lives. If we have to go right through Salt Lake City to get there, then so be it." Now it was Henry who was thinking out loud. There was something about Mr. Redford he trusted. They needed to find someone to trust.

"I hope you boys don't mind sleepin' in the barn. We have a good stand of hay in there. If you have good provisions you should be quite comfortable in there. Tomorrow morning, after James visits with us, I'll know better how I may be of help to you boys . . . and to you, Molly. You'll need to keep your animals out of sight, and you'll need to stay out of sight until he's gone. Molly you can spend the night in bed with Ann, but first thing in the morning you'll need to move to the barn as well. I don't want Haslam knowin' any of you are here until we've decided what's best."

Henry nodded his approval of Mr. Redford's plan. "I reckon your barn will be right comfortable. It sure beats settin' up tents out in this snowstorm."

All were silent for several minutes, lost in their own thoughts. Much of the tension the three young travelers had been carrying since the Sevier River had left them. The three Redfords at the table were carrying it now.

CHAPTER 80

SALT CREEK
(NEPHI)
UTAH TERRITORY

NOVEMBER 24, 1857
7:25 AM

Once the decision had been made, Tuck Wright and John Aiken were catered to in a manner the Prophet himself would have enjoyed. Several of the more compassionate women of the church (all the women in this town were of the church) set up a schedule to attend to the nursing and feeding of the wounded and battered Gentiles.

Their feet needed the most attention. Badly blistered and to some degree frostbit, various soaks and salves were administered several times a day. Steaming hot dishes, cakes, and pies were delivered in a succession so frequent that it was impossible for them to consume the bounty of it. Within forty-eight hours after having arrived in the sleepy little town, their swelling and discomfort had diminished appreciably.

Bishop Bryant offered the men the planned escort and introduced them to James Woolf and James Haslam. Woolf would be their wagon driver. Haslam had volunteered to go along as a bodyguard. Both men seemed affable enough, and the Gentiles thanked them for their assistance.

By the third morning after their arrival, the Gentiles had expressed a desire to head back in the direction of their two remaining friends. By now they had no illusions that strong forces in the territory were afoot and aimed at their destruction. They're only hope was that the loss of nearly all their material wealth would dissuade others from inflicting further mayhem upon them.

"I know Tuck and I are in your debt for all you've done for us these past few days. Unfortunately, the men that did this to us took everything we had of value. If you'd be so kind as to tally up what we owe we'll be sure, once we get back to California, to send back payment." John Aiken didn't expect there would be any argument about his proposal, being that it seemed to be the only reasonable offer he could make.

"I'm sorry, John, but that will not do. I hate ta be kickin' a man when he's down, but I happen ta know that you're carryin' a fine-looking six-shooter, an' Tuck here's the proud owner of a very expensive looking gold pocket-watch. I'd just as soon settle up with you boys right now as to have to wait for money over time." Timothy Foote's entire demeanor had changed from what it had been. His tone carried a resolve to pursue the matter further if necessary.

Guy Foote looked up as the discussion progressed and then looked away. He had grown fond of the two frontiersmen and had been proud of the way his family had selflessly aided them, above the efforts of all others, in their desperate hours of need. Now he felt only shame.

John looked at Tuck with a look that said "our troubles are not over." "Give me your pocket-watch, Tuck."

Placing the engraved gold watch on the hotel desk, he then laid his six-shooter next to it. "Either one should bring more'n enough to pay fer ten days in a place like this. Take yer pick but you can't have both." Aiken waited for the innkeeper's next statement.

Foote looked at the two items. He had hoped for both items and had been prepared to argue his point forcefully, if necessary. Instead of arguing about it, he silently reached for the revolver and withdrew it to the safety of the clerk's box.

Aiken picked up the pocket-watch, and as he turned to hand it to Wright, he said, "Now we have parted with the last friend we have on earth."

As the two men hobbled gingerly from the hotel toward the spring-board wagon and their awaiting escorts, Guy Foote heard John say to his friend, "Prepare for death, Tuck. We'll never get out of this valley alive." He patted the young boy on the shoulder as he passed him by.

There weren't many citizens on the street as the team and four men jostled northward on Main Street. Behind the windows of the stores and homes lining both sides, many watched as the two survivors left with their escorts. Even the compassionate ones were quite certain that the Gentiles were doomed. Many of them were already aware that O.P. Rockwell and his associates had already headed out in the same direction late the night before.

An hour and a half into the journey James Woolf pulled his team up to the cabin at Willow Creek. After reigning them to a stop he said, "I'm gonna need to unhitch the horses here an' walk them down to the spring to water. This is the last good water stop for some distance."

Wright and Aiken were in no position for easily unboarding. Their tender, still bootless feet were thickly bound in the last dressing that had been applied that morning. When Woolf had unhitched the team and proceeded to move them away from the wagon, James Haslam jumped off the wagon and walked several paces toward the old run-down cabin.

The cabin door flew open and out stepped Port Rockwell and Sylvanus Collett, each carrying double-barreled shotguns. Haslam then turned, and the three men raised their guns in unison, all aiming at the men Haslam had promised to protect. Rockwell let loose with both barrels at the same time into John Aiken. Collett took his time firing his shots in succession into Tuck Wright. He had been successful talking Rockwell into letting him have Tuck so he could exact revenge for Tuck having knocked his teeth out.

It was Haslam's job to finish off either of the men who might have managed to dodge the others' volleys. With the double-ott buckshot having been a lethal killer at close range, the operation went off exactly as planned. Haslam did not need to take part in the shooting.

The smoke cleared as the four men slowly converged on the mangled bodies of their targets. Both men had been knocked backwards by the blasts and now lay partially in the wagon bed, their legs twisted at angles only possible for the dead or the unconscious. Their tragic journey had finally come to end.

"Four down, two to go." Rockwell's tone carried all the reverence of a barfly in a darts match.

"Nice shootin'." Collett said with pride as if he was congratulating both Rockwell and himself.

"What shall we do with them?" said Woolf, eager to complete his assignment and report back to Bishop Bryant.

"There's a deep spring about four miles back. Take 'em back there, weight down their bodies with rocks, and sink 'em in the deepest spot you can find. Me, Sylvanus, and the boys are gonna head north from here.

We still got their two friends to take care of." Rockwell wasn't opposed to engaging in hard manual labor when called for. When he had subordinates to order around, which was often, he was quick to delegate.

Rockwell and Collett loaded the wagon they had parked behind the cabin with the plunder they had lifted from the Aiken party at the Sevier River. The property had been inventoried in the Salt Creek tithing office, and all agreed that it should be transported to Salt Lake City. Certain items left off the inventory found their way into the possession of those most involved in the transaction. About $15,000 worth remained, a considerable amount of wealth to consecrate to the church.

Haslam and Woolf did as they were told and reported back to Bishop Bryant. The bishop promptly swore them to a "blood oath of secrecy." Haslam had proven himself capable of keeping a secret. Young Woolf, however, was not about to miss out on the credit he was entitled to. Within days, most of the citizens of Salt Creek, a town that would eventually carry the name Nephi, had heard about the fate of the two Gentiles who had twice availed themselves of their hospitality.

CHAPTER 81

TEMPLE SQUARE
SALT LAKE CITY
UTAH TERRITORY

NOVEMBER 25,1857
3:00 PM

Mr. Redford was in the parlor with Hosea Stout and Molly Anderson when Henry and Cao arrived after having spent the previous night in the bowery stables. Redford and Stout had become friends a few years prior when Hosea had taken some law classes from the British barrister. Upon their arrival Molly, the brothers, and Mr. Redford had informed Stout of all they knew with respect to Milum Jones, the massacre, Rosmus Anderson, and what they only partly knew of the Aiken party. They were requesting an immediate audience with the Prophet. Hosea Stout assured them they would have one before business ended the next day.

Mr. Redford was a very persuasive man. Over the past several days he'd convinced Henry and Cao that he had friends in high places who had the power and character to put things right. He assured them that Hosea Stout, a former student of his, would mobilize the Christian values the LDS Church stood for by implementing the rule of law. He was also certain Stout could get them in front of the Prophet . . . the ultimate power in all the land. He'd guaranteed them there were still many good and decent followers of Joseph Smith who would not stand for the kinds of atrocities the brothers and Molly had witnessed.

"We sure are thankful that we listened to you, Mr. Redford. And we're grateful for your help too, Mr. Stout." Cao had been impressed that Redford had been able to arrange a meeting with such a powerful official. As territorial governor of the Utah Territory, and first president of the LDS Church, Brigham Young did have the power to set things right throughout this land of Deseret.

"My thanks as well, Mr. Stout, and will you please thank Lucretia for making me so comfortable in her room last night." Molly too had been pleased. She wanted so much not to be a burden to the brothers who were in at least as much danger as she. A favorable meeting with the Prophet afforded them their best chance of safe travel through the territory. There was also the opportunity of exposing the culprits and their obvious crimes.

Henry maintained his silence. For half the night, he and Cao had discussed the danger they might be walking into. He reminded Cao of Bishop Klingensmith's warning to be very careful whom they trusted. Might not the Prophet himself be in on the deceitful treacheries?

"You may thank her yourself, Molly. I expect you'll be returning here tonight after your meeting with the Prophet? I've asked his secretary to allot the remainder of the day for your meeting. The information you're reporting is of significant gravity and worthy of a full hearing." Stout had been a good listener, while revealing nothing of what he himself knew. He'd spent a considerable amount of time with the Prophet earlier this morning. He'd briefed him on the fact that the two Gentiles Ira Hatch had allowed to slip through his fingers had just delivered themselves into their hands.

"You'll look into the matter of Brother Haslam's involvement with the blood atoning of Brother Anderson? And if there is any connection between him and Brother Rockwell with respect to the Gentiles at the Sevier and in Salt Creek? I'm sure you understand my concern." Redford knew he was expending considerable capital asking his friend and pupil for such service. Hosea seemed more than willing to intervene on his behalf and did not seem troubled by it at all.

"Worry not, Brother Redford. I would hope my friends would do the same for me if one of my daughters were faced with a similar dilemma. Shall we proceed to our meeting with the Prophet? We dare not keep him waiting." Hosea Stout wanted to keep things on track himself and was more than a little anxious over how the Prophet was going to handle the highly charged and volatile meeting Stout had arranged.

"Will the Prophet be concerned with the presence of a young woman attending a meeting in the Beehive House?" Redford just wanted to avoid any potential embarrassment. Only the wives of ranking dignitaries were invited into the Prophet's personal residence, but never to discuss business.

Other than wife number one, Lucy Decker Young, his daughters, and a few maidservants, weeks at a time would pass without female visitors crossing the threshold of this house.

"He made it very clear to me that young Molly was to be included." Stout and Young already had discussed in detail how they wanted this meeting to transpire. Molly Anderson would be an important part of it. The six of them proceeded the short distance to Temple Square and Brigham's Beehive House.

* * *

Wilford Woodruff ushered the party into the meeting room, where Brigham sat behind his desk looking somewhat preoccupied. Within seconds of them having been seated, Brigham rose and very cordially greeted each one of his guests.

"Brother Redford, how long has it been since we were privileged to have your wisdom and intellect grace our humble social order here in Salt Lake City?"

"Why, it's been several years at least. I'm surprised you would even remember an old blowhard like me. I'm very flattered." Redford admired Young. A well-educated man, he appreciated, better than most, what the unschooled Prophet had accomplished for the Saints over the past ten years.

"Nonsense. I would be remiss not to remember a good man like you. Before we proceed, I would be most honored to make the acquaintance of your three companions." Young turned to Molly first.

"May I introduce Molly Anderson? Molly lived with us at Salt Creek for a time a bit over a year ago, after the unfortunate passing of her father. She is a wonderful young woman who aspires to a promising career in nursing. I can attest to her exceptional aptitude and will be disappointed if she does not pursue her dream." Redford was taking a bit of a shot at Cao in touting the young woman's ambitions.

"I'm afraid Molly's life has, once again, been stricken with tragedy. Her friends, Henry and Cao Young here, are from Pennsylvania and have witnessed some atrocities of their own. This is the purpose of our arrival here." Redford was also anxious to get on with the matter at hand.

"Any chance we might be related? I know the 'Young' surname is quite common in England." The Prophet was still making small talk. He knew his ancestry quite well. He was soon to have fifty plus of his own offspring. He was also overlooking, for the moment, Redford's comments about

Molly's aptitude. The Prophet had little use for the ambitions of women beyond their childbearing and homemaking capacities.

"No connection that I'm aware of, Mr. President," Henry answered while shooting a warning glance at Cao, challenging him to keep his mouth shut.

"No, I suppose not then. While I'm honored to make the acquaintance of all three of you, I can certainly understand your wanting to get down to business. Brother Stout has given me an account of the very troubling events you three young people have come upon. While I'm well aware of the unfortunate tragedy at Mountain Meadows, the killing of the gentleman at the Virgin River Gorge and the attack upon Mr. Anderson are new to me. Any light you may be able to shed on those two events could be of great benefit to me and to our people." The Prophet pulled up a chair as he was speaking and sat. It was obvious he didn't care who responded first.

Henry had gotten Cao to agree to let him do most of the talking. They had agreed that, although it was a gamble, their best chance of getting out of Deseret would be to elicit the protection of this man.

"Well, the man down on the Virgin River Gorge was named John Milum Jones. We found him stumblin' out a the desert near the Las Vegas Springs. He was in pretty bad shape, wounded and very dry. We got him well enough to ride and started back up this way with him, an' when we got just about to where the Santa Clara River feeds into the Virgin, a fella by the name of Ira Hatch shoots him right off the mule we'd lent him.

"Oh, him an' a couple of his boys said he shot him because he an' his folks in that massacred train had got the Injuns, the Lamanites, all stirred up by poisonin' some and killin' some others. Somehow, it jus' didn't seem right the way it went down, him shootin' Milum an' all." Henry was surprised at his own nervousness and struggled to control his discourse.

"Then we rode over to the Mountain Meadows and seen that what Milum had been tellin' us was true. There must a been over a hundred folks buried there, an' not too well buried neither. Big packs of coyotes were workin' at diggin' 'em up and draggin' 'em about. Looked to be quite a few women an' kids there. It was a horrible sight I'll never forget. Molly, you feel up to tellin' about what happened to yer stepdad?" Henry was somewhat intimidated by the powerful leader. He'd never before spoken to a man of such high status, and he certainly had never delivered so much bad news to one.

"Child, we will certainly understand if you'd rather not have your feelings harrowed up by recalling the sad account Brother Stout has already described to me earlier this morning." The Prophet maintained the demeanor of a compassionate father.

"I thank you for your concern, President Young, but I want to be of help if at all possible. My stepfather was with Ira Hatch when he shot the man Henry just described. Rosmus recognized the man was riding with Henry and Cao, but Brother Hatch wouldn't let him converse with them. On his way back to our farm on Coal Creek he passed by the same scene of killing that Henry just described. It upset him so that when he got back home he started telling people about what he saw. He said there were a good many of the men from Fort Clara and Pinto who had participated in the killing. They had taken an oath of secrecy not to tell anyone, even their wives.

"Brothers Higbee, Haslam, Macfarlane, and that horrible Mr. Rockwell showed up at the farm. Mr. Anderson was atoned because he broke the oath. But it was an oath he never even took. I've decided I can't live amongst people who could do any of the things we've described to you just now. I want to leave Deseret with Cao. We want to be married and live among people who would never think of cutting someone's throat just for telling the truth." Molly began to sob.

The Prophet turned to Henry so as to allow Molly to compose herself. "She's saying that a good many of the men of Fort Clara and Pinto had participated in the killing at Mountain Meadows. How would Brother Anderson have known this if he was not there when the killing took place?" Young was near nausea at the degree of information he was getting. It wasn't difficult for him to feign genuine disgust. However, he'd already heard it all in more graphic detail.

Neither Molly nor the brothers knew that Rosmus had been at Mountain Meadows during the siege but had left before the massacre. He'd also left with Ira's posse without knowledge that the Nauvoo Legion had arrived from Cedar City, though Thales Haskell may have told him about it. During the siege, all the Saints had been from Fort Clara, Pinto, or Fort Harmony.

"From what we'd heard from Molly and her mother, almost every man in Cedar City took part in it." For some reason Henry decided to leave Bishop Klingensmith out of the discussion. He'd made his mind up while sitting in the bishop's house that he was not going to let a sincere confession exonerate him for having committed such a crime. Henry was steadfast in his belief that everyone has to account for what they do. For some reason even he did not understand, he stopped short.

"I can understand all three of you wanting to leave Deseret after what you've been through. I wish there was something I could say that would change your feeling. I know there are some things that take many years to overcome, and I'm afraid the three of you have lived some of those things. You've been of great service to me . . . more so than you can possibly know. Now pray tell me how I may be of service to you." The Prophet was marking time at this point. He knew the presence of the three young people here in his home represented a looming threat to his church. He already knew what he needed to do.

Redford thought he could help summarize things for all concerned at this point. "Brother Haslam should be arriving with the two wounded Gentiles from Salt Creek today or tomorrow. Perhaps we can get to the bottom of his involvement when he arrives. These three have come to you because they fear for their very lives. Henry and Cao believe they are being hunted because Ira Hatch failed to kill them when he had the chance. Molly is petrified at the thought that Port Rockwell is planning to take her as his next plural wife, or worse. It is our hope that you will see the equity in providing these three safe passage out of Deseret. It is their wish to return to Pennsylvania."

"Is it true that this is your wish?" The Prophet looked intently at his three young guests. All three nodded in the affirmative.

"It is near December and winter is upon us. Attempting to travel over the mountains to the east is to risk certain death if you're so unfortunate to hit severe weather. Even moderate weather here in the valley usually means severe weather in the mountains. Is it your intention to travel over the mountains before next spring?"

"We've made it over the mountains in wintertime before. We made it over just a year ago in late January and early February. I reckon we'd just as soon take our chances in the mountains as stay here amongst some people that wants to kill us." Cao wasn't going to allow this part of the discussion to take place without his input.

"Last winter spring came early, as I recall. You're in the city now. Surely we can provide you with a safe haven until next spring. I'm not at all trying to disparage either you or your brother's survival skills. I'm sure you're both skilled frontiersmen. But surely you wouldn't place this fine young woman at peril just to prove you can make a challenging trek?" The Prophet knew where he wanted this discussion to go.

"I'm not leavin' Molly, no way. She stays with me. When we get back to Pennsylvania, we're gonna get married an' settle down. We talked this all out an' our minds are made up." Cao was setting his heels at odds with the most powerful adversary he could possibly confront. Molly reached for Cao's hand in a show of solidarity.

"I'll give you a choice. After what you've been through, there's no doubt you are owed this much. You can leave Deseret now and take your chances in the mountains. Or you can all stay here in Deseret and I'll see that you are provided a safe haven until next spring when you can travel over the mountains safely and enjoyably. I strongly advise you to avail yourselves of the latter option." The Prophet rose from his chair and began to pace while stroking his chin whiskers.

"I'll throw in a third choice. Allow us to place Molly in a safe home here in the city until next spring while you two make your journey to Pennsylvania. She can enroll in our nursing program. I'll ask Wilford to look into the possibility of providing her with a church scholarship. In the spring, once I've received word that you have made your destination safely, I will see that Molly obtains passage to join you." He figured that would throw Cao for a minute.

"May I suggest that Brother Redford and I be given an opportunity to discuss the alternatives with our three young friends before they are required to provide you with a decision?" This time it was Stout's turn to interject.

"Most certainly, Brother Stout. Take as much time as you need. When you've finished have Brother Woodruff here notify me of their decision." The Prophet shook hands with all the men present, kissed Molly's hand, and left the room. It would be up to Hosea Stout now to convince his three troublesome guests to accept the third option.

CHAPTER 82

POINT OF THE MOUNTAIN
UTAH TERRITORY

NOVEMBER 25, 1857
3:00 PM

After having traveled through the settlements of Provo and American Fork, Rockwell and Co. made camp near the little hamlet of Lehi on the banks of the Jordan River. The next day they were up early and on the trail again. With any luck they would be checking into accommodations on Whiskey Street in time for the dinner hour at the Globe Inn. John Lot and Joseph Harker took turns driving the wagon full of plunder while Rockwell and Collett rode point. Trailing behind the wagon was the string of four horses and four mules, which had formerly belonged to members of the Aiken party.

Collett was in a foul mood. His ambition had never risen above the level of smoke from his corncob pipe. Now, however, he smoldered at the thought that the bounty they guarded would be soon turned over to the Prophet's tithing office. He alone had suffered a beating and the loss of his teeth, already rotten though they were. His three companions had come through unscathed.

Rockwell sensed his sidekick's discontent, as Collett's nonverbal demeanor could not be hidden. "Don't you be grousin' about us turnin' this property over to the Prophet. Just be thankful he's the one we're workin' for. I wouldn't be takin' these jobs if I wasn't takin' 'em for Brigham Young. Far as I'm concerned, all the rest a these bishops, deacons an' elders can just as soon wipe my ass as ask me to do any work fer them. You jus' be patient. Turnin' this property over to the Prophet will come back to us ten-fold."

As Rockwell continued counseling his sidekick, the sight of two riders headed in his direction interrupted his guidance. As they came into view it became clear that it was George Grant and William Kimball, the two generals who'd convinced the Prophet to send Rockwell and Collett on this mission in the first place.

"Well, what do you know! Here comes the top brass. I wonder if they made this ride jus' to see us." Rockwell prepared himself to be disrespectful.

Grant and Kimball reined their horses to a stop. Kimball spoke first, "We've heard you boys had some trouble down at the Sevier with a couple of those Gentile spies."

"We didn't have no trouble. Someone's been tellin' tall tales." Rockwell loved it when he could head off a criticism aimed by those holding superior rank.

Grant was next, "Looks like Brother Collett's face is tellin' a different tale." The generals began to snigger. Collett began to turn purple.

"Why I think Brother Sylvanus looks better than he ever did. Don't tell me you boys is headin' down to Salt Creek to conduct an investigation of the whereabouts of those two Gentile spies." Rockwell had hit the mark exactly. Wilford Woodruff had dispatched the generals at the request of Brother Redford. They tried their best to hide sheepish looks. However, they couldn't hide their disappointment at, once again, not being able to discredit the rogue Rockwell. It was a desire both men would have enjoyed immensely.

"We just have to make a showing so the weak-kneed brethren think things are being handled properly. What we're really here to report is that the other two of their party are camped up a ways right about at The Point of the Mountain on the banks of the Jordan. They don't appear to be fixin' to break camp today. If you hurry you should be on 'em in about a half hour." Kimball was glad he could disguise his disappointment with something important to report.

"So you won't be throwing me to the wolves today, I guess. Why not just turn yer horses round an' give us a hand takin' care of these last two?" Rockwell was having fun.

"You shouldn't have any trouble handlin' 'em. There's four of you an' two of them. Should be easy for you to get the drop on 'em. We need to get to Salt Creek before the ruckus you boys started there gets out of control."

Grant hated Rockwell and wanted nothing to do with him. He was also afraid, and both he and Rockwell knew it.

"I understand, General. You go ahead an' take care a the ruckus. We'll continue on up the trail and hold up our part." Rockwell tipped his hat as if he was addressing a couple of ladies and smiled insincerely from ear to ear. The encounter couldn't have gone better as far as he was concerned.

* * *

Rockwell rode ahead to scout out the encampment of his next prey. He knew where the best campsites near The Point of the Mountain were and was able to scope things out from the high ground above A.J. "Honesty" Jones and John Chapman. They had set up a hunter's camp and had been embarking on hunting expeditions into the high country to the east. They'd been doing pretty well too.

They had a good-sized buck hanging from a tree limb. Several ducks and geese were curing as well. Chapman appeared to be skinning a big cat. The men would be well armed with rifles and shotguns at the very least. It did not appear they were belted with side arms.

It would do no good to ride up into their camp, affording them a warning. Men like this were usually good at preparing themselves against an attack. Stealth would be an important ally. Rockwell walked back to where he'd tied his horse and rode back to his three cohorts.

"We need to act now. Tie the mounts where I tell ya and foller me in from there. I want all three of ya to keep at least five paces behind me but not more than ten. Collett an' I will go in with side arms. Lot, you bring the shotgun. Harker, you pack the carbine. We'll be close in when the gunplay starts. I'll take out the first one. The three of you take out the one I don't."

Rockwell's men complied without question. Using the screen of a large boulder, the four assassins were within twenty yards of the Gentiles before they emerged into full view. Chapman was still at work skinning the cougar. "Honesty" Jones was tending the campfire trying to get it just right before boiling some fresh meat. A Bowie knife was Chapman's only weapon. Jones was holding a pot of cold water.

Before their targets realized they were at a disadvantage, Rockwell opened fire on Chapman. His first shot hit him square in the chest, knocking him backwards. Rockwell then stepped up closer to his target and continued to empty his forty-five-caliber revolver while his three confederates opened fire on Jones.

Jones, being about twenty yards further away, reacted quickly by throwing the full pot of water in the direction of his attackers. The pot and its contents misdirected Lot's first blast from his double-barreled shotgun. By the time he was able to discharge his second round, Jones had successfully evaded shots from Collett and Harker. Within seconds he was out of range of all but Harker's carbine, which promptly jammed.

"Well don't jus stand there! Go get him!" yelled Rockwell. He let the other three give chase while he surveyed his latest victim and the campsite for anything of value. Once his companions were out of view he began to rifle through John Chapman's pockets and stuff his own.

Jones reached the bank of the Jordan River a good thirty seconds ahead of his pursuers. He did not hesitate to leap into the deep, swift, icy current. By the time they arrived at the same spot, he had climbed out on the opposite bank and was running again, hoping to get out of range of that rifle.

Collett's pistol rounds were wide of his mark every time. Lot was able to pepper Jones with some double-ott buckshot a time or two, but by then he was so far out of range, and so full of adrenaline, he could barely feel the sting. Harker's jammed carbine was useless.

"Honesty" Jones' instinct was at first just to run. His immersion in the icy waters of the Jordan was a calculated risk. The men could not follow him on foot and keep their powder dry. He also gambled that they would not have the same motivation as he to pursue such a harsh course. Even if they pursued him on horseback, they would likely get soaked in the attempt. His gamble had paid off, and now he would immerse himself in the dense underbrush and eventually make his way back to civilization.

When Collett, Lot, and Harker returned to the camp they were expecting a dressing down. They had clearly not carried their weight.

"He got away, Port. Jumped in that ice-cold water an' swam like a harbor seal to the far bank." John Lot had been a sailor for the British Royal Navy before converting to the LDS Church and sailing to America.

"Well boys, since you didn't get yer man, yer gonna have to either bury this one or carry him over to that riverbank and toss him in." Rockwell began to reload his side arm. The others decided carrying John Chapman back to the river was the easier of the two alternatives.

"Sylvanus, let Lot and Harker pack him. I need you to go get the wagon and mounts. Looks like we have four more nice ones to add to the string." Once all three of his subordinates were out of sight, Rockwell resumed his pilferage of the Gentile camp. As he filled a saddlebag with the items he planned to carry back to his mount, he said, "Five down, one to go."

CHAPTER 83

WHISKEY STREET
SALT LAKE CITY
UTAH TERRITORY

NOVEMBER 26, 1857
6:30 PM

The four men arrived in Salt Lake City ahead of schedule, and after delivering the plunder to the church tithing office, they checked into the Globe Inn. Rockwell had deducted enough coin from the Aiken party to pay for two weeks' stay, including meals and entertainment, for all four of them. Though his companions couldn't be sure, he had taken a significant additional share for himself. He considered it executive pay.

Rockwell had reported that one of the Gentile spies had eluded his men and that the authorities should pass the word to be on the lookout for him. He would likely be penniless, unarmed, and in need of help in order to survive Deseret's cold November nights.

By the next day, word had come that a Gentile had shown up at old man Dalton's house and was shooting off his mouth to anyone who'd listen. He was saying horrible things about the church. He was saying that it was a bloody, greedy church that Christ would reveal as a church of Satan. Old man Dalton had helped the Gentile and his companions weeks before, but could no longer abide such a blasphemer under his roof.

Word of the Gentile, and the stink he was making, had already reached the Prophet. Hosea Stout showed up at the Globe Inn and told Rockwell that Bill Hickman was being placed in charge of dealing with Mr.

Jones. Ten minutes later Rockwell was banging on the door of the Beehive House.

Wilford Woodruff opened the door reluctantly. He disliked unscheduled meetings. More importantly, he disliked O.P. Rockwell. Most importantly, he was afraid of O.P. Rockwell.

"Brother Rockwell, what brings you to the . . . " Woodruff was interrupted.

"You know damn well what brings me, Woodruff. I wouldn't be one bit surprised if it was your sorry ass that convinced the Prophet to cast me aside." Rockwell knew that just about everyone feared and disliked him. He'd used this tactic on many people many times. His adversary would see him as having seen through him. As a result they would become even more fearful and intimidated.

The color drained from Woodruff's face. He tried to think of an appropriate response but he was too flustered to speak. He just stood there with his mouth agape. Rockwell's fists were clenched as he stepped forward slightly, in a looming and menacing manner.

"It was my decision to have Brother Hickman deal with the Gentile staying at Brother Dalton's! You have no call to address Brother Woodruff in such a manner!" Brigham Young also knew a thing or two about intimidation.

Rockwell was caught off guard, not having noticed the Prophet behind him. Defensively he tried to recover. "President Young, I've worked hard for days to deliver these Gentiles as you've asked. Is it too much to ask . . . " It was Rockwell's turn to be interrupted.

"IT IS TOO MUCH TO ASK! How dare you barge into my home and address my most trusted friend and ally in such an insulting manner. I know for a fact that you also malign my generals of the Nauvoo Legion. Oh yes! I've heard how you've had your fun at their expense. They hate you, and from what I can see it is for good reason. Now half the brethren in Salt Creek think you are a murderer and a thief. Have you any idea what a difficulty you've left for Bishop Bryant and his counselors to deal with?"

"And then we have to hear about that poor Anderson girl. You blood atone her father right in front of her and then you intimate that you may come back for her to be sealed to you? I will tell you now that the girl is in the care of Brother Stout's home where she will remain for some time. I tell you this so you will know that if you go within a city block of her while she is in Stout's care, I will have you driven permanently out from under my wing."

"You are out of line. You have been out of line. You and your hench-man have blundered your way across half of Deseret, botching nearly every attempt to put our Gentile adversaries out of the way. When I ask you to have someone used up, I expect it to be done discreetly. Many of the brethren are up in arms against you. Some are calling for your trial, some for your excommunication. And you have the audacity to charge in here as if YOU are somehow the injured party." The Prophet was notorious for dressing down his adversaries. This was the first time he had turned his tongue against Rockwell.

Rockwell dropped to his knees. "Please forgive me, Brother Young. I know now that I have failed you. Please forgive me." He began to shake as tears ran down his cheeks.

"It is from Brother Woodruff that you should beg forgiveness." The Prophet was not one to let a sinner off without having paid his penance.

Rockwell spun a half circle on his knees. He was realizing for the first time that this Prophet, the source of all his strength, was not someone he could afford to offend. "Please forgive me, Brother Woodruff. I acted self-ishly and without respect. Please forgive me and I will never let it happen again." He began to blubber like a five-year-old.

"I forgive you, Brother Rockwell." Woodruff knew a good deal when he saw one. He also knew that the fearsome Rockwell was a coward just like any other bully. He would never again allow himself to be intimidated by such a brute.

"Please rise, Brother Rockwell. All shall be forgiven. We have both spo-ken words in anger here today. Sometimes that is necessary before friends can go forward together again." Young figured his number one Danite had been sufficiently reined in.

"Now, Brother Hickman is over at General Grant's being briefed by him and General Kimball. Go over there and see if you can be of assistance. Be sure to watch your tongue in front of the generals. Most importantly, you must remember that the job belongs to Hickman now." The Prophet would need Rockwell someday again. His shepherd dog with sharp teeth had groveled sufficiently. His teeth must be kept sharp a little while lon-ger.

CHAPTER 84

DESERET HOT SPRINGS
SALT LAKE CITY
UTAH TERRITORY

NOVEMBER 27, 1857
4:30 PM

"Honesty" Jones had made his way into Salt Lake City much like John Aiken and Tuck Wright had been forced to make their way into Salt Creek. Fortunately for him, he did not have to contend with the seriousness of bullet or scalp wounds. He also had the advantage of not having to make the long trek barefoot. Yet his circumstance was far from enviable.

The weather had grown considerably colder, and his first few hours pushed him through a dangerous fight with hypothermia. Like his friends he knew that to stop moving meant sure death. Before his clothes could completely dry the sun went down. The night cover was a good thing for keeping his pursuers from locating him, but the cold intensified. His boots were not much better than bare feet. Jones was used to traveling horseback, and by the time he reached the first settlement, his feet were badly blistered.

He sought help from the first inhabitants he approached. Through a chattering set of teeth, he told them what had happened. They warmed him with a seat by their fire and hot drinks. Besides further indicting Rockwell and his companions, whom he had traveled with only briefly before separating some days back, he mentioned knowing Simon Dalton. This was the same old man Dalton who'd been kind enough to put him and his friends up while they waited to be cleared of spying several weeks ago. The good citizens knew of Dalton and immediately sent for him.

Simon Dalton had been nearby visiting friends. He corroborated much of the shivering man's tale, and the more that Jones described what had happened to he and his friends, the more the public consternation grew. Quickly word of the fantastic tale arrived at the Beehive House itself. Dalton had initially offered to provide sanctuary to Jones at his home in Davis County near Deseret Hot Springs until things could be worked out.

As Jones continued to piece things together for his eager listeners, Dalton became increasingly uncomfortable. The man with the moniker "Honesty" was implicating high-ranking church members of murder and theft. Then he began spewing angry invective at the LDS Church itself. This Simon Dalton could not abide. By the time he was approached by the Prophet's agent, Wild Bill Hickman, Dalton was more than willing to go along with the legendary Danite's suggestions.

The next day, before sundown, Dalton was to transport Jones in his springboard wagon to his home just past the hot springs. Hickman assured the old man he would take it from there.

It was a cold wintry day as Hickman and his brother-in-law, Morris Meacham, waited for the wagon to appear. A storm had moved in and was spitting snow as much as the extremely cold weather would allow. Hickman was happy to put up with the discomfort. He knew it would discourage others from venturing out into the remote location.

"I sure wish they'd get here. I don't know how much longer I can tolerate standin' out here." Meacham had been complaining bitterly for some time now.

"They'll get here soon enough. Then we'll be able to go back to General Grant's an' take some brandy." Hickman didn't look uncomfortable. He never did.

"Too bad we didn't think to bring some of his brandy out here with us. I could sure use a shot right now." Meacham pranced back and forth in front of Hickman.

"I'd actually thought about it but decided agin it. I generally don't imbibe before I do a job. Have to make sure my aim is true. Had I known it was goin' ta be this cold, I'd a broke that rule an' took my chances." Hickman went about his business with the same anxiety as a postman sorting mail.

The sound of hooves and wagon wheels interrupted their banter. Hickman looked at his brother-in-law and said, "Go ahead, Morris. You know what to do."

Morris Meacham stepped out into the wagon trail leading to the Dalton residence and raised both hands. "Halt!" he shouted.

Simon Dalton reined his team to a stop. The somewhat muffled report from Hickman's Yeager ruptured the wintry silence. Honesty Jones' hat flew off along with part of his head. Astonishingly, the California bear hunter and former constable did not fall. Instead he jumped off the wagon as if he was spoiling for a fight. He staggered forward toward Meacham, who looked back at Hickman for further instruction. With a grin Hickman motioned for him to pull his knife. This Meacham did just as Jones reached out toward his neck with both hands.

Wide-eyed and looking into the mangled visage of the man who was still coming, Meacham plunged his Bowie knife deep into Jones' stomach. The strength that had always been was no longer there for "Honesty" Jones. As he loosened his grip from his assailant's neck, Meacham withdrew his knife and used it to cut Jones' throat. "Honesty" Jones, the last member of a fine group of honest men, had finally fallen. It could be fairly said that they had all succumbed to the twisted purpose of religious fanaticism.

"Shall we get ourselves that brandy we talked about?" Hickman spoke while busying himself with rolling Jones' body into the ditch by the side of the road. He then began tying a rag to a fence rail.

Neither Meacham nor Dalton could speak. The scene of butchery and ghoulish chaos they'd just been a part of had disturbed them so. They continued to look at Hickman as if they hadn't heard a word of what he'd just said.

"Oh, don't let that little display he put on toward the end bother you. I figured it wouldn't be long before he went down no matter what you did with yer knife. I've seen men do strange things after being headshot lots a times. Still I prefer a headshot to anythin' else. It's the most sure way a puttin' a man down."

Meacham and Dalton were still speechless.

"This rag'll mark the spot. I need ta be gettin' back, boys. The Prophet has a couple more Gentiles he wants me to escort as far as Black's Fork. After we've had a little warm-up, we'll see if we can talk Port and the generals inta comin' out here an' givin' us a hand buryin' this one. There ain't no better time to be buryin' someone than when you got a fallin' snow."

Hickman finished tying his marker and hopped up onto the wagon seat Jones had been occupying a minute or so prior.

"That'll teach ya for standin' around Morris. Now that I got the warm seat, you'll jus have to settle for the cold one."

CHAPTER 85

TOQUERVILLE
SOUTHERN UTAH TERRITORY

SEPTEMBER 2, 1869
7:30 PM

It was with a sense of exhilaration the three men marched forward. They'd been walking for days without seeing any sign of civilization, and now the glow of hearth fires illuminated nearly all of the windows of the forty or so homes that lay before them.

"What town do ya think lies ahead of us, Oramel?" asked Seneca Howland of his brother.

"St. George, most likely. I'd have guessed Fort Pierce, but there don't look ta be a stockade. What's yer guess, Bill?" Oramel looked over at Bill Dunn.

"Yer guess is as good as mine. It don't matter a lick either, I suppose." Dunn replied.

It was Oramel Howland who knocked on the door of the first home that met their approach. Richard Fryer opened the door with a yank. Gruffly he asked, "Who might be pounding at my door on this dark night?"

"I'm Corporal O. G. Howland of Major Powell's Exploratory Expedition, a navigation of the Colorado River. With me are my brother, Private Seneca Howland, and Private William H. Dunn. We seek accommodation on behalf of our commission by the United States federal government." The party waited for a response.

"Just a minute. I'll be right back." Fryer slammed the door about as abruptly as he'd opened it. A few moments passed and he returned with his jacket on, a side arm strapped to his side, and a shotgun in his hands.

"Let's take a little walk over next door to my neighbor Eli. I'm jus' not comfortable allowin' three strange men into my home after dark. My wife's heavy with child." Fryer stepped outside and pointed the direction he wished them to proceed in with the barrel of his shotgun.

"We certainly understand. We'd want to handle the situation the same way if we was in yer shoes." Neither Oramel nor his companions had any intention of being anything but genial in their imposition.

The three men had indeed accompanied Major John Wesley Powell on his historic run down the Colorado through the Grand Canyon. Upon reaching a point that would forever after be known as Separation Canyon, these three had lost their nerve when faced with a cataract of immense size and fury. They were not the first to abandon the expedition as a result of the difficulties and dangers this watershed trip had posed.

Powell was not the kind of commander to browbeat his men into submitting to his will. He told them he understood. He even left one of his boats for them in case they found they could not scale the massive walls surrounding them. The rains had swollen the river so that its rapids appeared especially nasty. In a few days it might recede to the point that these three might be willing to return to the expedition.

Dunn and the Howland brothers had had enough. They found that it only took the better part of a day to scale the vertical canyon walls. With their packs and armaments they were well prepared to hunt their way back to civilization on foot if need be.

Richard Fryer rapped loudly on the door of his next-door neighbor, Eli Pace. "Open up, Eli! We got company in need of assistance."

Pace was more cordial in his greeting, the brusque Fryer being quite familiar to him. "How can I be of help, Rich?"

"These three say they're with the federal government. I think they're lookin' fer us to provide 'em with shelter fer the night. I told 'em I'm not comfortable offerin' it myself with the missus being with child an' all."

Eli N. Pace pondered the information Brother Fryer had imparted. He then said, "I'm in kind of a similar circumstance. What do you say we all head over to the Ward House an' see if the bishop is willin' to allow these boys to stay the night over there?"

Pace had recently been sealed to Nancy Lee, the daughter of John D. Lee. Due to his involvement in the Mountain Meadows Massacre, Eli's father-in-law had been evading federal authorities for the better part of the past twelve years. The bishop whom Eli had earlier referred to happened to be Isaac C. Haight, presiding bishop of Toquerville. Haight, for the same reasons, had also spent many of the past dozen years as a fugitive from searching federal officials.

Young Eli Pace armed himself as Fryer had. The five men proceeded toward the Ward House. The three members of the Powell expedition felt no alarm that their escorts had armed themselves. It was dark, and they were strangers.

As they approached the Ward House, Eli said, "I'll go get the bishop. You show the men to the Ward House. I think there's some food stocks and other supplies in the basement."

Haight's home was less than one block from the Ward House. Eli could see the stricken look on the older man's face when he explained the situation to Bishop Haight. He collapsed onto a chair as the blood drained from his features. He'd lived in fear ever since the massacre that the day of reckoning would someday come. Could this be the day?

Eli could see the look of desperation on his bishop. He knew the danger these men posed to his father-in-law. He knew that something needed to be done. Could this be his opportunity to be of assistance to his church?

"I think it best for you not to be seen by these men, Bishop Haight. We now have a telegraph working between here and St. George. The Prophet may be there to winter, as he likes to do this time of year. If you can get the telegraph agent to send a message to St. George, I will keep them occupied in the Ward House until we get a response." Like most young people, the use of modern technology would not be something Eli Pace would overlook.

"Yes! Yes! We need direction from the leadership. Very good, Brother Pace. I'll proceed as you suggest. Be careful what Brother Fryer divulges to these agents. You be careful as well." Haight seemed rejuvenated as hope returned. Since Mountain Meadows, he had been more reluctant than ever to relay orders down the line. The telegraph represented an opportunity to get the instructions straight from the Prophet.

"In a little while, I'll send Brother Fryer over to see if you have a response. If the telegraph is working properly, it shouldn't take long." With that Eli Pace was off. Haight was as well, but in the direction of the church's telegraph agent.

Over the next two hours the power of the Mormon theocracy shifted into high gear. While young Pace and Fryer entertained the Gentile agents in the basement of the Ward House with food and liquid refreshment, Bishop Haight exchanged a series of electronic communications with Deseret's equivalent of America's summer White House.

Elder Erastus Snow was the first to be notified of the Gentile's presence in Toquerville. Whether the Prophet himself was involved is not certain. The first message arrived with the basic information that three Gentiles identifying themselves as federal agents were in Toquerville seeking lodging and asking questions. The first response was to seek more clarification of the Gentile's purpose. Haight's response indicated that the agents had first contacted the son-in-law of John D. Lee and that it seemed their purpose was to conduct an investigation relating to the Mountain Meadows Massacre.

Perhaps there would have been a different result if someone other than Isaac Haight had been the initiator of this chain of communication. The final response was that "The Gentile agents must be used up," and, "A word to the wise should be sufficient."

Brothers Fryer and Pace had been successful in gaining the Gentiles' trust by the time the final response from St. George was received. Dunn and the Howland brothers had carefully stacked all their weapons on a shelf in the basement in front of their Mormon hosts. They had no reason to believe that their contacting Pace and Haight had set in motion this little Mormon community's worst response.

When Richard Fryer returned from a visit with Bishop Haight and handed the final telegram to his friend and neighbor Eli Pace, no further discussion was required. With their guests seated at the basement table, they drew their handguns and fired point blank into the backs of the heads of Seneca Howland and William Dunn. The spray of blood, bone, and brain matter temporarily blinded Oramel Howland. His vision loss became permanent as the young Mormons fired their second volley into Oramel's heart.

Before the sun rose the next morning, three of the first ten men to navigate the Colorado through the Grand Canyon were buried deep beneath the earthen floor of the Toquerville Ward House. Powell and his remaining five men successfully completed their mission two days after their separation from the three unfortunate defectors.

The rewards young Eli Pace hoped to achieve would be short-lived at best. He was shot in the heart under mysterious circumstances in January the following year. It would be ruled a suicide by a three-man inquest. One of three would be none other than Isaac C. Haight.

A few years later Richard Fryer, his wife, child, and a family friend would meet with a similar fate. The authorities would blame the triple murder on Fryer. Gunned down at the hands of the local constable, his death was ruled an act of justifiable homicide to prevent the further shedding of innocent blood.

Five days after the murder of Dunn and the Howland brothers, Elder Erastus Snow in St. George received an unsigned telegram informing him of the men's deaths. Shivwits Indians supposedly killed them for their having shot one of their squaws. Two years later Jacob Hamblin confirmed this story by acting as an interpreter for these Indians at a "powwow" with John Wesley Powell during his second expedition down the Colorado.

The Indians and Powell had no way of verifying the correctness of Hamblin's interpretations. Once again the Indians would get blamed. Evidence of the cover-up of the murder of Powell's men lay dormant for nearly one hundred twenty-five years, until 1993 when a letter by William Leany to Bishop John Steele surfaced.

A period of just over twelve years had elapsed as the last of the known victims associated with the events surrounding the Mountain Meadows Massacre were laid low.

* * *

In the spring of 1858, a federal army commanded by General Albert Sydney Johnston entered Salt Lake City and established Camp Floyd south of the place where Tom Aiken and Colonel Eichard were murdered.

In May of 1859, Pvt. Major James H. Carleton interred the remains of the victims at Mountain Meadows under a conical-shaped rock cairn that was fifty feet in circumference at the base and twelve feet in height. Atop the cairn a cross hewn from red cedar bore the inscription: "Vengeance is mine: I will repay, saith the Lord." Also erected was a slab of granite inscribed with the following, "Here 120 men, women and children were massacred in cold blood early in September, 1857. They were from Arkansas."

In 1859, Brigham Young, while visiting the site, ordered the cairn destroyed. Just prior to signaling the order he stated to his entourage, in a booming voice: "Vengeance is mine saith the Lord; I HAVE repaid!"

In the spring of 1859 Judge John Cradlebaugh convened an inquest impaneling a grand jury to investigate the Mountain Meadows Massacre and other crimes. His efforts to seek justice were frustrated at every turn by a Mormon population that simply would not embrace justice for the benefit of a Gentile. Gentile governor Alfred Cumming, a willing dupe for Brigham Young, assisted the Saints by ordering Johnston's troops to cease providing security to Cradlebaugh.

Nearly two years after their ordeal, seventeen children were returned to relatives in Arkansas. It is rumored that not all of the children who survived the massacre were returned. Their Mormon caretakers said that one or two might have died from wounds. A clear explanation was never forthcoming. Of those who did make it back, many suffered from eye diseases and some became permanently blind. Some said, "They cried their eyes out." Perhaps they had simply seen too much.

On October 16, 1859, John Brown's raid on the federal armory in Harpers Ferry signaled the beginning of the Civil War. It could not have been a more welcomed event as far as Brigham Young and his confederates were concerned. The Union needed to deal with the South. Abraham Lincoln said: "If Brigham Young will leave me alone, I will leave Brigham Young alone."

Within a few years the soldiers at Camp Floyd were redeployed. The federal judge replacement selections were more politically palatable to the Saints. For a while it seemed the Saints were beneficiaries of divine intervention. But time waits for no one.

The year 1861 marked the completion of the transcontinental telegraph. Within a few short years, nearly all the settlements outside Salt Lake City had effectively been put on line. In October 1864, Nevada became a state, confining the Saints into a much-reduced domain. Such reductions would continue until Deseret was but a fraction of its original size.

* * *

In 1866, the Civil War ended, the transcontinental railroad was completed at Promontory Point, and the first non-Mormon settlement in the territory was founded at Corinne, Utah. Brigham Young's iron grip on the population of Deseret was being pried free.

CHAPTER 86

COUNTY SEAT
PIOCHE
LINCOLN COUNTY
STATE OF NEVADA

APRIL 10, 1871
1:00 PM

The tall, dark-haired horseman reined his mount to a stop and dismounted in front of the county courthouse on this cool spring morning at the agreed-upon time. He pulled out his pocket-watch and checked the time. This was not an appointment he wanted to be early for. Straight up one o'clock, he was not the kind to keep his friend waiting.

"Afternoon P.B." Philip Klingensmith addressed P.B. Ellis, the county clerk, a man he knew well.

"Afternoon, P.K. You sure you want to go ahead with this?" Somehow Ellis knew that the business at hand today would have consequences far more serious than his typical work.

"I'm sure that I don't, but where do you want me?" P.K. carried a determined look as he folded his jacket over his arm.

"We'll go into my office, P.K." The little bureaucrat led the way, followed by the large, thickly muscled former Mormon bishop.

Thirteen and a half years had passed since he had participated in the most heinous mass murder in the annals of American history. A year after the massacre, he had been kicked in the head by a horse, resulting in an injury so severe it took nearly six months for him to recover. A year after that he asked his church to relieve him of all his ecclesiastical duties. He was the only church leader involved in Mountain Meadows who ever did so.

For the next ten years, he lived mostly in the saddle. Still valuable as a skilled ironsmith and mining authority, he was commissioned by the church to explore remote regions of the territory. Needing the work, and to make himself scarce, he helped establish settlements in Adventure, Pocketville, Rockville, Panguitch, the Muddy, and Toquerville.

It was hearing of the incident in Toquerville that settled it for P.K. Eli Pace, in his zeal to obtain his heavenly rewards here on earth, just couldn't keep his mouth shut about what he'd done for Haight, his father-in-law, Lee, and all the other participants. His verbal indiscretions cost young Eli his life.

P.K.'s confrontation with Molly Anderson and the two brothers shortly after the massacre made him aware that he was not going to be very good at keeping secrets. Somehow, the fact that Gentiles were still being "used up" and oath-breakers were still being "put out of the way" did not sit well with P.K. It was time to make a change.

By now P.K. had moved Hannah and her family to Bullionville, Nevada. His other wives, Betsy Cattle and Margaretha Elliker, and their families remained in Cedar City. Toquerville was the last settlement he founded for Deseret. He eventually heard about the murder of Powell's men and that of Eli Pace.

It would be in the state of Nevada where he would cease evading the responsibility that came with having participated in the Mountain Meadows Massacre.

Thinking he was sealing his fate, he told Judge Wandell first. It was Wandell who advised P.K. to provide the court with the affidavit of his account of the massacre. Then, a legal document would be of record if anything were to happen to him before the guilty were brought to justice. Ellis brought in a stenographer to swear him in.

P.K. told all he knew. He admitted to having shot one of the immigrants. In so doing he became the only participant ever to admit to having killed anyone at Mountain Meadows.

He told of Higbee ordering him to arm himself and proceed to the Meadows. He described the speeches made to the militia before the killing started. He recounted the argument between Haight and Dame the day after the massacre. His discussion with Brigham Young, Lee, and Charlie Hopkins was not left out.

Most importantly, he described the massacre as a military operation ordered by superior officers in command of the Nauvoo Legion. He finished by stating that, in 1857, it was his understanding that the commander-in-chief of the militia of the territory of Utah was Brigham Young.

CHAPTER 87

BEAVER
PANGUITCH
SALT LAKE CITY
MOUNTAIN MEADOWS
UTAH TERRITORY

SEPTEMBER 1874
TO
MARCH 1877

As a result of Klingensmith's affidavit and the passage of the Poland Bill, federal prosecutors could for the first time bring charges against those believed to have been involved in the massacre. Prior to the Poland Bill, only Mormon probate judges could convene murder trials in the territory of Utah. Two of the probate judges that had been assigned to Washington and Iron counties were John M. Higbee and John D. Lee. In September 1874, indictments for murder were entered against John D. Lee, William H. Dame, William C. Stewart, John M. Higbee, Isaac C. Haight, Philip Klingensmith, George Adair Jr., and Samuel Jukes.

In the middle part of November 1874, John D. Lee was captured under a pile of straw in a chicken coop at one of his homes near Panguitch. Marshall William Stokes had seen one of Lee's wives conversing with the chicken coop. He walked up to Lee's wife, poked his Colt revolver into the straw, and said, "I promise you, if a single straw moves, I will blow his head off."

Lee said from beneath the straw, "Hold on boys; don't shoot. I will come out."

Lee was confined for a time in the territorial prison, but was soon released on bail. The LDS Church would bankroll his defense.

On July 23, 1875, the first trial of John D. Lee commenced. Prosecutors decided to try Lee first, and then go after others. The Mountain Meadows Massacre was being hailed as the crime of the century, and the national attention paid to it would rival, for its time, the most sensational trials of today. Of the twelve jurors selected, eight were Mormons, three non-Mormons, and one apostate Mormon. Philip Klingensmith was the prosecution's star witness.

When he took the stand, the big Pennsylvania Dutchman appeared slow and depressed. As the questioning progressed he became more animated. The veins in his neck began to show as he relived the horror for the jam-packed courtroom. For the most part his testimony followed his affidavit. However, under examination, the details of the event, like Higbee's cutting of the immigrant apostate's throat and the like, came out. His answers under oath brought the picture of what had happened at Mountain Meadows into focus for an entire nation.

William Young, John H. Willis, Samuel Pollack, and James Pearce also testified. Each admitted to being on the field during the massacre. However, none would testify to having seen John D. Lee kill anyone.

Wells Spicer, Lee's defense lawyer, put up a spirited defense. He blamed the massacre on the immigrants themselves. It was their own behavior that provoked the atrocity. He claimed the Indians made Lee and the others do it. He claimed that Lee was the only one who tried to save the immigrants. Lee did not support the dishonesty of his defense when he wrote his last confession a year later.

On August 5, 1875, the case went to the jury. All eight Mormons and the apostate Mormon voted to acquit. The three non-Mormons voted to convict. By hung jury Judge Boreman ruled a mistrial. Lee would have to be tried again or cut loose.

The Mountain Meadows Massacre had now been played out on a national stage. The Gentile population of America had, until now, been willing to tolerate the church's unusual religious doctrine as an aberrant but harmless expression of one's civil rights. The national tone now changed and would demand that something more be done.

The prosecution determined that there would be a second trial. By now William H. Dame and George Adair Jr. had also been jailed. However, they would never be brought to trial. Brigham Young and his chiefs were at work determining the best course for the church.

Before the deal could be cut, on September 1, 1875, George A. Smith in Salt Lake City began gasping for breath. Doctors were called, but they could do nothing to help. One of his doctors claimed later that the apostle had died of fright. A white powdery residue had been found in Smith's room, but the prospect that someone might have poisoned such a beloved man was dismissed. After all, Smith was the most obese man in all of Deseret. Surely his poor physical condition must have led to his demise. Smith was fifty-eight years old.

Now that a link in the chain had been cut, the leadership could see their opportunity. Someone would have to pay for the horrid deed at Mountain Meadows. It had been said throughout Deseret, "Better for one man to die, than for a whole nation of people to dwindle in unbelief."

Lee returned to Beaver, under his own recognizance, on September 11, 1876. It had been exactly nineteen years since he played his part in the massacre. He was surprised to learn that his legal defense had been withdrawn. In addition, his long-time friend and the future U.S. senator William Hooper withdrew the $15,000 bond he had posted for him. This required Lee to be confined in jail when not in the courtroom.

This time the jury selection consisted of twelve Mormons. All non-Mormons in the jury pool were challenged and dismissed. This time the prosecution did not call Philip Klingensmith. In his place Daniel H. Wells, Sam McMurdy, Sam Knight, Laban Morrill, James H. Haslam, Joel White, Nephi Johnson, and Jacob Hamblin were called. All testified for the prosecution.

Wells' purpose at the trial, aside from keeping an eye on the proceedings for Brigham Young, was two-fold. He was to instruct the jurors during the trial's off hours and he was to testify that Lee held low rank in the church hierarchy both ecclesiastically and militarily.

Haslam's purpose was to prove that it would have been impossible for Brigham Young to get orders to Mountain Meadows in time to stop the slaughter. In subsequent years this claim would be shown to be false and it would be shown that Haslam had more than adequate time to make the ride from there and back.

Johnson, McMurdy, and Knight each testified that they saw Lee kill at least one woman. Hamblin's testimony was the most damaging of all. He said that Lee had told him all about the massacre a few days after it happened and that he admitted to cutting the throats of at least two young girls. He also insinuated that Lee might have admitted to doing more to the girls before killing them.

In subsequent years Johnson and Hamblin admitted to family members that they had received instructional letters from Brigham Young on how to testify. Even before these revelations, it was clear to Lee's counsel, and to Judge Boreman as well, that some kind of deal had been cut between the prosecution and the church. On September 20, 1876, after less than four hours of deliberation, an all-Mormon jury returned a verdict of "guilty of murder in the first degree."

* * *

On October 10, 1876, John D. Lee was sentenced to death. The execution was to be carried out at the scene of the crime, Mountain Meadows. Territorial law required that he be given the choice of hanging, firing squad, or beheading. Lee chose death by firing squad.

On March 23, 1877, a small crowd of dignitaries assembled to witness Lee's execution. He gave a speech that did not include an admission of guilt. He said he'd been faithful to his religion and that he'd done what he'd been ordered to do by his superiors. He complained bitterly that Brigham Young had sacrificed him in a most cowardly way.

Before his death, Lee told members of his family, "If I am guilty of the crime for which I am convicted, I will go down and out and never be heard of again. If I am not guilty, Brigham Young will die within one year! Yes, within six months."

Standing in front of his coffin, Lee was blindfolded. His last words were, "Center on my heart boys. Don't mangle my body." The commanding officer shouted "Ready, aim, fire!" Lee fell backward into his coffin, a dead man. Considering how the one hundred twenty men, women, and children had died there before him, his death was easy.

* * *

During the course of events leading up to and beyond Lee's execution, a series of communications were exchanged between Rachel Andora Lee and Emmeline Free. Tidbits from Lee's last confession were among them.

Lucretia and Emmeline Free had become close friends. Emmeline took ill and died a short time before Lee's final day, but had shared much of what Rachel Lee had sent her before she expired. Through a serendipitous chain of events, Lucretia and Molly Anderson had become close with Amelia Folsom, one of the Prophet's more recent plural acquisitions. All the while Molly continued her education in nursing and had become quite accomplished and in demand.

Molly's sad tales of the atoning of her stepfather, the disappearance of her fiancé, and her unrequited love had touched Lucretia and Amelia's hearts, and the two women of status had taken it upon themselves to quietly champion her cause.

The attorneys and judges working the Lee trial would have been staggered by the information these four women had been able to assemble of the facts surrounding the crimes of Mountain Meadows, the Aiken party, and Rosmus Anderson. By the time John D. Lee faced the firing squad at Mountain Meadows these women knew a great deal more than Hosea Stout, Wilford Woodruff, or the Prophet would have liked.

CHAPTER 88

ST. GEORGE
SOUTHERN
UTAH TERRITORY
SALT LAKE CITY
UTAH TERRITORY

APRIL 8, 1877
TO
AUGUST 29, 1877

April 8, 1877, was a blustery spring day in Saint George. It should have been a grand day of celebration for the Saints. For Brigham Young it was anything but that. The temple in St. George had been completed, and it was time for the Prophet, Seer, and Revelator to dedicate Zion's most inspiring structural creation. It would precede the temple in Salt Lake City by more than fifteen years. To this day it is a sight to behold.

Feeling old and angry behind his pulpit, Young excoriated his brethren from the Quorum of the Twelve on down. He was in an especially dark mood, and such moods had been increasing in frequency. In his wrath he pounded the podium with his cane, inflicting marks that still verify the attack.

Towards the end of his tirade a freak storm whipped up and increased in intensity to the point where Young had to reassure the congregation. "Sit down and calm yourselves and let the devil roar." It was unsettling, even for the Prophet, that such an upheaval should occur in concert with his intimidating oration.

Shortly after the dedication, bouts of diarrhea and vomiting struck several members of the Mormon leadership, including Young. Speculative rumor proliferated throughout Utah's Dixie that poisoning was behind it, an act of stealth motivated by vengeance over the execution of John D. Lee.

On August 23, 1877, after gorging himself at the Lion House on a meal of green corn and peaches, Young fell ill again. The assault of diarrhea and vomiting was relentless against the Prophet. For nearly a week he suffered severely and all his doctor's efforts failed to spare him agony. In one of his more lucid moments he called for Hosea Stout.

Amelia Folsom, the Prophet's fiftieth sealed wife, had led Stout into Young's room. As she left, she told him that the Prophet had requested to speak to him in private.

"Brother Young, I'm so sorry you're not feeling well." Stout was sincere in both his tone and in his heart.

"Are you really?" Young looked as terrible as death itself. The weakness in his voice was not enough to conceal the accusative intention it suggested.

"Have I somehow fallen into disfavor with you, Brother Young?" Stout was alarmed by his Prophet's tone.

"You never did tell me exactly how you were able to prevent Joseph's brother Samuel from ascending to the position I now hold. It's been more than thirty-three years and I have never asked you to divulge your methods during all that time. I think perhaps it's time, don't you?" It appeared and sounded like the Prophet truly might not have much time left.

"If it is your wish, it is my command." Stout had a sinking feeling that this discussion was headed in a bad direction.

"It is my wish, Hosea. It is my dying wish, if that is of any concern or consequence to you." Young was laboring under too much distress to be as menacing as he might otherwise have been.

"Very well then. If this is your wish, I shall tell you." Hosea gulped. He was about to divulge a secret he had not uttered to anyone since he lived in Nauvoo. "As I'm sure you will recall, Samuel was determined to claim a succession right to Joseph's holy priesthood. He had produced a notarized will declaring himself successor if both Joseph and Hyrum were killed. It was clear to me that a forgery had been committed. Acting as Samuel's nurse, I administered combination doses of arsenic and strychnine for a period of about a week until he succumbed."

"And now you've administered the same to me?" Young could barely speak.

"No! Never! What could possibly bring you to conclude such a treachery?" Stout was sincere. He knew he was innocent. He also knew he was in great danger if the Prophet believed such a lie about him.

"Samuel's death was described to me in explicit detail by his widow. I forgot all about it until lately. Now that I'm going through the exact same thing, I don't think it too far-fetched for me to conclude that I have been the victim of 'such a treachery.'" The Prophet struggled to maintain a strong voice.

Stout looked to the small table by the Prophet's bedside. There was an empty glass crowded among the other vials, elixirs, and medicines Young's doctors had been prescribing. At the bottom of the glass was a dried grainy residue of what appeared to be a white powder. He reached for the glass and sniffed what contents remained. The scent was unmistakable, even thirty-three years later.

"You did right you know . . . to Samuel that is. He was going to denounce celestial marriage . . . plural marriage. He was a Gentile at heart. He deserved what you did to him. Now the same has been done to me." At the end of each sentence Young would gasp for breath with tremendous difficulty.

As the Prophet grasped for his last ounce of strength, he tried to sit up, but could not. In his agony he cried out, "I command you in the name of the Lord Jesus Christ to find the responsible party, or parties, and submit them to God's wrath. Dear Lord! Dear Joseph! Joseph! Joseph!" Writhing in misery for the last time, the Prophet of the Church of Jesus Christ of Latter-day Saints finally let go. He had found peace at last.

Stout's mind was racing. He'd just witnessed the death of the Prophet. Although the event would not come as a big surprise to those waiting outside the room, Young's last revelation of being poisoned was as explosive an epistle as Stout had ever encountered. Who else might the Prophet have confided in with regard to the treachery he suspected? Had he shared his suspicions about Stout? Even though they'd never discussed it till this day, surely the Prophet had known of Stout's complicity in Samuel's death, and probably his methodology as well. Hosea needed to think.

He opened the door with a jerk, deciding to go on the offensive. "Amelia!" he shouted. He knew that Amelia Folsom had been disenchanted with her marriage of late. She had shared some of her discontent with him. He had felt there was an attraction between them. She had always been the Prophet's favorite, replacing Emmeline in that department. Emmeline had died a bitter woman because of Amelia Folsom. His more recent marriages to the younger Mary Van Cott and Ann Eliza Webb had initiated Amelia's displeasure. In spite of his feelings for her, before the finger could be pointed at him, he would be pointing it at her.

Amelia ran up the stairs and into the room. It was already becoming obvious the Prophet was dead. A thick line of drool flowing from the corner of his mouth to the base of his jowl had begun to slow and dry. His open eyes held the telltale look possessed by only those who have departed.

She stopped still, and her expressionless look told Stout that she was both aware of her husband's death and not terribly upset about it. This only confirmed his earlier suspicion that she was the likely suspect in the murder. "Tell me what you know of this!" commanded Stout as he thrust the residued glass up close to her nose so she would know that Hosea was aware of the poisonous odor.

In quick succession, Amelia was taken aback by the abrupt maneuver and then the odor. "I'm not sure I understand your meaning," she responded, as if she too was wondering if she was being accused of some sort of foul play. Her calm demeanor was due to her thinking that she and Hosea may now have the opportunity they had both always longed for. Until now, only the Prophet had had the audacity to speak to her in such a tone. For years he had been the only one who could do so without consequence.

"It's poison! Someone has poisoned the Prophet. The residue at the bottom of this glass, the white powder, where did you get it?" Stout's tone remained insolent, but he suppressed his desire to shout at the woman.

"If you're referring to the powder we've been giving him this past week, ask Lucretia. She provided it to me with explicit instructions of use." Amelia maintained the same startled look throughout their conversation, but now Stout could see she was not overly concerned for her own well-being.

Stout lowered the glass and glanced toward the Prophet. Her answer had hit him hard. "Why would Lucretia take it upon herself to prescribe medicine for the Prophet? He has four devout doctors working for him night and day."

"It was Molly Anderson. She said the doctors prescribed it. She is a very well-qualified nurse. She is quite used to administering doctors orders." Amelia was worried, as much for Lucretia and Molly as she was for herself.

Stout was momentarily stumped. His head was spinning with thoughts of conspiracy flowing through his entire household. Disaster lurked imminently from all potential elucidations.

"I'm going to see Molly and get to the bottom of this. Can I count on you to wait for me to get back here before you discuss with anyone what we've been talking about?" From her expression Stout knew she would comply.

"I think I should notify the doctors right away about . . . him, don't you think?" Amelia wanted to be sure her actions did not make the situation worse.

"Yes, yes, of course. I'll be back here as soon as I can." Stout and Lucretia had grown fond of Molly. Lucretia and Amelia were very close, and the affection for the Anderson girl had spread between all three of them. Sufficiently assured, Stout quickly left the room. Amelia proceeded to the doctor on duty downstairs.

Molly Anderson was studying her medical journals when Hosea burst through the door of her room. He immediately shut the door behind him, knowing that he would have but a short time to obtain the information he needed before the impropriety of his presence would raise his wives' suspicion. Thrusting the glass forward as he had done to Amelia and keeping his voice low he said, "I am told that you are responsible for prescribing this to the Prophet, who now lies mercifully dead after having spent the past week suffering an agonizing death."

As if she had been expecting this very confrontation she responded, "Did anyone happen to tell you what kind of death the Prophet arranged for my fiancé and his brother? I've been told over and over again that I can be sure that I will never see either one of them again."

He was beginning to understand. "Where did you come upon it . . . the powder you gave to Amelia?" Stout had a hunch he already knew.

"I discovered that you had an adequate supply of it in your stores of medicinal products in the basement. I didn't think anyone would die anytime soon if I were to run you short of it." The Stout family had come to realize long ago that Molly possessed a significantly higher than average intellect, and at times a sniping sarcasm.

Stout had a clear understanding now of what had transpired. Molly had been broken-hearted when she did not hear from Cao or Henry Young the spring and summer of 1858. Not long after that her friends began advising and encouraging her to move on with her life and to pursue her nursing career. They assured her someone else would come along. She was too pretty to be alone the rest of her life.

Molly was also too smart not to realize that she would never see Cao and Henry again. She also knew why. She knew that there were probably a number of good Saints involved in their disappearance. She could only be sure of one in particular and she wasn't the least bit sympathetic over the manner in which he had died.

"I'm going to talk to Amelia. Don't say a word about what we've discussed here just now to anyone!" Stout could see his only clear path forward now and it wasn't going to be "submitting the responsible party to God's wrath."

When Hosea returned to the Beehive House, things had already escalated to the chaotic frenzy one would expect following the announcement of the passing of the "Lion of the Lord." Reporters from news outlets from all over the nation converged for an exclusive on the expected event.

Hosea's eyes met Amelia's. She was acting the part of the grieving widow now, along with more than a dozen other widows, with tears streaming down their faces.

"They're asking if he had any last words. I told them that you were with him at the end." The way she said it, and the way she touched his arm when she said it, convinced Hosea that Amelia would not be divulging any aspect of their earlier conversation.

Assured the path he was taking was the best path for all concerned he said, "His last words were 'Dear Lord! Joseph! Joseph! Joseph!'"

The reporters scribbled away as they scurried off in the direction of the telegraph office. Hosea stood next to Wilford Woodruff as they observed the historic scene. Perhaps no two men in all the Utah Territory breathed a bigger sigh of relief as this chapter in the history of the Latter-day Saints came to a close.

CHAPTER 89

SONORA
OLD MEXICO

1881

He had been in the saddle for a long time. Home had not been a place to return to since he'd said good-bye to his families more than five years ago. It had been a long ride to Sonora, Mexico. Philip Klingensmith had become accustomed to long rides.

After the massacre, P.K.'s zeal for the church had diminished considerably. Before the massacre he'd lived among the people of the Southern Utah Territory for more than ten years and had earned the respect of nearly all. After leaving the church he had kept quiet enough about his religious beliefs that most treated him in an understanding manner. What else could he do but stay out of the way?

Upon the completion of the trial of John D. Lee, P.K. could no longer maintain the same degree of respect he'd earned by just staying silent. Now he was an apostate. He had broken the oath of silence. He was the reason the Gentiles were able to bring the Saints to trial. He had caused the entire nation to look upon the Mormon people with derision and contempt. P.K. was a hunted man.

Deeply ashamed of the role he'd played in the massacre, he could not bring himself to return home to what remained of his family in Pennsylvania. From the beginning, they'd tried to dissuade him from following the new doctrine they considered so aberrant. He had been too prideful to listen to them. He would not burden his people with his heavy baggage now.

He'd thought of the Nevada and California gold fields. A man with his expertise could do well in such an environment. But the Saints had returned to these areas in force since Mountain Meadows. The reaches of a vengeful people would be long and strong out there.

Mexico would be his sanctuary. He'd been good with languages and already knew some Spanish. Resources in this southern country were rumored to be great. The wrath of the Gentiles or the Saints would be subject to the laws of a different nation. Here was his best chance to evade the Avenging Angels . . . the Danites.

He thought back to the day after the first trial of John D. Lee. His testimony that day had changed his life forever. His affidavit had produced several threats on his life. Those who had threatened him had hoped he would refuse to testify at trial, the church would protect him, and all could be forgiven.

He remembered the reporter from the *Salt Lake Tribune* asking him for a statement. His published comment had been quoted accurately. "I know that the church will kill me, sooner or later, and I am as confident of that fact as I am that I am sitting on this rock. It is only a question of time; but I am going to live as long as I can."

His route to Sonora had been somewhat circuitous. His shortest route would be through Lee's Ferry, but that wouldn't do for P.K. Too many Saints on the lookout for him that way, not to mention much of what remained of Lee's family. He would take his chances through San Bernardino, and then head straight down.

His travels had been, for the most part, uneventful. At one point near the border he crossed paths with Isaac Haight. The two men just stared at one another with no words spoken between them. P.K. was not too concerned. Haight was trying to keep himself scarce too. Since they were headed in opposite directions and P.K. had told no one where he was headed, it was doubtful the former stake president would pose him any threat.

A mining operation near Sonora was his destination. There was a good chance his expertise would be of benefit and justly compensated. Mining camps were usually places where rough customers congregated. Any Saints among them would likely be "Jack" Mormons prone to whoring, gambling, swearing, and drinking. It was the devout ones P.K. thought it best to avoid. Not avoiding them could be a costly mistake.

Upon arriving in camp and contacting the mining superintendent, P.K. checked into a small room. Soon the call came that he would be given work in the assay department. The next day he was busy examining ore samples of new exploratory digs in the area. That afternoon while down in a prospect hole, he heard the click of a pistol hammers being cocked. P.K. turned to see who it was. He already knew what it was for.

"Well. Well. Look who we found down in a hole. Could it be the big shot bishop of Cedar City?" Lot Smith was enjoying himself. He hadn't distinguished himself in the eyes of the leadership since his predations against Yates and federal troops near Echo Canyon back in 57. That was about to change.

"Who's yer friend, Lot?" P.K. figured he might as well enjoy his last few minutes on this earth with some conversation. His only weapon was a small prospector's handpick. Smith and his friend had the drop on him. There was no way out.

"This here's my sidekick Sylvanus Collett, not that it's gonna do you any good to know that." Smith flashed a yellow toothy grin.

"Pleasure to make yer acquaintance, Mr. Collett." P.K. slowly tipped his hat. He thought it somewhat amusing that he would consciously refrain from doing anything to provoke these men. He knew they were going to kill him no matter what he did or said.

"I doubt it's gonna be much of a pleasure for you." Sylvanus tried to model his boss, but he could only muster a goofy, toothless grin.

"I'm surprised it turned out to be you, Lot. I thought it would more likely be someone like Ira Hatch or Bill Hickman. Did you boys come all the way down here after me, or did I just ride into the wrong camp at the wrong time?" P.K. wanted to enjoy the sun on his face for just a few more seconds.

"Bill's getting too old fer this kind a work and nobody trusts him anymore anyway. Ira's lost his stomach fer it . . . kinda like you I spose. The truth of it, bishop, is yer the best work around right now. The Prophet says the Lord just won't let him sleep well at night as long as yer walkin' the earth." Smith figured he'd indulge the sixty-five-year-old ironsmith for a moment or so. He loved having the advantage over men, especially when they were bigger and stronger than him.

"So you're working for John Taylor these days?" P.K. knew the score. President Taylor was as power hungry and vengeful as Brigham Young had been.

"That's right. I gotta make my money before that spineless Woodruff takes over." Lot Smith was feeling like the cat in a cat-in-mouse game. "Well, are you ready ta meet yer maker?"

P.K. took a deep breath. His life passed before him. He had known for a long time it would come to something like this. He figured he deserved it too. He was finally going to pay for what he did to Matt Fancher. He hoped it would be enough.

"To tell you the truth, Lot, I'd just as soon wait a little longer." P.K. figured that would do the trick, and he was right.

"Sorry, Bishop, but I got things ta do." Smith squeezed off the first round and just kept firing. So did Sylvanus Collett.

On their way out of the mining camp, Smith stopped by the mining superintendent's office. He walked in and told him that there was a dead man in one of the excavation pits over the south hill. "You might want to check it out. I think he's a Mormon from Salt Lake City."

About a month later an article printed in the *Deseret News* stated that Philip Klingensmith had been found dead in a prospect hole near Sonora, Mexico. Other news lines picked it up and used it to denounce the Mormon religion for, once again, resorting to violence to promote or protect its interests. The *Deseret News* responded by printing subsequent articles attacking the former bishop's character.

P.K.'s death marked the second and last time any of the participants at Mountain Meadows would pay the ultimate penalty for their involvement. Lee had been convicted in a court of law, and P.K. had, more than anyone else, provoked the conviction. No one would ever be charged with P.K.'s murder.

* * *

All the other participants would die naturally, or at least through causes unrelated to the massacre. Throughout their lives they received the support and protection of their church. Their penalties would be the indelible stain on their characters, the shame that would follow their families, and the haunting memories that would never allow them to rest in peace. Many would test the difficulty of deluding themselves that they had acted for the will of God as revealed by their very own Prophet, Seer, and Revelator.

After confessing to the murders of over fifty men and swearing that Brigham Young ordered almost every one of them, Bill Hickman would be indicted for the murder of A.J. "Honesty" Jones. Brigham Young, Morris Meacham, Simon Dalton, George D. Grant, O.P. Rockwell, and William Kimball would be indicted as well. None of them would ever be brought to trial.

Rockwell and Collett were arrested and charged with the murders of the Aiken brothers, Tuck Wright, and Colonel Eichard. Shortly thereafter, Rockwell, another man with many dangerous secrets, would make bail. After drinking Valley Tan Whiskey at the Globe Inn he fell ill with diarrhea and vomiting. He died the next day on June 9, 1878, before he could be brought to trial. A hundred and fifty years later Rockwell would continue to enjoy hero status in the state of Utah. As late as 2006 real estate developers would still be naming streets and parks after him to promote their product in the Beehive State. Such actions would stimulate little controversy.

Collett would actually stand trial for the charges but would be acquitted. Guy Foote and Reuben Downs testified for the prosecution. Foote's parents would contradict their testimony. When the prosecution attempted to enter the narrative Foote had written for John Aiken when he was in the care of his parents at their hotel, the judge would not allow it. His ruling was that such evidence was hearsay and therefore inadmissible.

After Hickman's confession, he and Hosea Stout would be charged with Yates' murder. It would never go to trial. None of the murders Hickman confessed to in front of a U.S. marshal would ever result in a trial.

After Rockwell's demise, Hickman fled to Wyoming, where good whiskey could be safely consumed. He would die quietly in Sweetwater, Wyoming, in 1883. He does not enjoy the same level of adulation in Utah as does Rockwell, even though evidence is strong that each man killed over one hundred men, many at the request of the Prophet. The only significant difference between the two of them is that Bill Hickman admitted to many of his dark deeds. Rockwell never admitted to anything.

Ira Hatch took a third wife a year or so after the massacre and relocated his families to Fruitland, New Mexico. He occupied his time with missionary work for the Indians of the region, and as an Indian interpreter. He stayed quiet and did his best to live out the rest of his life uneventfully.

Jacob Bigler and William Edwards would become bishops of Nephi and Beaver, Utah, respectively. Edwards would admit to his involvement at Mountain Meadows in 1924 by sworn affidavit approximately one year before his passing. His death April 24, 1925, would mark the passing of the last-known participant of the massacre.

Joseph F. Smith would become the sixth prophet of the Church of Jesus Christ of Latter-day Saints. His son would become the tenth. The church refers to the sixth prophet as the Son of a Prophet, a Prophet, and the Father of a Prophet. They say few men have enjoyed a more illustrious lineage. Rarely do they mention his involvement in one of the most horrific mass murders in the annals of American History.

Hosea Stout arranged for Molly Anderson to be quietly secreted out of the territory shortly after the death of Brigham Young. He would have her on a stage to Corrine, Utah, within forty-eight hours of Young's passing. She would arrive in New York City by passenger train two days later. Upon learning of Lucretia's involvement with Amelia and Molly, Stout was determined it was best for everyone that the citizens of Deseret believe a gorging of "green corn and peaches" to be the suspected cause of the Prophet's death.

Molly would remain in the big city for the rest of her life. She would pursue a successful nursing career at Bellevue Hospital, marry a doctor, and raise a family. She would follow with great interest news stories about federal prosecutors' efforts to bring additional perpetrators of the massacre to justice. Neither she nor anyone else would ever hear from Cao or Henry T. Young again.

As time marched on, the Mormon Church would move away from most, if not all, of the peculiar doctrines that caused so much of the American citizenry to recoil from it. In 1890, Wilford Woodruff, as the fourth prophet, would repeal plural marriage (polygamy) by revelation, and Utah would become a state five years later.

In 1978, the Prophet Spencer W. Kimball along with his counselors in the First Presidency, Marion G. Romney and N. Eldon Tanner, would repeal the prohibition against African Americans in the Holy Priesthood (men only . . . women of all races are prohibited to this day). In between, the church would steadily move away from blood atonement, communalism, theocracy, consecration of property, and millennialism.

By the beginning of the twenty-first century, the church and its people would become a beacon for capitalism, advanced education, Christian and family values, industriousness, and respect for the rule of law. Today their membership has grown to exceed thirteen million.

In 2007, one of their own has announced his plans to seek the Republican nomination for president of the United States. He appears to have a reasonable chance of success.

For one hundred and fifty years, after one of its prophets had orchestrated the crime of the century, the Church of Jesus Christ of Latter-day Saints, through its varied and abundant representatives, including those highest in authority, would continue to insist that Brigham Young had nothing to do with the Mountain Meadows Massacre.

Religious fanaticism, of another stripe, would strike America again, one hundred forty-four years later to the day, in a manner suggestive of the past. Their guiltless victims would be slain mercilessly by perpetrators overflowing with the spirit of a ruthless Prophet.

Printed in the United States
143444LV00002B/4/A